Wilbur Smith is a global phenomenon: a distinguished author with a large and established readership built up over fifty-five years of writing, with sales of over 130 million novels worldwide.

Born in Central Africa in 1933, Wilbur became a full-time writer in 1964 following the success of *When the Lion Feeds*, and has since published over forty global bestsellers, including the Courtney Series, the Ballantyne Series, the Egyptian Series, the Hector Cross Series and many successful standalone novels, all meticulously researched on his numerous expeditions worldwide. His books have now been translated into twenty-six languages.

The establishment of the Wilbur & Niso Smith Foundation in 2015 cemented Wilbur's passion for empowering writers, promoting literacy and advancing adventure writing as a genre. The foundation's flagship programme is the Wilbur Smith Adventure Writing Prize.

For all the latest information on Wilbur, visit: www.wilbursmithbooks.com or facebook.com/WilburSmith.

Tom Harper is the author of thirteen thrillers and historical adventures including *The Orpheus Descent*, *Black River* and *Lost Temple*. Research for his novels has taken him all over the world, from the high Arctic to the heart of the Amazon jungle. He lives with his family in York. For more information about Tom's books, visit www.tom-harper.co.uk.

WILBUR SMITH

WITH
TOM HARPER

GHOST FIRE

ZAFFRE

First published in Great Britain in 2019 by

ZAFFRE
80–81 Wimpole St, London W1G 9RE

A CIP catalogue record for this book is
available from the British Library.

Paperback ISBN: 978–1–78576–943–6
Export ISBN: 978–1–78576–944–3

Also available as an ebook

1 3 5 7 9 10 8 6 4 2

Typeset by IDSUK (Data Connection) Ltd
Printed and bound in Great Britain by Clays Ltd, Elcograf S.p.A.

Zaffre is an imprint of Bonnier Books UK
www.bonnierbooks.co.uk

To my constant love, my soulmate, my playmate, MOKHINISO. Spirits of Genghis Khan and Omar Khayyam reincarnated in a moon as lucent as a perfect pearl.

THE COURTNEY FAMILY

IN
GHOST FIRE

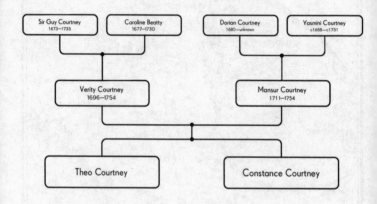

Sir Guy Courtney
1673—1733

Caroline Beatty
1677—1730

Dorian Courtney
1680—unknown

Yasmini Courtney
c1688—c1731

Verity Courtney
1696—1754

Mansur Courtney
1711—1754

Theo Courtney

Constance Courtney

Find out more about the Courtneys and see the
Courtney family tree in full at

www.wilbursmithbooks.com/courtney-family-tree

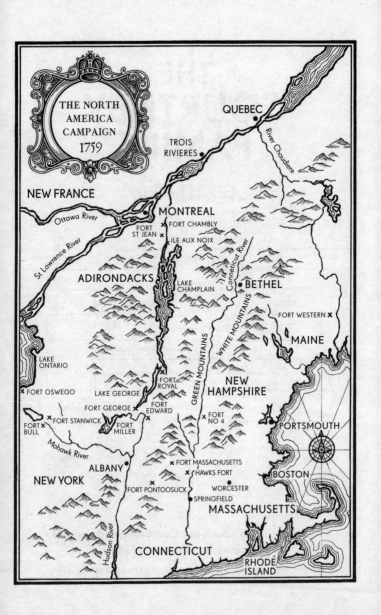

THE NORTH
AMERICA
CAMPAIGN
1759

QUEBEC

TROIS
RIVIERES

River Chaudiere

NEW FRANCE

Ottawa River

MONTREAL

FORT
ST JEAN × × FORT CHAMBLY

ILE AUX NOIX

St Lawrence River

ADIRONDACKS

LAKE
CHAMPLAIN

Connecticut River

BETHEL

FORT WESTERN ×

MAINE

WHITE MOUNTAINS

LAKE
ONTARIO

× FORT OSWEGO

LAKE GEORGE

FORT
ROYAL

GREEN MOUNTAINS

NEW
HAMPSHIRE

FORT GEORGE ×

FORT
EDWARD

× FORT
NO 4

PORTSMOUTH

FORT
BULL × FORT STANWICK
×

FORT
MILLER

Mohawk River

ALBANY ●

× FORT MASSACHUSETTS

× HAWKS FORT

BOSTON

NEW YORK

× FORT PONTOOSUCK

WORCESTER ●
● SPRINGFIELD

MASSACHUSETTS

CONNECTICUT

RHODE
ISLAND

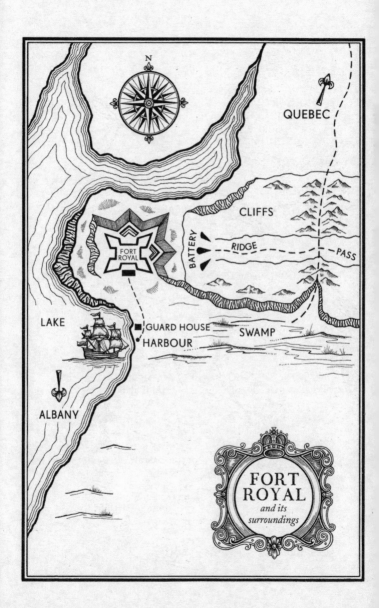

Fort St George, Madras, India
1754

The two children climbed the wall and dropped into the garden. The evening air was ripe with the midsummer scent of jasmine flowers and coconut oil burning in the lamps that had been lit. Long shadows hid them from view as they crept towards the big house.

They were brother and sister. The girl, the older of the two, had long fair hair that hung loose down her back, though she was of an age when more modesty would soon be required. The Indian sun had tanned her skin golden. She had a woman's curves, but a soft, girlish face that brimmed with mischief.

'Why have we come here, Connie?' asked the boy. He was taller than her, of which he was proud, though a year younger. He was sturdily built, already taking the shape of the man he would become, with a mop of tousled red hair and intelligent brown eyes. His skin was darker than hers, a bronze that could pass for Indian as easily as European.

Constance crouched behind a terracotta urn. 'Mr Meridew is hosting an assembly this evening. Gentlemen only.'

'But that will be the most boring party in the world,' Theo complained. 'Old men talking about the price of cotton all night.'

'They have not come to talk business, Theo. I had it from my hairdresser, who had it from her sister, whose cousin is a cook in the house, that Mr Meridew has hired a troupe of nautch-girls to dance. I am told it will be so scandalous that the men have been talking of little else all week.'

'You want to break in and see what they do?'

'Don't you?'

'Of course. But . . .' Theo was not a coward, but he had a practical streak. Painful experience had taught him that if they were caught it was he who would feel the strength of their father's anger.

Constance's green eyes sparkled. 'I dare you,' she said. 'They say the nautch-dancers are the most beautiful women in the world. You will be of age soon. Are you not curious to see the mysteries of the feminine form?'

Theo swallowed. Constance was dressed in Indian style, with a bright sari wrapped around her and draped over her shoulders. She had mastered the intricacies of the garment so that it clung to the contours of her body, shifting easily as she moved. She wore nothing underneath, yet she had a slimmer waist than many a woman who trussed herself up with iron stays and whalebone busks. Her young breasts swelled under the fabric.

To Theo, the complexities of women's undergarments were a mystery more profound than the algebraic equations his despairing tutor tried to make him work out. But he could not fail to notice the changes in his sister over the last two years – and it made him uncomfortable when she spoke so frankly. He knew women should not say such things.

'Or are you frightened?'

Her eyes met his, flashing with the challenge. Theo swallowed his doubts. He could never resist his sister – however many times it ended with him bending over in their father's study.

'I'll go first,' he said defiantly.

Keeping low, he ran to the house and flattened himself against the wall. It was a grand building, as befitted the richest merchant in Madras, designed in the fantastical style that was unique to the British in India. A broad veranda was supported by Grecian columns; onion domes flanked classical pediments. It stood about half a mile from Fort St George and Madras, though near enough for its occupants to hear the surf crashing on the beach that fronted the city walls.

From the sounds within, Theo guessed the party was taking place on the first floor. He recalled a grand ballroom there from his only visit to the house, trailing along behind his father.

A shadow flitted past one of the ground-floor windows. Theo ducked. He could see the carriages and palanquins lined up on the driveway. With so many of Madras's finest citizens assembled, the house would be full of servants. He could not hope to get up the stairs unseen.

A carved stone elephant stood on the terrace. It was almost as tall as Theo. He climbed onto a flowerpot, scrambled onto its back, then hoisted himself on to the roof of the veranda. Just in time.

As his legs disappeared over the edge, a light swept the terrace. A Sikh watchman was making his rounds with a lantern. Theo flattened himself against the roof and waited until the danger had passed. He edged to the nearest window and peered inside.

There was no glass – in India, it was an unimaginable luxury. Wooden blinds hung in the opening, protecting the room from the dust and heat of the day. Theo heard the soft pulse of a drum, and the sinuous playing of breathy flutes. He pushed his fingers between the slats and prised them apart.

The smell of sweet tobacco billowed into the night, so suddenly that Theo nearly choked. He covered his mouth to stifle a cough. He saw the merchant princes of Madras lounging on cushions, sucking lustily on their hookah pipes. Most had removed their coats and wigs, but even from behind Theo recognised nearly all of them. They passed through his father's office, or the family godown, almost every day.

None of them noticed Theo. Their gazes were fixed on a troupe of dancing girls swaying and spinning in time with the music. They wore saris, like Constance, yet theirs were made of a cloth so fine it was almost transparent. Theo stared at the dancers, hypnotised by their movements. Their hips writhed; their breasts undulated under the gauzy fabric. One, in particular, fascinated him: a slim young woman with almond eyes, her oiled skin gleaming in the lamplight.

The dancers unwound their turbans. Long black hair spilled over shoulders, falling over breasts.

The men clapped appreciatively and shouted encouragement.

The throb of the music seemed to grow faster, more urgent. All the dancers moved as one, but Theo's eyes were fixed on the girl with the almond eyes. She tied her turban cloth around her hips, then wriggled out of her sari, pulling it from under the makeshift belt. The flimsy cloth unravelled from her body and trailed away, like a veil.

All that covered her was the band of cloth around her loins, and her black hair brushing her breasts. She pressed her palms together, swivelling her hips, and Theo's chest tightened. Her hair swayed from side to side, caressing her breasts and offering tantalising glimpses of the dark brown nipples beneath.

Theo was so entranced he didn't hear the sound behind him.

'She's beautiful,' whispered Constance.

Theo whipped around. 'What are you doing?' he hissed. 'You should not be seeing such things.'

Constance pouted. 'I know what a woman's body looks like.'

Theo could feel he was losing control. He knew they should go, but he could not bear to look away. In the room, the girl had untied the knot in the cloth around her waist. She held it against her skin, spinning behind it, offering snatches of bare flesh. Theo glimpsed the curve of her buttocks, the smooth arc of her belly tapering away between her thighs.

Suddenly she let the cloth fall to the floor. At the same time, she flicked back her hair, and her nakedness was revealed.

Theo was open-mouthed. Her breasts were firm, gleaming with the oil she had rubbed on her skin. Between her legs, the girl's sex was smooth and exposed, a plump, mounded cleft meticulously plucked free of any hair. He had never seen such a thing before. Warmth spread through Theo's loins. His manhood strained against his breeches, so hard he thought it might burst.

The men inside had risen to their feet, whistling and cheering. One stood in front of the window, rubbing the crotch of his breeches and blocking Theo's view. The girl disappeared from sight.

The pang of loss was too much to bear. Theo scrabbled to his feet, careless of anything except one more glimpse of that beautiful naked body, still gyrating in time with the music as if it was the most natural thing in the world.

'Get down,' hissed Constance.

She tugged on his belt. Theo resisted, but Constance was stubborn. She grabbed his ankle and pulled it from under him.

The roof tiles were slippery with the evening dew. Theo lost his balance and fell, sliding down the slick pitched roof on his stomach. He flailed for a handhold, but there was nothing to grip. He felt his legs go over the edge. He hung there for a moment, dangling in space. Then he dropped.

He landed hard, knocking over a flowerpot. A stabbing pain shot through his ankle, and he cried out despite himself. The flowerpot rolled away, bounced down the steps and shattered.

Constance jumped down after him, landing softly as a cat. 'Oh, Theo,' she said, 'are you hurt?'

Shouts came from the front door, and lantern beams swept across the lawns. Theo tried to rise, grimacing with pain. Rapid footsteps approached the corner of the house.

'You must go,' said Constance. Her eyes were wide, alive with excitement. 'If they catch us, we will be in such trouble.'

'What about you?'

'I can take care of myself.'

With a flick of her wrist, she flipped a fold of her sari over her head, covering her face. In an instant, she was unrecognisable.

Theo ran. Each step was agony, but he forced himself to go on, spurred by the fear of what his father would do to him if he was caught.

The terrace was now awash with light. The music had stopped. Merchants were hanging out of the upper windows to see what was happening. Below, the terrace, which had been empty a few moments ago, was crowded with onlookers. Every servant had come to witness the commotion.

The master of the house pushed through the throng in a fury. He had spent months planning the evening. He had promised his guests that they would enjoy private sessions with the dancers afterwards, in consideration of favours they had done him, and now everything was ruined. Someone would pay.

As he looked around the assembled crowd, his gaze paused on Constance. He saw only another veiled servant – and he had so many servants, he could not be expected to recognise all of them. It would never have occurred to him that an Englishwoman would disgrace herself by donning native dress. He turned his attention elsewhere.

At the far end of the garden, a shadow disappeared into the rose beds.

'After him!'

Theo blundered through the bushes. Thorns drew beads of blood on his arms, the hard earth jarring his swollen ankle. He could hear the men pursuing him, and he redoubled his efforts to escape. He came to the wall and reached up to haul himself over.

It was too high. He stretched on tiptoe, gritting his teeth as a flash of pain shot through his ankle. The guards were closing on him, their lamps casting dappled shadows through the rose bushes.

Theo's fingers scrabbled for the top of the wall. He couldn't find a purchase. He tried to jump, but his foot would not take the pressure. The bushes rustled as the guards charged through. Forcing himself to breach the pain barrier, Theo jumped again. His ankle felt as if it had snapped – but he made it. He hauled himself up the wall, flailing and kicking.

Firm hands grabbed his legs and tried to pull him away. He fought, lashing out with his feet. His shoe connected with something soft, and he heard a grunt of pain. His fingers could not keep their grip. He came away from the wall, landing in a heap on top of the guards. Before he could run, they held him in a tight grip.

They dragged him onto the lawn and shone a lamp in his face. One was bleeding from his mouth where Theo had kicked him.

'Theodore Courtney,' said Meridew, in a voice that carried the full weight and dignity of the United

Company of Merchants Trading to the East Indies. 'Wait until your father hears of this.'

• • •

Mansur and Verity Courtney were sitting in their parlour, playing chess, when Meridew arrived at the door. Their house was a short distance from his. They had an uneasy relationship with the East India Company, and Mansur did not want to be too close to the walls of Fort St George.

Mansur raised his eyebrows when he heard the angry knocking on the door. 'Are we expecting callers?'

'I thought all of society had been invited to Mr Meridew's gathering.' Verity moved her knight, taking her husband's bishop.

A large Sikh in a bright red turban entered the room. His name was Harjinder, Mansur's guard and stoutest servant. He had served the family since before Constance was born.

'Theo-sahib has returned,' he announced.

Mansur rose. 'I wasn't aware he had gone out.'

Theo stood on the doorstep between two sepoys. Meridew waited beside them, red-faced with fury. A large gathering of Indians and Englishmen crowded behind them.

'I was not expecting so many callers at this hour,' Mansur said calmly.

'He broke into my garden, clambered onto my roof and interrupted a private entertainment I was hosting for the most eminent citizens of Madras,' said Meridew.

Mansur considered this. 'I wish I could say that does not sound like my son.'

'And what was the nature of this entertainment?' asked Verity, innocently. She was behind her husband, peering over his shoulder.

Meridew blanched. 'I would rather not say in front of a lady.'

'But if I am to punish my son, I must know the nature of the offence.'

Meridew tried to catch Mansur's eye. 'If you and I could discuss this in private – between gentlemen, as it were . . .'

'My husband and I have no secrets from each other,' said Verity.

She fixed Meridew with a stare that brooked no argument. Meridew flushed and looked away.

'I am sure the entertainment must have cost a great deal of money,' added Mansur. 'If you send your man to my office in the morning, I will see you are properly compensated.'

Meridew took the offer for what it was – a bribe. 'I dare say you know best how to discipline your own children,' he muttered.

'I promise you it will not happen again,' said Verity. She shot Theo a dark look. 'Will it?'

'No, Mother.'

'What were you thinking?' Mansur exclaimed, as soon as the door had closed on Meridew. 'Where did you get such a ridiculous idea?'

The truth was, it had been Constance who first heard about the dancers, and Constance whose curiosity had insisted they try to peek in. But Theo would not betray her. There was still a chance she might have escaped unseen.

'I heard some of the boys talking about it,' he lied. 'I . . . I wanted to see the nautch-girls.'

Mansur and Verity shared a parental look.

'I understand a boy your age will have certain . . . interests,' Mansur said awkwardly, 'but you cannot embarrass us like this. Our family is not so secure here that we can afford to antagonise the Company.'

Theo stuck out his chin. 'I don't give a fig for the East India Company.'

'Go to your room.'

Theo made to argue – but one look at his father's face convinced him to think better of it. He stomped up the stairs.

Mansur turned to Verity and sighed. 'He is a growing young man, with a young man's desires,' he reflected. 'It is natural he should want to see such things.'

'But not in such a manner,' Verity responded tartly. 'Soon Constance will need a husband, and if it is said that her brother goes around ogling native women from rooftops, there is not a reputable family in the whole Presidency who would countenance such a match.'

Mansur grinned. 'Of course, my love, you would never have dreamed of marrying a disreputable young man. You would not have *countenanced* it, Cousin.'

Verity glared at him. She and Mansur were cousins, though they had grown up unaware of each other's existence. Their fathers, the brothers Dorian and Guy Courtney, had been mortal enemies. But from the first moment Mansur spied Verity through a telescope, on the deck of her father's ship, he had fallen absolutely in love with her.

'I conducted myself with the utmost decorum,' said Verity.

'You leaped onto my ship during a sea battle, and left your father clutching a fistful of your blouse, so keen was he to keep you from me,' Mansur answered.

Guy Courtney, Verity's father, had been a monster, who beat his daughter savagely and abused her for his own purposes. Later, he had tried to kill the whole Courtney family. When he had held a knife to Mansur's baby cousin Jim's throat, Mansur's aunt Sarah had shot him dead.

'I wonder how Sarah and Tom are faring,' Verity mused.

Mansur sucked on his hookah pipe and didn't reply. Thinking about Tom and Sarah, their son Jim and grandson George, reopened old wounds he preferred not to dwell upon.

Verity read the expression on his face. She rose. 'I should see that Constance is all right. I hope she has not been disturbed by all the commotion and Theo's foolishness this evening.'

But when she put her head around Constance's door, everything was as it should be. Her daughter lay in her bed, her golden hair spread across the pillow, breathing softly in her deep, untroubled sleep.

• • •

The next day, Mansur received a summons from the governor to attend a meeting of the East India Company council. The note came with no explanation, and even the offer of a silver *fanam* could not prise any more information from the servant who had brought it.

I hope this is not about Theo's escapades, Mansur thought, as he mounted the steps of the governor's mansion in Fort St George. Officially, he and the East India Company were competitors. Though they had developed a tacit understanding that benefited both parties, Mansur preferred to keep the Company at arm's length whenever possible. They, in turn, rarely allowed him into their confidence.

But now the whole council was waiting for him – all the most senior traders and officials in Madras. They sat around a long mahogany table in an airy first floor room with high windows. Dust marks on the wall showed the outlines of the swords and muskets that had once been on display, at a time when the Company needed to proclaim the force of its arms. Now even the shadows were barely visible, poking out behind the paintings that had replaced them.

Mansur had dressed, as usual, in the Indian style. He wore billowing *shalwar* breeches of striped silk, a fitted coat of cotton dyed bright green, and a turban threaded with gold. Silk slippers with pointed toes completed the ensemble – yet none of the men in the room gave his dress a second glance. They were used to the eccentricities of their fellow merchants. Some, in private, would wear similar garments when they visited clients or their mistresses. In the heat, tumult and sensuous living of India, men behaved in ways they would never dream of in London. Mansur, with his Omani blood, they considered more than half Oriental anyway.

There were a dozen men on the council, none of them above forty and most nearer twenty. Their faces were burned red by the sun or too much liquor, their young bodies prematurely aged and gaunt from the diseases they had survived. But all had the same glint aflame in their eyes: a hunger for fortune that would never be sated. For all their affability, there was not one – Mansur knew from personal experience – who would not sell his own daughter if he could make twenty per cent.

They had no loyalty to their employer. They wielded the power of the East India Company, and drew their salaries punctiliously, but every man earned ten times more by cheating the directors in London. As much as they traded on the Company's behalf, the best goods and the fattest profits always somehow accrued to their own accounts.

And the man to whom they looked to facilitate their commerce away from the jealous eyes in Leadenhall Street was Mansur Courtney. With a fleet of ships, and a network of agents that stretched from Canton to Calcutta to Cape Town, they could rely on him to move any cargo anywhere, with the utmost discretion. All for a very reasonable fee.

At the head of the table, Governor Saunders banged his fist on the arm of his chair to bring the meeting to order. He was sweating.

'I received intelligence today from London. War has broken out in America. We have fought an action with the French at a place called Fort Necessity, on the frontier of the Virginia colony.'

There were murmurs of alarm as the men took in the news. Mansur knew they would not be thinking of casualties and loss of life. Each man would be computing in his head the impact on his balance ledger. Would demand for tea from the colonies fall? Would the price of saltpetre, the crucial ingredient in gunpowder, rise? Several of the merchants edged towards the door, each wanting to be first to reach the market and profit from the news, before it became widely known.

'We must not think we will be immune,' continued the governor. The room quietened. America might be ten thousand miles away, and Fort Necessity was no doubt some tiny stockade in a trackless wilderness. But the threads of commerce, and of empire, had made a web around the world. A twitch in one, however distant, could reverberate to the ends of the earth. And there were Frenchmen a great deal closer than America.

'When the French garrison at Pondicherry hears of this, they will no doubt seek to take advantage. They may be marching on us already.'

'Then let us march to meet them,' said a man named Collins. He was the youngest in the room, fresh to India and only appointed to the council on the strength of his father's connections. His cheeks were still milky white, not yet tempered by the Indian sun. Mansur had seen the type before: he guessed he would not survive the first monsoon.

His suggestion fell on silence.

'The French have two thousand men,' said the governor.

'We have six hundred,' persisted Collins, transported by dreams of glory. 'And one stout Englishman is worth at least five Frenchmen.'

'Our official complement is six hundred,' Saunders corrected him. 'Our actual numbers are . . . fewer.'

He did not like to say exactly how many fewer. As far as the account books were concerned, he was still drawing pay for all six hundred men.

'Battles in India are not fought as you read in the histories of Europe,' Mansur counselled him. 'They love the pomp of war, here, but not the barbarity. They will fire a few shots at us, and we will gallantly return fire, and then they will offer to retreat upon receipt of a certain sum of money. Which – after a respectable amount of haggling – we will consent to. It will hurt us in the pocket, but nothing worse. Until then, we shelter safe behind our walls.'

The men around the table nodded, grateful to Mansur for speaking good sense. Only one, standing at the back of the room, did not share the general approval. He wore a plain black coat, with none of the lace or ornament of the merchants' clothes, and no wig. He stepped forward.

'You have something to say, Mr Squires?' said the governor. He had already half risen from his chair, eager to get to the market. By now, his factors would have had almost an hour to use the intelligence to stake various advantageous positions.

'The west wall is no better than sailcloth,' said Squires. He was the fort's engineer, a plain-speaking Yorkshireman, who baffled his Company colleagues with talk of ravelins, revetments and lunettes. 'The only way the wall will help us is if it falls down on our enemies.'

The governor frowned. A chatter of consternation swelled around the table. 'Surely you are exaggerating.'

'If you'd read one of my reports, you'd not be so surprised,' Squires retorted. 'It was no better than a garden wall when they built it, and no one's done any upkeep since. 'Tis no fortification at all. The only thing that keeps it upright is all the shacks and houses the blacks have built against it.'

'The directors in London voted two hundred thousand pounds for the improvement of the fortifications,' said Collins.

'I never saw a penny of it,' said Squires.

'Then where did it go?'

'That is hardly the question before us now,' the governor interrupted hastily. He would not have welcomed a lengthy investigation into where the money for the fortifications had gone. 'What matters is that we do not panic the populace, or give succour to our enemies, by revealing our weaknesses.'

'Our enemies will find them out soon enough,' muttered Mansur. Saunders didn't hear him.

'We will not be cowering behind walls, like women,' the governor insisted. 'A few shots, a show of valour, and honour will be served. Then we will be able to get back to business.' He stood, concluding the meeting. 'Good day, gentlemen.'

The merchants nodded heartily. Squires, the engineer, stood alone, staring pensively out of the high windows.

As the others hurried from the room, Mansur sought him out. 'Are the defences really so bad?'

Squires nodded. 'And the siege may be harder than you and our esteemed governor think. The French have their eyes set on the world. America, India, the East – they mean to take all our commerce. I would move your family into the fort, if I were you.'

'You said the walls availed us nothing,' Mansur protested.

'Better than being caught by the French in your home,' said Squires. 'A storm is coming, and we must seek what shelter we may.'

• • •

'Are you sure this is necessary?' said Verity. She stood by her harpsichord in the middle of the drawing room, surrounded by baggage. Furniture had been covered with dust sheets, while a small army of servants bustled about filling the chests, boxes and valises that littered the room. The house looked as if a typhoon had torn through it.

Mansur kissed her forehead. He smiled, so she would not realise his concern. 'What do you see through those windows?'

Verity did not have to look. Beyond the shady veranda, a line of trees fringed the road and the river. Past those, visible between the powder mill and the hospital, the angular towers of the western defences projected from the walls.

'If the French come, our house will make a fine artillery platform.'

'"If the French come,"' Verity repeated. 'We do not even know that they will. And this is our home.'

'I am taking no chances.' Mansur lowered his voice. 'I lost my own father too young because he was stubborn in the face of danger. I will not let my pride orphan my children.'

Mansur's father, Dorian, had lived an extraordinary life. Captured as a boy by Arab pirates, he had been sold into slavery to a prince of Oman, who had afterwards freed Dorian and adopted him as his son. Thus, through many adventures, Dorian had become a Muslim known as al-Salil. But he had made a mortal enemy of another of the prince's sons, Zayn al-Din, who had poisoned his father, usurped the throne, and later sent a man to murder Dorian's wife, Yasmini.

Mansur touched his eye socket, a gesture Verity had seen many times before. It still hurt when he was tired. He had found his mother's killer and fought him at the mouth of one of the great rivers of Africa. Although the man had almost ripped his eye out, in the end Mansur had disembowelled him, and watched sharks devour his corpse.

Mansur picked up a curved dagger mounted above the mantelpiece. It had been his father's. The scabbard was ivory, traced with gold and studded with jewels.

'I lost my father needlessly. I came to Madras because I was done with wars and fighting. I do not want my children to grow up without their father.'

Verity's face was sombre. 'In this world, it is a possibility we cannot ignore, whether the French come or no. How many of the writers and factors who arrived from London last summer have survived the year? Half, maybe? We must reconcile ourselves to the fact that we will not be here to protect them for ever.'

'But they are so young,' protested Mansur. 'Who would look after them if we were gone?'

Their eyes met. He knew what she would say even before she spoke.

'There are always Jim and Louisa.'

Jim was Mansur's cousin. They had grown up almost as brothers in Cape Town. Then Jim had fallen in love with an escaped convict woman, and the whole family had had to flee. Eventually, they had settled in an uncharted bay on the south-east coast of Africa, and built a compound they named Fort Auspice. Because Jim had many enemies, its location remained a secret known only to a few trusted friends.

It was more than ten years since Mansur had visited.

'You should make your peace with Jim,' Verity insisted. 'It is time to forgive. Jim and Louisa would not recognise Theo and Constance – and their little Georgie must be a strapping young man by now. I am sure they miss you.'

Mansur picked at one of the gems in the dagger, his thoughts far away. 'I curse the Elephant Throne,' he whispered.

His father, Dorian, had lived an extraordinary life, in the course of which he had become the heir to the Elephant Throne of Muscat, in Oman. But it had been taken from him.

'My father should never have tried to reclaim the crown,' said Mansur. 'It was sheer vanity.'

'It was not,' Verity rebuked him. 'Your father never wanted the Elephant Throne for his own glory. He went back because he felt obliged to serve his people. They were crying out for a fair and honest king.'

Mansur blew a thin cloud of smoke out through his lips. 'Still, he should not have gone.'

It had been a disaster. Early on, Dorian had suffered a wound that festered, but he had hidden the true extent of his suffering even from Verity and Mansur. He could not afford to appear weak before the desert-hardened sheikhs of Oman, whose support he needed in the war for the kingdom. In the crucial battle, in the thickest fighting, Dorian had fallen from his horse. Too weak to remount, he had been dragged away by his enemies and killed. Mansur and Verity had had to flee for their lives.

'It would have been different if Tom and Jim had come.' While Dorian and Mansur sailed for Muscat, the rest of the family had stayed in Africa. Afterwards, Jim and Mansur had quarrelled bitterly. Mansur blamed Jim for not coming to help, while Jim blamed Dorian for leaving before he was fully recovered. Their friendship could not survive it. And so Mansur and Verity had sailed for India. With a Courtney's instincts for commerce, Mansur had built up a tidy business trading across the Bay of Bengal, all the way to the East Indies and China. He had prospered. But he had never repaired the breach with the family he had left behind in Africa.

Mansur said nothing for a long time. They had had this argument many times, and he had never yielded. But now emotions he had kept pent up for years roiled inside him. Imminent danger – fleeing his home with his family in peril – had unleashed feelings that peace had let slumber. What was more important than family?

He put the dagger down on a table next to Verity's harpsichord. He smiled. There had been another harpsichord, and another house, and another flight a long time ago, pursued by soldiers of the Dutch East India Company. It was a time when he and Jim had been friends.

'You are right, my love – as usual. After this season, when the monsoon winds change in our favour, I will make the voyage to Africa. It will be good to go fishing with Jim again. And Theo and Constance will be astonished to find the cousins they have no memory of.'

• • •

'I'm bored,' Constance declared. 'Who could have imagined that war should be so tedious an affair?'

She lounged on a chaise in a white cotton sari, examining her reflection in a hand mirror. She was practising making faces, affecting different attitudes and studying their effects. Her hair hung in braids; her cheeks glistened with perspiration. Her French grammar book lay untouched on a side table.

She pouted at Theo. 'At least you could run away and join the army.'

Theo looked up from his book. 'Do not think I have not considered it. I am as bored as you are. But Father would find me soon enough. I cannot leave, any more than you can.'

They had been cooped up inside the fort for almost a month. The house they had taken belonged to a Company trader who was away in Bengal; his agent had been happy to let it to Mansur in consideration of a debt the trader owed.

For the first fortnight Theo and Constance had complained relentlessly about having to leave their home on nothing more than a rumour. Then the French had arrived. They had made camp near the great pagoda to the south, and erected gun batteries around the town. As Mansur had predicted, the Courtney family's drawing room now hosted two nine-pound field guns.

A dull boom echoed through the town. It had been going on for days now, though it still startled Theo each time. The French did not prosecute the siege with any great vigour: they rarely fired more than three shots an hour.

'I do not know how Mother can sleep through that,' said Theo. Verity was upstairs, having adopted the Indian fashion of napping after lunch.

'Perhaps growing up in so many sea battles she got used to it,' said Constance. 'At least she was allowed some excitement.'

'Father says we must carry on as if nothing was happening.' Theo turned to his book. It was *The Life, Adventures and Piracies of the Famous Captain Singleton* by Daniel Defoe. It was his favourite book. The tale of the pirates trekking into the undiscovered heart of Africa made him long for adventure, and to see those exotic landscapes for himself. His father had told him many stories of his escapades on that mysterious continent as a boy, which further ignited Theo's restless imagination. But it was hard to concentrate on fictitious pirates when real French gunners were trying to pound your home into rubble.

'I have always preferred *Moll Flanders*,' said Constance. 'Twelve years a whore, five times a wife, including once to her own brother, transported to America, yet she still grew rich and died comfortable. That is the sort of adventure I should like to have.'

'Mother says it is very unsuitable,' said Theo. He did not like hearing his sister use words like 'whore'.

Constance examined her face in the mirror again. 'Perhaps one day I will be a kept woman and marry for an obscene amount of money.'

'What a ridiculous notion. I want to marry a woman I love, like Mother and Father.'

Constance said nothing. Suddenly she put down her mirror and stood. 'Enough. Why should we speak of adventures in books when there are real adventures happening right on our doorstep? I want to go and see.'

Theo closed his book. 'Harjinder will never let us out.' Mansur had posted the guard at the mansion's door, with orders to allow none of the family to leave without his express permission.

'Surely you will not let that get in our way.'

Despite himself, Theo's eyes drifted to the window. Constance caught his gaze.

'What will Mother say if she wakes and finds us gone?' he said.

'We can be back before she wakes and she will be none the wiser. Or you can tell her yourself, if you are too afraid to come.'

'I'm not afraid.' He could not let her encounter danger alone. He put down his book and lifted the damp mat that had been hung over the window to cool the air. Constance swung her slim legs over the sill and dropped gracefully to the ground outside. Theo followed.

At that hour of the afternoon, the city was quiet. Most of the British inhabitants were asleep.

'Where shall we go?' asked Theo.

'Up to the walls. That will give us the best view.'

'But they will be guarded,' Theo objected.

She stuck out her tongue at him. 'I know a way.'

'How?'

'Follow me.'

She led him along the wide, sandy streets, keeping as much as possible to the backs of houses, and the alleys behind the Company warehouses. The buildings ended suddenly in a group of shacks and crumbling storerooms, crammed so close upon each other that it took Theo a moment to realise the brick wall behind was actually the outer wall of the fort.

'Lift me,' Constance ordered.

Theo cupped his hands and hoisted her onto the lowest roof, then hauled himself up behind her. The outbuildings made a giant staircase that they could scramble and clamber up until they pulled themselves, dusty and sweating, onto the rampart.

Theo ducked behind one of the battlements, but Constance stood fearless, leaning forward to peer out through the embrasure.

'Get down,' hissed Theo. 'What if someone sees you?'

'Who?' countered Constance. 'Father says the garrison is stretched so thin they can only man the main towers. And if some soldier comes by, I shall simper and smile and clutch his arm, and he will be convinced it is all a great misunderstanding.'

'The French?'

'I am sure they are too gallant to fire on a lady.'

At that moment, a puff of smoke and fire blossomed from the French lines. They heard the boom a moment later, felt it reverberating through the walls under their feet. A spray of sand fountained up from the plain below, as the cannonball fell harmlessly short.

'You see?' Constance exulted. 'There is nothing to worry about, little brother.'

'Don't call me that.'

Theo rose and peered out cautiously. Fort St George and the town of Madras had been built on a sandbar, a long finger of land crooked down the coast, separated from the mainland by a tidal lagoon. Across the strand, behind the lagoon, he could see the French encampments dotted among the palm trees around the great pagoda: rows of tents, baggage wagons, and stores. A makeshift parade ground had been cleared, where a company of fusiliers was being drilled. In front, native labourers had dug a row of entrenchments, where half a dozen guns sat mostly idle. Theo could see the gun crew lazily sponging out the gun that had just fired. The Company gunners in the fort showed no great desire to retaliate.

'If Father was commanding he would have fired four broadsides before the French had reloaded once,' said Theo, with a touch of family pride. Mansur had often told them how he had rescued their mother from her wicked father, how he had commanded his own sloop and engaged Guy Courtney's flagship, running right under her guns. Since Theo had first heard the story, sitting on Mansur's knee, he had longed for the thrill of battle. Yet now, confronted with the reality of guns aimed at him, it seemed more complex than Daniel Defoe made it sound.

'Keep down,' he told Constance. 'We should not expose ourselves to danger needlessly.'

'That last shot did not come within fifty yards of the walls,' said Constance. Her eyes were bright and wide, her face flushed. 'They are out of range.'

'You are enjoying this,' Theo said in wonder.

She turned to him, one hand resting on her chest. 'Of course. Isn't it thrilling?'

The cannon fired again.

• • •

The blast echoed through the fort. The crystal chandelier shivered and tinkled as Mansur entered the house. All the blinds were drawn, and the doors closed against the afternoon heat. Shafts of sunlight lanced through, showing eddies of dust in the air. However much the servants swept and cleaned, you could never escape it in this country.

'Verity?' he called. 'Constance? Theo?'

His anxiety increased as he climbed the stairs – though he told himself there was no reason for alarm. They would be sleeping, as they always did at this time of the day. And the house was well chosen – far back from the western walls and the French guns.

He opened the door to Constance's bedroom. It was empty, the bedsheets stretched tight and untouched. Uneasy, he tried Theo's room. The same. Perhaps they were with their mother.

Verity lay stretched out on her bed in a thin cotton shift, fast asleep. Even now, approaching forty, she was the most beautiful woman Mansur had ever seen. He thanked God every day for the chance that had brought them together.

But worries drove those thoughts from his mind.

'Where are Constance and Theo?' he asked, shaking her awake.

She rubbed her eyes. 'Are they not in their rooms?'

With greater urgency, they ran through the house, throwing open doors and calling for their children. It took them only minutes to realise that Theo and Constance were not at home.

'Where can they have gone?' wondered Verity. 'They knew they were forbidden to leave without permission.'

Another bang shook the house: louder, this time, as the English gunners decided to return fire. The vibration agitated the dust, spinning it into angry swirls in the sunbeams.

'The walls,' Mansur realised, with a jolt of horror. 'You know what Theo is like – always playing at soldiers. He will have gone to see the battle.'

'And Constance?'

'He must have taken her with him.' Mansur was already at the door.

Verity hurried after him. 'They will be exposed to the full force of the French artillery,' she fretted.

Mansur remembered the engineer's warning: 'They are in more danger from the walls they are standing on.'

He led her at a run across the parade ground in front of the governor's house, then past the church and the well. The scent of pepper, tea and spices surrounded the warehouses, but he did not notice. Cannon fired again, several shots so close they almost rolled together in a single noise. The French had increased the tempo of their attack, and the English responded in kind.

I pray we will not be too late, he thought.

They reached the bastion at the south-west corner. A sepoy sentry at the foot of the stairs made to stop them, then thought better of it. Mansur raced up the steps.

At the top, an English lieutenant blocked Mansur and Verity's way. The men at the guns, naked to the waist and dripping sweat, stared in surprise at the new arrivals.

'What the deuce are you doing?' shouted the lieutenant. 'This is no place for civilians. We are fighting a battle.' But looking along the walls, Mansur had seen what he was seeking. He pushed the lieutenant aside – harder than he intended. The officer stumbled, screaming as he fell against the scalding hot barrel of the cannon. By then, Mansur was beyond him, Verity too. Her skirts swished past the astonished gunners.

Mansur raced along the wall, his feet tripping on the uneven stones. 'Theo!' he shouted. 'Constance! Come down this instant. It is not safe.'

From the French lines, the cannon roared again.

* * *

At first Theo and Constance didn't hear their father's shouts. They were watching the French, and the sound of the guns had dulled their hearing. Then Theo noticed movement from the corner of his eye. The anxiety he had been feeling turned to horror.

He tugged on Constance's dress. 'They have spotted us. We will be in such trouble.'

Smoke from the bombardment drifted along the wall. The haze obscured the figures running towards them, but as they drew closer and clearer, Theo felt an ominous sense of familiarity.

'Father?' His gaze shifted to the figure behind. 'Mother?'

The rush of guilt was so great it drowned everything else. He turned and ran, no longer a young man but a boy who wanted to hide. He heard his father shouting at him to stop, screaming something about his safety, but he blocked it out. He didn't hear the cannon fire, or the louder sound that rose, like thunder, behind him.

His mother's scream cut through it all. Whether he heard it, or simply felt it ring in his bones, he paused. He turned.

The wall behind him had disappeared. The rampart he had been standing on seconds earlier was obliterated, collapsing on itself in an ever-widening hole. Bricks cascaded down, like water released from a dam, vanishing into the cloud of powdered mortar and dust that rose out of the rubble and engulfed it.

Theo ran back, holding his sleeve against his mouth. He paused at the edge of the hole. Loose bricks slithered and tumbled beneath him. How could one cannonball have wreaked so much damage?

'Go back.'

The voice was so faint, he hardly heard it above the settling stones. He didn't know where it had come from. He looked down.

His father was below him, clinging to a fragment of wall that had somehow remained upright. Further down, a bundle of limp white fabric lay at the bottom of the hole, pinned under the rubble, like a discarded rag. It was Verity.

'Get back,' Mansur hissed. Falling bricks had knocked out his teeth and left his mouth a bloody mess. His face was ghostly white with dust. 'Save yourself.'

'I can reach you,' said Theo, obstinately. He lay flat and stretched out his hand as far as he could. Mansur tried to reach back, but the pillar of bricks swayed at the least movement.

The gap was wider than it looked. Even at full stretch, Theo's fingertips came up short. He edged further out. Loose bricks fell from under him. He was inches from his father's hand. But he could feel the void opening beneath him. Another movement might bring the whole wall crashing down.

'Go back,' croaked Mansur. His precarious perch tottered on its foundations.

'I can save you,' Theo insisted. He reached further. His fingers brushed Mansur's but could not find a grip.

The rampart shivered. Theo, lying on his stomach, felt the vibrations in his skull, like a ringing bell. The French had not been idle. They had seen the damage they had caused and trained all their fire on it. Another cannonball slammed into the wall. More bricks shook loose and the shaky pinnacle Mansur had clung to gave way with a crack and started to collapse.

Forgetting all reason and safety, Theo lunged. Too late. Mansur was already falling away from him, slipping beyond his reach even as his hand stretched out. Mansur mouthed something that Theo could not understand. He wondered if it might have been 'Constance'.

Theo felt the slightest brush on his fingertips – then nothing. Mansur fell into the cloud of dust and smoke and disappeared.

There was nothing to stop Theo following him. The cannon fire had weakened the rampart he lay on, and his final lunge had taken him beyond safety. He didn't care. He had lost the two people he loved most in the world, and there was nothing left for him. Too late, he remembered the last word framed on his father's bloody lips. *Constance*. If he died now she would be left alone in the world. His father's dying wish, and Theo had failed it.

His thoughts flashed through his mind in an instant. As the full weight of guilt and failure hit him, he suddenly stopped falling. For a second, he seemed to hang in mid-air.

He looked around and saw a red-faced sergeant staring down at him, one hand locked on Theo's belt.

The sergeant hauled Theo back and laid him on the rampart. The ground felt heavy and solid beneath him. Before he could get up, Constance ran over and hurled herself onto him, cradling his head to her breast. 'I thought you were lost,' she said. 'I thought we were lost.'

More soldiers had arrived. The sergeant was shouting, telling them they must get away to safety. But Theo and Constance were unreachable, locked in a private world of grief. Theo was crying, adding shame to his misery: he should not be so womanly. But his parents had gone. He felt such despair that it was breaking his heart.

When he told Constance what had happened, she howled with anguish. She was inconsolable, and Theo held her tight, rocking her like a baby. Their world had exploded, shattered in an instant, hopes and dreams in fragments, loved ones pulverised. This was the bitter, brutal reality of war. Theo saw his fate anew through his tears, as the dust stung his eyes, and it was broken and twisted. How could he rebuild his life?

'This is my fault,' Constance whimpered. 'We should have been safe at home. If I had not led us here . . .'

Theo gripped her wrist too hard. 'Never say that again. We both came. We are both equally to blame. I will not let you take this on yourself.'

She brushed a lock of hair from his eyes and wiped the tears off his cheek. 'Thank you. We will have to look after each other now.' She started sobbing again.

There was a terrible void inside him, growing until he thought it would swallow him. 'Promise me, Connie. Promise me, whatever happens, you will never leave me.'

'I promise.'

'Never ever?'

'Never ever. I promise.'

Below, a party of sepoys began to pick through the rubble to recover the lifeless bodies of Mansur and Verity Courtney.

• • •

'We must learn the lessons Providence teaches from this tragedy,' said Governor Saunders sombrely. 'Mansur Courtney and his amiable wife must not have died for naught.'

He looked around the silent council room. The French bombardment had stopped; the only trace it had left there was that one of the paintings on the wall hung askew. He would tell the servants to straighten it.

The men at the table looked around without emotion. Death was ever-present in India, a cost to be borne, like spoiled goods and bribes. And every one of them had owed Mansur money.

'I have this afternoon sent envoys to the French commander under a flag of truce,' Saunders continued. 'He has agreed to accept our surrender, then ransom the city back to us. After some discussions, we have settled on a ransom of one and a half million gold pagodas.'

There was a sharp intake of breath in the room.

'Naturally, the money will be provided by the directors in London. After the Courtneys' deaths, they can have no doubt that we defended the Company's interests beyond the demands of honour – maybe even of prudence.'

The men in the council chamber relaxed. The siege would be lifted, London would pay, and they could return to making their fortunes. Mansur Courtney had not died in vain.

Squires, the engineer, looked up. 'And what of the children?'

Theo and Constance sat in the hall outside the governor's office. Theo's eyes were swollen and dark. The hours since Mansur had slipped away from him had been a waking nightmare, replaying the horror again and again.

Constance's grief took a different shape. After shedding her tears, she sat perfectly still, her face pale and emotionless. She stroked the nape of Theo's neck, the way his mother used to when he was small. It made him flinch as if he'd been burned.

'What will they do with us?' he asked, in a distant voice.

'I don't know.'

The door opened and a servant in the governor's livery beckoned them. Theo stood.

'Be strong,' Constance said, squeezing his hand. 'I rely on you, now.'

Theo nodded.

They stepped into the governor's office. Saunders ushered Theo and Constance to two chairs opposite his desk and gave them what he hoped was a sympathetic look. The boy was distraught; the girl seemed collected, her green eyes cool and poised. More than a girl, he corrected himself: the pert breasts swelling under the lace of her bodice were those of a woman now.

Saunders wondered if perhaps he should keep her in Madras after all.

He adopted a solemn expression. 'Words cannot express my sorrow for your loss. Your father was a good man, an admired colleague and – I flatter myself – a friend. Your mother was an ornament to our society. We grieve them deeply.'

Constance inclined her head in acknowledgement.

'But now you are orphaned.' He leaned forward over the desk and fixed Theo with a hard stare. 'What possessed you to take your sister up on the walls during such a bombardment?'

Theo's cheeks burned crimson. Part of him wanted to cry out, to explain: 'It wasn't my fault. It was Constance's idea.' But he could not do that to her. 'I wanted to see the battle,' he lied.

'I hope you never see another. War is a terrible thing, not for children,' Saunders lectured him. 'You have paid a dreadful price to learn that.'

He poured himself wine from a decanter. 'But now, as chief magistrate of the Presidency, I must decide how best to provide for your care and education.'

'What are your plans for us?' asked Theo.

Saunders surveyed him with a benevolent gaze. 'You have a cousin in Calcutta, I believe, a young man named Gerard Courtney.'

'We have never met him,' said Constance. 'His father and ours were not close.'

Saunders waved away her objection. 'But he is one of the most able men in India. His father – your uncle – is Christopher Courtney. Though I should more rightly say Baron Dartmouth, now that he has claimed his ancestral title. He was the richest man in India before he retired to London. In his son's household, you will want for nothing.'

Suddenly his face was not friendly. 'You have lived a comfortable life, my dear. I think you do not understand that the world outside our walls can be capricious and cruel – especially for those without a fortune. I will do what I can, but I cannot protect you for ever.'

That was not strictly true. He *could* keep Constance in Madras and take considerable pleasure from exercising his rights as her guardian. But that would not serve his greater purpose. 'Unless you have any other family I might consider?'

Constance bit her lip. Somewhere on the southeast coast of Africa had once lived her great-uncle Tom and great-aunt Sarah, with their family. But she had only met them once, as a tiny child, and she had no idea how she could find them now. The location of their settlement, in an uncharted bay on an almost uninhabited stretch of coast, had been a carefully guarded secret. For all she knew, they might be long since dead, or have moved away. And how could an orphaned sixteen-year-old girl, who had lived in India almost her whole life, make a passage to Africa with no one but her younger brother for company?

'We will go and stay with Cousin Gerard,' said Constance, feeling the weight of the decision. She knew India, knew its rituals and the levers of influence. She would find a way to ensure that she and Theo survived.

'A wise decision. I will arrange for your passage by the first ship to Bengal.'

Constance fixed him with her green eyes. So frank and knowing, they could not possibly belong to a girl of her tender years. Saunders felt a tightness in his breeches.

'What will happen to our inheritance?' Constance asked.

'It will be placed in trust until you come of age,' Saunders assured her. 'I myself will serve as one of the trustees.' He raised a hand to stop any protest. 'I feel I owe it to your father. It is the least I can do.'

He felt no guilt as he said it. Life was business, and these children were merely an asset that fate had put in his power. An asset of considerable value – and he would make sure he profited from it. By the time he had finished with Mansur's estate, there would not be two *fanams* left in the Courtney children's inheritance.

And that was if they lived long enough to claim it. The city of Calcutta had been built on a foetid swamp. The addition of two hundred thousand souls, with all their filth and squalor, had not improved its healthfulness. A pair of youngsters, newly arrived, might not survive the winter there – let alone the long, feverish summer.

Constance was watching Saunders with her sharp, appraising eyes. For a moment, he had the uncomfortable feeling that she could read his every thought. He dismissed the notion. She was little more than a child, a mouse in a world of wild cats.

But still her look unsettled him. He was right to send her away. He would have enjoyed breaking her in, but business always had to come first. The boy, too. He was a model of his father: the same tousled red hair, the same handsome looks. He might be damaged now, but Saunders could see the strength growing into his face and his body. He might become a formidable adversary.

A smile spread across Saunders's face. He hastily rearranged it into a look of pious concern. 'God speed to Calcutta.'

• • •

Ten miles from the governor's office, dust billowed off the road as the ox teams hauled the French artillery train towards Pondicherry. The soldiers sang lustily, despite the heat. They had bloodied English noses and were marching back richer than they had come. What else was war for?

A black horse galloped towards them through the dust. Its rider wore a plain grey coat without markings.

The major at the front of the column drew to the side of the road to let the artillery pass. A new commander had been dispatched from Paris, Major General Corbeil, and he wondered if the rider had news of him. It would be a fine thing to be able to present the general with this spectacularly profitable victory on his arrival. Perhaps a promotion would be in order.

'Who are you?' he interrogated the rider. 'Have you a message?'

The rider said nothing. Fixing the major with a piercing stare, he raised a gloved hand and brushed it against his coat. The layers of dust that had coated it fell away. Underneath, the cloth was white, not grey, and as the hand swept it clean it revealed brocade and gold lace. The uniform of a major general in the army of Louis XV.

The major swallowed and saluted. 'I am sorry, Monsieur Général. I did not know.'

The general gestured to the column. 'What is the meaning of this?' His face was puce with rage. 'Why are you retreating?'

'Retreat? Monsieur, this is a victory.'

'It is defeat,' spat the general. 'Ignominious failure – a wasted opportunity. When I write to Paris, I will see to it that you spend the rest of your career scrubbing latrines in the fever islands. You had Madras at your mercy, and you did not press the advantage.'

'Honour was satisfied. Six men and a woman – including an English merchant and his wife – died in our bombardment. It would have been ungentlemanly to make them suffer further.'

Without warning, Corbeil leaned forward and slashed the major across the cheek with his riding crop. 'You should have driven every English man, woman and child into the sea, or massacred them on the end of your bayonets until the ocean ran red with their blood. You should have bombarded the walls to rubble, burned their mansions and stripped the city's carcass so bare even the rats would find no pickings.'

The major clutched his face, but Corbeil rapped him again with the riding crop, leaving a white welt across his fingers. 'Look at me when I speak to you.'

The major's hand came away sticky with blood and dust. He gaped at the general.

'But have you not heard the news from Europe, Monsieur? There is no war. Our government has commenced negotiations with London to resolve the hostilities in North America without resort to arms.'

The major wiped his cheek on his sleeve, leaving a crimson stripe across the white cloth. As the shock receded, anger and indignation swelled in his breast. He had humiliated the English, earned the French Compagnie des Indes one and a half million pagodas, and all in a war that had never been declared. He was a hero. Honour demanded he should call out the general for a duel, to avenge the insult and protect his reputation.

But when he looked into the general's pitiless eyes, honour did not seem so important.

'If you will excuse me, *mon général*, I must keep my men moving.' The column had ground to a halt, the men distracted by the entertainment of their arguing superiors. The major grabbed a whip from one of the ox drivers and started lashing the men, cursing furiously. 'Get moving. If we are not in Pondicherry by nightfall, I will flog the flesh from your backs until I can see your ribs. On with you.'

He cantered to the head of the column as it lumbered into motion again. Corbeil watched from the roadside. A smile curled his lips. Anger was good: it served his purpose.

He didn't care what was said in Paris or London. Diplomats would talk, but they would fail, as they always did. In the end, France and Britain would go to war again, as they had for the last seven hundred years.

But this time the prize would be the world itself.

The ship's crew didn't see Calcutta as it came into view around a bend in the wide Hooghly River. The men were intent on their tasks, watching the sails for any shift in the breeze, or scanning the water for hidden dangers. At the stern the captain, the master and the pilot huddled around the wheel in deep concentration. The river was shallow, filled with treacherous sandbars that shifted with every storm. Along the way, sun-blackened hulks warned of the perils of straying from the shipping channel.

The only people who could afford to admire the view were the knot of passengers clustered by the starboard rail on the quarterdeck. They were a strange society: blue-coated clerks and writers come to make their fortune with the East India Company; soldiers returning from leave; Armenian merchants chattering in their own cryptic language; women from England eager to find a husband.

Theo and Constance stood among them. Theo strained his eyes as their new home came in sight. The imperious wall of Fort William towered over the ghats at the riverside, long and straight, stamping its authority on the twisting river. An enormous Union flag hung limp from the flagstaff, next to the church spire and the grand classical façade of the governor's house. Elegant mansions stretched along the river front for a mile in each direction, set in splendid gardens sloping down to the water. Beyond the dockhead, big East Indiamen swung at anchor against the lazy current, while the small local craft called budgerows darted nimbly between them, their oars like centipedes' legs.

Constance squeezed his hand. 'What do you think, Theo?'

'It looks just like home,' he exclaimed.

And yet it was different. Instead of the ocean surf pounding the beach, there was the slow brown river oozing by. Instead of handsome red stone, the fort was built from whitewashed brick. From a distance, it looked radiant in the sunlight, but as they came closer Theo saw it had yellowed in the damp and heat, like curdled milk. The humid air weighed heavily on him and gave him a headache. The city was indisputably magnificent, but as soon as the gardens gave out, the jungle pressed close on every side.

A cannon fired a salute from the fort. An elephant screeched its wild cry. Theo shivered.

'I am certain you will be very happy here,' one of the clerks said to Constance. He was a gangly man, with ginger hair and a lisp, but he had managed to secure the coveted place next to her at the rail. Ever since the ship had weighed anchor from Madras, the young men on board had attended her, like moths around a candle. If she dropped her scarf, a dozen gallant arms reached to pick it up before it touched the deck; if the level in her glass dropped a fraction of an inch at dinner, someone was on hand to refill it. Of all the commodities that the East India Company's ships carried, few were so valuable – or so rare – as eligible English ladies.

'I am sure it will be delightful,' said Constance, with a bored smile.

Their arrival had brought a throng of people to the ghats in front of the fort, keen for whatever news the ship might bring. As the jollyboat rowed the passengers to the wharf, the sight lifted Constance's spirits. The confined world of shipboard life did not agree with her, the same dull faces night after night, making the same tedious conversation over the same hard food. She wanted crowds, novelty and dancing.

Theo, sitting beside her, wanted none of those things. Every night, he dreamed the same nightmare: his father's hand slipping away, and brick dust filling his lungs. He burned with the shame and injustice of it. All he wanted was a chance for revenge.

The boat bumped against the wharf. The noise from the crowd as they reached the top of the steps was overwhelming: traders and relatives asking for news, porters, hawkers and prostitutes offering their services. Theo shrank back.

One man cut through the crowd. He was tall and handsome, with tousled fair hair and a firm stride. Through the jostling elbows and barging shoulders, he moved with ease and an unshakeable smile, as if the scene was simply a marvellous entertainment. He made straight for Constance and Theo.

'Cousins!' he exclaimed. He kissed Constance on the cheeks and gazed at her face. His eyes were hazel, flecked with green, and already crinkled at the edges from squinting too much in the Indian sun.

'Cousin Gerard, I presume,' said Constance.

'Words cannot express my sorrow at the circumstance that brings us together.' He spoke softly, but the force of his words carried over the hubbub around them, as if they were alone on the dock. A tear welled in Constance's eye. Before she could blink it back, he reached up and wiped it gently away. 'I did not realise how grown-up you were,' he said. His eyes seemed to bathe her in light, warm as the sun.

Perhaps it was the heat, or the shock of being on land after weeks at sea, or the irretrievable loss of her old life and family, but suddenly Constance felt giddy. The world spun around her and darkness speckled her vision, as if she was going to faint.

Then Gerard turned to Theo, and the world returned. The clouds lifted, and the ground under her feet stabilised.

'You must be Theo.' Gerard shook his hand, firm and businesslike. 'Come.'

Two dozen native porters fell in behind them to carry their baggage. Gerard offered Constance a sedan chair, but she refused with a gracious smile. 'After that ship, I am grateful I can take ten paces without falling into the sea.'

Theo observed the city as they walked. Though far younger as a city than Madras, Calcutta was already larger in every dimension. The houses were grander, the gardens more elaborate. Even the streets seemed busier, which he had not thought possible. He was seeing the city in the throes of its own invention – or reinvention. Every other building seemed to be swaddled in scaffolding, either half built or half torn down to add some newer, grander design. The city throbbed with a restless, adolescent energy, which mature Madras had long since outgrown.

Gerard brought them to a large mansion on a wide avenue near the edge of the town. A doorman in a crimson turban, with a scimitar at his side, flung open the high double doors. Three footmen appeared, each carrying a cup of sherbet, while various butlers and factotums bustled about in a chaos of orders and commands.

'Welcome to my home,' said Gerard. He took Constance's hand. 'I hope you will soon feel it is your own, as well.'

'I do so look forward to meeting your family,' said Constance.

Gerard looked pained. 'I fear I must disappoint you. My mother passed away some years ago while my father, as you know, has removed to London to take his seat in the Lords. I have two sisters, but they are married and far away.'

'You live here by yourself?' marvelled Theo.

'For the time being.'

'How old are you?'

Gerard laughed. 'Twenty-five. You think I am too young for such an estate? Perhaps you are right. But in this city life is lived to the full. Time is too short to do otherwise. Fortunes are won or lost in an instant.'

'There is no Mrs Courtney?' Constance enquired.

'Alas, no.'

'No attachments or connections that cause tongues to wag?' she probed. 'If we are to live under your roof, we must know if we have stepped into the domain of a notorious rake.' Her eyes sparkled.

Gerard grinned, sharing the joke. 'If you hope to uncover a scandal, I fear you will be disappointed. There are few eligible ladies of sufficient quality in Calcutta, and the demands of business leave me little time to press my suit.' He began climbing the grand staircase, lined with portraits of his ancestors. 'I am in no hurry to marry. I am happy to wait for love to find me.'

He opened a door. The three maidservants lined up inside curtsied. 'This will be your room, Constance. I have taken the liberty of appointing some maids for you, but if they prove unsatisfactory I will happily find you others.'

'You are too kind,' Constance murmured. She took in the large room with its rich carpets teak furniture and ornamental hangings, the high, airy windows fitted with carved sandalwood screens. After weeks of sleeping in a cot in a cabin the size of a coffin, the space felt immense. The bed alone could have slept four abreast.

'Where is my room?' asked Theo.

Gerard put his arm around his shoulder. 'You will not live here.'

'But—'

'I have made special arrangements with the governor that you will take up a position as a writer for the Company. It is a little irregular, at your age, but given your circumstances and the family connection, I was able to prevail. You will have lodgings in Writers' Row, inside the fort, with the other bluecoat boys.'

'But I want to live *here*,' said Theo, obstinately. 'With Connie.' He stared beseechingly at his big sister.

'You must do as our cousin says,' she said. 'It will be for the best.'

Gerard ruffled Theo's hair. 'If you are as clever as I hear tell, I dare say you will soon own a house to make mine look like a mere cottage.'

'But I could live here and still work in the fort. It is no distance.' Through the window, he could see the Palladian façade of the governor's house a stone's throw away.

'It is not just about learning the ropes. Living with the other writers, you will come to know them intimately. You will make connections and friendships that will be invaluable to your career.'

'You must, Theo,' said Constance. She was keen that Theo embrace the opportunity to further himself. 'And, as you say, it is no distance at all. We will surely see each other almost as often as if we lived in the same house.'

Theo's face flushed dark. He turned away, his thoughts in turmoil. He kicked at the frame of a door and tried to marshal the raging demons in his head. He wanted to be with Connie. He had promised to protect her at all times, and she had pledged never to leave him. But a higher calling was making itself heard, its voice a shriek, like a bird of prey with blood on its talons. His father and mother had been slaughtered and vengeance burned in his soul. A bookish life was a mockery.

'Then I will join the army,' he said.

'That is not the right path for a gentleman,' Gerard cautioned.

'I do not care about being a gentleman. I want to fight the French.'

'You will do as I say.' Gerard's friendly demeanour had vanished. His tone was harsh and threatening.

Theo was unbowed. 'You cannot stop me.'

'You are my ward – you are mine to command.'

'I will volunteer.'

'The commander of the army is the president of the council,' said Gerard, with a bitter laugh. 'He will not accept you.'

Theo looked at Constance. How could she stand there, fanning herself, while their cousin bullied him like this? 'I will run away.'

'You will not,' said Gerard, and now his voice trembled with something truly dangerous. 'Whom could you go to? Where would you run? You are an orphan now – my charge – and if you embarrass me I swear you will pay a price you cannot afford. You will join the Company, and you will excel in every endeavour to bring credit upon yourself, and on me. Do I make myself clear?'

Fury boiled inside Theo. He felt an overwhelming urge to swing at his cousin, to bloody that haughty face. Then he remembered Constance. She would be living in Gerard's house. As his ward, their cousin would have absolute power over her. Any insult that Theo inflicted, Gerard could take out ten times over on Constance. Was that what he had meant by 'a price you cannot afford to pay'?

Without a word, Theo turned and stamped down the stairs.

'You must not think badly of him,' said Constance. 'After all we have suffered, he is fragile.'

'Of course,' said Gerard. 'He is very loyal to you.'

Constance smiled. 'He takes his duties as a brother very seriously. He always thinks it is his job to protect me.'

'You do not look as if you need protecting from anyone,' said Gerard, with a wink. 'But this will be for the best. Standing on his own feet, and making his way in the world, will help him to put his sorrows behind him. Forgive me if I sound callous, but that is the way of things.'

'You do not sound callous. I think you are very generous.'

'I am glad you are here,' he said quietly. 'My father is an austere man, and since he left I have been too busy with other things. The house could use a woman's touch. Life will be gayer from now on.'

Constance squeezed the plump mattress. Suddenly, she longed for nothing more than to sink into it. 'I hope so. Perhaps it is selfish, but I feel I deserve a little happiness now.'

• • •

When Theo first saw his quarters in Writers' Row, he wanted to run away. It was as far from Gerard's opulent mansion as could be imagined. Two spartan cells, one with a bed, one with a desk, both covered in dust. Giant ants scuttled about the floor, while the furniture was ridged with the veins of woodworm. For long moments, he entertained fantasies of fleeing Calcutta and making his living as a mercenary at an Indian court, where even Gerard couldn't reach him.

Then he remembered his obligations to Constance. He must do this for her, and find a way to fulfil his destiny.

His pay was five pounds a year, plus three pounds' allowance, with which he employed two servants. In return, he was required to calculate sums and enter them in the ledgers, inspect cargoes and inventories, ensure the appropriate paperwork reached the correct file, and attend church twice a day.

In the first month, the work overwhelmed him. Most of Theo's leftover allowance went on lamp oil, as he scribbled in the ledgers long into the night, cursing the figures that obstinately refused to add up. In daytime, bleary-eyed, he tried to assess the quality of a bale of cloth, while a crowd of merchants harangued him with their sales patter until his head hurt. He put the wrong papers into the wrong files, then could not find them when they were needed. He began to look forward to the compulsory church services, simply so he could nap for a few minutes without feeling a rap across his knuckles or hearing angry voices shouting in his ear.

But he was determined to win this game. Since he had been a baby, his nursery had been the godowns and marketplaces of Madras, trailing dutifully after his father. He had learned how to haggle almost as soon as he could talk. The endless ritual courtesies of Indian conversation tripped off his tongue. Unlike most Englishmen, he understood that the stock phrases were not merely empty convention but a way of building trust; that the tone a man used to answer your question spoke far more than the words he said. Soon, the merchants who came to Fort William to sell their goods sought him out especially. They gave him the best prices, because they liked doing business with him, and the skills he had learned from his father ensured he acquired the best goods. He was not afraid to unravel a whole bale of calico to see that the fabric in the middle was as good as that on the outside, or to invite the tea merchants to brew a cup with their wares, in case it had been bulked out with sawdust or straw. His reputation as a sharp operator grew: the dishonest merchants shunned him, preferring men who would connive with them in cheating the Company, but the honest ones adored him because he would pay fairly for top quality.

Eventually, he mastered the ledgers. He had a good head for figures. If he was offered cloth at six rupees the yard, he knew instantly how much the bale would cost, and how much profit he would make if the prices in London stayed constant, or if they dropped a halfpenny. It was when he had to tot up the figures on paper that the numbers swam in front of his eyes. After a time, he hit upon a solution. He taught one of his servants the English names for numbers, and thereafter did his accounts by lying on his bed, listening to the servant read the figures aloud, then shouting out the tallies.

Though they lived almost in sight of each other, he did not encounter Constance very often. Even in a universe as small as Calcutta's, there were different orbits that rarely intersected. Her life, breathlessly recounted in her letters and on the rare occasions they met, was an endless round of assemblies, card parties, rides and dancing. She no longer walked but travelled in a palanquin carried by eight stout Hindus, with a servant girl running beside her whose only responsibility was to smooth out her petticoats. Or she would drive herself in a landau that had been shipped from England, cracking the whip while Gerard lounged beside her.

'Cousin Gerard is so good to me,' she confided in Theo, one Sunday afternoon. It was evening, and they were walking in the public gardens around the great reservoir known as 'the tank'. 'He has practically made me mistress of the house.' She had banished to the attic the old pictures of ships and battles and replaced them with Indian paintings in bright and exotic colours.

'I hope he is not too forward,' said Theo. Living in Writers' Row, in the constant company of two dozen boys all under the age of eighteen, had given him a breakneck education in all manner of experiences that had nothing to do with commerce. It had made him very protective of his sister's honour. More than once, he had had to defend it with his fists in impromptu bouts with the other boys behind the carpenter's yard.

Constance linked her arm in his. 'He is a perfect gentleman. And, I declare, he thinks no more of marriage than of going to the moon. I could walk past him wearing nothing but my petticoats, and he would not look up from his papers.'

'Connie!' said Theo, shocked. He did not like his sister even thinking of such behaviour.

Her eyes danced. 'Do not play the innocent. I heard from Henry Lushington's sister that you had been seen three times last week with a certain Indian girl at a punch house in Black Town.'

Theo was instantly transported back to the sensuous, smoky dark rooms, the heady scent of nutmeg and spices, the voluptuous girls and, in particular, the sweet young maiden who had taken a shine to him, her soft, supple skin like the finest silk on the tips of his fingers. He shivered. 'That is different.'

'Indeed – for if I were seen unchaperoned in a punch house with a native, I would be drummed out of our society.'

'That is not what I meant.'

'Why should the rules not be the same for women and for men? We are all creatures of flesh and blood.'

Theo flushed scarlet. 'To protect your virtue.'

She laughed. 'Rest assured, brother, my virtue is safe. I believe our cousin intends to marry me off to a sea captain or a Company trader. He has begun correspondence with Governor Saunders in Madras concerning our inheritance. He says he fears it is being ill-used in our absence, but I think his true worry is that I shall have no dowry, and he will be left with an old maid to feed all his days.'

'I wish he showed so much concern for me.' Though Gerard frequently had business in the governor's house at Fort William, he almost never visited Theo. 'Sometimes I think he deliberately snubs me.'

'He means it kindly,' said Constance. 'He wants you to learn habits of self-reliance. Also, he does not want it to be said that you rise only because of your connections. He is very sensitive to this point: his own father, Uncle Christopher, meddled constantly in Gerard's life, and his friends resented him for it.'

'It does not seem to have harmed his career,' said Theo, thinking of the great mansion.

Constance slipped her arm out of his and kissed his cheek. 'I must go. We are invited to supper with the Manninghams, and I will be late for my hairdresser.'

• • •

As time passed, and as Theo's masters noticed every week the balances in his ledger outshone those of the other bluecoat boys, he began to travel away from Calcutta, sometimes for days, visiting distant suppliers. He enjoyed seeing more of the country, though the pace of the expeditions infuriated him. Even the shortest trip in India required all the pageantry and pomp of a royal progress. Musicians led the column with trumpets and drums, while the merchants rode in howdahs on the backs of elephants. A detachment of soldiers followed, together with scores of the local servants known as *peons* and *hircarahs*. Wherever they went, hordes of the native inhabitants clustered around them. Sometimes they were lucky to go five miles in a day.

On most of these trips, Theo was attached to a senior agent named Deegan. He was a Scotsman, who had lived in India longer than anyone could remember and insisted he would die there too. 'This heat and the liquor are all that holds my body together,' he maintained. 'If I went back to a Scottish winter, the cold would snap me in two.' He had given himself over to the Indian way of life. He dressed in loose Indian clothes, his head wrapped in an enormous turban, and ate the most pungently spiced curries Theo had ever tasted. He kept an Indian wife, though rumour insisted there still existed a Mrs Deegan back in Edinburgh.

'Once ye've had black, you never go back,' he told Theo, with a wink. They were sitting in the agent's house in one of the trading stations, lounging on cushions. 'Softest bonny pussy you'll ever feel.'

He handed Theo the stem of the hookah pipe. Theo took a long drag of the vaporised mu'assel, a syrupy tobacco mixture, with molasses, vegetable oil and a fruit flavour. The hit made him light-headed and gently relaxed. He said nothing.

'I blame it on the clothes they wear. Our bonny Englishwomen are parcelled up in their busks and stays, pinched in so tight it makes them tough as old leather. Now your Indian girl, all she has is soft cotton wrapping her boobies, as close to nature as the Good Lord intended.'

Theo thought of Constance, the way she'd fought with their mother over wearing her sari. Since they had arrived in Calcutta, he had only ever seen her wearing immaculately starched English dress.

Deegan sucked on his pipe and blew a smoke ring. 'D'ye ever go down to the riverbanks, early in the day when the native women wash?'

Theo shook his head.

'They bathe fully dressed, you know, but when they come out, oh, laddie, those wet clothes hide nothing. You see all their beauties and graces.'

'I am usually at morning prayer,' said Theo.

'Aye,' grunted Deegan. 'And that's the tragedy of it. This Company would rather you were locked up in chapel, staring at the floor, than observing what's happening around you.'

'I am not sure the governor would see it so.'

'Course he wouldn't.' Deegan drained his glass of arrack and gestured at the serving girl to pour more. 'The Company has grown fat and complacent. The governor is a fool, and the council filled with men who are so busy lining their pockets they do not see what is in front of their noses.

We are guests in this country, though you would not know it from the way we lord it over them. There are a few hundred of us, against millions of Indians, but we presume to think we're untouchable.'

'The Indians profit too much from our trade to confront us,' said Theo. It was the sort of opinion he often heard in the mess hall at Fort William.

'The Indian has his pride, just like any man. Some more than most. You know that our local prince, the nawab, is dying?'

'I have heard rumours.'

'Aye, there are always rumours. There are rumours that his heir, his grandson, has the temper of Nero and the appetites of Caligula. There are rumours he has seen that the Company treats his grandfather like a lackey and means to teach them manners. There are rumours that a French general has been seen skulking around his court, and no one troubles to think it significant because no war is declared yet. Have you heard the story that our esteemed Governor Drake is gathering an army in Calcutta to attack the French settlements upriver?'

'That is preposterous.'

'Of course it is. Our fat fart of a governor could-nae find his own cock in a brothel, let alone start a war. But why are people saying it?'

'To discredit us?'

'Aye. The French know we've no cause or hope to attack 'em. But if they make out we do, and the nawab believes 'em, he'll not be best pleased. Can't have his guests brawling in his own front room.' He took another long pull on his pipe. 'Did you notice nothing amiss in the market today?'

'I thought we got surprisingly good prices.'

Deegan nodded. 'That we did. But only because we agreed to pay cash. If we had asked for credit, they would have turned us away.'

'Why?'

'Because they do not think we will be here in six months' time to honour our debts.'

He belched – a noxious gas of curry, arrack and tobacco. His turban had slipped. Years of alcohol and sunburn had left his nose as red as a pepper. He looked what he was: a foolish, dirty old man. How could anyone take his warnings seriously against the supreme assurance of young men like Gerard Courtney?

Yet still Theo wondered.

• • •

Major General Corbeil was sweating. Even in the shade of the nawab's pavilion, the still air was boiling. The French general tugged at the collar of his starched white uniform, cursing the heavy cloth. If he found the tailor who had made it, he would pull out his fingernails.

The young nawab, Siraj-ud-daula, lounged on golden cushions on the throne he had recently inherited from his grandfather. His plump, rounded body reminded Corbeil of the pears that grew in the orchard on his family estate in Normandy. He fidgeted incessantly with the rings on his fingers, each one bulging with precious stones as big as musket balls. He looked bored.

Corbeil tried to master his face, to hide the sneer that rose so naturally. The nawab was a fool, devoted to sensuality and cruel pleasures. But he might be useful.

'I am grateful to Your Highness for inviting me to witness this entertainment,' he said.

In front of the royal pavilion, a naked man was trying to run away from an elephant. He had large chains shackled to his ankles. One was attached to a stake in the ground; the other was fastened to the elephant's leg. Mounded earth walls made a rough arena encircling them, lined with the crowds who had come to watch.

The elephant lumbered around the arena in a broad circle, pausing every so often to scratch the dust with her trunk. The chained man shuffled along behind her.

'This is too slow,' the nawab complained.

The court officials looked anxious. They could not afford to displease their master, or they might find themselves suddenly joining the prisoner in the arena. It had happened before. Urgent commands were given. Bare-chested men with spears ran into the arena, prodding the elephant's flanks. With a honk of outrage, she gathered pace.

The prisoner had to run to keep up. If he allowed the elephant to get too far ahead, he would be torn apart by the two chains. At the same time, the weight of the chains slowed him down. His run consisted of awkward, jerky motions, like those of a puppet with a broken string.

'What was his crime?' Corbeil enquired. He didn't care: he was making conversation.

Siraj took a piece of mango from the silver plate beside him. 'I do not trouble myself with details. Whatever it was, he is guilty. An example must be made.'

He stared at his French visitor, daring him to disagree. But Corbeil had seen men die in a hundred terrible ways, for good reasons and bad and none at all. Many had died cursing Corbeil's name, his pitiless eyes the last thing they saw. He didn't care about an Indian peasant. 'When men defy their rulers, the punishment should be exemplary,' he said.

'Indeed.' The nawab leaned forward. Mango juice dribbled from his moustache. Before it reached his chin, a servant with a napkin wiped it away.

Corbeil lowered his voice. 'You will not tolerate one thief or criminal in your kingdom. Yet in Calcutta you allow hundreds of them to steal from you with impunity.'

There was an 'Ooh' from the crowd as the prisoner tripped – but he recovered his balance and kept running. Weighed down with chains in such stifling heat, Corbeil wondered how long the man would last before his strength failed.

'The English do not respect you,' the Frenchman continued. 'In the bazaars and the marketplaces, they say you are not half the man your predecessor was. They mock you as a spoiled child. They cheat you on the taxes they are obliged to pay. They think you are too stupid to notice and too weak to stop them.'

Corbeil paused. He wondered if he had gone too far. Siraj's face was almost purple with fury. No one had ever dared to say such things to his face. He had had men mutilated and killed for less.

In the arena, the prisoner was losing his battle to keep pace with the elephant. He tripped and sprawled on the ground, distracting Siraj. He tried to scramble to his feet but was yanked off balance by the taut chain and dragged through the dust after the elephant. The chain attached to the post unspooled behind him. The crowd cheered.

'What do you think they do with the money they cheat out of you?' Corbeil asked Siraj. He had used the goad. Now it was time to dangle the carrot.

Siraj turned his attention to the Frenchman, keeping one eye on the arena.

'There is a strongroom in Calcutta, in the governor's mansion, where the governor keeps his treasure,' Corbeil continued. 'All the money he has defrauded from you – many millions of rupees. He sits there at night, counting his coins and laughing at the man he stole them from. He sees your face stamped on those coins and spits on it to polish them. But he will regret his arrogance when you march into his strongroom and force the coins down his throat until he chokes.'

On the ground, the elephant stampeded in circles. The chain attached to the prisoner's leg wound tighter and tighter around the stake.

'Is it not right that you should be given what is owed you, Your Highness?'

A scream drew their attention. The elephant was rampaging in circles, but the man lay in a crumpled heap, like a bloodied rag doll. His severed leg, spewing gouts of blood, was still attached to the end of the chain behind the elephant. It flew into the air, bouncing on the ground, like a piece of meat trailed before a pack of hungry dogs. The crowd roared and cheered, their bloodlust given full release. The baying became demonic – they wanted more.

'In a test of strength between a man and an elephant, there can be only one winner,' Corbeil said. 'You have let the English flout your rules too long. Now it is time to crush them.'

The broken prisoner dragged himself through the dust, though he could not escape. The chain on his one surviving leg fixed him to the stake in the middle of the arena. If he could reach it, he might be able to cling on and avoid the elephant's stamping feet.

The elephant was charging again. Every man in Siraj's court craned his neck to see if the prisoner would reach safety.

But at the final moment, summoning one last gasp of strength, the man leaped forward, straight into the elephant's path. The crowd gasped as the man's body exploded in a haze of red.

The prisoner disappeared in the clouds of dust beneath the elephant's pounding feet. Everyone watched intently. Moans could be heard, and a fug of disappointment descended. The mahouts corralled the elephant and slowed it to a walk. The dust settled. The prisoner lay flat and limp, like an old pillow.

Siraj slumped back on his cushions and gulped wine from his cup. 'He did not give much sport,' he complained. 'Next time, I wish to see the prisoner fighting for his life.'

Corbeil gave a smile. 'If that is what you wish, Your Highness, then that is what I shall give you. In Calcutta.'

A hungry gleam came into the nawab's eye. He belched and nodded. 'In Calcutta.'

• • •

Theo and Deegan returned to Calcutta on a Tuesday afternoon. It was June, and the monsoon was coming. In the last days before it broke, the heat was driven to such impossible heights that every movement was an ordeal. The humidity weighed on the air in Theo's lungs, and even changing his shirt five times a day he was always soaked with sweat. Every day he felt as if he was pushing a boulder up a mountain, the effort greater and greater, waiting for the moment when the burden would lift.

They crossed the bridge over the Maratha Ditch and entered Calcutta. The ditch was a defence that had been dug some years earlier, when the Company had feared that the brutal Maratha

Army might attack the city. But the threat had passed before the ditch was finished, and it had been left incomplete. Now it was overgrown, filled with dirt and rubbish. It could barely keep out the gaunt cows that grazed freely on the outskirts of the city.

'If you go back to the fort now, you'll be in time for church,' Deegan pointed out. 'Take yourself off to a punch house and, if anyone asks, tell them I had you totting up my books.'

Theo nodded gratefully. After the liberty of travelling with Deegan, he was not yet ready to return to the tight routines of Fort William.

It was mid-afternoon, and Calcutta was sleeping. The streets were almost empty, the shutters on the great houses closed as their British masters and mistresses slept out the heat of the day. The monsoon still had not broken.

Theo wanted a drink – but the punch house did not appeal. The only people there at this time of day would be the worst drunks, a smattering of men who had failed in the Company's service, and new arrivals he would rather avoid. He needed water to wash the dust of the road from his mouth before he could stomach liquor.

He was a few minutes from Gerard's house. Without thinking, he found his weary legs carrying him past the twin tamarind trees at the house's gate and up the steps. The windows were shuttered.

The doorman moved to intercept him, shouting urgent protestations that his master was not available. Theo had lived long enough in India to learn the habits of command. He stared down the doorman, and, with a contemptuous toss of his head, barged past.

The doorknob was so hot it was scalding and Theo had to wrap his hand in his shirt sleeve to turn it. Inside, the hallway was dim and cool. A servant woke from the chair he had been sleeping on and hurried forward, but Theo silenced him with a look. At this hour, Constance would be asleep upstairs. He could surprise her, as he had so many times as a small boy, sneaking into her bedroom and leaping on her like a tiger.

He took off his shoes and padded quietly up the stairs. More servants emerged from the shadows, like cats, watching him pass, but none tried to stop him. They could lose their jobs in an instant if they so much as looked at an Englishman in a way he did not like.

Theo walked down the wide corridor and came to Constance's door. A low, rhythmic thumping came from inside – probably one of the shutters banging on its hinge. But there was no wind. Perhaps a servant was beating dust out of the carpet. Standing at the closed door, his hand resting on the handle, he could hear soft grunts, and an occasional throaty moan. Maybe the carpet-beater had struck a hand while holding up the carpet.

It was a strange time to be cleaning the carpets. He opened the door.

The carpet lay on the floor where it always did. The shutters were closed and fastened securely. As he had supposed, Constance was in her bed. A canopy of gauze curtains hung around her, so that in the dim light she was little more than a silhouette sitting upright.

Then the opening door pushed a current of air into the stillness of the room. The breeze lifted the thin curtains, while light from the doorway fell on the bed and illuminated it like a theatre stage.

Constance was naked. She knelt up, back arched, one hand cupping her breast and the other rubbing the gleaming wet tuft of fair hair between her thighs. Her eyes were closed, her head tipped back and her mouth open in a rapturous expression, making exotic mewls of pleasure.

She was not alone. She was straddling a man, though his face was hidden by the pillows. His hands clutched her buttocks, squeezing and pulling as he thrust himself into her, so hard it made the whole bed shudder. The sound Theo had heard was the headboard, banging against the wall.

'Connie,' he cried.

Theo would never forget the look she gave him. It was not shame, or guilt, or contrition: her green eyes blazed with deep, pure anger. She did not grab the sheets, or even cover herself with her arms. She stayed where she was, her lover still inside her.

'You should have knocked,' she said calmly.

Theo stared. In the dull light, Constance's lithe white body seemed to glow. Her breasts were shapely and firm, the nipples bright red with excitement. He thought the emotions welling inside him might tear him apart.

The man under her pushed himself up and twisted around.

'Can a man not take his pleasures in peace?' Gerard said irritably.

Theo stared at the floor. His certainties about the world were collapsing. And yet he knew what he must do. There was no room for thought or compromise.

He forced himself to look Gerard in the eye. 'I demand satisfaction.'

Gerard squinted at him. 'Damned selfish of you, when you interrupt before I've had my own satisfaction.'

'I mean I am challenging you to a duel.'

'Don't, Theo,' murmured Constance.

'A duel?' Gerard echoed. 'For what?'

'You have dishonoured Constance.'

'Honour is nothing but what other people believe. No one need know.'

His insouciant tone was too much for Theo. 'God damn you, sir – this is my sister.'

'Theo!' The sharpness in Constance's voice was like a slap. 'Stop behaving like a prig. Go downstairs, have the servants fetch you some tea, and I will be down presently.'

'You want me to sit in your parlour while you are upstairs with . . . *him*?'

'You are not my father or my guardian. You will not tell me what I can do, or where I should take my pleasures.'

'Your pleasures?' Theo felt sick. The sultry, stultifying air pressed on him, like a funeral shroud. He needed space, light, room to breathe. How could he have been so naïve? 'Are you to be married?'

She shrugged. 'We have not talked of it.'

'How long has this been going on?'

'Long enough.'

Her lack of shame fanned his anger. Phrases that had been drummed into his head through all those compulsory hours in church came effortlessly to his lips. 'Are you such a wanton harlot?'

'Is that what you think of me?' Constance turned on him. 'You and every other man in this settlement – are you such paragons of continence and virtue, with your Indian *bibis* and dancing girls? If you married every girl who ever came to your bed, you would have more wives than King Solomon.'

Theo had no answer. He had never conceived of a woman speaking like this – let alone his own sister. 'I am leaving Calcutta,' he said, hardly knowing where the words came from.

Constance put her hands on her hips. 'Do not be such a fool.'

Theo was trembling. 'I cannot stay in this city while you whore yourself out to all comers.'

That brought a flush of colour to her cheeks. He wanted to hurt her, to make her feel as wounded and betrayed as he did.

'Do not speak to your sister in that way,' Gerard warned him. He swung himself out of bed and stepped towards Theo. He was naked. 'Whose honour are you really concerned for?'

'Connie's,' said Theo.

'Do you think anyone cares what happens behind closed doors in White Town?' Gerard's manhood swung between his legs, still engorged. 'Without gossip to occupy them, the women of this city would drop dead from boredom. They have been speculating about your sister since she stepped off the ship from Madras. It is nothing but rumour. But if you start accusing her of fornication, calling me out for a duel, it will be the greatest sport they have had in years. The guardian who seduced his ward – son of the great Baron Dartmouth, no less. The brother who shamed her in order to protect her honour. The cousins who fought a duel. Win or lose, there would be nowhere you could go in all Bengal to escape the taint. There would not be a man in the world who could think of marrying your sister. And you think that would be serving her honour?'

Theo stared at him, so full of anger and despair he did not know what to say. Gerard met his gaze, even and unflinching. Behind him, Constance had pulled on a gown.

'I hate you,' Theo spat at Constance.

'This is not your life,' she said softly.

'Then I want no part of it.'

He could bear it no longer. He turned and fled.

• • •

Theo ran to his rooms in the fort and hastily packed his possessions in a bag. His servants weren't present: he left them a note, and coins for a month's wages.

He did not expect to find anyone at the offices in the governor's house. The Company men would not return to work until half past seven in the evening, if they came at all. He went anyway and wrote a brief letter of resignation, which he left on

Deegan's desk. He would miss the old Scotsman's company – but the red-hot fury burning inside him would not relent. He was headstrong, his world polarised into good or bad, life or death, with nothing in between. He felt a crushing emptiness. Connie's betrayal had left a chasm in his heart, and he was desperate to fill it with meaningful purpose.

As he came out on the landing, he heard voices from the council chamber on the top floor of the mansion. It sounded as if all the members were in attendance, voices raised in heated debate. He wondered why they were convening in the middle of the afternoon. In all his time in Calcutta, he had never known anything interrupt their afternoon recreation.

Amid the clamour, he heard Gerard's voice. If he saw his cousin again now, he would kill him. He ran down the stairs, out of the door, through the river gate, and along the wharf to the landing stage. All his possessions in the world were in the canvas bag on his shoulder, and he did not know where he would go. He felt as if he had been orphaned a second time. Part of him longed to go back, to hug Constance and listen to her telling him everything would be all right. But he remembered her naked body gyrating on top of Gerard's, the look of abandon on her face, and the rage rose inside him again.

He stepped into one of the budgerows that clustered at the foot of the steps, like ducks waiting to be fed. He thumped down on the thwart, burying his head in his hands, and sat for several moments before he realised the boatman was waiting for him to say where he wanted to go.

Some twenty ships were anchored in the Hooghly. Theo pointed at the closest, a handsome vessel with her gun ports picked out in green and gold, and the red-and-white-striped Company flag fluttering from her high-backed stern.

They came alongside and received permission to go aboard. When the officer of the watch heard what Theo wanted, he looked at him as if he was mad. 'Passage to England?' He pointed to the sky, and the limp pennant hanging lifeless from the masthead. 'The monsoon will break any day. We cannot sail for three months.'

'Then can I take a cabin on board for my quarters? Please?' He could not countenance returning ashore, where the sideways glances and whispered rumours would follow him everywhere. Escape was his only option.

The lieutenant peered at him closely. 'Are you wanted for a crime? Because if you are, upon my word I will have you clapped in irons and sent to the Black Hole in Fort William.'

'I have committed no crime. I . . .' Theo hesitated. 'I have been unlucky in love.'

The lieutenant looked more interested – more for the whiff of gossip than sympathy, Theo suspected. He shrugged.

'Board will be one pagoda a month, in advance. The passage to London is twenty pounds, but you may pay that to the purser when we are ready to sail.'

Theo knew he was being cheated. The look on the lieutenant's face said: *If you are so desperate to live in a stifling cabin, on a ship that cannot sail, on*

the hottest day of the year, I will make you pay for it.
Theo did not care. He reached into his purse and
counted out three golden pagodas. The Company
had taught him well, and in addition to his salary
he had made several well-judged trades on his own
account. He could afford to live, like an outcast,
on this ship until she sailed for London. Perhaps
in that time he might work out what he could do
when he got there.

• • •

Theo lay in his cot, staring at the ceiling. He
wanted to sleep, to obliterate the thoughts tearing
him apart. Again and again, he saw the shameful
sight of Constance's naked body, her ecstasy as she
rode Gerard. It made him want to be sick. Why did
he care so much? He was confused.

A boat bumped alongside. A moment later, footsteps thumped across the upper deck. He heard
muffled conversation. Was it Gerard? One of the
Company agents come to retrieve him?

A shout came down the companionway. 'All
hands on deck.'

Theo lay still, hardly daring to breathe. What if
Gerard had decided to accept his challenge, after
all? Whether with swords or pistols, his cousin had
a formidable reputation that Theo had only remembered belatedly. He listened to the bare-footed sailors moving through the ship, assembling on deck.

If they had come for him, it would not do to
be taken in his cabin, like a cat in a sack. Honour
demanded he should at least confront them.

Honour. The word tasted like bile in his mouth.

He climbed the companionway ladder. On deck, the sailors were assembled in rows, their backs to Theo, while a perspiring soldier with a colonel's epaulettes on his red coat addressed them.

No one paid Theo the least attention.

'The enemy has already taken our settlement upriver at Kasim Bazar,' the colonel was saying. 'They have captured the artillery and taken the governor captive in chains.'

The crew heard the news impassively. They were merchant sailors, not navy men. They could service their guns if attacked, but they had little interest in other people's fights.

'Siraj-ud-daula, the nawab, is marching on Calcutta with five hundred elephants and fifty thousand men.'

Murmurs of surprise and unease rippled through the crew.

'Fight them yourself,' called one of the sailors. 'You've got a garrison.'

'This beastly climate has taken its toll on our men. I make no bones about it, we are under strength. We need more soldiers.'

'How many have you?'

The colonel flushed. 'All told, some four hundred and twenty men.'

'What about the militia?'

'That is including the militia.'

'Four hundred men against fifty thousand?' said one of the sailors.

'Fifty thousand darkies,' said another. 'One charge of grapeshot and they'll run all the way to Bombay.'

'According to our reports, there are French officers in the nawab's army. They will teach the blacks to fight.' The colonel looked around the assembled tars, taking in their hard faces. 'Who will join us?'

No one spoke.

'There are women and children in the fort,' the colonel pleaded. 'Do you know what the nawab will do if he captures them?'

Theo stepped forward. 'You say there are Frenchmen with the nawab?'

'So we are informed.'

'Then I am with you.'

It was the easiest decision he had ever made. All he wanted was to fight, to find some outlet for all the rage and hurt inside him. If Gerard would not give him satisfaction, he would take it out on the French. It would be some measure of revenge on the nation that had murdered his parents. And if he died in battle – defending Constance – perhaps then she would see how wrong she had been to betray him.

'I'll come.' One of the sailors jumped down from the shrouds where he had been listening. 'The French killed my brother in a raid. I'd welcome a chance to repay the debt with interest.'

He had an unfamiliar accent, like a West Country burr but deeper. He stood beside Theo and gave him a wink.

'Any others?' The colonel scanned the faces in front of him. 'Will no one answer the demands of honour?'

Honour. Theo flinched to hear the word again.

'In any event,' said the ship's captain, 'I cannot spare more of my crew. I am short-handed already.

And if the fortress falls, and you have to evacuate the inhabitants, you will need every man to work this ship.'

'Evacuate?' The colonel gave a braying laugh, the sound of invincible confidence. 'It will never come to that.'

• • •

Theo and the other volunteer clambered down the side into the boat that had brought the colonel. Half a dozen more men sat waiting, gathered from the other ships in the river. All too few against the army of fifty thousand that was approaching.

'Nathan Claypole,' the other volunteer introduced himself. He was tall and loose-limbed, with sinewy muscles honed from climbing masts and hauling ropes. He wore his brown hair tied back in a short queue, and thick hooped earrings. His forearm carried a tattoo of a snake wound around an anchor, expertly inked but spoiled by a thick scar that split it in two.

'Theo Courtney.'

Theo remembered what the man had said about his family. 'I was sorry to hear about your brother. Did he fight in the war?'

'Not any war that was ever declared.' Nathan plucked out an earring. To Theo's surprise, he unscrewed one end of it, revealing a hollow inside. Carefully, Nathan pulled out a plug of tobacco and stuffed it into his pipe. 'I come from New Hampshire. America,' he added, in case Theo did not know. 'My family settled there before I was born.'

That explained the accent. 'Is it near Virginia?'

'Not especially. Have you been to Virginia?'

'I have read about it in a story.' It was in *Moll Flanders*, Constance's favourite book. He did not want to think of that. 'I have heard it is a wild country,' he said.

'Aye,' said Nathan, thoughtfully. 'In summer, with the sun in the trees and the rivers overflowing with salmon, it can feel like paradise. There is a kind of freedom, I suppose. But it brings dangers.'

'To your brother?'

Nathan lit his pipe, puffing at it until the bowl glowed red. 'The laws are not held in such high regard on the frontier. With so much for the taking, every man thinks it should be his. A few years back, the French in Québec allied with the local Abenaki Indians. Sent a raiding party down, without warning. They fell on our homestead and killed my brother, his wife and their children. I was at sea. I had no news of it until almost a year after it happened, and then I was on the wrong side of the world.'

'I am sorry,' said Theo. 'My parents died when the French bombarded Madras.'

Nathan puffed on his pipe. 'I thought of returning home, joining the militia to gain some measure of revenge. But that would not bring my brother back. Perhaps now I can make amends.'

Theo nodded. If his parents had not died, he would not have come to Calcutta, and if he had not come here, he would never have lost Constance to Gerard. 'The French took everything from me.'

'Then let's hope we can pick out a few of them among the fifty thousand Indians.'

• • •

'And there were no others willing to enlist from the ships?'

Governor Drake sat at the head of the table in the council room, a long chamber that spanned the full width of the building. It could have held a hundred men, though only ten sat at the table, each in an upholstered mahogany chair wide enough for three. Through the long windows, those on the right side of the table could see the full panorama of the fortress walls, and the shipping that plied the river – the source of their wealth. Whatever titles the Mughal emperor might bestow, however many nawabs and nizams he might appoint, these men were the true kings of Bengal. And they knew it.

Drake was the governor, thirty-four years old and as unpopular as any man so rich could be. At his right and left sat his two deputies, Messrs Manningham and Frankland, resplendent in the newly tailored uniforms of a colonel and a lieutenant colonel. They were Company men, merchants, with no more military training than the youngest child in the fort. But there was glory to be won, and they were determined it should be theirs. There were also practical implications. Siraj would travel with his full court treasury. If they captured it the spoils would be divided according to rank.

The governor's question hung unanswered in the long room.

'Numbers do not matter,' said Manningham. He had been a colonel for a day and he was convinced he had mastered the art of warfare. 'One taste of our grapeshot will send the darkies scurrying for the hills.'

'It would – if we had any grapeshot.' The speaker was Deegan, still dressed in his Indian coat and turban. In the emergency organisation of the garrison, he had been assigned the job of quartermaster.

'According to our ledgers, we have at least a thousand rounds of grape,' said Manningham.

'We inspected the magazines today,' Deegan answered. 'Worms had got to the canisters and devoured them whole.'

'Then we will load our guns with regular shot and blast them to bits. I assume the worms have not eaten the balls.' Manningham looked around the table, sharing the joke at Deegan's expense.

'Oh, we have shot,' said Deegan. 'But the powder's wet as a tart's knickers, and in this weather it won't dry properly until November.' He took grim pleasure in delivering the news.

The others accepted it in silence.

'Then what should we do?'

The governor turned to the fort's engineer, a florid Irishman named O'Hara. 'You have inspected the town's defences?'

O'Hara puffed out his cheeks. 'I have.'

'And?'

'The town is indefensible.' There were murmurs of shock and disbelief. 'The ditch we started digging some years back is now choked with scrub and rubble. In any event, it was never completed.

We must focus our efforts on the fort. That is not ideal either.' He walked to the north windows and pointed to the large mansions that ringed the fort. 'As you can see, we are hindered by those buildings, which command our defences.'

'I will remind you, sir, that "those buildings" are our homes,' said Colonel Manningham. 'That is my house you are pointing at.'

'And from your bedroom, enemy marksmen will have a clear field of fire straight into the fort.'

'Then what do you propose?' said Governor Drake. 'We cannot simply remove them.'

'Demolish them with explosives.'

Frankland laughed out loud – a high-pitched giggle that trailed off as he realised O'Hara was deadly serious.

'But that is preposterous!' Manningham exclaimed. 'Do you have any idea how much my house is worth?'

'More than your life?' asked O'Hara.

'There is no question of demolishing the houses,' said Drake, trying to quell the outraged babble that had erupted around the table. 'We must not let Siraj and his army get within a mile of our homes. Where can we hold them off?'

O'Hara unrolled a map of the city and spread it over the table. The others crowded round. 'The nawab's army will approach from the north. I propose we put a small garrison here' – he tapped a place on the north edge of the city – 'in the guardhouse at Perrin's Garden. A redoubt there should hold up the enemy a little while.'

'As soon as the nawab sees we mean to fight, he will offer terms,' said Drake, confidently. 'He needs the Company and the money we put in his treasury.'

'If the redoubt is overrun, we will fall back.' O'Hara continued as if Drake had not spoken. 'We will barricade the main avenues to the north, east and south of the fort, and place batteries there.'

'Let Siraj try to advance,' cried Frankland. Powder from his wig had made a soggy crust on his golden lieutenant colonel's epaulettes. 'We will paint the town with his blood.'

'Should the barricades fall, we will retreat to the fort. And God help us then,' O'Hara muttered under his breath.

The warning was lost as Drake banged the table to conclude the meeting. 'I believe that will do. Colonel Manningham, prepare your men for battle. In a week, I wager, we will all be heroes.'

Throughout the discussion, Gerard Courtney had not spoken, studying the papers before him in silence. He was not interested in the petty politics of the council: he did not take sides, because he despised them all equally. Nor did he care for gaudy uniforms and trumped-up ranks. It was the substance of power that he cared about. What troubled him was that he could feel its absence in the room.

Manningham took his arm as he was leaving. 'You know your young cousin has volunteered for my army? I found him aboard ship. I believe he intended to quit Calcutta.'

There was a devious tone in his voice. Even now, Manningham would seize on any gossip to embarrass his trading rival.

'Theo had an unfortunate encounter with a woman he loved. You know how young men can be.'

'I dare say. A little taste of battle will do wonders for his heart – make a man of him.'

'I am sure your leadership will inspire him.' An idea began to form in Gerard's mind. 'Actually, I feel he has the makings of an excellent soldier. I wonder, would it be possible for you to give him a position where he could earn a full share of the glory? If you were to do me this favour, I would be greatly in your debt.'

Manningham took the hint. A debt from Gerard Courtney was always a useful card to have up one's sleeve. 'I shall see to it at once. Too many Indians and foreigners in our army for my taste. They need Englishmen to stiffen their spines. I will give him command of a battery on the west tower.'

'I am obliged. But I fear Siraj's army will flee before they come in musket shot of the fort. I was hoping for somewhere the boy can taste a little more action.' Gerard pretended to think. 'How about the redoubt you spoke of, at Perrin's Garden?'

The colonel stared at him. 'But that redoubt is our most exposed position. I fear, sir, it is a post from which the men may not return.'

'A suicide mission,' said Gerard, calmly. 'But a man might win honour and renown.'

'Well – yes.'

'Then give my cousin the command. There are Frenchmen in the nawab's army, and it was the French who killed Theo's parents. I assure you, he would make any sacrifice to gain his revenge. He will never yield on a point of honour.'

Manningham wiped his brow. He had a gift for sniffing out cunning and treachery: he could sense it now, and it worried him that he did not understand the game. Did Gerard Courtney think that, by putting his cousin in the front line, he would gain a share of the glory?

It did not matter. When the reports were written back to London – copied to the newspapers – they would record that Colonel Manningham had led the defence and gallantly repelled the Indian hordes. He did not intend to go anywhere he might come in range of the enemy's guns.

'I shall speak to your cousin at once.'

• • •

Theo and Nathan stood on the wharf below the fortress walls. The low sun shone on the river, casting a vivid orange light that made the ships, the water and the fort the colour of flame.

Theo squinted at the bill in his hand. 'It says there should be twenty-four guns in this battery.'

They had counted them all, twice. There were fewer than half of that number. Some of the gun carriages had been eaten by woodworm and collapsed; others had accumulated so much dirt they would need boring out. Several had simply disappeared.

'The Company calculates that every penny it spends on defence is a penny less profit,' said Nathan. 'They are about to receive a full accounting for their parsimony.' He took out his sheath knife. He held the blade in front of one of the cannons, angling it so that the steel reflected sunlight into its mouth. 'What do you see?'

Theo knelt and peered down the barrel. 'There are strange markings.' In the flickering light, he could see that the inner bore of the gun was pitted with hundreds of tiny holes.

'Honeycombing,' said Nathan. 'These guns fire salutes every time a ship weighs or drops anchor. But the crews have been lazy. They have not swabbed them out and cleaned them as they should. The powder residue reacts with the dampness in the air and eats away at the casting. If you fired a ball, the barrel would shatter like glass.'

Theo was horrified. 'Are all the guns like this?'

'Some. Others are worse.' Nathan led Theo along the wharf to a pile of long nine-pounder cannon barrels, stacked like sawn logs behind a collection of empty water barrels. 'These were never taken into the fort – who knows how many years they have sat here? They have corroded so badly you could not even get a spark down the touch-hole.'

Theo stared at the pile of metal, flakes of rust scattered around it like sawdust. Dreams of glory faded. 'How are we meant to fight the nawab with this?'

'Mr Courtney?'

Theo jumped to attention as Colonel Manningham strode across the wharf, still stiff in his new coat. Theo marvelled that the tailors had had time to run up such elaborate uniforms when the threat was so close.

'The governor has given orders that you are to be commissioned as an ensign, with immediate effect.'

Theo's face glowed. At last he would get the chance to prove himself.

'You will join the garrison of the redoubt at Perrin's Garden.' Manningham put a hand on Theo's shoulder and looked him in the eye. 'It is a weighty responsibility for one so young. I fear the brunt of the attack will fall on your post.'

'It will be an honour, sir. Thank you.'

'And me, sir?' enquired Nathan.

Manningham gave him a vacant look. 'You, too.'

The colonel retreated inside the fort. Nathan gave Theo a crooked look. 'Do you wonder why they are so keen to put you in the front line?'

'I hope because they trust my courage,' said Theo.

'Have you been in battle before?'

'In Madras, when the French attacked.'

'But in the thick of a fight, when men come at you from every side, and the only difference between your life and theirs is the sword in your hands?' Nathan touched the scar that bisected the tattoo on his arm. 'Our ship was boarded by pirates once, off Madagascar. We were fighting for our lives. It was a terrible thing. No man knows how he will fare until he is in that situation.'

'The Indians will not press the attack. Everyone says so.'

Nathan kicked the gun carriage. The wood creaked; the whole assembly shuddered. 'Then let us hope everyone is right.'

• • •

They marched out that evening, two miles north, to where the frontier of the city met the jungle.

Their commander was a lieutenant named Cole, so newly commissioned that the shining brass buttons on his coat bore traces of the grease they had been packed in. He had a high-pitched giggle, which he let out every time a gun went off from the enemy camp. Theo wondered if it was supposed to reassure the men.

The redoubt was a small gun platform on the banks of the Hooghly, overlooking a gully where a rivulet flowed into the river. It had embrasures for six guns, but only one pointed north. The others faced the river.

'Typical John Company,' said Nathan. 'They were more worried about other merchants sailing upriver and stealing their commerce. They never conceived that their hosts might take against them.'

'Not that it makes a great deal of difference, with these feeble guns,' said Theo. There were two cannons, but they were not much better than those he'd inspected on the wharf. On the first shot, the gun carriages would most likely disintegrate from the recoil. Worse, they were naval guns, made to be aimed at tall ships, and they would not depress low enough. When the enemy came, the shot would sail harmlessly over their heads.

Theo crouched behind the walls of the redoubt and peered into the night. The enemy was not far off. The jungle was lit up like a great city, with all the watch fires and torches of the army camped inside. Sounds of war drifted from the trees: the rasp of whetstones sharpening blades, men discharging pistols to check the priming, the trumpeting of elephants and the crash of trees as they broke paths through the forest for their artillery.

'That does not sound like an army planning to retreat,' said Nathan.

'Do you think they will attack tonight?' asked Theo. Though they had barely known each other a day, he felt reassured by the lanky American's calm presence.

Nathan lit a match from their lamp and put it to the bowl of his pipe. 'The nawab will attack in daylight.'

Lieutenant Cole gave his high-pitched giggle. 'What would an American sailor know of Indian warfare?'

Nathan sucked on his pipe. 'I know about men. The nawab will attack in daylight so that everyone can see his victory. He means to make an example of us.'

'Then he has another think coming, by God,' scoffed Cole. He looked to the men, hoping for a huzzah. Twenty-four blank faces stared at him.

Crammed into the guardhouse of the redoubt, their body heat and the high temperature of the night made the room an oven. No one slept.

'Worse than being in the Black Hole,' said one of the soldiers. The Black Hole was their nickname for the gaol at Fort William, a tiny cell where petty thieves and drunkards were sent to pay for their crimes.

The night drew on. The sky turned grey, then pink, as the sun rose beyond the forest. Now Theo could see the landscape ahead of them: the gully in front of the redoubt that served as a defensive ditch, the demolished bridge that had spanned it and the high road disappearing into the forest a hundred yards distant.

He loaded his musket and checked the priming on his pistols. Behind the loopholes, the men thumbed the edges of their bayonets, and laid out cartridges to grab when the fighting began.

'They will come soon now,' said one of the soldiers, a small *topass* of Indian and Portuguese parentage, with floppy dark hair. 'Before the heat is too great.'

The day had begun, but across the ditch the mouth of the forest was still dark and empty. Drums beat from within it, accompanied by clashing cymbals and sometimes a trumpet blast. But no one came.

'Where are they?' Cole fretted. 'Have they decided to run away?'

As if to mock him, a shrill, chilling scream rose from the jungle, like a man being flayed alive. Theo almost let off his pistol with the shock of it. A thousand more voices took up the cry. The jungle trembled, as if the trees themselves feared what was coming.

'Ready your weapons,' Cole ordered.

The nawab's army came out of the jungle. They were led by men from the *ghosia* caste, crazed warriors who painted themselves white and daubed themselves with ashes, so that they took on the appearance of walking skeletons. They capered and scampered, howling their battle cry.

Behind them came the main body of the nawab's army. His banner, a white flag with a golden crescent, fluttered above them.

'There are hundreds of them,' gasped Theo.

'Some two thousand, by my reckoning,' said Nathan, surveying the advancing line.

Theo stared. He felt a trembling in his veins, but it was not simple fear. It was something he had never felt before: anticipation, excitement, an energy rising through him like fire. The thrill of battle. He *wanted* the enemy to come. He gripped his musket tighter. 'At least we won't lack for targets.'

'That's the spirit,' said Nathan. He rested his gun on the parapet and sighted it. Unlike the others, who carried British-made smooth-bore muskets, he had equipped himself with an Indian jezail. With its heavy, rifled barrel, it could take a stronger charge, delivering the bullet further and more accurately than any musket could.

He fired. Two hundred paces away, one of the nawab's officers collapsed, blood spurting from his eye socket.

'That was . . . incredible,' said Theo.

Nathan winked. 'I grew up on the frontier. Shooting and praying were the only entertainment we were allowed.'

'Then we may need both your talents before the day is out.'

The Indian line advanced. Some carried muskets, which at this distance they fired in the air, but most brandished scimitars, pikes and cutlasses.

'Let us give them a taste of English lead!' Cole shouted. His face was a sickly green. 'Ready.' He raised his sword.

'They are still too far away for muskets,' Nathan murmured to Theo. 'You will just be wasting shot and letting them closer while you reload.'

'Aim.'

There was a metallic clang as Cole's sword dropped to the ground. He sank to his knees, then toppled over on his side. Blood spilled from the perfectly round hole that had been punched through his forehead.

Twenty-four sepoys craned around. One was so shocked he discharged his musket. The others stared, dumbfounded. Across the battlefield, the enemy rushed on.

Suddenly Theo realised all the men were looking at him. What did they want?

'You are an Englishman,' Nathan whispered in his ear. 'They expect you to lead.'

It felt like the longest moment of Theo's life, though it lasted only an instant. How could he, who had never seen battle, command these men? He was just a boy.

Above the approaching army he glimpsed fluttering white banners. Probably the nawab's, but Theo also saw the white flag of the King of France. The enemy.

The fire returned to his veins. He grabbed Cole's bloodied sword and raised it. 'Aim!' he shouted, with the biggest voice he could muster.

Several of the *topassees* glanced back over their shoulders, thinking of flight. Theo could not let that idea take hold. He marched to the nearest, slapped him across the face and pointed forward. 'The enemy is that way, damn you.'

Whooping and chanting, the opposing army rushed for the ditch. Theo's heart pounded as if about to burst the buttons on his shirt. He was desperate to give the order to fire. But he knew he had to make the first volley tell.

The front rank had reached the ditch. The *ghosias* leaped down on the rubble of the collapsed bridge, lost in the madness of battle, but the men behind hesitated on the edge. The line contracted, like a giant snake, as those further back pressed up against them.

'*Fire!*' shouted Theo.

Twenty-four muskets fired. The noise deafened him. The smell of the smoke brought back memories of Madras, lying on the rampart, hand stretched out, watching his father fall inexorably away . . .

But he had to live now. Through the clearing smoke, he saw bodies cartwheeling down into the ditch. Some had been struck by the volley. Others were pushed forward by the crowd of men behind and trampled underfoot.

'*Fire!*' Theo shouted again.

Nathan gave him an approving look. 'You learn fast.'

'I fear I have little choice.'

It could easily have become a free-for-all, the sepoys and *topassees* firing and reloading as fast as they could. But Theo would not let them. Again and again, he forced them to wait for his command and fire in unison. He knew from his travels with Deegan that nothing intimidated Indian troops so much as British military discipline. He hoped the impact of regular volleys, each falling like a hammer blow, would blind them to how few troops he had.

'It seems to be working!' he shouted to Nathan. His ears were ringing from the constant barrage – he had to shout at the top of his lungs to hear anything at all.

'Aye,' said Nathan. Their enemy still had not crossed the ditch. They hung back, terrified of the onslaught from the redoubt, while Theo's men crouched behind the walls. The bank of the ditch was piled high with bodies.

In the dark shadows of the jungle, a light flashed. A deeper roar boomed over the battlefield. Theo barely heard it, but he felt it like a punch in the gut.

The corner of the redoubt's wall exploded. Theo was knocked off his feet by the shock wave, a blast of superheated air that threatened to tear off his limbs. A cloud of debris flew at the defenders. Two died instantly, struck in the face by jagged lumps of brick. More went down, blinded or stung by dust and sharp fragments. One grazed Theo's cheek, half an inch from his eye. When he touched it, his hand came away wet with blood.

They have cannon. Theo scrambled to his feet, dragging up two sepoys by the scruffs of their necks. All around him, men lay dazed and bleeding.

'Up!' he shouted. 'Up!' He took a fallen musket, jammed it into the nearest man's hands and pointed him to the embrasure. The cannon had given the attackers new hope: they were already pouring forward down the ditch, leaping over their fallen comrades.

The cannon fired again. The whole building shuddered with the impact. A section of wall wobbled, like a kite in a breeze, then toppled over.

Three of the men, who had yet to rise after the first hit, were crushed under the rubble.

There was no time to dig them out. Theo found Nathan and bellowed in his ear, 'Can you see the gunners?'

Nathan peered through the swirling smoke and dust. Nodding, he bit the end off a cartridge and tipped the powder down the rifle barrel. He wrapped the bullet in a patch of greased leather and shoved it in with the ramrod. The fit was so tight it took all his strength to get it down. He unstopped his powder horn, poured a small charge onto the pan, and snapped the frizzen shut.

The process took less than twenty seconds.

He aimed the rifle into the jungle, cushioned the stock against his cheek, and fired. Theo didn't see if it hit, but Nathan seemed satisfied. He reloaded, quick as ever, and fired again.

Theo crawled along the wall, ducking behind the piles of rubble as he exhorted his men back to their places. Musket balls rattled off the stonework.

'We need reinforcements.' Theo spotted the youngest boy in his company, a lad named Eli barely thirteen years old. 'Run to the fort and tell the governor I need more men now.'

He said it loudly – partly because of the noise, but also so all the men would hear. He wanted them to believe that help was coming, that if they could hold on they would be relieved. They needed hope.

It was a lie. The fort was two miles away. In that heat, the boy would need at least half an hour to reach it, longer to go through the company hierarchy and speak to anyone who mattered. Even if the governor agreed straight away, it would take at least two hours to assemble the reinforcements and bring them to the redoubt.

Theo was down to seventeen men. They could not hold out nearly that long.

Trying to disguise his dismay, he picked up a musket and started firing. There was no time for ordered volleys. Men fired as fast as they could. In the glare of the high sun, the barrels became so hot that they scalded any skin that touched them. The men sluiced their guns with buckets of water, which turned to steam almost the moment it touched the burning metal.

The cannon had ceased firing, though whether because of Nathan's marksmanship it was impossible to tell. The attackers had swarmed over the gully and were so close that it would be impossible for the cannons to fire without hitting their own men.

Once again, Theo cursed the complacent minds that had built the redoubt without considering it might be attacked from the land. The walls were too low, the attackers too many and the defenders too few to keep them at bay. For every man the sepoys killed, three rushed forwards to take his place. They had reached the walls. Theo dared not raise his head over the parapet for all the musket fire coming at him. When he did, he saw a sea of snarling faces, their owners jabbing and stabbing with their weapons.

He knew they could not defend themselves for much longer. But neither could they flee. Once they broke ranks, the nawab's army would charge them down and tear them apart. All he could hope to do was delay them long enough to afford the men in the fort time to prepare their defences.

Firing and reloading, firing and reloading, he thought of Constance. Would she weep when she heard he had died to save her? Would she know that she had driven him to this?

Still the enemy came. Now the battle was fought hand to hand, with blades and bayonets and anything they could grab. Bodies piled up on the rubble of the collapsed walls, so that there was no longer anywhere to hide. Theo fought with a borrowed sword, hacking and punching and stabbing with no technique except blind desperation.

An Indian vaulted over the remains of a battlement, brandishing his scimitar. Theo's arm was so weary he could barely lift his sword. He brought it up just in time to parry the stroke, but too slow to move to the attack. The scimitar flashed again, a numbing blow that shivered up his arm. The sword flew from his sweaty hands, spinning away across the blood-slicked rampart.

The man raised his scimitar. Theo tried to step back, but the press of fallen bodies behind him left no room to move. His opponent bared his teeth, stained red with betel juice.

And then his head disintegrated in a spray of blood, like a melon crushed under a cart wheel. Whatever had struck him ploughed on, cutting a bloody gash through the crowd on the rampart.

Theo picked up his sword. Only then did he dare look out, through the western embrasure towards the river. The sight made his heart leap. An East Indiaman had come up, her boats straining to hold her against the current, like dogs on a leash. Her guns were run out. One flashed as she fired again, and another ball ripped through the attacking hordes.

Victory turned to panic as the nawab's army realised their flank was exposed. They began to fall back, giving Theo's men precious seconds to reload and deliver a volley of musketry. From the rear, the Indian captains bellowed at their men to stand their ground and press home the assault.

It was futile. Standing on the corpses of their fallen comrades, exhausted from intense fighting in the heat, the army had had enough. They poured back across the ditch, sped on their way by more shots from the exultant defenders.

Theo embraced Nathan, who was using his jezail's greater range and accuracy to pick off a few of the stragglers. 'We did it.'

'They will come again,' he warned.

'With luck, our reinforcements will arrive first.'

They were both wrong. The nawab's army stayed skulking in the jungle, giving Theo time to repair the redoubt's defences as best he could. He kept gazing back down the high road towards Fort William, looking for the telltale plume of dust that would announce their relief. None came.

Late in the afternoon, Nathan volunteered to scout out the enemy positions. Theo was reluctant, but Nathan persuaded him. 'I grew up playing hide-and-seek with French fur-trappers and Mohawk Indians, with my scalp as the forfeit if

I lost. I think I can keep out of the way of a fifty-thousand-strong army.'

Theo watched as Nathan crept across the battlefield, darting between the stumps of trees that had survived the fighting. He moved with lithe grace, alert to any danger, and disappeared into the forest.

He returned half an hour later. 'They've gone,' he announced.

'You're sure?'

'Men, elephants, cannon – everything.'

Theo stared at him in absolute joy. 'Then we have won.' He was already seeing himself at the ball the governor would give to celebrate, the saviour of Calcutta. He imagined the look on Constance's face. 'Everything they said about the Indians – that they could not stand up to English discipline, that they have no stomach for a fight – was true.'

The men cheered; some let off their guns. Nathan did not join them. He looked thoughtful.

'Come.' Theo clapped him on the arm. 'When we get back to Fort William we will open a cask of rum.'

A movement caught his eye. Someone was coming up the road from the fort. He smiled, thinking how sick they would look when they realised they had missed the battle.

It was Eli, the boy he had despatched earlier. He was running, his face so red Theo feared he would faint. He staggered the last few paces and fell in a sweating heap at Theo's feet. He was trying to say something, but his parched mouth could not make the words.

'Fetch water!' Theo shouted. Anxiety pricked him. Why had no one else arrived? Surely word of their victory had not spread so quickly.

The boy gulped down the water. 'Easy,' cautioned Nathan. 'Too much too quick will be worse than none at all.'

Eli looked up, his face dripping. 'Governor's respects, sir. You're to fall back to the fort at once.'

Theo stared at him. 'But we have won.'

'Siraj has taken his army round to the east. They've crossed the ditch at Cow Cross Bridge and made their camp on the Dumdum road. If you don't retreat now, you'll be cut off.'

Some of the men had gathered close and heard the news. Others, too tired to move, lay slumped out of earshot. Theo turned to address them. Heat and despair made him want to be sick, but he knew he must not let it show.

'On your feet!' he shouted. 'We have bloodied Siraj's nose enough for one day.'

And all for nothing, he thought bitterly.

• • •

The next day, they watched Siraj's army move into position. Camel trains brought up ammunition, ton after ton, while elephants hauled the great guns to their batteries. From the high point on the east wall of Fort William, Theo saw the nawab's camp stretching almost to the horizon, the richly decorated tents of the noble officers like gilded islands among the tens of thousands of men bivouacked in the open.

Even now, Governor Drake maintained that the nawab wouldn't attack. 'He is a peacock, spreading his tail-feathers,' he said confidently. 'Alas, if he wishes us to play the hen, he will be disappointed.'

Theo had no such illusions. He had bound his wounds, but blood still seeped through the bandages, drawing flies. The nawab's men had died in their hundreds in front of the redoubt, and still kept coming. They would not give up the fight now.

Neither was there much hope that the fort could sustain a siege with the whole populace of White Town crammed within its walls. There was no shelter, no water for washing, and not enough latrines; the entire fort stank of human effluent. That brought flies in their thousands, including the bugfly – a tiny beetle that emitted a pungent, sulphurous smell. They settled on anything that was motionless. Theo saw one child with his face almost invisible beneath a mass of crawling insects.

The governor and council were nowhere to be seen. They stayed in their chamber, watching the catastrophe through the long windows. They wrote letters and memoranda; they argued around the table.

'Why do they not evacuate?' Theo wondered. He was on the walls with Nathan, helping his men barricade the gaps in the wall with bales of cloth taken from the Company warehouses. Though Theo had received no rank or promotion, the men had accepted his authority with simple certainty. He was their leader.

To the west, the fleet of ships sat placidly anchored in the river. Only a musket shot away, but it might have been ten thousand miles. With the naked eye, Theo could see the crews swabbing decks and polishing brass, playing fiddles and dancing jigs. It was as if the devastation of a great city was not happening a few hundred yards off their neatly painted sides.

'The governor still thinks Siraj is shadow-boxing.' Nathan looked away from the ships to the cauldron of misery in the courtyard below. 'His English mind cannot comprehend the idea that an Indian would dare force the issue.'

'You seem to comprehend it well enough.'

Nathan shrugged. 'I grew up on the frontier, where titles and the colour of a man's skin count for nothing. We have Indians there, too, and I can assure you that ours yield to no one when it comes to warfare.'

'Is that why you left?' Theo asked. 'Because of the Indians?'

'I got bored of praying and shooting.' Nathan lifted a roll of calico and jammed it into the embrasure. 'So I ran away to sea.'

'But what about your parents?' Theo asked.

Nathan took a swig from the flask of rum he kept in his powder bag, and offered it to Theo. 'I know how you lost yours. It must be hard for you to understand why a man would choose to leave his family. Mine were easier to lose than yours, by the sound of it.'

The rum burned Theo's throat, but he was glad of the moisture. 'Will you go back?'

'If I have a choice in the matter.' Nathan shot a wry look towards the nawab's camp. 'Not for my parents, but I would like to see my sister Abigail again.'

Theo didn't answer. He was thinking of his own sister, and if they would ever repair the bond that had been broken. He had seen her only once since he had returned to the fort, sitting with other women wrapping powder cartridges for the defence. She had not noticed him, and he had not spoken to her. No matter what had happened between them, he wanted her safe. He would do everything he could to get her out alive.

Gerard had stayed in the council room with the other merchants. That was just as well: even thinking about him incited Theo's rage.

'What is that?'

Nathan was pointing south, to the jumbled roofs of Black Town. Smoke was rising; high flames licked the evening sky.

'They have set the bazaar on fire.' The warren of tight-knit alleys in Black Town hid what was happening, but Theo could hear pandemonium from the streets. Another fire started, further east, then another. The screams of women rent the air.

'Siraj has unleashed his army.'

They both knew what that meant. Black Town was an open target: Governor Drake would not have considered defending it, even if he'd had the men. Most of the inhabitants had fled, but – judging by the shouts and wails – many had stayed.

'They will seek shelter here,' Theo realised. He ran down the steps at the south-east bastion. By the time he reached the gate, it was trembling under the impact of the crowd pressing and pounding against it from the outside.

Gerard Courtney stood in front of it. He had his back to the gate, facing down the gaggle of sepoys remonstrating furiously with him.

'Outside are our families,' one implored. 'You must save them or Siraj kills them.'

'Out of the question,' snapped Gerard. 'If we let them in, they will overwhelm us. We do not have enough supplies for ourselves, let alone thousands of homeless blacks.'

One of the sepoys stepped closer. Gerard edged back against the gate. 'Why do we fight for you, if you do not help our families?'

'You fight because we pay you. Now get back to your stations, before I throw you in the Black Hole for mutiny.'

The sepoy took the bayonet from his belt and held it bare-handed. In the gang of men behind him, Theo saw the gleam of knives.

'For God's sake open the gate,' Theo begged.

Gerard glanced at him. His eyes narrowed. 'Do not involve yourself in this, cousin. This is a Company matter and I have the authority.'

Theo thought about that. He nodded. Before Gerard could react, Theo stepped forward and punched him square on the jaw. His cousin's head snapped back and thumped against the gate. Gerard slumped, unconscious, to the ground.

The sepoys stared at Theo uncertainly. 'I am in command here now,' he announced. 'Take Mr Courtney to the governor's house and see he gets medical attention. Tell them he was struck by falling masonry.'

Two of the sepoys dragged Gerard away.

'Now open the gate.'

Almost before he said it, the sepoys lifted the bar and heaved. It took all their strength to move the gate against the crush of people pressing on it. As soon as it was open a crack, women started pouring through: a trickle at first, but soon a torrent. Their clothes were torn, their faces black with soot and bruises.

'You may regret this,' Nathan murmured in Theo's ear.

Theo watched a woman in a torn sari push by. She had a baby clasped to her chest and a small child clinging to her hand, struggling to keep up. Three more children pressed close behind, holding her dress so they wouldn't get lost in the fray. He imagined them as orphans, as he and Constance had been. 'I will not regret it.'

• • •

The city burned all night. Black Town was constructed mostly of wood and straw: it burned quickly. The flames danced so high they flickered on the clouds so that the sky itself seemed on fire.

At first light, Theo looked out to see a smoking ring of ash and devastation. Only the houses closest to the fort had survived, the church and the great traders' mansions. Scorch marks covered the white façades and smoke billowed from the windows where some of the shutters had caught fire.

'Have you seen your cousin this morning?' asked Nathan.

'I do not think he has left the governor's house since last night.'

'I would avoid him, if you can. The fact that we are fighting for our lives will not stop him having you shot for mutiny, if he finds you.'

'I fear Siraj may save him the effort.'

The boom of a cannon echoed over the desolate landscape. To the east, beyond the church and the theatre, puffs of white smoke blossomed from the batteries Siraj had erected.

'They're coming.'

Theo gazed around. He did not need a manual of warfare to understand the danger. The Company mansions that ringed the fort were all at least a storey higher than the ramparts, and easily within musket range. If the nawab's army gained control, they would be able to pour fire down on the defenders. For the hundreds of women and children huddled on the parade ground, it would be a massacre.

'Get the men,' said Theo. 'We will take up position next to the church.'

When Nathan returned, Theo was surprised at how many men he brought.

'You are earning a reputation,' Nathan explained. 'They have heard how you defended the Perrin's redoubt. They want to serve under you.'

'I hope we do it to more purpose this time,' Theo answered. He could not help but feel honoured by the men's regard – but also the weight of responsibility. The men had chosen to fight for him. He owed it to them to lead them well.

They left the fort by the east gate and took up position in one of the mansions overlooking the main avenue and the park. Looking down from the upper windows, Theo saw how the battle had already ravaged the park. Trees had been felled and dragged into the road to form rough barricades, while shallow ditches criss-crossed the lawns and flower beds. They served no purpose that Theo could see: they had been begun in panic and abandoned in haste, without connecting to any other defences. More like an open grave.

He shivered and banished the thought. He cradled his rifle – like Nathan, he had adopted one of the Indian jezails taken from the battlefield – and sighted it down the road towards the nawab's camp. It was eight in the morning, and his shirt was already soaked with sweat. 'It will be a hot day's work,' he predicted.

Afterwards, his memories of the battle that followed were fragments, like a waking nightmare. Intense vivid images were interrupted by blank spaces, as if all sensation had been stripped bare. The worst moments, when the battle was hardest, were knots of insanity: between the noise, the smoke, and the repetitive actions of firing and reloading, there was no specific recall except the feeling of terror and proximity to his own death. Likewise disjointed were the interludes when the enemy paused – sometimes for hours at a time – and Theo and his men would sit around the bedrooms and drawing rooms of Calcutta's eminent citizens, unable to relax because the attack might resume at any minute. What had they talked about?

He remembered his men cleaning their muskets with port from crystal decanters and wiping down the barrels with silk napkins. He remembered one of the men finding a pink crêpe dress hanging on the back of a door, putting it on and capering around the room, while the others laughed and shouted lewd comments. He remembered an Indian soldier suddenly bursting through a door that should have been guarded, as surprised to see the English as they were him. Theo had put his pistol to the man's temple and blown his brains out at point-blank range. He remembered fighting with Nathan, side to side or back to back, saving each other's lives so often they barely thought to mention it.

But always the momentum was retreat. They were pushed out, first, of one mansion, then another. They fortified positions but were out-flanked and forced back. There was no talk now of the nawab's army fleeing. The attackers fought like tigers, and however many Theo's men killed, there were more to take their place. The houses that the Company merchants had refused to raze became battlefields. The fighting went from room to room, and if the attackers could not crash through a door, they smashed through the walls instead, or set the building on fire.

Theo and Nathan fought all that day, and through the night, and into the next day. By the following afternoon, it was clear their position was indefensible. They left the last house by setting light to the powder in Theo's flask as a diversion, then jumping out of the first-floor window and sprinting across the open ground to the fort. Bullets rattled around them – some from their own men, on the fort's walls: they did not recognise the blackened, ragged figures fleeing towards them.

With the remnants of their men, they gained the shelter of the walls and managed to squeeze through the gate before it slammed shut.

The fort was unrecognisable from when they had left it. A day and a half of sustained bombardment had battered great breaches in the walls. The bales of cloth and mattresses they had used to block the gaps had burned; some were still smouldering. The governor's mansion was a jagged stump, open to the sky – every one of its precious windows had been smashed.

The parade ground was strewn with bodies and body parts. The nawab's French gunners had targeted their cannon with murderous precision. In the packed courtyard, there had been nowhere for the refugees to flee. They had sat motionless, while the cannonballs carved bloody trails through their midst.

A corpse lay at his feet: a slim young woman in a green dress. She might have been pretty, once, but there was no way of knowing. Her head had been shot clean off her slender neck. The rest of her remained untouched, apart from the flies. Her dead fingers clutched the book she had been reading. There was not a drop of blood on the gold lettering down the spine. *The Fortunes and Misfortunes of the Famous Moll Flanders.*

What if that had been Connie?

The thought cut through Theo's heart. Exhausted from days of fighting, suddenly all he cared about was his sister. In the heat of battle, he could not protect her, like he had promised. She might be dead already, one of the bodies strewn around him, and the last words he had spoken to her had been cruel and angry.

In a frenzy, he began searching through the corpses. Flies swarmed in protest like a black mist. It was like wading through Hell. He stared into lifeless eyes in heads that had been separated from bodies and tugged on arms that pulled away from their sockets. He trampled on torsos, legs, stomachs and hands, the fingers stiff with rigor mortis and outrage.

'What are you doing?'

Nathan's calm voice checked the madness and brought Theo to his senses. He stared at his friend. 'Looking for Connie.'

'You should try the waterfront. The governor has ordered all the women to evacuate the city.'

Theo pushed through the crowds that clustered around the western gate that led to the ghats and the river. Desperate to get through, he started using his shoulders and elbows more aggressively, pushing people out of his path. It was impossible: every person in the fort was trying to squeeze onto the wharf. What if Connie was already there? What if she left, before he had had the chance to make his peace with her? What if he would never know what had become of her?

There had to be another way. He left the crowd and ran to the stairs that led up to the rampart, moving quickly before the nawab's marksmen sighted on him.

The wall was empty. From its height, he could look down onto the wharf outside the fort. Every inch was crammed with humanity, a crush of women and children pressing towards the budgerows that bobbed against the pilings. Soldiers had been posted to organise the evacuation, but they were overwhelmed by the tide of desperation. Some women lost their footing and fell into the water. Others jumped, swam to the boats and tried to haul themselves aboard, while angry hands pushed them away.

Theo scanned the crowd, searching for Constance. In the sea of dark hair and headscarves, her fair tresses would stand out like a beacon. He strained his eyes. Nothing.

'There.' Nathan had come up behind him. He was pointing to the river, where one of the budge-rows had already set out.

Theo's heart leaped. There she was! She had her back to him, but her fair hair and pale skin were surely unmistakable. 'Thank God,' he breathed. The boat was so overloaded that her gunwale almost touched the river. Many passengers were squeezed aboard and some hung out over the water, clinging to the others to keep from falling in. With no room to move their oars, the rowers made tiny crablike movements, barely enough to keep the heavy-laden boat moving.

But Connie was safe, he was convinced of it. Soon she would be aboard one of the East Indiamen that waited implacably at their moorings, ready to carry her away from this charnel house.

Further along the riverbank, beyond the walls, a dark shape flew into the air. Trailing a plume of black smoke, it arced over the water, struck the river with a hiss and vanished.

'Fire arrows!' cried Nathan.

Another flew up, and another, all bending their lethal arcs towards the overcrowded boat. Theo ran to the end of the wall, thinking he could disrupt the archers with flanking fire. But they were hidden behind one of the mansions and he had no shot.

He had to save Connie.

He would never get through the river gate. The arrows had sent the crowd into a frenzy. Panicked women on the wharf were fighting to get into the fort, while those inside – ignorant of what was happening – pressed equally hard to get out. Theo couldn't jump down. The wall was too high, and the wharf was too wide for him to clear it into the river. He would break his legs.

More arrows hit the boat. One struck a woman through her back, setting her dress on fire. The boat rocked as the other passengers scrambled desperately to get rid of her. She clung on, but they prised her fingers off and dumped her in the water. The fire went out – but she was drowning. Theo saw her arms flailing frantically as the boat pulled out of reach.

He had to get to Connie.

A low wall blocked the end of the wharf. In peacetime, it stopped thieves gaining access. Now, it kept out the attackers. But it had not been built for defence. It was only half the height of the main rampart, jutting out below where Theo stood.

Theo squeezed through an embrasure and jumped down onto the top of the wall. It was narrow, a foot wide, but he landed cleanly. The boat had edged further away, but it was still within range of the fire arrows. They hissed down all around it, sending the passengers into terrified convulsions that threatened to spill them all into the water.

Nathan had followed him down. From here, they could easily leap to the ground outside the fort, get round the back of the mansions and engage the nawab's archers. It would buy precious time for Connie's boat to reach the safety of the big ships.

Theo was about to jump, when his heart missed a beat. The boat, prickling with arrows like a stuck pig, had caught fire at her stern. The women on board shrank away from the flames, but there was nowhere to go. The crowded vessel overturned and her passengers tipped into the river, screaming and thrashing. The water boiled around them, while their skirts bloomed in the water. The heavy fabric weighed them down, sucking them under.

Theo had lost sight of Connie. The boats at the wharf were already overloaded: there was no space, and they would be too slow to reach the drowning women.

He threw aside his musket, stripped off his ammunition pouch, and dived off the end of the wall into the river. He took a mouthful of the brown, silty water, spat it out and kicked off.

The river was wide, and the boat had capsized a distance away. The water stung his eyes and the teeming chaos never seemed to get any closer. Behind it, the hulls of the East Indiamen, with their immaculate paintwork and gilded sterns, rose high above the carnage. Their crews clustered at the rails, watching and pointing, like spectators at a bear pit. *Why didn't they lower their boats?*

Arrows started to fall around him. One struck inches away, so close that the water splashed his eyes. He trod water, checking the faces near him. There were fewer women now, their motions less frantic as they tired. One girl with wide brown eyes slipped below the surface, leaving a trail of bubbles.

Something hit his shoulder. He turned and saw a woman's corpse floating face down, bumping up against him. Three arrows stuck out of her back. He pushed her away, but the current returned her to him. He wrestled her out of his way, fighting the cold, rubbery skin until she drifted downriver.

'Connie!' he shouted, taking more mouthfuls of river water. 'Connie!'

Some of the women had managed to reach the upturned boat and clamber on top of it. Others clustered around, trying to cling on. A vicious fight for survival had taken hold. The women on the boat fought off the others, battering the hands that reached for the hull with broken pieces of oar.

On the far side of the boat, Theo caught a glimpse of fair hair. He shouted Connie's name again; the head sank and was blocked by the upturned hull. Theo swam towards her. His body, battered and bruised from days of fighting, summoned one last effort of will.

Suddenly pain exploded through his skull. Something struck him hard and full in his face. A jealous defender had lashed out with an oar. It swung again. A hollow crack echoed in his ears as it collided with the back of his head.

The last thing Theo remembered was water flooding his mouth and entering his lungs, mingling with the blood, as he rolled over and lost consciousness.

• • •

Theo woke with the sun in his eyes. He was lying on his back, on hard planks that made him feel every bruise and wound on his body. Rigging and spars made intricate patterns above him as they rose towards the clouds.

He felt as if a powder charge had gone off inside his head.

Constance.

He opened his eyes again and sat up. The pain doubled, like a hot lance probing his eyeballs, so bad it made him want to vomit. He fought it back. He must find her.

The deck was crowded with men and women in every state of despair. Sailors moved between them, fixing lines and trimming the sails. He could not see Constance.

'So they left you a few brains in your skull,' said a voice behind him.

It was Nathan, sitting on a chest, filling his pipe with the tobacco he kept in his earrings. His smile could not hide the concern in his face.

Theo touched the back of his head. A lump was swelling like an ostrich egg. 'How did you get here?'

'The same as you.' Nathan touched his shirt, still damp. 'I followed you in. And when they swung at me, I managed to duck.'

'You saved me?'

'So far.'

'And Constance?'

Nathan fiddled with his pipe. 'The ship lowered her boats – too late for many, but not for all. They rescued everyone they could.' The look on his face broke Theo's heart. 'I'm sorry.'

The pain in Theo's head throbbed harder, but he hardly noticed in his despair. Why had he been so angry with her? Why had they parted in hatred?

He should have drowned – not her. He rose unsteadily to his feet and stumbled towards the rail. He would end it now.

Staring over the side, he saw water rippling past her hull. The ship was moving. Nathan's hand clamped on his shoulder. 'There were others I could have saved from the water,' Nathan murmured. 'Do not make me regret my choice.'

The rebuke brought Theo back to himself. 'Where are we?'

Calcutta had disappeared. Off both sides of the ship, the riverbanks showed jungle and small villages, with the peak of a pagoda occasionally breaking through the trees. Gaunt cows trampled muddy paths down to the water to drink.

'The nawab sent boats loaded with burning straw to try to set us alight. The captain felt it was necessary to remove ourselves downriver.'

Theo followed Nathan's gaze, along the row of cannon that lined the main deck. All were tied down tight, their tampions still wedged in their muzzles.

'One broadside would have turned the nawab's boats to matchwood.' Theo's despair hardened to anger. 'What sort of coward is the captain?'

'He was obeying orders.' Nathan pointed aft, where a thin, stooped figure stood in earnest conversation with two young women, who were impressing on him their desperate gratitude. 'Colonel Manningham took charge of evacuating the ladies personally – and when they were aboard, he felt honour-bound to chaperone them to safety.'

Theo strode aft. The two young women recoiled at his approach, sensing his fury, while Manningham raised his chin contemptuously and stared him down. His shirt was immaculate, not a speck of blood or black powder sullying its starched white front.

'Mr Courtney.' He sniffed. 'I am glad you have woken at last.'

'You must turn this ship about.' Theo gestured to the cannons, impotent and unused. 'With these guns, you could stop the nawab dead.'

Manningham coloured. 'My duty is to the ladies aboard this ship.'

'But there are hundreds of men and women still trapped in the fort.'

'They will have to look to their own protection.'

Theo could hardly believe what he had heard. He saw another vessel on station a few cables behind their ship – and another beyond, and another. The whole fleet from Calcutta seemed to have followed Manningham's lead and deserted the city. 'If you do not put about, you will condemn hundreds of loyal Company servants to their deaths.' He glanced at the ship's wheel on the quarterdeck. He wondered if he could grab it, force the vessel to come about. But that would be madness. Even if he was not stopped, you could not turn a great ship as if it was a landau. In the treacherous shallows and mudbanks of the Hooghly, he might ground the vessel – or worse.

Manningham read his thoughts. A sneer of triumph spread across his face. 'The last time your superior gave you an order, you disobeyed. You assaulted Gerard Courtney. Now, you will pay the price.'

Unseen, four sailors had come up behind Theo. They seized his arms and legs, lifting him off the deck so that, no matter how he fought, he could not move.

'Take him below and clap him in irons.'

They carried him to the brig, a tiny cell in the bowels of the ship, and shackled him to an iron ring.

Alone in the dark with his regrets, only one thought consoled Theo.

At least Connie will suffer no more.

• • •

Constance watched the tragedy unfold from the second floor of the governor's mansion: the desperate, overcrowded boats, the rain of flaming arrows, the carnage when the boat caught fire and overturned. She noticed the fair-haired woman among the dark-complexioned fugitives and guessed it was Mary Butler, a merchant's wife from White Town who had been her friend. She did not see Theo dive into the water, and by the time he reached the boat he was another bobbing head among many.

'It is too terrible,' she breathed. She knew how easily it could have been her in the river. Some of the women had clambered onto the upturned boat, defending their position by jabbing oars at others who tried to claim their place of safety. It didn't save them. The arrows fell with relentless accuracy, killing them anyway. Some caught fire.

Others died where they lay, clinging to the boat even in death.

Constance turned away from the window. Belatedly, the anchored ships had begun to lower their boats, hauling up the few survivors who had made it out of range of the arrows. Her friend was not among them.

'What are you doing here?'

Gerard had entered. Hours of grim fighting had broken his usual confidence. He looked unutterably exhausted, bleeding from his cheek where a musket ball had come within an inch of ending his life. Constance ran to him with a cry and embraced him.

'I told you to go to the ships,' he admonished her. And then, 'Thank God you did not.'

'I could not abandon Theo. He always made me promise I would never leave him. Even after everything that has happened . . .' She fingered the pendant she wore at her neck, a pearl set in gold that had belonged to her mother. 'If we die, it will be together.'

'I fear you are mistaken.' Gerard had picked up a telescope and was studying the river. He pointed to the nearest of the big ships, the *Dodaldy*, where survivors were being lifted on board. 'There is your brother.'

Constance snatched the telescope from him. It was true. Theo was standing on the deck, conversing with another sailor. There was no mistaking his shock of red hair.

She looked away, trembling.

'Your loyalty was misplaced,' said Gerard, drily. 'You would not abandon your brother, but it seems he had no such scruples.'

She looked again. She couldn't help herself. The sailor walked away. Theo turned towards Fort William and Constance – his features were close through the glass, his face full of despair. For a second, he and she stared at each other across a distance that had suddenly become unbridgeable.

Then he disappeared behind the hammocks stuffed into the ship's netting. Constance passed the telescope back to Gerard.

'So now it is us,' she said, in a voice as cold as stone. Even with the naked eye, she could see sailors running up the rigging to unfurl the sails. Others were fitting the spokes to the anchor capstan, readying the ship to get under way. 'I never thought he would run away.'

'He keeps eminent company,' said Gerard, running his eye over the ship with the spyglass. 'I can see the gallant colonels, Manningham and Frankland, aboard that ship. Governor Drake has fled too.'

'What shall we do?' asked Constance.

'We cannot leave even if we wanted to.' All along the river, the East India fleet was following the *Dodaldy*'s lead and making sail. 'There is no way out. We will have to fight, and trust to Providence to save us.'

The building shuddered as a cannonball struck home. Constance put out her hands to steady herself against the windowsill. 'I trust nothing any more.'

• • •

The fighting continued through the night. The nawab's French gunners had brought their cannon closer, making embrasures in the church and the mansions from where they could target the buildings inside the fort with lethal accuracy. It was impossible to sleep. Constance drifted between the governor's mansion and the parade ground, only dimly aware of the progress of the battle. Men with ladders tried to gain the walls by stealth. A Dutch sergeant mutinied and deserted with his band of mercenaries. A fierce attack was mounted on the river gate but was repelled. Constance watched it all with the indifference of a spectator. All she could do was await her fate.

Next morning, the fort's commanders assembled for a final council of war in the ruined council chamber. The roof had been torn off, so it lay open to the sky; the long mahogany table was strewn with rubble, and the gilt mirror on the wall had cracked into a thousand shards. Heavy clouds pressed down, kettling in the immense heat that refused to break.

With the Company leadership having deserted, seniority fell to a man named John Holwell, the chief magistrate. He was a serious man, a veteran of India, whose lined face and grey hair belied the fact he was only forty-five. More than one man around the table could not help wondering how the battle might have gone if he had been in command from the start. Now it was too late. He sat in an upholstered chair at the head of the table, with Gerard and the other surviving merchants on either side.

'The first order of business,' Holwell announced, 'is to record that in the absence of Governor Drake, and colonels Manningham and Frankland, I am duly elected president and governor of Fort William and its Presidency.'

The clerk to his left had managed to salvage the minute book from the carnage. He recorded it in a neat copperplate hand, tutting where the dust made fat gobs of the ink, or when the shiver of another cannonball made his letters wobble.

'What is the butcher's bill today?' Gerard asked.

'We lost twenty-five killed and seventy wounded overnight,' said the surgeon. 'Some thirty have also deserted to the enemy.'

Holwell did the sums in his head. 'There cannot be more than two dozen men able to hold a musket.'

A silence fell, heavy with despair. Everyone knew there could be only one conclusion. No one wanted to voice it.

Holwell sighed. 'I had hoped that if we held out long enough the ships might return.' A bite of anger came into his voice. 'God knows a single sloop could have laid waste to the nawab's forces, and given us safe passage out, if only they had been willing to fight.'

He gazed around the table. 'Now our hopes have expired. The fleet is not coming. I will send an envoy to the nawab under a flag of truce and sue for peace.'

No one disagreed. Looking at their reflections in the cracked fragments of the great mirror, it was obvious that any notions of honour or glory had been crushed, like the brittle bricks of the fort's walls.

'You must not concede too much,' Gerard warned. 'The nawab is cruel and greedy. If he finds out how desperate we are, he will offer no quarter.'

Holwell nodded. 'I will send the message this very hour, offering surrender with dignity, if he will guarantee safe conduct.'

Outside, the city looked like the Day of Judgement. Smoke turned the air black, while a red glow tinged the sky, like a false sunset, from the burning buildings. Dust clogged every pore and made eyes weep. Everything was broken. The families that crowded the courtyard, still in their hundreds despite all who had died, were like lost souls awaiting punishment.

Gerard found Constance curled in a ball, in a corner of the fort where the walls offered a modicum of shade. She looked up with dead eyes. 'Why have the guns gone silent?'

'We are negotiating our surrender.'

'What will become of us? Will the nawab's men . . .?'

She put her hand over her breasts and lowered her eyes. For the first time in weeks, Gerard remembered how young she was: sixteen. With her fair hair and golden skin, she would be a tantalising prize for the victorious army.

Gerard had heard many stories of the nawab's appetites. It would do no good to tell Constance now. 'He has made his point and won his victory,' he said, with more confidence than he felt. 'It suits his purpose to appear magnanimous. He must know that our masters in London cannot leave this insult unavenged. If he is merciful, it will go easier with him later.'

Constance tugged up the bodice of her dress. She had not changed in three days. With the heat, the damp fabric clung to her body like a second skin, revealing her curves. She felt hopelessly vulnerable.

A shout rose from the sentries on the wall. Gerard ran to the broken rampart. An Indian *jemmautdar*, wearing the vivid blue turban that signified high rank in the nawab's army, was approaching over the broken ground between the ruined houses. One of the sentries aimed his musket, but Gerard pushed the muzzle down even before the *jemmautdar* had spread his arms wide in a gesture of peace.

Through signs and a mix of broken languages, he explained that if they ceased fighting, his master the nawab would graciously consent to discuss the terms of their surrender.

'We need his word that he will deal with us honourably,' Holwell shouted down.

The *jemmautdar* bared his teeth in a wide white smile, nodding emphatically. A bargain was made. The *jemmautdar* retired. A hush fell on the fort, uncanny and nerve-racking for being the first time there had been quiet in four days and nights. Even the wailing of the children seemed muted in the hot, exhausted silence that gripped the courtyard.

'I do not trust him,' Gerard told Holwell. 'We should keep our men on guard.'

Holwell shrugged. 'We must not give the nawab any reason to question our sincerity. Besides, we have so few men there is little we could do.'

'He will take it as evidence of weakness,' Gerard warned.

Holwell looked at him through glassy eyes. 'No Indian prince would dream of going back on his word once he had agreed a truce. They would rather negotiate than fight.'

'If I had a rupee for every man who said that and is now lying dead with an Indian blade or bullet in his belly, I would have a lakh,' said Gerard, acidly. A lakh was one hundred thousand rupees.

'We have no choice.'

The minutes ticked past in the long, hot afternoon.

The few dozen soldiers in the garrison left the walls and lounged on the parade ground with their families. Heat, hunger and exhaustion had paralysed them all.

Gerard sat on the ramparts, scraping a whetstone over the blade of his sword. His head ached from thirst; each rasp of the stone was like a knife through his skull, but he could not help himself. He had to drown out the menacing stillness that had settled on the city. In the shells of the surrounding mansions, shadows flickered behind broken windows. He heard noises of rubble shifting within.

'It does not feel like peace,' said Constance. She had come up to find him, carrying a small bowl of water. He drank it in a single gulp and regretted it immediately. It only made him more aware of his thirst.

Gerard no longer had the strength to argue. He offered Constance his sword. 'If they come, and betray us, and we are separated, put this through your heart. It will be a kinder fate.'

Constance pushed it away, glaring at him with her wild green eyes. 'Do not presume to tell me how to spend my life. You forget. My parents died a brutal death, my brother abandoned me, and I am still here. I will not take the coward's way. As long as I breathe I will fight.'

'I did not mean—'

A single cannon shot shattered the calm. Before the ball struck home, the ruined mansions around the fort had erupted with men, pouring out of their hiding places and racing across the broken ground to the fort. They carried scaling ladders made of lashed bamboo, which they raised to the fractured ramparts.

'They have played us false,' Gerard cried. Pushing Constance back, he levelled his pistol at the first man on the ladder and fired. Blood spread through the attacker's turban as the bullet penetrated his skull. He lost his grip and fell into the throng below.

But there were thousands more, climbing ladders all along the fort's walls. Gerard could not hold the rampart alone. Down in the courtyard, the refugees and off-duty soldiers were waking up to the danger. Constance had fled. Gerard looked to the stairs – but the way was blocked with men who had already gained the walls. Smoke and flame licked around them. The nawab's archers had shot burning arrows into the bales of cloth and mattresses that jammed the gaps in the wall. The dry fabric erupted in sheets of fire.

A bare-chested warrior came at him with a heavy curved sword. Gerard sidestepped the blow and moved forward, tripping his opponent as he stumbled past. He sliced through the man's hamstrings, and left him behind as he charged towards the stairs.

There were too many men in the way. Half a dozen of them, looking for slaughter. They saw Gerard and bared their teeth. Others were closing behind him. There was no way out.

Flames lit the rampart. One of the bales of cloth had come loose and rolled onto the walkway in front of him. It cut him off from the men ahead – but the men behind had him trapped.

Gerard had no choice. With a grimace, he kicked out into the flames. The heat scorched his leg, but he ignored the pain. He felt his boot connect with the roll of cloth in the centre of the fire. With a second kick, it started to roll forward.

The walls angled down towards the river. Helped by the slope, the burning bale of cloth gathered speed, tumbling along the rampart like a fireball. The men in its path dived out of the way. Some flattened themselves against the walls; others, panicking, leaped down into the courtyard, preferring to break their bones rather than risk the all-consuming fire.

Gerard ran behind it, shielding his face against the heat. He was so close he could feel his skin blistering, but he didn't dare drop back. He had nearly reached the stairs.

Men were closing in behind him. He vaulted over the edge of the wall onto the stairs below. He landed halfway down, turned over with the impact, sprang up and ran the rest of the way.

The besieging army had managed to open the gate. Thousands more men were careering into the fort. All that held them back was the massive press of bodies already in the courtyard – the elderly, the wounded, the women and children who had sought refuge. They had no chance. The nawab's troops cut them down like grass. They themselves had suffered terrible losses, and now they avenged their fallen comrades with all the savagery of a victorious army.

'To me! All Englishmen, to me!' Above the din, Gerard heard Holwell's voice roaring defiance. The new governor at least meant to end his tenure more honourably than his predecessor. He had gathered a small knot of Company men and loyal sepoys around the flagpole – and among them was Constance.

The sight of her gave Gerard new impetus. He fought his way to her, slashing and hacking at anyone in his path. The fighting was so desperate, a sepoy by the flagpole nearly ran him through with a bayonet without realising who he was. Then the bayonet drooped, and the sepoy reeled away, clutching his throat where a spearhead had torn it open. Gerard took his place in the line. His eyes met Constance's – but only for an instant. He had to defend himself against an incoming blade, and the battle consumed him.

They were outnumbered a thousand to one. Yet Gerard fought, cutting and parrying every stroke that wished him dead. Beside him, a Dutchman took a bullet through his brain and collapsed. A young ensign, who had been a writer with Theo, was dragged out of position and hacked to pieces in front of his comrades. Blood soaked the parade ground.

One by one, the last defenders were whittled down. The knot of men tightened around the flag-pole, fighting almost blind in the smoke descending from the burning walls.

A man with a scimitar swung at Gerard. He lifted his sword to block it – but there was no strength in his weary arm. He caught the blow clumsily. The shock shivered down the blade; his hand let go the sword. His enemy stepped back, raising the sword for the killing stroke. Gerard was defenceless.

The blow never came. The man seemed to stand there for an eternity, so long Gerard almost willed him to end it. Then he stepped back, lowering the sword while keeping it pointed at Gerard's chest. Gerard breathed hard. Was it a trap?

The mob of soldiers surrounding them eased away. Commands were shouted. With remarkable discipline, the soldiers shuffled into lines, arranging themselves around the slaughtered bodies at their feet.

A trumpet blew. Drums beat. A phalanx of guards in burnished armour marched through the river gate from the ghats, making a corridor that led to the open ground in front of the writers' building. Men scurried to drag corpses out of their path.

'Have we surrendered?' Gerard asked, but no one heard him.

More trumpets sounded. A dozen African slaves entered, carrying a litter so large it barely squeezed through the narrow gate. On it, a man in a white silk robe lounged on plump pillows. He had a pretty face, almost feminine, with pouting lips and long-lashed hard eyes, which took in the scene of his conquest without pity.

Three men rode in behind him on immaculately groomed horses, adorned with embroidered harness and silver buckles that tinkled like bells. Two were Indians of high rank, their robes sewn with pearls and gold thread, and ornate ceremonial daggers tucked into their sashes. The third, to Gerard's shock, was European, a man with a hooked nose and dark eyes, dressed in the uniform of a general in the French Army.

The slaves halted. More servants came and unrolled a carpet so that the nawab would not sully his feet on the bloodied stones. Others brought in a throne draped with tiger skins. The nawab descended from his litter and seated himself on it.

He swept his eyes over the ruined fort. He spoke loudly and firmly so all the men could hear, no doubt praising their courage and success. Often, he was interrupted by cheering from his men, and chants of *Allahu akbar*. The tattered Union flag was cut down from the flagpole and replaced with the nawab's banner.

The nawab turned his gaze to his prisoners. He beckoned them forward.

'Keep back,' Gerard whispered to Constance. 'You must not let him notice you.'

Holwell, the governor, approached the throne. Gerard, and two of the other Company men who had survived the final onslaught, fell in behind him. Against the pristine finery of the nawab's retinue, they made a sorry, shabby picture. The army jeered and whistled, then abruptly fell silent at a gesture from their prince.

The nawab spoke quickly and angrily. The French general walked his horse forward and translated in heavily accented English.

'His Excellency Siraj-ud-daula is most displeased with your insolent resistance. You have cost him over five thousand men, and more than eighty of his bravest officers.'

If he admits to that, he must have lost three times as many, Gerard thought. It was no consolation now.

'Because you defied your rightful overlord, your city and all its possessions are forfeit.'

'We agreed to negotiate a surrender,' Holwell protested.

The Frenchman frowned. 'His Highness did not accept your offer. He has taken this city by right of conquest, and all that is in it is his.'

'And what becomes of us?' asked Holwell. His mouth was so dry the words barely carried.

'You will remain here as prisoners. If your Company values your lives, perhaps one day they will ransom you.'

Siraj waved them away. The audience was over. He turned his attention to the wrecked governor's mansion. He looked displeased. Gerard guessed he had meant to take over the magnificent building for his own quarters. There was also cold malice in the nawab's eyes.

At a word from him, men ran forward with torches, soaked with pitch to make them burn more fiercely. They threw them through the mansion's broken windows on every side of the house. Flames caught hold of the carpets and the furnishings, licking up the walls and devouring them.

The nawab watched the fire with a mixture of contempt and sadness. With another blast of trumpets and drums, he ascended his litter and was borne away by his slaves and his guards. The general rode after him. The prisoners were herded to a grassy patch of ground near the barracks at the south-east bastion. There were fewer of them now: perhaps a hundred and forty, Gerard guessed. They were a mongrel bunch of every race: English merchants and soldiers, Dutch mercenaries, Indian sepoys, half-Portuguese *topassees*, even a Negro. Constance was the only woman. During the audience with the nawab, the other women and children who had survived the massacre had been allowed to slip away. The nawab did not want extra mouths to feed.

A few men with clubs and scimitars stood watch over the prisoners, while the mansion burned and the rest of the fort was looted. The writers' spartan cells were stripped bare. One man cut the silver buckles off Gerard's boots, and the brass buttons from his breeches. Every bale of cloth and sack of spices that survived in the warehouses was carried off. Gerard could tell by the looks on their faces that what they wanted above all was the East India Company's treasury that they believed must be hidden somewhere. He wondered what Drake and Manningham had done with it.

Shadows lengthened. The sun sank below the walls, though it made no difference to the heat.

The monsoon refused to come. Many of the men had not drunk since that morning and were almost dead with thirst. Gerard gestured to their guards that they needed water. They obliged, and brought a cask, but when broached it turned out to be rum. That did not deter the prisoners, who drained it with thirsty gulps, grateful for anything that would numb their pain and their thirst.

The liquor made them angry. They started fighting among themselves. The watching guards found it amusing, cheering them on. One of the prisoners, a burly sergeant with a sunburned nose, took it into his head to charge at the guards. The attack was so unexpected that he managed to wrestle away a cudgel, knocking one man out and sending two more reeling. Other prisoners, primed with drink, piled in. For a moment, it seemed that the battle might break out again.

Gerard glanced around. Could they slip away in the distraction? The gate stood open, only fifty feet away.

But the fort was filled with the nawab's men, and they had heard the commotion. There was no way past. In a short time, the sergeant had been disarmed and given a bloody beating to discourage him from any further rebellion. An urgent conversation followed between the captains of the guards.

Gerard pulled Constance closer to him. 'If we are not careful, they will decide we are not worth the trouble of being kept alive.'

'*Est-ce qu'il y a un problème?*'

An assertive voice cut through the argument, silencing the guards. The French general had returned. He eyed the prisoners with a vicious disdain that chilled Constance more than anything their Indian captors had said.

The guards explained the situation. From the snatches he understood, Gerard gathered that they resented the French general's intrusion. They were minded to let the matter lapse.

But the general had other ideas. He crooked a finger and beckoned Holwell forward. 'Where is the prison in this fort?'

Holwell made a gesture behind him, where a shaded arcade lined the wall. Most of the rooms inside were barracks, but one had been walled off and fitted with a door and a grille to make a small cell. The Black Hole.

'How many can it hold?'

Holwell shrugged. 'I have never been inside. A dozen men, perhaps.'

Corbeil nodded, considering his options. He barked orders. The guards started rousting the prisoners from where they'd been sitting, forming them into a line and herding them to the arcade.

The prisoners were dazed and battered. Some were drunk. They had been fighting for days, and their resistance was exhausted. They filed into the gaol like sheep.

The cell was too small. As soon as the first prisoners reached the back wall, the space was filled. More came in, an endless stream, with much pushing and jostling of elbows. Those who had sat were forced to stand or risk being trampled. Those outside could barely squeeze in, but the guards beat them with the flat of their swords to force them forwards.

Holwell saw the danger. 'For God's sake,' he pleaded, 'do not put us in here. This is not a prison but a death sentence.'

The French general stood to one side, watching through the arcade. 'Your fate will be a warning to others who think they can defy the might of *la France.*'

He turned away, as the guards beat and kicked the last of the prisoners into the cell. Gerard had not thought it was possible they could all fit. The iron gate slammed shut and was locked. The guards left. By now it was nearly dark. The only light came from the governor's mansion, still burning like an enormous pyre and casting ghastly, flickering shadows on the frightened faces packed inside. The sound of the *azan* echoed over the broken city as the *muezzin* called the victorious faithful to their sunset prayers. His keening voice made it sound like a lament for the fallen.

For long, disbelieving minutes, the prisoners were silent as their predicament sank in. Then the panic started and the claustrophobia was infectious. A hundred and forty odd men – and Constance – were crammed into a cell meant for a tenth that number. There was not even space to collapse. They stood upright, held by the press of bodies around them, like meat packed into a crate. There were moans and screams, muffled by expiring breath, gasps for air.

Gerard's mind raced. How long would the guards keep them there? The only air coming in was through the bars at the front of the cell, and one tiny window high in the outside wall. There was no water.

The night was pregnant with the oncoming monsoon. Sunset had brought no relief from the immense heat of the day, while the burning building across the courtyard added its own diabolical warmth to the inferno. Those at the back of the cell pushed and shoved, but the room was so tightly packed that movement was almost impossible.

'Keep calm,' said Holwell. 'With God's grace, if we stay resolute, we will all survive this ordeal.'

The first deaths began within the hour. Some died with their arms in the air, still gripping the hats they had been waving to make a breeze. Some died in silence, and some died weeping for their mothers. Men by the windows hammered on the bars to get attention. 'For God's sake,' Holwell gasped, 'you cannot leave us like this. We need air – and water.'

By now, every man had managed clumsily to strip off his shirt, and many their breeches as well. Those with hats rolled them up and fed them through the bars, holding them out like begging bowls and clamouring for a drink. The guards arrived. After some discussion, they agreed to bring water, which they poured into the hats for the prisoners to draw into the cells. Much of it spilled going back through the bars, and what little remained caused vicious fighting as men tore at each other to drink it. The guards were entertained by this human bear pit and they fetched more water to goad the prisoners into further acts of frenzied barbarism.

So many bodies together undulated restlessly, panic turning some into juddering marionettes, limbs and body functions losing control. Gerard and Constance were pulled apart. He tried to cling to her, but the chaos was inexorable. He let her go, and lost sight of her in the darkness.

Terror gripped him. Gerard had grown up the son of the most powerful man in India, a cruel father without a trace of love in his heart. He had steeled himself to loneliness, acquired an iron-clad inner strength. But in the dark, squeezed into that hell of humanity, with no room for even the sweat to run between them, he felt as if his very soul was being crushed to nothing.

Constance was a few feet from him. She could have reached out and touched Gerard. But her arms were pinned to her sides, and she could not see him in the dark crowd. She, too, felt horribly alone. Theo had abandoned her. The nawab did not care if she lived or died. The guards would take bets on her life, and the men around her would trample her into the stones if it meant saving themselves. Never before had she understood the utter indifference of the universe so completely. There was no grace and no redemption. Nobody cared for her.

Instead of despair, the hideous reality made her angry. Anger made her feel alive. She nursed the rage, like a spark in a tinderbox, the one certainty in the wreckage of her spirit. She would not let the nawab win. She would not let Theo escape while she perished. She would defy them all. She would walk out of this cell alive even if all the others were dead. And then, when she was free, she would never again give any man power over her.

The human current that agitated the crowd was forcing her inwards, away from the windows and the hope of air into the dark, dead centre of the room. She fought back, jostling and squirming. The weight was relentless. Stony faces came out of the darkness. An old Scotsman named Deegan, one of the merchants she recognised from the governor's banquets, lolled over her. His arms involuntarily rubbed her breasts through the soaked fabric of her dress. His head swooped down, mouth open as if to kiss her. She recoiled, but there was nowhere to go. His lips brushed against hers, so warm it took her a moment to realise there was hardly any life in them.

She tried to scream, but there was not enough air in her lungs. She tried to wriggle away, but he was pushed against her, insistent as a lover. She ducked her head aside, so that his face fell nuzzling against her shoulder. He sagged down on her, threatening to suffocate her.

The spark of anger was turning to ash, becoming terror. She would never escape. She saw that the fate that had brought her here was tightening the screw on her life, and now it would finish the job. Her heart raced. Her chest heaved to breathe.

She thrust her foot between the dying man's legs and raised it until she felt his knee. With all the force she could summon, she stamped down. His mouth twisted in a silent scream. Constance stamped again, and again. The bone snapped; the leg buckled. Deegan sank towards the floor. Now she could free her arms. She placed them on his shoulders and pushed, forcing him to slither down her front until he reached the floor.

He knelt in front of her. His dying eyes stared up, imploring her for mercy. Her heart trembled, but only for a moment. She had to live.

She kicked and jabbed until he disappeared into the darkness at her feet. She climbed on top of his sprawled body, raising herself above the mass of people and savouring a few heady seconds of air and space around her. It never crossed her mind that she had killed a man.

The night wore on and more people became limp and waxen and died. As each man passed away his bowels opened, discharging noxious fluids. The floor became a lake of blood, sweat, vomit, urine and faeces befouling their ankles. The air was rank and men fainted from breathing it, collapsing and drowning in the pools of rancid effluvia.

By pushing aside the living and trampling the dead, Gerard had managed to force his way to the high barred window set in the wall. Revived by the air from outside, he had enough energy to fight off anyone who tried to displace him. He sucked the sweat from the sleeve of his shirt to moisten his tongue.

Eventually he fell into an exhausted stupor. He was not quite dead, but surely not alive, not awake, never asleep but semi-conscious in the place of stasis before death, clinging to the window bars like a shipwrecked sailor. Whether he lived or died he did not care. He was entering Hell.

. . .

The guards came before dawn. Gerard's head drooped, images swam before his eyes, terrible visions of loss and destruction. He could barely focus on reality in the shifting nightmare. He thought the guards had come to mock again, but then he heard the jangle of keys. They were banging the door. They could not open it because of the pile of corpses jamming it shut. He floundered towards it, crawling over the dead three or four deep. He tried to move the slippery corpses that blocked the exit, but he was too weak.

Bones snapped and flesh was crushed, limbs skewed in unnatural angles. Eventually the guards forced the door wide enough for a man to pass through. Gerard crawled outside, gulping air so deeply it made him retch. A fresh dew glistened on the parade ground. He flung himself onto it, lying on his belly and desperately licking the grass.

Behind him, a furious argument was raging among their captors. A *jemmautdar* – the one who had offered the false truce the day before – was berating the guards. The nawab had not meant this to happen. Servants, from the untouchable caste, were already hauling the bodies out and flinging them onto handcarts. Clouds of flies descended on them.

The *jemmautdar* stood over the feeble survivors, arms folded, his lip curled with disgust. Half naked, smeared with grime, they were almost indistinguishable from the dead. Gerard counted twenty-three of them.

Twenty-three out of a hundred and forty.

Constance was not among them. He did not grieve her loss: he felt nothing, except the pure relief of being alive. He thought he saw her body being thrown into one of the carts, but he could not be sure. He wanted to remember her as she had been, but he would rather erase all memory.

The *jemmautdar* was speaking. His guards moved through the survivors, pulling out Holwell and four of the senior Company men. Either they did not recognise Gerard, or they did not know who he was. They left him lying with the others.

The *jemmautdar* gestured to Gerard's group. He pointed to them, and then to the gate, which stood open and unguarded. His meaning was clear. *Go.*

With energy he had not known he had, Gerard pushed himself to his feet and hobbled out of the fort. One of the handcarts rattled past him, and he averted his eyes. They were no more. He was alive.

At the waterfront, Gerard found a boat whose master was eventually persuaded to co-operate by Gerard's promise of a handsome payment on their safe arrival. He had heard rumour that the rest of the English – Manningham, Drake and those who had escaped on the Company ships – had taken refuge at the Dutch settlement of Fulta, some twenty miles downriver.

Gerard clambered on board with the other survivors, and let the boatmen ferry them away from the smouldering city.

He did not look back.

• • •

The Dutch trading post at Fulta was small and shabby. The ships that had abandoned Calcutta swung at anchor before a low town screened by trees. It could not possibly hold the dispossessed population that had descended on it in the past week. They camped in the open, on a great bend in the river where mudflats sloped down to the water, adding their waste to the already stinking mud.

Even on the East Indiaman, across the wide river, the stench was overpowering. The ship's captain had released Theo from the foetid brig, but the air on deck was foul. The smell permeated everything. Theo had been there three days, and still found it oppressive. 'If we ever get home, I will never be able to look at a chamber pot without thinking of this place,' he told Nathan. But where could he call home? Calcutta had been destroyed. He had nothing in Madras now. His parents and his sister were dead. The small stretch of planking on the ship's deck was as much a home as he had in the world.

Nathan did not answer. He lay stretched on the deck, a handkerchief covering his face. Despite the heat, he was shivering. There were dangers in the camp that could not be avoided. Almost as soon as the refugees arrived, a fever had broken out. Despite the captains' best efforts to quarantine their ships, it had spread on board. Half of the passengers were sick, especially those who had recently arrived in India. Every day, a dozen or more bodies were thrown overboard.

Theo put his hand on Nathan's brow, and felt the heat boiling inside him. He tipped a cup of water to his friend's lips and poured some on the handkerchief to dampen it. He had to keep his friend from slipping away. 'Tell me about your home,' he said to Nathan, 'since I have none.'

Nathan didn't open his eyes. For a moment, Theo feared he might already be dead. When he spoke, it was as if he was dreaming.

'It's the winter I miss,' he said softly. 'So cold you have to smash the ice in your basin to shave in the morning, but you don't mind because it's so beautiful. So clean and pure, when the snow's just fallen, you think it's wiped away every bad thing in the world.'

Theo, who had spent his life in the tropics, could not imagine such a thing.

'You take boiling maple syrup, pour it out on the snow and it hardens to candy. We eat it with spice-bush tea, and it warms you right through.'

He shivered again. 'What I'd give for some spicebush tea now. I'm so cold, Theo. They told me India was supposed to be a hot country.'

Theo held his friend's hand, as if the grip would keep Nathan from slipping away. 'What about your family?' he asked. At some stage, he thought, he would have to write them a letter explaining how their son had died in a festering backwater of a distant continent.

'My parents won't grieve me,' Nathan murmured. 'They'll see it as divine justice for the sinful life I've led.' He coughed. 'Perhaps they're right. I'll miss my little sister, though. Abigail. You remember her name? You'd like her.'

'Perhaps one day you can introduce us,' Theo said, with false confidence.

Nathan shook his head. 'Not now. But – have to – give her . . .' He trailed off, worn out from the effort of speaking. At the same time, a challenge sounded from the bow. Looking over the side, Theo saw a crowded budgerow heading for their ship. The men aboard were filthy. He did not recognise them as Englishmen, until the man at the prow hailed them.

'Permission to come aboard.' Even in his feeble state, his voice carried an air of command across the water.

'Who are you?' called the officer of the watch.

'Gerard Courtney. These men and I are the last survivors of the fall of Calcutta.'

The men clambered aboard. Red sores had boiled up all over their bodies. Some were so weak they had to be hauled in the bosun's chair, but Gerard mounted the ladder unaided. The men and women on deck stood apart to make way, as if touching these soiled wraiths would contaminate them.

The captain had the crew use the pumps to sluice down the new arrivals, then took them below and gave them fresh slops to wear. As they re-emerged, people clustered around to hear their story, desperately seeking news of family and loved ones.

Theo had no desire to see Gerard again – but in the confines of the ship, it was unavoidable. Gerard found him an hour later, tending Nathan.

'So these are the rewards of cowardice,' said Gerard. 'I suppose I cannot blame you. Better men than you fled their post.'

Theo ran his gaze over Gerard's frame. Although washed and in a clean shirt, he still stank of the gaol, while the red pustules on his skin made him look like a plague victim. 'I suppose you covered yourself in glory.'

'I am not here to prolong our quarrel. I came to tell you your sister is dead.'

Theo stared at him dully. 'I know. I tried to save her. That is how I ended up here.'

'But that is nonsense,' said Gerard. 'She died the night before last, in the press of the Black Hole.'

Theo was astonished. 'She drowned in the river, when the boat overturned.'

'You are mistaken. I was with her. I saw them pull her corpse out of the prison yesterday morning.'

Theo went grey. He searched his cousin's face for any hint of deceit, wanting to see a lie so he would not have to believe it. All he found was truth. Neither man had the strength for dissembling. 'Yesterday morning?' he repeated huskily.

'You have heard what the nawab did to us?' Gerard asked. Theo shook his head. Gerard told him. 'Constance was there.'

Theo closed his eyes. In his heart, he knew it made no difference. He had thought Connie was lost – and now she was. But at the same time it changed everything. Theo could have stayed if he'd known better. He could have protected her to the last. Perhaps if he had been there, he could have saved her, or at least died in her place.

His one consolation had been that he had done everything he could for her. Now that that had been ripped away, he had nothing. Chance is a brutal master. He gazed at Gerard, hating the man who had destroyed his last illusions. 'What will you do now?'

Gerard leaned against the mast. 'The directors in London cannot let this insult pass. Siraj has sown the wind, and now he will reap the whirlwind. It will be a fight to the death. Either we will rule all Bengal, or we will be expelled from India for ever.'

'You will stay and fight?'

Gerard's lips spread a little, a faint indication of his old confident grin. 'If we fail, I have nothing left to lose. But if we win, think of the opportunities. The richest province in the Indies would be ours, ripe for the picking.' He held out his hand. 'I am sorry for what happened with Constance. Perhaps if you were older you would understand better. But we both loved her, in our way. We should honour her memory by avenging her death.'

His hand stayed outstretched. Theo stared at it – but all he saw was Constance's naked body writhing above Gerard's. That quarrel had been the cause of all their misfortune. Without it, he would never have left Connie at the fort. Her death was all Gerard's fault.

He spoke slowly and clearly: 'If we were standing against all King Louis's armies, and you and I were the last two men left, I would kill you myself rather than fight beside you.'

Gerard's eyes flashed with anger. Then he shrugged his shoulders and withdrew his hand. 'As you choose.'

Theo turned his attention back to Nathan, who had lain silent while they spoke. His breathing was quieter, his eyes closed. But the moment Gerard had gone, they opened. 'What will you do?' he croaked. He had heard the conversation.

'I do not know,' said Theo, honestly. Then, in despair: 'I wish I were dead.'

Nathan grimaced. 'It is poor manners to wish that in the presence of a dying man. If you were lying in my bones, you would not be so eager to throw your life away.'

Theo blushed. 'I'm sorry.'

Nathan raised himself a little on the rolled-up shirt that served as a pillow. His hand pawed at the gold hooped earring he always wore.

'Take it off.'

Theo undid the clasp and pulled it out of Nathan's ear.

'The cap,' Nathan hissed.

As he had seen Nathan do before, Theo unscrewed the cap from the hollow hoop. Threads of tobacco tumbled out. But there was something else, rattling inside at the bottom. He tipped it into his palm and stared.

Two tiny stones winked and sparkled in his hand. Their cut facets threw rainbow points of light onto his skin. 'Diamonds,' he breathed. He closed his hand quickly before anyone else saw. 'But . . . where did you get them?'

'In – the house,' Nathan wheezed.

Theo took a moment to understand what he meant. 'In the battle?' He remembered Nathan disappearing for a moment during the frantic fighting in the mansions. He must have found the jewels in some lady's dressing room, forgotten in her flight. 'You stole them?'

'Only fair. Owners – won't miss.'

Nathan tapped Theo's closed fist. 'My sister,' he whispered.

'You want me to take these to your sister?'

'One for you. One for her.'

'In America?'

'Yes.'

Theo stared over the ship's side. Beyond the muddy river, beyond the squalid camp and the gabled roofs of the Dutch houses at Fulta, his gaze rose to the distant hills. This was the only country he had ever known: a land of heat and dust, teeming cities, unbearable poverty and inconceivable riches. Could he sail away to the far side of the world, a dim frontier of snowy forests and savage peoples?

Could he bear to stay?

He dropped the diamonds carefully back inside the earring, making sure the cap was screwed in tight. He removed his belt and put it into his mouth, biting down firmly. Then, gripping the ring's clasp, he drove the pin into his earlobe. Warm blood spurted out and trickled over his hand, but he bit harder on the belt until he felt the pin prick through to the other side.

The pain and the blood felt cleansing, consecrating his decision: the birth-blood of a new chapter in his life.

A few drops of blood fell on Nathan's face, shocking splashes of colour against the grey skin. Theo started to wipe, but as his hand touched Nathan's cheek he paused. The skin was cold. Nathan's eyes were closed, and his chest was not moving. Theo put his ear against his mouth and felt no sign of breathing.

Another wave of guilt surged through him. He had not been there for his friend's last moments. Once again, he had failed the people he loved best.

But then he saw the expression fixed on Nathan's face: the calm smile of a man at peace. He knew what Theo had decided. He had died passing on a part of his soul.

Theo unrolled the handkerchief and covered Nathan's face. In the west, on the far side of the continent and across the oceans, the sun was setting. He stared in the direction of the sunset's horizon, shading his eyes but absorbing the promise of its golden light.

That was where he would go.

• • •

The road out of Fort William was strewn with the detritus of battle: rubble that had been blasted from the fort's walls, spent cannonballs, pieces of furniture looted from the mansions and abandoned. The cart being manhandled along the track was overloaded, weighed down with numberless bodies.

It was grim work, but the men were used to it. Undertaking and grave-digging were unclean professions, confined to the lowest caste – they were the untouchables, avoided and shunned since to touch them would be to acquire the pollution they carried. The men could imagine no other life. They sang as they worked, lifting down the corpses and lining them in the pit, a former defensive ditch hacked out of the ground. It was too shallow, but no one cared about formal ceremony.

Some of the bodies were so heavy it took four men to carry them, and the gaunt gravediggers were contemptuous at how fat the hat-wearers had become on the profits of their trade. Only one corpse gave them pause, that of a woman among the scores of men they had buried. Her skin was marble smooth; her beauty obvious even in death. One of the men unlaced her bodice and pulled open her dress to reveal the white breasts underneath. But his companions chided him: enough sullying of the dead, they said. They carried her respectfully and laid her gently in the grave with the others.

They took their shovels and began to fill the grave with red earth.

Constance had barely noticed the jolting journey to the burial ditch. She vaguely sensed pressure lifting as the pile of bodies on top of her was unloaded, felt space and swaying as the men lifted her out of the cart. But if it registered at all, it was only as ripples on the edge of her deathly dreams.

She dreamed she was at the bottom of a deep well, staring up at a full moon. Then the moon became Theo's face. He reached down to pull her out, but however far she stretched her hand would not reach. He grew angry. He shouted and swore at her, but there was nothing she could do. She would be trapped for ever.

A spray of dirt and grit struck her face. The shock sprang her from her dream. She opened her eyes as another spadeful of earth hit her. She tasted soil in her mouth.

She tried to sit up, but she had no strength. More debris rained down, hard heavy clods that bruised her skin and piled around her, compacting her body into the grave. She was being buried alive.

She wanted to scream, but there was not enough breath in her lungs. She writhed and twisted and moaned but the soil kept landing.

And then it stopped. She heard muffled voices through the earth that clogged her ears. Rough hands pawed at her and scraped away the mounds of dirt.

Half a dozen men stood around her, naked but for dirty cloths around their waists. They stared with wide eyes. Her pale skin and white gown made her appear like a *petni* – a vengeful ghost risen from the dead. One of the men brandished his spade at her – superstition had it that iron would ward off an evil spirit.

Constance stood unsteadily in a cascade of loose earth. The gravediggers retreated, fearful of this grotesque apparition. They cowered and muttered.

She wanted to run but her limbs were too stiff. She swayed, dizzy with sudden life and freedom. How had she managed to rise from the dead? One of the men struck her bare leg with the blade of his shovel. The wound it made began to bleed. She was human, flesh and blood. The men grabbed her and dragged her along the road to the fort. Had she arrived earlier, she would have met Gerard Courtney stumbling out of the gate and making his way to the ghats. But she was too late for that. None of her people saw her.

The gravediggers presented her to the *jemmaut-dar*, who gave a calculating grin and barked a series of orders. Guards took her, more roughly than the gravediggers, leading her back towards the nawab's camp.

She wondered if she'd died after all, if God had judged her for her carnal sins with Gerard and sent her to the outermost depths of Hell. The city they led her through was a carcass of the elegant Calcutta she had known. The houses were smashed, and corpses littered the streets. A sulphurous haze hung over the city. She could hear singing, shouts, and the screams of women as the victorious soldiers took their pleasures. Soon, she realised with a chill, it would be her screams.

'*I am alive*,' she told herself, again and again. '*I am alive*.' She clung to the possibilities opening to her. In the Black Hole she must have lapsed into a coma, unconsciousness saving her from death after the prison's horrors. She began to relish her good fortune.

The nawab's camp was almost deserted. The army was looting the city. The guards took her through lines of empty tents, to the great golden pavilion in its centre: a constellation of separate apartments joined by shaded walkways. Guards made a cordon around it, and men in splendid uniforms sat atop elephants at the four corners.

A dozen serving girls were waiting for her in one of the chambers. The guards withdrew a short distance: Constance could see their shadows rippling on the canvas outside the door.

The women surrounded her. Without preamble, they tore off her dress, pointing and smirking at the tuft of fine blonde hair between her legs. She was too exhausted to care. They filled a steaming bath and ushered her in. She went eagerly, but the moment she touched the water she cried out in agony. The bathwater was like being stabbed with a thousand hot needles. The women held her down, oblivious to her screams, scrubbing every inch of her clean. It felt as if they were peeling off her skin.

They dried her on soft towels and rubbed perfumed oil over her body. They brushed her hair until it shone, letting it hang loose down her back. They dressed her in a cotton sari woven so thinly it hid very little. It reminded Constance of what the nautch-dancers had worn at the Company party in Madras. The memory would have made her cry but she could not summon the tears.

She had no resistance. Her mind had shut down, separated from fear or hope. She buried her spirit beyond anyone's reach. She became a detached observer of her own life, as if she were floating outside her body, watching her life unfold with mild curiosity.

Guards returned. They led her along the covered walkways, through other tents where women lounged like cats on carpets and cushions. They stared at Constance without pity or scorn, but through narrow, appraising eyes. Musicians plucked at instruments, and the air was thick with perfume.

They came into the grandest tent of all. Constance's bare feet vanished into the thick carpets. The walls were hung with gilded mirrors and painted screens, which showed naked women cavorting in complex sexual positions. The only piece of furniture was a wide bed, which stood in the centre of the room, like a sacrificial altar.

Abruptly, the guards pushed Constance hard in the small of her back. She stumbled forward against the bed. Before she could right herself, they lifted her arms and legs and spread-eagled her face down on the mattress. She struggled, but they held her fast. One of the women had followed the guards, bringing bands of cloth. Methodically, she tied the cloth around Constance's wrists and ankles and fastened each to the corner posts of the bed.

Then they left her.

Bound and alone, Connie pressed her face into the pillow. If she twisted her head she could see the figures on the painted screens, women bent unnaturally while bare-chested men penetrated them in imaginative ways. She closed her eyes and tensed, listening hard. The carpets were so soft, she might not even hear an approach.

She lay there for a long time. If that was part of the nawab's sadism, or if he was simply busy seeing to his conquered city, she didn't know or care. After the Black Hole, she was beginning to learn endurance.

She began to test her bonds. The harem mistress knew her job and had tied them fast, but Constance persisted. She flexed her wrist, back and forth, working the cloth loose, tensing at every noise.

With a tug, her hand came free. She rolled her wrist to get the blood flowing again. Now she could pick at the knot that held her other hand.

But even if she freed both hands, her feet were still tied. And there was little hope of escaping with so many guards about.

Something caught her eye. There was a crack in the headboard. She shuddered to think what might have caused the damage. She saw a long split in the wood and prised at it with her fingernails. The wood was strong but, with persistence, she broke it off. Now she had a splinter, about nine inches long and as thick as her thumb, tapering to a jagged point. It was a makeshift weapon, hard enough to drive into the nawab's eye or belly. She would not have to worry about getting close enough.

Outside the tent, she heard the guards snap to attention. She tucked the splinter under her chest, then replaced her hand in the cloth loop.

The folds of the door-hanging swished gently as someone entered. The carpet softened his steps, but she could hear him approach. His armour clattered as he moved, then stopped. She heard the rasp of buckles, a heavy thud as the armour dropped to the floor, followed by cloth on skin as he stepped out of his tunic.

She could smell him: stale perfume, sweat and *bhang*. The bed creaked and sagged as he clambered on to it, positioning himself between her outspread thighs. She could feel the heat from him, inches away. Her body clenched, but she tried to relax.

He ran his fingers through her fair hair. Then his grip tightened. He twisted her hair around his fingers and yanked sharply, pulling her head back. She felt sharp cold steel pressing against the base of her spine where her buttocks spread apart.

The point of the blade pricked through her gauzy dress. He cut through the fabric, splitting it open. He ripped it apart, leaning forward so his erect manhood pushed against her. She braced herself.

With a cry of horror, he let go of her hair and jumped back. She could not see what was happening. He was shouting and cursing. Guards and servants came running, fearful that their master had been attacked. Constance quickly pushed the splinter aside and let it drop under the bed.

The nawab screamed in disgust and left the room. The guards began a furious consultation among themselves.

Constance risked pulling her hand out of the cloth loop. Craning her head, she caught a glimpse of her back in the mirror on the wall and gasped. Every inch of her skin had erupted in vivid red boils. Rolling on her side, she saw they were down her front, too, her belly, her thighs and her breasts. She looked like a leper, or a plague victim.

She began to be very afraid. With her beauty intact, she had some value to her captors. Without it, she had nothing. She saw the guards gesticulating as they spoke, their hands on their swords. Were they were debating whether to keep her for their own amusement, or to cut her throat? She wished she hadn't let go of the wooden splinter. She would rather kill herself than let them touch her.

One of the guards drew his sword. Constance tensed, anticipating a fatal blow, or perhaps they would elect for a slow death, the sensuousness of her gradual bleeding away.

But the guard did not strike her. He cut through her bonds and gestured to her to get up.

He took her by her neck and pushed her onto her knees. He stood over her and lifted his tunic, grabbing the sides of her head with both hands. The other men crowded around, offering encouragement. Constance shut her eyes. The guard's erect manhood pressed against her face, angry and obscene.

'*Qu'est-ce qui se passe ici?*'

A shout from the door and the scene froze. A French officer had entered, red-faced with anger. '*Laissez-la partir maintenant!*'

The guards did not speak French, but they understood the expression on his face. He tapped the epaulettes on his shoulder – Constance did not know what rank they signified – and berated them in a mix of French, Arabic and Bengali.

Then she heard another voice. Constance turned her head.

It was the French general with the cold eyes. He spoke angrily, first to the guards and then to the French captain. 'What are you thinking, you imbecile?' he shouted in French. 'You jeopardise our standing with the nawab over a mere *woman*?'

The captain stiffened. 'I am sorry, *mon général*. I felt it would be improper to allow these native savages to molest a European woman.'

'She is an *English*woman,' the general raged. 'I would not care if the nawab fed her to his dogs. But now I must let one of my officers lose face before these savages. And that is *insupportable*.'

Unobserved, Constance watched the general in one of the mirrors.

He was not a handsome man. His eyes were small, his lips fat, his nose hooked, like an eagle's beak. His mousy brown hair was cropped short without regard to fashion or appearance, as if he had used a sabre to chop it off himself. Yet there was power in his face, an ugly strength that held Constance's gaze even as he repelled her.

'Take her out of my sight,' he said to the French officer. 'And if you ever force my hand like this again, I will serve you to the nawab for his pleasure. He likes men, too.' He made a crude gesture. 'Your arse would please him greatly.'

The captain nodded. 'Very good, monsieur.'

The guards retreated. The French captain approached Constance. He cupped a hand under her chin and lifted her face to look at him. '*Mon Dieu,*' he said to himself. Then, still in French: 'For God's sake, cover yourself.'

Constance pulled a sheet off the bed and wrapped it around her. She rose unsteadily to her feet. 'Who are you?' she asked, in French.

He clicked his heels. 'Captain Lascaux,' he introduced himself. 'I serve on the staff of General Corbeil.'

'How did you . . .?'

'When I heard that the nawab had captured an Englishwoman, I feared the worst. I hastened here immediately. Thank God I was not too late.'

He was young, barely twenty, with a wide-open face that had not yet hardened to the ways of the army.

'I owe you my honour and perhaps my life,' she said. 'But why as a Frenchman do you want to save an Englishwoman in distress? I thought your country hated the English.'

He frowned. 'We hate their warlike ways, their superciliousness, their presumption and their arrogance, but we do not hate their women.'

Constance sensed warmth in his smile. She needed to trust him.

'We are not barbarians,' he told her. 'I give you my word as a French officer you will be treated correctly from now on. I will arrange a safe passage to our settlement at Chandernagore. From there, it will be possible to return to your people. Or . . .' He hesitated '. . . you are welcome to stay with me.'

Her skin burned, her head ached, and she felt sick to her stomach. Theo had abandoned her. Gerard must have died in the Black Hole. She was alone and defenceless, a pretty plaything for any man who chose to violate her at a whim. Or simply to cut her throat because it amused him.

In the cell, she had sworn never to let a man have power over her again. But that had been folly built on despair. In the hard light of day, she could see the truth. The world was a battlefield where men clashed, like swords, sharp and vicious: women were nothing more than targets for their blades.

A woman could not fight them on her own. But she was not helpless. Swords could be wielded, if you flexed the right muscles and could stand a little pain.

She had noticed the way the captain blushed when he looked at her. She forced herself to give him a shy smile. 'I want to stay with you.'

It was late in the day when Theo walked along the road into the township of Bethel. It had taken him a full year to get here – a year honouring a dead man's last wish. The sun shone golden from a blue sky, but there was a chill in the air, the first breaths of autumn. He could smell ripe apples and freshly cut grass, and the scent of woodsmoke wafted nearby. He was alone.

These were the last steps of a journey that had taken him across four continents: from Calcutta to Cape Town; from the Cape to the docks at London; from London to Boston, and finally to this American wilderness. The young man who had landed on the quay at Boston harbour was unrecognisable as the tentative child who had left Madras two years earlier. His adolescent frame had taken shape, bulking out with strength and muscle. His bright red hair had mellowed to copper, and his features had hardened. It was still a friendly face, but with an underlying seriousness of purpose. Men and women had smiled when they passed him in the Boston streets. But the men did so with a certain respect, while the women would look again when they thought he did not notice.

Theo had signed as a landsman on an East Indiaman and worked his passage to London. He had enjoyed the work and the camaraderie with the crew. In London, he had exchanged one of Nathan's diamonds for a tidy sum in gold, but when it came time to sail to Boston he preferred life in the fo'c'sle with the other hands, rather than in the roundhouse or the stern cabins with the gentlemen passengers. On the main deck, no one asked after your family or your connections: he was free of his past.

He was near his journey's end and that gave him an extra bounce in his stride. He was ready to discharge his obligation to Nathan, and to begin the rest of his life. He did not know where it would lead him – but autumn, with its harvest and succulent fruits, was ripe with the promise of new beginnings.

A cloud seemed to cover the sun as he entered the village. The nip in the air turned sharper – or perhaps it was the looks he received. Men and women with pinched, furrowed faces gazed at him with undisguised suspicion as he passed. Theo stared back. Growing up, he had never seen a white man working with his hands or carrying anything heavier than a book. Yet these people, respectably dressed, were digging vegetables, drawing water and cutting wood in the way that only a servant would have done in India.

The houses straggled along the road for almost a mile, but they did not go deep. Goats and pigs grazed in the back gardens, and beyond the split-rail fences the forest pressed close. It was a precarious place, carved out of a frontier that had not yet yielded.

Halfway along the road, in the centre of the village, there was a white clapboard church, a duck pond and a muddy green. Something that appeared to be a life-size cross stood between the church and the pond, but its purpose was not religious. It was a pillory, raised up on a wooden pole, so that all the villagers could see the unfortunate miscreant. It looked well used.

Theo gave it a wide berth. But as he strolled closer to the church, he saw that a menagerie of animal heads had been nailed to its walls: wolves, foxes, mink and even a small bear. They made a macabre sight.

He remembered what Nathan had said: *Shooting and praying were the only entertainment we were allowed*. He wondered what living in such an unyielding place did to people.

A crow flew up from the tower as the church door opened. A priest stepped out. He wore a black suit, with a starched white collar, and a black hat over his close-cropped white hair. He wandered from the church and stopped in front of Theo, blocking his path. 'A visitor,' he said, with no trace of welcome.

'I am looking for the Claypole family,' Theo told him.

The priest sucked his teeth. 'You know Ezekiel Claypole?'

'I knew his son.'

The past tense, and the expression in his voice, left no doubt why he had come.

The priest nodded. 'Last house as you leave the village.' And then, 'The town of Bethel keeps its business to itself. Claypole and his son were not close. You will not need long.'

The priest went back inside the church and closed the door. The fox nailed beside the frame watched Theo with dead eyes, mocking him.

The Claypole home was a good way beyond the village. The road turned into a rutted single track, hemmed in so close by the trees that the sun had not dried the mud. The light began to fade. Theo wondered if he'd missed the house, or if he should turn back and try again in the morning.

A shadow caught his eye in the forest. Theo's hand moved quickly to his belt. In London, he had spent some of Nathan's money on a new suit of clothes, and a fine pair of matched pistols. He peered into the undergrowth.

It was a girl. She was squatting by a tree with her back to him, examining the ground. She wore a simple grey dress, with a white apron, which she held out in front of her, like a basket. Her hair was pinned under a white bonnet. She was engrossed in her work.

She plucked something from among the tree roots and sniffed it, then added it to the stock in her apron. Theo raised his hat. 'Good day, mistress.'

She started, stood and spun around. She dropped her apron, a look of terror on her face; mushrooms spilled all over the forest floor. 'Why did you sneak up on me? I thought you were an Indian,' she cried.

Nathan had told him about the dangers of the native Indians: *I grew up playing hide-and-seek with French fur-trappers and Mohawk Indians, with my scalp as the forfeit if I lost.* No wonder she had been frightened. He spread his arms to show he meant no harm. 'As you see, I am only a visitor.'

'Who are you?' She backed away, suspicious of this stranger.

For a long moment, Theo didn't answer. Now that she was standing, he could see she was taller than he'd thought, almost his own age. Her skin was smooth and creamy as butter, though flushed now with surprise and embarrassment. A strand of glossy dark hair had escaped from under her bonnet and hung down over her eyes, which were as blue as an August sky.

Theo replaced his hat. 'I am sorry I startled you. My name is Theo Courtney. And though I am not one of your Indians, I have just arrived from India.'

She laughed, a pure, joyous sound that seemed to banish all the gloom in the forest. Then she remembered herself, and composed her face, blushing even harder. 'How do I know you mean me no harm?' She eyed his features, perhaps to see where she could inflict the most pain if he attacked her.

'I come in peace,' he said.

'Show me your hands.'

He held them up.

She examined them from a distance. 'I can read palms, and the stories they tell are astonishing. I can see you have had a hard journey in your life so far. You have suffered loss and grief, your heart is bruised, but I think your soul remains pure.'

Theo was aghast. He saw her face soften.

'I pray you will forgive me. Mother says I do not behave properly, like I should.'

'I should be asking your forgiveness.' Theo pointed to the mushrooms on the ground. He started collecting them, placing them in the apron the girl held out. He moved clumsily.

His fingers brushed hers. He felt a shiver go through him, but she recoiled so suddenly he thought she would let go of the apron again. Her eyes met his with a reproachful gaze that relaxed into something tender as she saw the innocence on his face. 'We do not meet many strangers in these woods,' she said.

'What is your name?'

'Abigail Claypole,' she said shyly.

Theo let out a long sigh. He had known it from the moment he had looked into her eyes – so similar to Nathan's. 'Will you take me to your home?'

'Why?'

'I have brought something for your family.'

He could see she was curious. But she was from New England stock, people who kept their thoughts to themselves. Without more questions, she led him down an animal trail through the trees. Theo's heart beat faster. He had travelled halfway round the world for this moment, but now that it had come he wanted it to be over. He would shatter the girl with news of her brother's death.

They came out in a meadow. Blackened stumps poked through the long grass where the trees had been burned and felled to clear it. A cluster of buildings stood at the far edge, near a stream: a shingled barn, a low house made of split logs, and a few storage sheds. An orchard of apple and pear trees grew in front of the house, and a fenced vegetable plot beside it. A woman in a shapeless grey dress was bringing in laundry from a line, scolding the small child who played around her feet.

Two dogs raced out from the porch of the house. They were huge, grey brindled mastiffs. They galloped across the clearing and stopped three paces from Theo, barking and snapping. The menace in their powerful bodies and slavering jaws made him tremble. He suspected that if he had not been with Abigail they would have torn him to pieces.

At the sound of their barking, the woman with the laundry looked up. She put her fingers in her mouth and let out a sharp whistle that silenced the dogs immediately.

'Claypole,' she called, in a piercing voice. 'A visitor.'

Her husband appeared from inside the barn with a pitchfork, followed by a youth of about seventeen. Their faces were so similar, from the close-set brown eyes to the crooked chins to the scowls they wore, they could only have been father and son. There was a resemblance to Nathan, but different, like fruit from the same tree that had gone off.

The man pulled his straw hat over his eyes and leaned on his pitchfork. The dogs trotted over and stood beside him, hackles still raised. 'Don't much care for visitors.'

'This is Mr Courtney come from India,' said Abigail.

Claypole gave Theo a long, appraising look that conceded nothing. 'That's a mighty long way from Bethel.'

'I was a friend of your son, Nathan.'

Claypole said nothing. But clearly Abigail had felt the emotion behind Theo's words. With a gasp, she cried out, 'What has happened to him?'

Claypole glared at her.

His wife slapped her daughter's wrist. 'Do not speak when your father is in conversation.'

Theo held his hat in his hands. 'It is true. Nathan is dead.' He hadn't meant to say it so baldly. But he had been walking all day, and this hostile reception at the journey's end had disconcerted him. 'I am sorry,' he added.

Abigail let out a long, terrible moan and ran inside the house, sobbing. The dogs growled. Her mother twisted her hands in her skirts, while Claypole's knuckles tightened around the pitchfork handle. He made no move to comfort his wife but exchanged a wordless glance with her. 'Best you'd come inside.'

• • •

The house had a single room, low and smoky. A long rifle hung above the fireplace; animal skins dangled from the beams. A stitched sampler on the wall said 'God is Love.' Claypole seated himself in a high-backed chair beside the fire, while the others perched on rough stools. Mrs Claypole poured cups of crude apple brandy, called applejack. 'Tell me about my son,' she said.

The smoke and the applejack made Theo's eyes water. 'Have you heard of the loss of Calcutta?'

'We don't get much news of doings in other parts,' said Claypole.

As briefly as he could, Theo explained what had happened. The more he spoke, the more he felt the weight of their disbelieving gaze. In that cramped room, talking of India – of nawabs and monsoons, of sepoys and elephants – he felt like Gulliver describing Lilliput. He described the siege and the fighting, pausing only to emphasise how Nathan had saved his life. With the Claypoles watching, he hardly dared look at Abigail, but he was always conscious of her presence.

'Also, he asked me to deliver *this*.' He took the leather pouch from around his neck and tipped out the diamond. In the dim room, it lay dull and inert.

'It is a diamond from India,' Theo explained, in case there was any doubt. 'Nathan wanted you to have it.'

He held it out to Abigail, enjoying the look of wonder on her face. She reached for it.

A sharp hand slapped her. Mrs Claypole plucked the diamond out of Theo's palm.

'It is vanity,' she said severely. 'We have no need for such trinkets in these parts. We are godly folk. I do not know what Nathan was thinking.'

'His last wish was that Abigail should have it,' Theo said.

'I will trouble you to address my daughter with respect,' Claypole warned. 'She is Miss Claypole to you.'

'It must have been that heathen, foreign air that gave Nathan the notion,' his wife continued. 'If that is why you came, to impress my daughter with riches, I am afraid you have wasted your journey.'

'I came because of the debt I owed Nathan,' Theo answered. 'And to fulfil your son's dying wish. Does that count for nothing?'

Perhaps he should have guessed, from Nathan's description, how they would react. Even so, it shocked him that they should be so dismissive. That little stone could transform their lives, yet they treated it as if it were the seed of the devil. He wished he had given it to Abigail when he met her.

It was too late for that. Mrs Claypole dropped the diamond into the pocket of her apron without a second glance.

'Nathan ran away from us seven years ago.' Claypole puffed on his pipe, stroking the bowl the way Nathan used to. 'We will not take his charity. What he did, he proved he was no son of ours.'

'Not like dear Caleb,' said his wife. Her gaze went to the wall, where a framed charcoal sketch showed a young family: two children, a mother and a father whose face bore an unmistakable likeness to Nathan's. A posy of fresh wild flowers lay on the shelf below it. 'He was a good boy. The Lord took him from us too soon.' A tear escaped her eye.

Claypole rose from his chair. 'Thank you for bringing us news of Nathan's death,' he said formally. 'God speed on your journey.'

The meeting was over. Theo stood, wondering where he was supposed to go. Through the cabin's tiny windows, he could see night had fallen. He thought of the twisting road back to town. It would be easy to get lost in the woods.

'Do you mean to cast Mr Courtney out of our home?' cried Abigail. It was the first time she had spoken since they had come inside, and for a moment Theo feared Claypole would strike her for her trouble. But she carried on undaunted. 'He has travelled thousands of miles on our account. Will you not even give him a bed for the night?'

'Go to the stable,' snapped her mother. 'It is past time for milking the cow.'

Abigail stood, defiant. 'Will you?'

'This does not concern you.' Her mother was angry. 'It is not seemly.'

'This does concern me. Nathan was my brother, and Mr Courtney was his friend.'

Neither woman would retreat. Claypole stood silent as mother and daughter faced each other across the cramped room. Theo feared they would come to blows. He stepped between them. 'I have enjoyed your hospitality long enough. If you would be so kind as to lend me a light, I will have no trouble finding my way back to town.'

He didn't look at Abigail. Claypole fetched a lantern while Theo waited outside. Abigail disappeared into the barn while her mother busied herself in the house with much banging of pots and utensils.

'Jebuthan will show you to the road,' said Claypole, indicating his son. 'You will find your way from there.'

'I am obliged. And the lantern?'

'Leave it at the store in town. I'll call for it when I am there.'

Theo nodded. He glanced towards the barn, hoping for one last glimpse of Abigail.

Claypole gave him a crooked look. 'God speed, Mr Courtney. I did not look for you to visit us, and I do not expect we will meet again. No doubt your business will take you far from Bethel tomorrow.'

He had made his meaning plain.

Theo smiled ingenuously. 'Thank you for the hospitality. I am sorry to have been the cause of grief.'

The boy led him through the trees without a word. The dogs accompanied them. Theo didn't realise they'd reached the road until the boy stopped and pointed to his right. He handed Theo the lantern and disappeared.

The only hint of the road was the water lying pooled in the ruts, which gleamed in the lamplight. Theo followed it, walking slowly and listening hard. He was not worried about Indians or bandits. He was hoping that Abigail would come after him. He held her face in his mind, remembering every detail: the curve of her lips, the lock of hair that had escaped her bonnet, the flush of her cheeks when she defied her mother. He would have given everything he owned for a few more minutes alone with her.

But she didn't come. Soon, he saw the lights of the village ahead, few and faint against the immense forest that surrounded it. The residents retired early. He banged for ten minutes on the door of the boarding house, and when it opened, the surly landlady offered him only a mattress on the attic floor.

He had travelled many miles that day and his limbs ached with weariness. But it was hours before he fell into a deep, dream-laden sleep.

• • •

Next morning, when he had washed and eaten a meagre breakfast, Theo explored the town. The rest of his life stretched before him, but he was in no hurry to leave. He had dreamed of Abigail in the night.

An idea had begun to form in his mind. After lunch, he took the borrowed lantern and headed back towards the Claypole farm. When he reached the turning, he left the road but did not approach the buildings. He skirted around the clearing, keeping within the undergrowth and hoping the dogs did not get wind of him.

Smoke puffed from the chimney of the main house.

He heard Mrs Claypole's voice inside. Was Abigail in there? He moved further around, trying to see through the door of the barn. What if she was away in the fields? How long could he wait? He was downwind of the house, but he did not want those ferocious dogs to scent him.

A door slammed. A moment later, Abigail came past the side of the house and went into the barn. She fetched a pail of milk and poured it into a butter churn that stood outside. Seating herself on a log, she began rhythmically raising and lowering the plunger into the barrel.

Theo cupped his hands and made a hooting noise that he hoped sounded like an owl. Abigail looked up in surprise, which turned to alarm when she saw Theo waving at her from the bushes.

He ran across and knelt beside her. They were at the back of the house, and there were no windows on that side. He was hidden from view – as long as no one walked around the corner.

'Why did you come?' Abigail whispered, clearly afraid.

'I wanted to see you.'

Her face creased in pleasure mingled with pain. 'I wanted to see you too, but if Mother or Father finds you are here . . .'

He gestured to the barrel. 'Keep churning. They will hear it if you stop.'

She resumed the rhythmic plunging. There was silence, except for the thud of wood on wood. Theo stared at her. Her simple beauty made his heart feel too big for his chest. He was short of breath. How could he be so instantly smitten? The long, harsh road of fulfilling his promise to Nathan had stripped his spirit bare. He craved a soft female presence, but he couldn't think of anything to say.

'Tell me more about Nathan,' Abigail said. 'What sort of man had he become?'

'I barely knew him,' Theo reminded her.

'Yet you came so far for him.'

'I owed him a debt.' Theo thought back to Calcutta, half a world away. 'He was strong, calm and brave beyond measure.'

'No wonder you were his friend. You sound much alike, I can tell.'

Theo flushed. Did this woman have special insights? He glanced at Abigail to see if she was teasing him, but her face was sincere. Their eyes met, open and unguarded. Something mystical seemed to pass between them: an understanding beyond words that resonated to Theo's core.

'You should go,' said Abigail. Her voice was hoarse. She had forgotten the butter churn. 'Father will be furious if he finds you here.'

Theo knew she was right. He didn't move. 'He seems very strict with you.'

'Everyone in Bethel is strict. That is why Nathan ran away.'

'And you?'

She gave a wry smile and he saw rebellion in her eyes. 'I do not fit in here. Like Nathan, I am a restless soul. But it would not be ladylike to run away to sea.'

'We would not have to go to sea. There are many places we could go. We—' He broke off as he realised what he had said. Abigail stared at him in shock and wonder. Everything was happening so fast. This was not what he had planned. Her aura seemed to draw him in – he was helpless to resist.

The sound of a dog barking brought him to his senses. He leaped to his feet and grabbed the lantern as Claypole came striding around the corner with the dogs at his heels. He was carrying his long rifle. Suspicion burned on his face as he looked between Theo and Abigail. The gun started to come up. Theo wished he had not left his pistols at the boarding house.

The gun held steady, angled at Theo's midriff. The dogs bared their teeth but did not attack. Claypole seemed to gather his emotions. 'Mr Courtney.' He tipped his hat a fraction. 'I thought you had left our town.'

'I came to return your lantern.' Theo thrust it forward.

Claypole pursed his lips. 'There was no need.'

Theo wondered how Nathan could have grown to be so loyal and generous from such a bitter seed. He nodded to the dogs and the gun. 'Have you been hunting?'

'No,' said Claypole.

There was a silence, the only sound Abigail churning the butter.

Claypole jerked the gun. 'Obliged for the lantern. Now you should go. You'll want to be getting far away from Bethel.'

'I have a mind to linger in this area a little longer,' said Theo. 'I believe there is fine hunting to be had.'

'Have a care,' Claypole warned. 'There are many dangers hereabouts. A man who goes in those woods and don't know what he's doing, he might find himself dead right quick.'

'Perhaps fishing is more to his taste,' said Abigail, looking up from the butter churn. 'Are you a fisherman, Mr Courtney?'

As a child, Theo had sometimes dropped a line into the lagoon behind Madras. He had never caught anything. But he sensed a hidden purpose behind her words. 'On occasion.'

'The best fishing around here is at Shaw's Pond,' she said. 'Pa says the fish rise near midnight. When there's a full moon, you can almost pluck them out of the water with your bare hand. Isn't that right?'

Claypole grunted. Theo tried to meet her gaze, but she had returned to the churning. 'Perhaps I will try my luck.'

Claypole scowled. 'Full moon's not until next week. Mr Courtney will be far from here by then.'

It wasn't a question.

• • •

Theo had no intention of letting Claypole threaten him. But next morning he found everything had changed in the town. The looks he drew in the street, always suspicious, were now so sharp they prickled his skin. At the boarding house, the landlord informed him that he would need the bed back that night.

'But what have I done wrong?' Theo demanded. 'Yesterday I was a welcome guest. Today I am treated like a diseased dog.'

The landlord wiped a tankard with a dishcloth. He would not meet Theo's eye. 'You may be new arrived, but you've made enemies quick enough.'

'Enemies? Surely you cannot mean Mr Claypole.'

By now, the tankard was so bright Theo could have read a newspaper in its reflection. The landlord mumbled something about it not being right to talk of other folk, and how Theo's business was his own.

'If this is how you treat visitors, then it is a wonder you have any custom at all!' Theo exclaimed. He had seen only one other visitor at the boarding house, a furrier from Massachusetts. 'I do not know what you intend to do with my bed, for you surely cannot need it for your guests.'

But there was no reasoning with the man. Theo left that afternoon – watched, he was certain, by every pair of eyes in the township. He had little doubt that news of his going would reach Claypole before he crossed the town boundary.

The next township was called Easton, some fifteen miles distant. Theo stayed for five days. The people were friendlier than in Bethel. His money was good, and in the evening, conversation could be had around the common table. Theo relayed the news from India and from London. In turn, he learned of the situation in the colonies. He was astonished to find out how two continents on opposite sides of the globe could weigh on each other. The battle at Fort Necessity, which had prompted the French to attack Madras, was a spark that had lit a long fuse. In Europe, King Louis XV of France and King George II of Great Britain had talked of peace, but in America the fighting had never stopped. Now the pretence of negotiations had finally broken down, and war had been declared.

North America was the only place in the world where the British and French shared a land border.

'The new prime minister, Mr Pitt, says he will take the fight to the French anywhere in the world,' said one of Theo's companions. 'He calls it war, but really he wants their trade. He has sent ten thousand men from England, and more are coming from all over the colonies. There is a captain in Lexington, raising a new regiment of New Hampshire men.'

The others nodded and agreed it would be a war like no other.

'But will we win?' asked another man, glumly. He was a backwoodsman, with buckskin trousers and mud under his fingernails. Beer dribbled down his beard. 'Easy for Pitt to give orders in London, but our frontiers are not the neat battlefields of Europe. It takes a different kind of fighting to win a war in the back country – and the French are past masters at it. Even before you count their Indian allies.'

'An English redcoat is worth ten Indians,' said one young hothead. He wore lace cuffs and had just arrived from Boston.

'They said much the same in Calcutta,' Theo said quietly. 'And it cost many men their lives.'

'And it will cost us here,' agreed the backwoodsman. 'We treat the Indians as slaves, but the French treat them as men.'

'And the French have a chain of impregnable forts right down to our border,' added another man.

'No fort is impregnable,' scoffed the hothead.

'Tell that to George Washington.'

There was much laughter at that, which Theo did not understand. 'Colonel Washington is a Virginian. He built a fort in the wilderness two years back named Fort Necessity,' his neighbour explained. 'The French took it and destroyed it. Washington surrendered.'

'I have heard of it,' Theo said tightly.

'A year later, Washington returned with an English army to attack the French outpost at Fort Duquesne. The French and Indians ambushed them. We lost a thousand men, and Washington retreated again.'

'If he is the best we can do, we are in for a hard war,' said the backwoodsman morosely. He looked at Theo. 'You're young and have seen battle. Will you enlist?'

'Are you trying to make me take the King's shilling?' Theo asked, in mock outrage. He drained his glass and pretended to examine the bottom.

Unscrupulous recruiting sergeants had been known to drop a coin into an unsuspecting man's drink and claim he had accepted enlistment when he fished it out.

The laughter was free and easy, and the conversation moved on.

Theo passed a few pleasant days in Easton. On the fifth afternoon, he left with a day's provisions, a tin of worms he had grubbed from the soil, and a fishing line.

• • •

Abigail told herself she was being foolish. She said it aloud that morning, milking the cow. She said it again in the afternoon, scraping the linen over the washboard. She thought it silently at supper, trying to avoid her mother's piercing gaze. And she repeated it over and over to herself as she lay in her bed, fully dressed, waiting to be sure everyone was asleep.

Before she went to bed she stared up at the stars in the pitch-black night sky. They were like diamonds on black silk, celestial messages decipherable only to those who could read their language. Ships could navigate from the stories the stars could tell, and Abigail read her destiny in the shimmering starlight. It filled her heart to bursting.

Her hint about the fishing had been so subtle, Theo might not have understood. Or he had understood but did not want to go, or had not realised she meant him to come tonight, the night of the full moon. Perhaps he did not know where to find Shaw's Pond, or was too frightened of her father.

She had looked into his eyes, and seen a spark – a mirror of the desire that she had tried so hard to keep from showing in her own face. She had to believe he would come.

And what if she *was* being foolish? It would cost her nothing but lost sleep, and damp shoes, and a beating if her father caught her.

She rose and crawled across the attic floor, feeling her way around her sleeping brother. She descended the ladder on tiptoe, terrified the rungs would creak. Embers in the hearth cast a low red glow; the only sound was her father snoring in his bed.

She did not put on her boots until she was outside. The night made her skin taut with cold. She wished she had brought a blanket, but she did not dare risk going back inside. What time was it? She had said midnight to Theo, but there was no clock in the house and she had no idea if she was late or early. What if he left because he thought she was not coming?

She knew she was being foolish. She went anyway.

The full moon lit her path. As a girl, she had ranged far and wide through the forest, often following Nathan on his foraging expeditions. When she had turned fourteen her mother had forbidden it, saying it was unbecoming for a young woman to be out on her own. But the trails had not changed. She flitted along them, never tripping. An owl hooted; a grazing deer looked up in surprise, then went back to its meal. Twice, she thought she heard a twig snap behind her, or the rustle of leaves. She waited, holding her breath. At this time of year, the Indians should have moved on to their winter hunting grounds, but you never knew who might be out in the forest.

She was jumping at shadows. She hurried on.

Shaw's Pond was a pool in the river that flowed down from the mountains at the foot of a waterfall. The weight of water coming over the cliff had hollowed out a bowl in the rock, deep and clear and surprisingly placid. Stone ledges surrounded it, making it easy to scramble in and out. In the hot summer months, all the local children went swimming there.

The moon shone on bare rocks and still water. The foaming falls glittered like a river of diamonds, roaring loud in the quiet of the night. The place was deserted.

Abigail's hopes collapsed. She *had* been a fool – a fool to come all this way for a dream of a man she barely knew. The night's cold teeth sank into her bones. It would be a long walk home.

A hand touched her shoulder, so unexpected she shrieked.

• • •

Theo had arrived before sunset. He walked softly, watching for others on the path, but met no one. He ate his bread and drank the ale he'd brought. Then he settled down under his blankets, inside the trees where he would not be seen. He watched the sun set over the great river valley in a pageant of gold and copper. The forest stretched to the mountains, and the mountains to the horizon. It was like no country he had ever seen or imagined, blank and untamed in a way that India, with its teeming multitudes and ancient civilisation, never could be. He felt it deep in his soul, a fierce sense of belonging. This was where he could write his life.

He did not have a timepiece, so he did not know how long he waited. Raised in distant cities, the night sounds of the forest were alien to him. Every bird and animal that stirred the undergrowth made him think she might be coming. Each time, he was disappointed.

He was a fool, he told himself. He'd thought he had heard a suggestion in her tone when she described the pond, but he had been mistaken, inventing things he wanted to be true.

Then he saw her.

She glided out of the forest without a sound. She stood on a rock, and the moonlit waterfall made a curtain of light behind her. Her dark hair fell loose down her back, framing her face and her wide, longing eyes.

He rose and went to her and put his hand on her shoulder. She shrieked with alarm and spun around, losing her footing. She stumbled forward. Theo caught her. He pulled her to his chest and wrapped his arms around her.

'You came,' she cried. 'I thought . . .' Her voice trailed off.

'I read your meaning.' Theo grinned, and gestured to the fishing rod leaning against a rock. 'You know I am a keen fisherman.'

She could barely speak for happiness and relief. 'I know this is wrong, but I thought I would never see you again and I could not bear it.'

'Neither could I. But I am here now, and so are you.' He touched her cheek. 'You are cold.'

He took her hand and led her to the edge of the water. They sat, legs dangling over the silver pool. The moon cast a spell that made everything – rocks, trees, water – strange and magical. He wrapped the blanket around them both and held her close.

'I heard you left Bethel,' she said.

'I found I had outstayed my welcome.'

'Father took against you. And I think Mother guesses how I feel. She gives me such spiteful looks – she would rather I were dead than thinking of you.'

Theo squeezed her tighter to him. 'She may have to get used to me. I am thinking of making my life here. Maybe as a fisherman.'

'Do not joke about such things.'

'It was no joke.'

She shivered. 'You do not understand. They will never let you stay. Father is an elder on the parish council, and you have seen how he can turn the township against you. They will hunt you out.'

Theo took her hand in his. 'Even if I am married to his daughter?' He was heedless of his impulsiveness. The emptiness inside him yearned for fulfilment.

Her hand was like ice. She pulled it away.

'Do not speak of marriage,' she whispered, so softly he barely heard her over the rushing waterfall. 'I am already engaged.'

A piece of granite seemed to pierce Theo's heart. 'I see.'

'Mother arranged it for me. He owns the neighbouring farm – recently widowed.'

'Do you love him?'

'No!' she cried. 'He is a man in my father's image. He never puts down his Bible, unless it is to pick up his gun. When we took tea with him to agree the betrothal, he gave me one look, as he might give a cow at auction, then talked to Father of land prices and theology.'

'Then do not marry him.'

'I have no choice.'

A silence settled between them. A startled bird flew, squawking, out of the forest, but Theo did not notice. 'Why did you bring me here?' he asked.

'I wanted to see you again.'

'So you could tell me you were betrothed?'

'Not only for that.'

She pulled away, so suddenly he thought he must have offended her. She stood and stepped back from him.

'Did I . . .?' There was such a confusion of emotions in Theo's chest he could not speak.

Abigail put her hands to her neck and undid the collar of her dress. Her cold fingers fumbled with the laces. Theo didn't move.

She parted the dress and pulled it down to her ankles. She wriggled out of the white shift she wore underneath, then stepped away from the pile of discarded clothes. She stood on a rock overhanging the pool, entirely naked, her skin so white and lustrous she seemed to be made of moonlight.

Theo gaped. Reverentially, his eyes traced the lines of her body. Her young breasts standing firm and full, the nipples hardening to the touch of the cool night air. The swell of her hips, the curve of her thighs and the darkness in between. Her bare feet on the mossy rocks.

Yet her face was the loveliest of all. He looked up. Her eyes caught his and held them.

'Don't you dare look away,' she said.

Theo obeyed.

'I wanted to feel a man look on me with love. Not as some sinful object, to be treated with less care than he gives his livestock.'

'You are beautiful,' Theo said simply. 'The most beautiful woman I have ever seen.'

He sensed she was waiting for something more. He stood. He hesitated, but she smiled, inviting him on.

He put his hand on her breast, soft as silk. He let his fingers slide down her skin to the cleft between her legs. She gasped.

Unbidden, he thought of her father carrying his long rifle. 'If he finds out about this . . .'

She put a finger against his lips, while her other hand undid the buttons on his shirt. 'Do not speak of that. Please. For one night in my life, let me call my body my own.'

They lay together under the stars, cushioned by the mossy ground. She cried out when Theo entered her, but only for a moment. Soon it turned to moans of pleasure, as she coaxed him ever deeper inside her. She wrapped her legs around his thighs and urged him on, agile and eager.

They climaxed together, their bodies shaking in unison as he emptied himself into her.

* * *

It was a cold night, but Jebuthan Claypole was snug under his blankets. When he heard Abigail stir, he wanted to believe it was nothing. A call of nature. Nothing to make him leave the warmth of his bed.

But his mother had told him to keep close watch on Abigail, and he could not fail her. As soon as he heard the front door close, he slid down the ladder and went to the window – in time to see his sister vanish into the forest.

It was the path that led to Shaw's Pond.

He dressed and followed her. The pathway was difficult to see and she moved quickly – it would have been easy to lose both her and the trail – but Jebuthan had grown up in the same woods, tracking and trapping animals for days at a time. Even so, she almost caught him twice, when he stepped on a stick or knocked a low branch. But he stayed stock still, and she was too eager to move on to pay keen attention.

He slowed when he heard the falls ahead and crept the last few yards to the rocks that ringed the pool. Crouching in the shadows and the undergrowth, he saw everything – abominable things that even the fieriest preachers would only hint at darkly in their sermons. He crossed himself, reciting every prayer he could think of. It was hideous, the works of Satan as he had never imagined them. Yet he could not take his eyes off it.

At last Theo and Abigail had sated their lust. Jebuthan ran back to the farm. His father woke in an instant, an instinct honed from living on the frontier. Two words were enough to make him understand the situation. He snatched the rifle off the wall.

'Fetch the dogs.'

• • •

Theo and Abigail lay in each other's arms, naked and spent. Their bodies glowed with heat under the blanket he had pulled over them.

'Is that the sin the preachers hate so fiercely?' Abigail said in wonder. 'Surely such a thing cannot be wrong.'

'Not when it comes from love.'

The night was drawing on. Soon Abigail would remember her family, and the life they had waiting for her. Theo clung to her, pressing her skin against his, wishing he could hold her back from the world that wanted to claim her.

'Come away with me,' he said suddenly.

'Do not say such things,' said Abigail. 'If my parents find me gone from my bed, they will have me put in the pillory.'

'Then why did you agree to meet?' Theo asked.

'To taunt me with one night of bliss? I would rather

you had never come than leave me to be tormented by this memory.'

'One night is all I am allowed.'

'Allowed by whom?' he demanded. 'Will you let your life be governed by others? I lived that way for a time, doing as my guardian told me. All it brought was heartbreak. You must choose for yourself.'

'I cannot.'

But Theo could feel her heart beating faster against his chest. Was she softening? He stared into her eyes. 'I would go to the ends of the earth to be happy with you,' he said. 'If not in the colonies, then in England, or India, or even China.'

'Those are only names on a map.'

'They are real places. Some of them I have already been to. I can take you anywhere in the world, so long as we are together.'

'You make it sound so easy.' She was on the verge of tears. 'I have never been further than Easton.'

'It takes only one step to begin a journey.'

She lay still for a long time. Theo's hopes faded. He had tried his best and it had not been enough.

When her answer came, it was barely louder than the wind in the trees. Theo was not sure he had heard aright. 'What did you say?'

'Yes,' she whispered. And then, more confidently, 'A thousand times yes.' She hugged him, her eyes sparkling. 'As long as I am with you.'

'I will never let you go,' Theo promised.

He gave her a long, penetrating kiss. She responded eagerly, pressing herself against him.

'Can you do it more than once?' she asked shyly.

Theo was already stiff with desire again. He lifted her buttocks, angling her towards him – then paused.

Abigail moaned with impatience. 'What is it?'

'I thought I heard a dog barking.'

He sat up, listening hard. It came again – unmistakable.

'It sounds like Father's dog,' said Abigail. 'But how—?'

'We must go.' Theo jumped up and put on his shirt. Abigail pulled on her dress. She headed for a path away from the clearing.

'The dogs will track us through the forest,' Theo warned. He looked over the moonlit pool. 'If we crossed the river . . .'

'There are no paths on that side,' Abigail answered. 'We must make for Bethel.'

'But people will see us there,' Theo objected.

'Yes, indeed,' said Abigail. 'And that will be the only thing to stop my father murdering you.'

* * *

Claypole and Jebuthan came out at the rocks by the pool. The moon was low in the sky; a faint light was breaking in the east. Claypole looked around the empty scene.

'You sure what you saw, boy?' He pointed to the fishing rod leaning against a stone. 'Not a man doing a spot of night fishing, and your imagination run away with you?'

'I saw it,' Jebuthan insisted.

The dogs circled the clearing, sniffing and growling. One picked something up in his jaws, brought it back to his master and dropped it on the ground. It was Abigail's shift.

Claypole's face twisted in fury. 'The little whore,' he hissed. He let the dog nuzzle it, taking the scent. 'She will pay for her harlotry.'

The dog barked and sprang away down the track towards Bethel.

• • •

Even in the panic of the moment, Theo marvelled at Abigail's knowledge of the landscape. Little moonlight filtered through into the forest, but she moved effortlessly, flitting down paths he could barely see. The grey smudge of her dress led him on, like a ghost.

There was no way of telling how far they had come, or how far they had to go. It was like running in a nightmare. Branches and briars slashed at Theo's face and legs. Roots and stones tripped him. And always he had the dogs on his heels, closer and closer until he was convinced he would feel their jaws on his leg at any moment. He tried not to look back.

They reached a fork in the path. Abigail stopped.

'Leave me,' she gasped. 'I will delay him. If he finds us both, he will kill you.'

Theo grabbed her wrist and looked deep into her eyes. Images of Calcutta flashed through his mind. 'I will not leave you. Whatever happens, we will stay together.'

They had no time to argue. At that moment, the dogs came around a bend in the trail, snarling shadows in the grey pre-dawn light. With howls of triumph, they charged towards Theo and leaped at him.

Theo grabbed a fallen branch and swung it at them. He clubbed the lead dog in mid-air, a heavy blow on the head that deflected the animal away from him. It fell to the ground, whimpering. The second dog halted, hackles raised and growling. Beyond, Theo heard running feet crashing down the track in pursuit.

Undaunted, Abigail pushed past Theo. She went to the dog and knelt beside it, stroking the back of its neck. The dog stopped growling.

'Run,' Abigail told Theo.

This time, Theo didn't hesitate. He saw light ahead, dawn rising beyond the edge of the trees. He ran faster. Suddenly his feet were no longer on the forest trail, but trampling the earth of a recently ploughed field. Houses appeared. He vaulted a rail fence and ran through an orchard. Frightened chickens squawked and flapped; a cock crowed.

He came out onto the road in the middle of Bethel. There was the boarding house, and the duck pond, and the church with the tall pillory in front of it. The dead animal trophies nailed to the church wall watched Theo mockingly. *We did not escape*, they seemed to say. *Can you?*

Surely Claypole would not violate the sanctuary of a church.

Claws clattered on the stony road behind him. Theo heard barking and snarling. He turned and grabbed a large stone from the ground.

But the dog had learned. It delayed a fraction of a second. Theo pulled back his arm to hurl the rock but overbalanced and the dog leaped on him. Its full weight slammed into his chest and knocked him to the ground. Before he could get up, the dog was on top of him, paws planted on his chest, growling and snapping at his throat. Theo writhed and rolled, but the dog had its prey at last and would not be shaken off.

A shadow fell. Claypole stood over him, breathing hard. The fury on his face transformed into grotesque triumph as he saw his enemy brought to bay.

'Call off your dog!' Theo shouted.

Claypole spat in his face. 'You think you can make free with my daughter?' He pulled a knife from his belt, its curved blade wickedly sharp. 'I will make sure you never touch a woman again.'

He turned to his son. 'Hold his ankles.'

Jebuthan did as he was told. Claypole knelt beside Theo. He hooked the tip of the blade into the waist of Theo's breeches. The cold steel pressed against Theo's belly. He flinched.

'That's right.' Claypole leered. 'Next time you feel a lustful stirring in your loins, think of this.' He jerked the knife. The breeches fell open. He pulled them down to Theo's knees and gave a derisive glance at Theo's shrinking manhood. 'Can't believe my daughter would throw herself away on a little thing like that.'

He put the knife between Theo's legs, forcing them apart. With the flat of the blade, he lifted Theo's balls, so that the knife was against the base of his scrotum. 'I done this plenty of times on hogs,' Claypole said casually. 'Shouldn't be too different. Easier, given the tiny size of the thing.'

Theo saw in his eyes that it was no idle threat. 'Please, God, no,' he begged. 'You cannot do this to me.'

Claypole slapped his face so hard that Theo tasted blood. 'Do not take the Lord's name in vain. His name is an abomination in your mouth.'

Theo screamed, hoping it would draw attention from some of the shuttered houses along the street. Surely someone would come and talk Claypole out of his madness.

Claypole caressed Theo's testicles with his knife. It was so sharp, some of the hairs came away on the blade. He looked into Theo's eyes, savouring the fear he saw.

Theo had stopped screaming. He clenched his teeth so he would not bite off his tongue when the cut came. He could not even struggle, or he would slice himself on the knife that pressed firm and insistent against his manhood.

Claypole's ugly face shone with righteousness. 'I warned you not to come back. Now you'll learn your lesson.'

A ringing broke through his words: the bell on the church steeple. A door slammed. Theo heard footsteps, a slow and measured tread along the road. He tried to twist his head around but could not move far enough. All he saw was sky, and the roofs of the church and surrounding houses.

Claypole looked up. His hand froze, the knife still tight against Theo's skin.

'Peace, Goodman Claypole,' said a voice. Theo recognised it: the black-suited priest he had met on his first day in Bethel.

'Do not interfere, Reverend,' Claypole warned. 'Go back in your church.'

The priest didn't move. 'You cannot do such a thing on the Sabbath.'

'He seduced my daughter and made a whore of her,' Claypole declared.

Theo heard shocked murmurs ripple around him. Villagers had emerged from their homes, some still in their nightgowns. They gathered round, keeping a safe distance. All wanted to see. None wanted to be called as witnesses afterwards.

The priest stared at Theo. 'Do you deny it?'

Theo said nothing.

'Do you know the Tenth Commandment?'

Theo had recited it a hundred times in church in Calcutta. Even with a knife at his balls, he remembered it effortlessly. 'Thou shalt not covet thy neighbour's house, thou shalt not covet thy neighbour's wife, nor his manservant, nor his maidservant, nor his ox, nor his ass, nor any thing that is thy neighbour's.'

'Clearly, that would include his daughter. You have broken God's law, and you are guilty of fornication.'

'And, by faith, he will not do it again,' growled Claypole. He tensed his arm. Theo closed his eyes. The knife seemed to throb against his taut skin.

'No,' said the priest, '"Vengeance is mine, saith the Lord." We are governed by laws, not the whims of men, however justified their outrage.

The punishment for fornication is the pillory, Goodman Claypole.'

Claypole's eyes smouldered. He stared at the priest with black hate. For a long moment, which felt like half a lifetime, Theo feared Claypole would castrate him to spite the priest. He saw Abigail watching from the crowd, held fast by her brother. Her eyes filled with tears, but she said nothing. It would not help Theo's cause.

With a grunt, Claypole pulled the knife away. Relief flooded through Theo so hard he thought he would be sick.

'Blessed are the merciful,' said the preacher. 'I leave you to see that your daughter is properly chastised, for the father is the head of his household as Christ is the father of the Church.'

Claypole glanced at his daughter – a murderous look that made Theo fear for her life.

'For the fornicator, I sentence him to stand in the pillory during divine service, with his ears nailed. Thereafter, he is to be branded on both cheeks with the letter "F", as a fornicator, so that all the world shall know his crime and his character.'

Men ran forward from the crowd. They hauled Theo up and half carried, half dragged him towards the pillory. Theo remembered it from the day he had arrived in Bethel: a tall post, with a platform of about six feet for the offender to stand on, and a crosspiece above with holes to lock his arms and head in place. It loomed against the sky, like a cross ready for crucifixion.

There was some delay while a ladder was fetched. As the villagers jostled, Theo suddenly heard a vicious voice in his ear. 'Do not think you have escaped justice so easily,' hissed Claypole. 'After church you will be pelted with refuse. It is not unknown for a few stones to be thrown by mistake. A well-aimed rock between the eyes will be the last thing you ever know. I will bury you, and my only regret is that you will not see what I do to my whore of a daughter.'

The ladder came. Theo was forced up to the platform, prodded on by a pitchfork. The boards were old and well trodden, with a broad stain that looked like dried blood. Two crosswise boards stood in a frame, with holes for Theo's neck and wrists.

A bailiff came up. He locked Theo's head and hands between the two boards. A hammer and nails were passed up. Theo writhed and squirmed, but he was fixed in place. The bailiff put the nails against his ears and drove them through into the wood with one meaty blow apiece. Theo was almost too tired to scream. Blood flowed from his ears, running down the pillory and dripping onto the boards. The pain was so excruciating he felt he would pass out.

Then the townsfolk went to church, and Theo was left alone.

The pillory was set at a height that meant he could neither kneel nor stand but was forced to stay bent over in an awkward stoop. Soon his back was in agony. The heavy board pressed on his neck and made it hard to breathe. Claypole's last promise echoed in his ears. All he could think of was Abigail. He should never have gone to Shaw's

Pond. He should have known what her father would do if they were discovered.

The minutes dragged by. He had not known time could pass so slowly. The church bell rang the quarter-hours, and he almost went mad waiting for the next chime to sound. One hour passed, then two. *How long did the church service last in this place?*

But what did he have to look forward to? While he stayed in the pillory, he was racked with pain. When the service ended, he would be pelted with rubbish. Claypole would have his chance to knock him dead with a well-aimed stone – and even if he did not, it would not be the end of the ordeal. They would take him down from the pillory, tearing off his earlobes and leaving them nailed to the wood, then burn the letter 'F' into his cheeks. He would be mutilated for ever.

Though how long would that be? Would Claypole ever let him leave Bethel alive?

A crow flew from the church steeple and landed on the crossbar that held him. He heard the flutter of wings as it preened its feathers over his shoulder.

A sharp jab of pain made him cry out. The bird had hopped onto his head, and its talons were digging into his skull. Panic gripped Theo. He stamped his feet on the platform and flapped his hands as much as the pillory would allow. He bellowed like a bull.

The bird flew off and settled in a tree. But it came back. Theo shouted and squirmed again, but this time the bird was not so cowed. It retreated to the edge of the platform, watching Theo with a beady black gaze.

What if it went for his eyes?

The bell rang again, so suddenly that the bird rose squawking into the air. The church door had opened. The congregation filed out and formed a semicircle around the pillory. Some disappeared to their homes and returned with buckets of dung, rotten fruit and kitchen scraps. In the crowd, Theo saw Claypole stoop and pick up a large, round stone from the road. He hefted it in his hand, like a gunner weighing up a cannonball. He leered at Theo and sliced a finger across his own throat.

The preacher addressed the villagers, detailing Theo's crimes. Theo searched the throng for Abigail, but could not see her. At least she would be spared witnessing his ordeal.

An egg hit his cheek and exploded over his face. Bits of shell and yolk lodged in his eye. A rotten apple struck him on the jaw, smearing brown pulp on his chin. The platform was high up, but the people of Bethel were practised. Some of the more spiteful children aimed for his ears, making the blood flow freely around the nails.

The mess on his face blinded him. It entered his mouth and nose with a taste like vomit, making him gag. The pain tore through his head. A hard pebble rattled against the woodwork an inch from his face. He braced himself for Claypole's *coup de grâce*, though doubtless he would bide his time. He would want Theo to suffer as long as possible.

In his misery, he did not hear the horn sound. He didn't realise that something had changed, until the baying crowd had fallen silent. Instead of their jeers, he could hear unexpected music: fifes and drums playing – of all things – 'The Grenadiers March'.

Regimented feet marched onto the green, then stopped abruptly. Theo opened his eyes, though with his hands fastened he couldn't wipe them. The slime on his face ran down into them unchecked.

Soldiers had arrived. A dozen men, in blue coats with red facings, and squat tricorn hats. They carried long Brown Bess muskets. Behind them, in a more ragged line, stood a column of unarmed men in civilian clothes.

A captain in a mud-spattered coat reined in his horse. He barely glanced at Theo. 'By order of His Majesty King George II, and Governor Wentworth, I am authorised to raise a new company of New Hampshire volunteers to fight in the war against France.'

The villagers eyed him sullenly, angry that he had interrupted their sport. The captain continued unabashed. 'Any man who enlists will receive a bounty of three dollars, a full uniform, including coat and stockings, and a musket.'

No one answered him.

'The French are coming. With their Indian allies, they will spare nothing: your homes and farms, your crops and livestock, not even your wives and servants.' He adopted a more convivial tone. 'Are there no stout-hearted men in Bethel? In Easton, I had so many recruits I could scarce write down their names fast enough. Surely the men of Bethel are no less bold than those of Easton. Surely the same martial zeal burns in your breasts. Would you have your sweethearts turn their backs on you, and seek solace in the arms of Easton men when they come home from the war garlanded with glory?'

He looked around the village green and saw only hostility.

'I had heard the men of Bethel enjoyed a better reputation for valour.' He circled his horse. 'Perhaps I will enjoy more success in the next town.'

Theo opened his mouth, spitting out gobs of rotten fruit and offal that had lodged there. 'Wait,' he cried. 'I will volunteer.'

The captain squinted up at him. 'Who is this man?'

'A criminal,' said the preacher, stiffly.

'What was his crime?'

'Fornication.'

The captain gave a braying laugh. 'If that barred a man from joining the army, our ranks would be thin indeed. Bring him down and let me look at him.'

One of his corporals ran up the ladder. Stabs of pain tore through Theo's ears as the corporal worked the nails loose, but the lobes stayed intact. The moment he was freed from the pillory, he collapsed and nearly fell off the platform. The corporal had to carry him down.

Theo's head swam with pain, but he forced himself to stand upright in front of the captain. He waited, covered with filth and bleeding from both ears, trying to ignore the hostile crowd around him.

'What is your name?' asked the captain.

'Theodore Courtney.'

The captain gestured to the pillory. 'A criminal, eh. Were you guilty?'

'Yes, sir. I am in love.'

'Well, the army can cure you of that. Have you fought before?'

'At the defence of Calcutta, in the army of the East India Company. I commanded a redoubt in the front line.'

'And lived to tell the tale.' The captain gave him a keen look. 'Not many men can say the same.' He reached into his purse and pulled out a shiny coin. He tossed it to Theo, who had enough wit to pluck it out of the air. The captain turned to his corporal. 'Enlist Mr Courtney in the muster book – then throw him into the duck pond. I will not have my men stinking like a midden.'

'You cannot do that,' said the preacher. He had stepped out from the crowd, with Claypole beside him. 'His sentence has not been carried out in full.'

The captain stared at him. 'You have no jurisdiction over a soldier of the Crown. He has taken the King's shilling. He is subject to military law.'

An angry murmur pulsed through the crowd.

'Justice must be done,' said Claypole, showing the blade of his knife.

The captain peered at him. 'Who is this man?'

'The father of the girl Mr Courtney debauched,' said the preacher.

'Indeed. Well, if she resembles her father in any way then I would say Mr Courtney was doing her a rare favour.'

Before Claypole could register the insult, the captain clicked his tongue and his horse moved off. A murderous look came over Claypole's face. The preacher put a restraining hand on his arm, and the corporal glared at him in warning. Theo turned his back.

The band struck up again, a bright and jolly tune that sounded out of place in the grim village. The new recruits fell in behind them.

'Onwards,' called the captain. 'We will bathe Mr Courtney elsewhere. We have a long march ahead before we rendezvous with the army at Albany.'

• • •

Theo washed himself in the river and they gave him a new suit of clothes. Pain racked his body from his hours on the pillory, but he had no time to recover. The captain set a brisk pace. Theo stumbled along at the back as best he could.

They slept that evening on the outskirts of another village. The captain took lodgings in town, while the men pitched tents in a meadow by a river. Theo noticed that the recruits' tents were in the centre of the camp, surrounded by the regular soldiers.

He was relieving himself into a patch of bushes after supper, when the corporal came up beside him and unbuttoned his breeches.

'A friendly word in your ear.' The corporal directed a prodigious stream of piss into the bushes.

'I couldn't help noticing the way you was looking at the forest. Almost like a man thinking of leaving us.'

Theo tried not to let the guilt show on his face. In fact, he had been thinking of Abigail, wondering when he could slip away from the company and retrace his steps to Bethel.

The corporal focused on his business. 'You've got that sweetheart you left behind, ain't you? Must be quite something, worth taking that punishment for.'

Theo nodded.

'I only says it in case you've forgotten you've joined the army now. Leaving ain't a matter of walking off. It's called desertion, and the punishment for that makes the pillory look like a tap on the cheek. You understand?'

He buttoned himself up and returned to the campfire. He posted extra sentries around the camp and looked into Theo's tent twice before the lantern was put out.

They marched for three more days. The weather grew cooler. The leaves were beginning to turn orange. Theo thought constantly of Abigail – what would Claypole have done to her? – but he had no chance to escape. After India, he had thought he was done with soldiering, yet now he had no choice. On the march, the corporal made sure there were always men around Theo; in the evenings, he made a show of placing the pickets.

On the third evening, Theo sensed something different. There was no village nearby for the captain to retire to, not even a farm. They camped together in a glade in the forest. The corporal spent longer than usual posting the sentries and seemed more preoccupied with what was beyond the camp, rather than the men inside it.

'There's Indians in these parts,' he explained, sitting at the campfire sharpening his bayonet.

'Are they hostile?' Theo asked.

Sparks flew from the whetstone. 'Some's with us, and some's with the Frogs. Sometimes you can't tell the difference until you feel the touch of their steel carving up your scalp.'

Theo shivered. The forest seemed darker than ever.

'You ever fought Indians?' one of the men asked Theo. He was a farmer's son named Burwell, with rough hands and a beard already grown full.

'Only in India. They fight on elephants.'

There followed an incredulous discussion about elephants. The men around the campfire could not imagine such a thing. But Burwell had a point to make.

'Indians on elephants, you'd hear coming through a forest, I reckon.'

Theo thought of the din he had heard at Perrin's Garden, the blast of drums and elephants and war cries that announced every Indian army. 'You hear them anywhere.'

'Our Indians ain't like that. They move through the woods like ghosts, and all you'll notice is a strange prickling feeling down the back of your neck. Until they want to be seen.'

There were murmurs of agreement around the fire. Burwell continued, 'Just don't let them take you prisoner. They'll scalp you alive, and not even trouble themselves to put a bullet in you to ease the pain.'

'What is "scalping"?' Theo asked.

'It's what they do to them they kill. They cut down to the bone of your skull, then peel off the top of your head – skin, hair and all. Take it as a trophy, proof of the kill. You go in their villages you see dozens of 'em – hundreds, sometimes – hanging off their tents and longhouses.'

'It sounds barbaric,' said Theo.

Burwell leaned forward. Firelight flickered over his face. 'That's not the worst of it. One man I heard of, the Indians opened his chest and cut out his heart. Ate it right in front of him as he died. Says it gives them the strength of their enemy.'

'Enough,' said the corporal. 'You'll give young Mr Courtney nightmares.'

Theo had no nightmares that night. He barely slept. Each time he began to drift off, some new noise from the forest snapped him awake again. He lay with his knife beside him. When one of his companions returned from a call of nature, Theo almost stabbed him in the belly.

When dawn broke, Theo's relief was only tempered by his fatigue. He spilled his breakfast, fumbled with his pack, and tripped constantly as they marched along the road.

Worse, he had ended up beside Burwell, who had an inexhaustible supply of stories of Indian atrocities, which he shared in intimate detail. Decapitation, mutilation, torture and murder: Burwell recounted them all with savage relish.

Suddenly, Theo heard a rush of air, and a sound like a wet kiss. Burwell went quiet.

For a moment, Theo was glad for the relief from Burwell's chatter. Then he noticed an arrow sticking through Burwell's throat. Blood geysered from the wound.

Burwell collapsed. A volley of musketry tore through the company. The captain's horse reared and he was thrown to the ground. Several of the men were already down, wounded. An arrow plucked Theo's hat clean off his head.

He could not see who was attacking them. The musket shots seemed to have come from the bushes by the roadside, but no one was there.

At that moment, the bushes came alive. They were blinds, disguised to look like natural growth and mask the men behind them. The Indians emerged hollering, taking full advantage of the confusion.

The column had no chance. Half the soldiers were carrying fifes and drums; the rest had no time to unsling their muskets before they went down. The volunteers at the back, unarmed, fared no better. Some stood frozen with shock, gaping at the Indians, until a bullet or an arrow caught them. Others fled down the road. They didn't make fifty yards.

Theo ran to one of the fallen soldiers. The musket was still on his shoulder, with the strap buried under the man's body. He cut the strap and grabbed the gun.

An Indian, bare-chested and painted with strange designs, stood over him wielding a vicious axe. The part of Theo's brain that had been listening to Burwell's stories identified it as a tomahawk. There was no time to load his musket, no time even to think. Theo brought the gun up like a staff, as the Indian brought down his tomahawk. The blade buried itself in the wood of the stock and stuck. Theo wrenched it away, reversed the musket and clubbed the Indian's face.

Before his enemy could rise, Theo ran to the forest, carrying the musket with the tomahawk still lodged in it. Bullets flew through the trees, gouging clouds of splinters out of the trunks. He'd been seen. He ran on, twisting and weaving through the thick forest. The shots died away.

Shouts and running footsteps took their place. The Indians were following him – and however fast he ran, they were faster. They moved through the forest like wolves. The musket weighed him down. He dropped it, and continued running, though he was now defenceless. Glancing back, he saw men close on his heels. An arrow flew past his shoulder and stuck in a tree trunk beside him.

He started to swerve again so they could not get a clear shot. It slowed him down further, pushing through thick undergrowth. The Indians fanned out, choosing easier ways to encircle him.

Theo found an animal track. It was narrow, but at last he could stretch out his legs and run full pelt. He looked back, hoping he was putting some distance on his pursuers. To his horror, he saw that one of the Indians was on the same track and closing fast. He brandished a tomahawk in one hand, and a scalping knife in the other.

Theo put his head down and sprinted for all he was worth. His foot landed in a patch of leaves that lay scattered over the path. He stepped forward and—

Something clenched around his ankle, so tight and sudden it pulled him off his feet and sent him sprawling face-first to the forest floor. He kicked to free himself but couldn't escape. His leg was hanging in a noose about a foot off the ground. The noose was suspended from a sapling, which had sprung up from the pile of leaves and now stood quivering.

He had stepped into a trapper's snare.

He still had his knife: he could have cut himself free. But he had no time. The Indian, seeing his target fallen, bounded forward with a whoop of triumph. There was nothing Theo could do. The Indian stood over him and raised his tomahawk for the killing blow.

Burwell's words echoed in Theo's mind. 'Whatever you do, don't let them catch you alive.'

With a deafening crash, the Indian's body snapped forward as a bullet struck between his shoulder blades. Theo twisted around. The corporal knelt between two trees, a dozen paces away, his musket to his shoulder.

Theo leaned round and fumbled with the snare, trying to free his foot.

'Give me your knife,' he begged the corporal. But the corporal was frantically reloading. More Indians were coming, stalking through the forest. They made a ring around Theo and the corporal, closing tighter.

The corporal started to panic. He jerked the musket from one man to the next, trying to cover them. He could not shoot them all.

'One step closer and I will shoot,' he shouted.

The Indians did not falter. The corporal aimed his musket at the nearest, a broad-chested man with a proud face, and many feathers hanging from his single lock of hair. He was naked, except for a loincloth. His head was shaved but for one lock of hair and painted red down to his eyes. He walked towards the muzzle of the gun and did not flinch.

The corporal glanced at Theo. But Theo was still caught by the snare and could do nothing to help him. With a cry of despair, the soldier reversed his musket and put the barrel in his mouth. The weapon was so long, he had to grab a stick to reach the trigger and push it down.

The Indians gathered around the corpse and examined it. An angry exchange ensued. From the gestures they made, Theo sensed they were frustrated that the bullet had blown off the top of the corporal's skull, ruining their trophy.

They still had Theo. They set a guard over him, and left him in the trap while they went back to the road. He did not dare look at his captor. Every moment stretched like an eternity while he waited for the touch of steel against his scalp. All the misery in his short life played through his mind, and he cursed the fates that had brought him there.

Screams sounded from the road. Not all of his companions had died in the first onslaught. When the Indians returned, each had two or three fresh scalps, still dripping blood, tied to his belt. Theo thought he recognised several as coming from men he'd shared a tent with. He vomited into the bushes.

They also brought a prisoner – an Easton man named Gibbs. Theo wondered why they had kept this man and himself alive. Burwell's stories suggested plenty of possibilities, all of them horrific.

The Indians freed Theo from the snare but bound his hands. They put a branch between his arms, like a turning spit. They did the same to Gibbs. With a man on each side of the prisoners holding the ends of the poles, they set off into the forest.

Chandernagore, India
1756

The city was fine enough, Constance supposed. Almost a mirror image of Calcutta, it had been built by the French some twenty miles upriver from the English city. Like its counterpart, it spread around a bend in the Hooghly river. It boasted imposing brick mansions, expansive warehouses, tall-spired churches and a fort with many guns: all the necessities of European civilisation.

But it was not like Calcutta as she had known it. Or maybe it was she who was different. Things she had hardly noticed before now drove her to despair: the stink of mud and human effluent; the heat; the insects that crawled over every crumb of food and kept her awake at night; the empty words and dull platitudes that passed for conversation among the French society. She moved through it in a daze. Her corset always felt too tight, however much she loosened it. She struggled to breathe, as if a scream was trapped inside her.

She lived with Lascaux, the French captain who had rescued her from the nawab's camp. She owed him a debt of gratitude – and she had nowhere else to go. She repaid him as women had always repaid men. She made herself as beautiful as she could, and let him squire her around town to the balls and levées and entertainments that made up the social calendar. Lascaux held her arm with the proud air of a man who could not believe his luck. His fellow officers teased him mercilessly. They seemed to find enormous fun in the situation, though Constance did not understand the joke. Her French was improving, but not fluent.

'They are just jealous I have secured the affections of the most beautiful woman in the city,' Lascaux told her, with a kiss.

He was good to her, and as gentle as could be expected. He was stolid and reassuring. She could not deny that, compared to Gerard Courtney, with his sly intelligence and wicked wit, Lascaux was as dull as a block of wood. Nor was he handsome. His wiry dark hair stuck out at odd angles, his skin was marked with pox scars, and he seemed to have been born with his mouth fixed in a permanent pout. She did not care: it was not a question of love. Constance wanted never to touch another man.

But a woman must make compromises to get what she needs.

Constance made herself smile for Lascaux, laughed at his *bons mots* and put on the fine gowns he bought her. When her boils had subsided, and she could do so without being physically sick, she allowed him to kiss her. Sometimes she let him fondle her breasts, but never anything more. When he tried to go further, she always withdrew with a demure frown and a regretful 'I must think of my virtue, Monsieur.' She enjoyed seeing the pained frustration on his face. It felt like power.

She knew she was lucky to be alive. Yet a part of her soul remained inaccessible, still locked inside the Black Hole. The press of the crowds at the balls and parties made her feel faint. If someone brushed against her in the throng, she had to bite her lip to keep from crying aloud.

Even the smell of the air made her nauseous. Sometimes she woke drenched with sweat, sobbing in the darkness. Once, when Lascaux had come to her room and tried to calm her, she had almost scratched his eyes out.

She had to escape India.

One day, Lascaux returned from his barracks with a sombre look on his face. 'My regiment has been summoned back to France.'

'But that is wonderful news.' Constance moved towards him, her face lit with the first sincere smile she had felt in months. 'I am so bored of India.'

'I thought you liked this country,' said Lascaux, surprised. He pulled back, avoiding her gaze. 'The army has decreed that our sweethearts and, er, native friends must stay behind.'

Constance's eyes blazed. '*Sweethearts?*' she spat. 'Is that what I am to you? Just a common soldier's whore?'

She said it so fiercely that Lascaux retreated in something like fear. He stiffened. 'Mademoiselle, I have never treated you with anything other than the greatest courtesy. I hope you did not mistake my attentions for anything more significant.'

'It seemed significant enough when you had your hand down my bodice.' Anger coursed through Constance, so much it made her tremble. It was like a key turning a lock inside her. The part of her being that had been inaccessible, the black box in her soul, was suddenly opened. She had thought there was nothing inside but a dark hole. Now she realised it was filled with fury, powder that only wanted a spark.

But . . .

Beneath the rage there was something even more profound: her instinct for survival. Lascaux was her only ally in the world. Attacking him would harden his heart and drive him away. Without him, she would have nothing again.

There were other ways.

'Forgive me,' she said humbly. 'If I spoke hot words, it was the heat of love, not temper. Do you not see that I love you?'

He stared at her. Constance crossed to him and wrapped her arms around him. She wanted to hit him, but she resisted the urge. Instead, she pressed her breasts against his chest, rubbed her midriff against his groin. She felt him stir under her touch.

'You are everything in the world to me,' she said. Her voice shook with emotion. 'I would do anything not to be parted from you.'

Her hand slipped around his back and down, cupping his buttock. Gerard Courtney had been an imaginative lover, and she had been an enthusiastic pupil. She had learned what men liked and how to pleasure them in ways that the stolid captain from Bordeaux could scarcely imagine.

He sagged against her, yielding to her skilful fingers. 'There are things I must tell you.'

'The only thing that matters is that we are together. Is that not so?'

She kissed him, letting her tongue flutter over his lips like a butterfly. She undid the buttons of his shirt, sinking to her knees as she went and planting little kisses on his throat, his chest, his belly. She tugged open the fly of his breeches and slipped her hand inside.

Lascaux moaned with pleasure.

'The adjutant will not give you a berth on the ship,' he said. He was struggling to speak. 'There are only places for . . .' He gasped as her fingers ran over his balls, exploring the crevice between his legs. '. . . wives.'

Her tongue flicked the tip of his shaft. 'What can we do?' she wondered, in a voice so plaintive she sounded like a little girl.

'Perhaps . . .' Lascaux gasped. 'Perhaps there is a way.'

Constance paused. She gazed up at him, eyes wide and brimming with gratitude. 'You mean it? We shall be married?'

Lascaux hesitated. Constance took his balls into her mouth and sucked on them gently. 'You know if we were married, I could deny you nothing,' she whispered. 'As my husband, you could make me do anything you desired.'

Lascaux shuddered so hard she thought he might climax at that moment. She eased away, watching his tumescent prick throb with frustrated longing.

'We shall be married,' Lascaux gasped.

Really, Constance thought, as she took him in her mouth, *men were not hard to govern. All a woman had to do was swallow her pride.*

There was a handsome cathedral in Chandernagore, but they did not have the wedding there. Lascaux did not want a big ceremony. 'You know how the others tease me for falling in love with an Englishwoman,' he explained. Instead, they found a sea captain in one of the taverns by the riverbank, and had him marry them on his quarterdeck, according to maritime law. There were no guests – only a Swedish boatswain who stood witness – and no reception. But Constance gave Lascaux a wedding night he would never forget.

A month later the newly-weds embarked for France. From the stern rail, Constance watched India dissolve into the horizon and did not feel the slightest tug of regret. She wondered what had become of Theo, if he had been killed in the fighting, or escaped, or died of fever. The question hardly mattered. When she had needed him most, Theo had failed her.

Instead, she turned her mind to France. She practised her French until she was fluent. She peppered Lascaux with questions: about his family, his home, the weather, the society, the fashions. Partly this was because she knew he would expect it of an eager and dutiful wife, and she wanted to please him. But it was more than that. France loomed in her imagination as a sort of Promised Land, a place where she could forget who she had been and remake her future.

But the more Constance asked, the more Lascaux withdrew. He had less and less appetite for conversation. As they passed Spain and beat across the Bay of Biscay, he sank into gloom. The night before they docked at Lorient, he did not even respond to her advances in bed.

'Is something wrong?' Constance asked.

He turned away from her. 'The colonel is insisting that I go to Boulogne as soon as we dock. A fool's errand, but there is no arguing with him. I am sorry, my love.'

'But you are due your leave.'

'He insists. It will be only a week or two. I will find you lodgings at an inn, and return as soon as I can.' He rolled over and kissed her forehead. 'You will barely notice I am gone.'

The ship docked at Lorient on the morning tide. Before dawn, Constance was dressed and on the poop deck, breathing in the air of her new home. It was cool and damp, like nothing she had ever known in India. Soft grass grew on the banks of the Blavet estuary, while beyond she could see well-ordered fields full of green. A ripe new world.

A crowd had assembled on the quay to greet the ship's arrival. Constance scanned it, wondering what sort of people she would meet in this unfamiliar country. Surely they could not all be as dull as Lascaux.

One person in particular caught her eye. 'Who is that woman waving at you? The fat one with the ugly child on her shoulders.'

Lascaux, standing beside her, didn't look. 'She must be one of the sailors' wives.'

'No – she is waving directly at you. Look.'

Reluctantly, Lascaux turned to where Constance had pointed. The boy on the dock put both arms in the air, waving them frantically. Lascaux replied with a small, embarrassed twitch of his hand.

Constance looked between the three of them: the woman, the child and Lascaux. Closer now, she could see that the boy had wiry dark hair, and a pouting mouth that was a perfect miniature of Lascaux's.

She saw everything.

'That is your wife.' She gripped the rail until her knuckles went white. 'Your son.'

Lascaux said nothing.

'Do you deny it? Shall I ask her myself?'

Lascaux's mouth flapped open. He made a sound in his throat, like a toad. 'I did not know she would come,' he croaked.

The key had turned in Constance's heart again. The fury flooded into her. It took an effort to keep her voice down, so she would not humiliate herself in front of all the passengers. 'Why did you marry me, bring me here, if you already had a wife?'

'You made me do it,' said Lascaux, feebly.

'And what did you intend to happen when we returned to France? Did you think you could keep this from me? That I would be satisfied to live as your mistress? Or were you going to leave me at the inn here, and never return?' She saw the truth in his eyes. 'You would have abandoned me, like some weeping Penelope waiting for her gallant husband's return.' She shook her head. 'I have been such a fool.'

'You must understand—'

'Hold your tongue.' Constance thought quickly. 'How much money have you?'

Lascaux blanched. 'What has that to do with anything?'

'*How much?*'

The day before, the regimental quartermaster had given the soldiers their back pay for the last six months. 'A thousand francs.'

'Give it to me.'

'That is impossible,' Lascaux protested. 'My family depend on that money to live.'

'Perhaps you should have given more thought to your family before you married me.'

He put out his chin. 'I refuse.'

The ship shook as the hull bumped against the pier. The spectators gave a huzzah. Down on the wharf, Constance could see Lascaux's wife staring at her husband. She had noticed him deep in conversation with Constance, and had a dark look on her face.

'If you do not give me the money, I will go to your colonel and inform him that you are a bigamist. Then I will go and introduce myself to your *other* wife. She will be fascinated to hear what you got up to in the exotic Indies.'

'You would not dare,' whispered Lascaux. He had turned away from Constance, and was waving at his son with jerky movements, like an automaton.

'You have not the least idea what I would dare to do. I have survived torments you could not imagine.' She leaned closer. 'Give me the money, and you will never see me again. You can go back to your dumpling wife and your fat son and pretend to yourself you never knew me. Or lose everything.'

'Half,' he pleaded. 'Leave me half of it at least.'

'You may keep a quarter. And that is my final offer.' She dropped her hand to the crotch of his trousers and tightened her fingers around the bulge until he had to blink back tears. 'What is it to be?'

Constance stepped off the ship with a spring in her step, seven hundred and fifty francs richer, and a free woman. Lascaux's wife watched her with narrowed eyes. As Constance walked past, she jostled the woman's shoulder so hard she nearly dropped her child.

Constance offered the woman her most dazzling smile. 'My apologies, madame. Do give my fondest regards to your husband. He is magnificent.' Without waiting for a reply, she moved on, leaving behind a furious wife, a bawling child, and a stammering captain, whose reunion with his family was not at all what he had dreamed of.

Constance did not look back. At a dockside inn she found a stagecoach drawn up, waiting for passengers off the boat. It would leave in half an hour.

A middle-aged man in a bright scarlet coat stood outside the inn, smoking a pipe and watching the shipping. The style of his dress, the cut and weave of the fabric, was so instantly familiar from Chandernagore that Constance guessed he must be a merchant with the French East India Company.

He tipped his hat to Constance and gave her a smile. His teeth were black from too much sugar. 'Where are you bound, mademoiselle?'

'Madame,' she corrected him. 'I am a married woman.'

His smile faltered, but only a little. 'Your husband is a lucky man.'

'He is dead.'

'My condolences.' The merchant did not sound very sorry.

'He was lost at sea.' Constance did not sound very sorry either. 'It happens.'

'Then perhaps you will permit me to escort you to your destination.' He saw her hesitate. 'Of course, chivalry demands that I should pay your fare.'

The merchant's breath was stale with tobacco and he wore far too much perfume, but Constance did not mind. Even with seven hundred and fifty francs in her purse, she would have to be frugal in this new country. And a woman must make compromises to get what she needs. 'That is most kind.'

He hooked his arm through Constance's. 'May I have the honour of your name?'

She thought for a moment. Lascaux was a liar, a coward and a bigamist. The marriage was a fraud: she would not bear his name one moment longer. But neither could she go back to being plain Constance Courtney.

'I am Constance de Courtenay.' It had a pleasing French ring – maybe too much, judging by the merchant's impressed reaction.

'Are you related to the Courtenays of Burgundy?'

'Only distantly,' she said vaguely. 'My mother was English.'

'How exotic. And where are you going?'

She was in an unknown country, without friends or property. She needed somewhere she could make a new beginning, reinvent herself. Somewhere to leave behind her past and forget for ever the broken woman who had crawled out of the Black Hole.

There could be only one destination.

'I am going to Paris.'

• • •

Theo would never have believed that men could travel so quickly through a trackless wilderness. The Indians went on, hour after hour, with a lolloping stride that never seemed to tire them. Soon Theo's feet were blistered raw, his boots shredded on the rocky ground. Agonising pain ran through his body. He tried to keep up, and when he couldn't, the Indians took the rod between his arms and dragged him along.

As best he could guess, they covered fifteen miles that day – and more the next, through laurel thickets that made the going hard even for the Indians. They camped at night without fires, and though they shared their rations equally with the prisoners, there was never enough to stop the ache in Theo's stomach.

And always nagging was the desperate fear of what they meant to do with him.

On the fourth day, they reached the top of a cliff. The leader signalled a halt. He was the man who had faced down the corporal's musket. From what he had overheard, and whispered conversations with Gibbs, Theo learned that his name was Malsum. The feathers in his hair were battle honours, and there were more than Theo could count.

Malsum advanced to the cliff edge and let out a long, keening call. Before it had died away, he repeated it again, and again, a string of cries that echoed off the valley below.

'Each halloo signifies one scalp they have taken,' Gibbs said to Theo.

Answering shouts came from the bottom of the cliff. Muskets were fired into the air. The returning warriors descended the cliff path, emerging into a clearing where their village stood. More Indians came out to greet them, with many women and children among them.

The Indian village was ringed by a rough palisade. Inside, low wooden sleeping platforms covered with straw roofs surrounded a curved longhouse, made of arched saplings roofed with bark. Animal hides were strung on poles to dry; others hung from the frames of the buildings.

Theo took a closer look. They were not animal hides hanging from the buildings but human scalps.

Malsum and his men dragged the two prisoners to a patch of beaten ground outside the longhouse. An old man wrapped in a blanket sat cross-legged on a bearskin. He had a porcupine quill through his nose, and many strands of shells around his neck.

'That is the sachem,' whispered Gibbs. 'He is the chief of the village.'

The sachem spoke formally with Malsum. Much of it seemed to be ritual, recited from memory, but

Theo sensed an underlying battle going on beneath the exchange.

The sachem struggled to his feet. He examined Gibbs closely, then turned to Theo. His face was wizened, his eyes clouded with age, yet when he looked into Theo's eyes, Theo felt he was peering deep into his soul. He spoke – low words that had no meaning to Theo. He surmised he was being asked a question, that his life might hang on the answer, but he had no words to reply.

The chief turned away. A decision had been taken. Gibbs was dragged to a wooden post and tied fast against it. Theo was led to one of the wooden platforms. The ropes around his hands were tied to the frame, but he was able to sit down. His captors left him, joining the crowd that had gathered around Gibbs. Malsum was cleaning his knife on his loincloth. Nearby, a woman tended a glowing bed of coals with a pot sitting on them.

Malsum cut Gibbs's clothes away. The Indians peered at his nakedness. In a blur of strokes and hands, he flashed his knife around Gibbs's head. Gibbs screamed. A ring of blood oozed from his skull. Malsum clenched a fistful of hair, twisted it around and pulled.

With a sucking sound, a floppy scrap of hair and skin came away, leaving a bloody tonsure. Gibbs's screams were diabolical, echoing endlessly across the empty wilderness.

Malsum thrust his trophy in Gibbs's face, then held it aloft in triumph.

Gibbs's screams never stopped. Even with his head sliced open, he was still alive. A woman brought the clay bowl that had been sitting over the coals and passed it to Malsum. Malsum upended it over Gibbs's head. Hot sand poured into the open wound. Gibbs writhed and jerked like a madman. He banged his head against the post, trying to dislodge the burning sand or to dash his brains out. The bonds would not let him move.

The torture lasted for hours. Every person in the village took their turn, even the children. They cut and tore pieces off his body; they burned him; they drove nails into his flesh. Theo closed his eyes but could not block the terrible sounds. The question gnawed at him: *what will they do to me?*

The sun set. The Indians built a pyre around the post and set it alight. Gibbs was still living: Theo saw his body moving in spasms as the flames consumed him. He had never thought he would count it a mercy to see a man burned alive.

He barely slept. When he did, his dreams were so terrible he was glad to wake from them – until he remembered where he was.

At dawn the Indians seemed in no hurry to attend to him. They brought him a bowl of maize meal and meat, which he devoured. He wondered at the significance of this act of nourishment.

Mid-morning, the Indians gathered in front of the longhouse. Many were armed; even the children carried sticks. Again, Malsum and the chief seemed to be at odds. Malsum spoke angrily, stamping his feet and beating his chest. The chief faced him down, yielding nothing. Theo wondered if they were discussing his fate.

A decision was reached. It evidently dissatisfied Malsum, which gave Theo hope, until he saw what was going to happen. The whole population of the village lined up in two rows opposite each other, making a corridor in between. The warriors held their tomahawks and war clubs, while the women and children brandished sticks and cudgels. A woman untied Theo's hands. A man handed him a birch pole, about six feet long.

All eyes turned to Theo. The Indians beat their clubs and sticks on the ground, raising clouds of dust and chanting a strange song. Theo gripped his staff. He saw what he had to do, even before the chief pointed to the space between the lines. They wanted him to run the gauntlet.

The line was almost a hundred feet long. There was no way he would survive the ordeal. But he would not let them say he died a coward. Indians were approaching with sharp sticks to herd him forward. Without waiting for them, he walked to the line of his own free will. He raised the staff in both hands and took a deep breath. He felt as if he was standing on the edge of a cliff.

He stepped in.

The first blow almost knocked the staff out of his hands. He twisted to block it, but that left his other side exposed. A stick jabbed him in the kidneys and sent spasms of pain through his back. He staggered forward. A small boy stuck out his leg, tripping him. Theo stumbled and would have fallen if he had not caught his weight on his staff. That meant he was in no position to stop the next hit, a sharp crack across his shoulders.

Another buckled his knees. An impact almost broke his arm. They came from every direction. No matter where he turned he couldn't defend himself.

The end of the tunnel was far away. He had not gone three steps. He sank to his knees.

But through the haze, he realised something strange. No one was striking his head, where he was most vulnerable. Was that to prolong the ordeal, so that he did not pass out too soon?

Leaning on the staff, he pushed himself up. The weight of blows raining down on him almost forced him back to the ground, but he hunched his shoulders and pushed through the pain. He flailed the staff wildly. One step, then another. He saw a club sweeping in to his ankles and hurdled it, making three more strides.

Every inch was an ordeal, every step forward a triumph. But they were hard won victories. A mist of pain threatened to overwhelm him. An Indian warrior swung his war-club at Theo's ribs. Theo barely had strength to thrust out his staff to block it.

The staff snapped. And in that moment, Theo saw his chance. Taking the two halves, one in each hand, he windmilled them about so that the Indians had to get out of his way. Space opened around him. Summoning the last of his strength, he charged forwards. There was light and space ahead. Ten paces away. Five. He was almost there.

A towering figure stepped into his path. Even in the fog of battle, Theo recognised Malsum's face. He was unarmed. Theo swung the two halves of the broken staff at him, but Malsum caught them and twisted them out of Theo's hands. He knocked Theo's legs from under him. Theo dropped like a stone. He tried to rise, but Malsum kicked dust in his eyes. Theo clutched his face, leaving himself exposed.

A blow struck the side of his head and his vision went black.

Theo didn't know how long he was unconscious. Maybe only seconds. When he opened his eyes, the Indians were standing around him and the blood still flowed from his wounds. But the ordeal seemed to be over. No one tried to hit him. He was alive.

But what did that mean?

'Let me go!' he demanded, spitting out the words through the blood in his mouth. The Indians either didn't understand or they had other plans. They grabbed his arms and dragged him to the open space in front of the longhouse. Looking down, Theo saw dark specks of ash on the ground, the remains of Gibbs's pyre.

He would not show fear.

They made him kneel. Two of the Indians held him, while Malsum stood over him. He raised a knife for the crowd to inspect and intoned some ritual incantation. Theo remembered what he had done to Gibbs. He braced himself.

Malsum grabbed a lock of his hair and pulled his head forward. Theo refused to cry out. He felt the steel against his scalp. Blood trickled down the side of his face. The pain was negligible compared with the fire racking his beaten body.

Locks of his hair rained down over his shoulders. The knife's edge scraped over bare skin. Perhaps they were not scalping him: were they shaving him? When they had finished, they stripped him naked and took him down to the river to wash him.

They dried him and dressed him in the breech clout and buckskin leggings of their own fashion. They daubed red paint on his bald head, and lightning streaks of red and blue down his chest and cheeks. They hung strands of beads and shells around his neck.

The Indians led him back to the stockade and presented him to the sachem. The old man addressed the tribe with stern, sonorous words. In his guttural, alien voice, it took Theo a moment to realise he was speaking a form of French.

'We have beaten the white man out of your spirit and washed it out of your blood. From today, you are our kin and our family, a warrior of the Abenaki tribe.'

Theo was stunned. Not knowing what else to do, he bowed. Would he really be allowed to live? Why had they chosen him?

A woman came forward out of the crowd. She looked to be about Theo's own age, with glossy dark hair braided down her back and an almond face that would have been pretty, if not for the ferocious scowl that distorted her features. She wore a silver amulet shaped like a bird of prey.

The sachem took her hand and placed it in Theo's. 'This is Mgeso,' he announced. 'Your wife.'

'My wife?' Theo wondered if he'd misunderstood.

'Her husband was killed in the battle.' The chief poked his finger into Theo's chest, smudging the paint. 'You take his place. His home, his weapons, his wife – everything. I think you strong. Your spirit is good.'

Theo stared at the woman uncertainly. She gazed back, her dark eyes haughty and implacable. Beyond her, he saw Malsum watching him with barely hidden fury.

Theo might now look like an Indian, but how could he possibly act the part?

His adoption was a cause for celebration. The feast went on into the night. Theo could not understand how these people, who had tortured his companion so cruelly the day before, could now welcome him as one of their own. They fed him venison, which they dipped in a succulent concoction of bear fat and sugar. They gave him a pipe to smoke, a mix of tobacco and sumac leaves that made him choke. There was singing, and dancing, and a great many speeches that Theo could not understand.

At the end, they carried Theo and Mgeso to one of the thatched sleeping platforms. Theo wondered if the feast had also served as a sort of wedding, for there was much amusement and nudging among the women of the tribe. They withdrew into the darkness, leaving Theo and Mgeso alone.

He looked at her uncertainly. What was he supposed to do now? Through all the celebrations, she had remained stony-faced and silent.

'Perhaps we should go to sleep,' he suggested in French.

She reached down and lifted her short dress over her head. Underneath, she was naked. She smelt of the forest.

Dazed and bruised, Theo could only stare.

They lay down and she straddled him. Slowly, she reached behind her head and unbraided her long plait, combing it out with her fingers. Her breasts rose and fell as she stretched her arms behind her.

She shook out her hair and bent forward over him. Her long hair brushed his skin; her nipples touched his stomach, making him shiver. She slid lower, so that her body rubbed against his. She took him in her mouth, caressing his manhood with her tongue. And all the while, her dark eyes never left Theo's.

Her gaze unsettled him – but his body could only respond to her expert caresses. He grew hard. She pulled herself up again, letting him feel the wetness between her legs. Spreading herself, she sank down on his erect manhood. She sat straight-backed, hardly seeming to move, yet inside Theo felt her pulsing around him, coaxing him with tiny movements that made him groan with desire.

And still she held his gaze, no hint of emotion crossing her face. She had him trapped, exquisitely. She gripped him inside her, drawing him to the edge of climax and suddenly easing off.

She was toying with him.

Theo did not want her like that. There was no privacy on the sleeping platform. Every pair of eyes in the village would be watching and listening from the surrounding darkness, eager to know what sort of man Theo was.

It would have been so easy to surrender and wait for her to give him release. But even on the brink of orgasm, he thought that it would demean him for ever in the eyes of the tribe. Overcoming his body's desires, he lifted her off and threw her down on the mat beside him.

Her eyes widened in surprise. Her face flashed with anger, and he felt a surge of satisfaction that he had broken through her reserve. She lashed out, dragging her nails down his back and drawing blood. She grabbed her comb and tried to stab him with it, but he knocked it out of her hand and pinned her arms. She kicked and writhed, but he was stronger. He rolled her onto her stomach and spread himself over her.

He was still erect, his manhood unsated. He re-entered her. With three quick, brutal thrusts he climaxed. She shuddered and went still.

For long moments they lay together naked. Warmth glowed off her, sweat pooling between their bodies.

Theo rose onto his knees. He stared into the darkness. He could feel the eyes on him, even if he could not see them. He wondered what they thought.

'I will not be your plaything.' He was speaking to Mgeso, but in a voice loud enough to carry to every corner of the village. 'Next time you come to my bed, come because you desire me. I would rather sleep alone than with a woman who does not respect me.'

Mgeso wrapped herself in the blanket and scurried away to wash herself. Theo lay flat on the platform, entirely spent. He listened to the night. Had he turned the tribe against him by his treatment of Mgeso?

The night offered no answers.

• • •

The next morning, Theo was surprised to find the tribe busy preparing to leave. Weapons were wrapped in skins, possessions bundled in blankets. He pulled on his unfamiliar clothes, the buckskin trousers with the sharp porcupine frills, and the ruffled shirt. He touched his head, still shocked to feel the smooth skin where his hair had been. His body was stiff and he groaned with the pain from his weals and bruises.

From across the clearing, Malsum glared at him. Mgeso stayed with the other women, averting her face whenever Theo looked at her. He went down to the river where some of the men were loading canoes. He started picking up bundles and passing them down. The others accepted his help wordlessly.

'Where are we going?' he asked in French.

Most of the men ignored him, but one – younger than Theo, with a friendly face – turned and answered, 'We are going hunting.'

'Hunting what?'

The youth shrugged. 'Whatever the spirits send us. Deer, buck-elk, raccoon . . . The hunting moon has been and gone. It is time to come down from the mountains.'

'You speak French very well,' Theo complimented him.

'There is a French priest who has a mission school at St Lawrence. I went there to study. My father says we must learn all we can about the Europeans, or they will conspire against us.' He smiled shyly. 'I do not mean to be rude. You are one of us now.'

Theo nodded, though the words made him uneasy. He saw his reflection in the river and flinched at the stranger who stared out of the water. With his head shaved to a single lock of hair, the ornaments protruding from his ears and nose, the unfamiliar clothes, he looked an authentic Indian. The bronzed skin he had inherited from his father completed the picture. How could he return to civilisation now – even if he found his way through the miles of wilderness? The French would take him for an Englishman, while the English would shoot him on sight as a French ally.

The sachem had won. Theo was a member of the tribe, whether he desired it or not.

'I am Moses,' said the young Indian, who had been watching Theo.

'That does not sound like an Abenaki name.'

'The priest at the mission school splashed me with water and gave me this name. My Abenaki name is . . .'

He said something so long and unpronounceable that Theo smiled. Moses looked wounded.

'I am sorry,' Theo apologised. 'I fear the Abenaki blood does not yet run strong enough in my veins that I can remember that. I will call you Moses.'

They slid the canoe into the water. Theo marvelled at how light it was: four men could lift it with ease, though it must have measured nearly forty feet long. The hull was made from a single piece of elm bark, bent around hickory ribs and sewn together at the ends. It felt so thin he was sure a single sharp stick could rip it open.

'Why did the old man save me?' he asked. 'Why did you not kill me like Gibbs?'

'The sachem had a dream the night before you came. A child was alone in the forest. All the women were tending the crops, and the men were away hunting. A wolf stalked the child. Closer and closer, until the child was almost in his jaws.'

Moses had dropped into a crouch, his body swaying, as if he himself was the wolf, not just retelling an old man's dream.

'But as the wolf was about to devour the child, a hawk swooped out of the sky. He wrapped the child in his mighty wings. He pecked and clawed at the wolf's eyes, avoiding the beast's jaws, until the animal fled. Then he flew away.'

Moses was staring at Theo in a most disconcerting way – as if he could see something Theo wasn't aware of.

'Next day, you arrived in the village. The sachem looked into your eyes, and he saw the hawk. It means you will be a mighty warrior and save our tribe from some great calamity.'

At that moment, lost in a hostile wilderness, every muscle in his body aching, it seemed a preposterous idea. Theo thought better of saying so. If the Indians wanted to believe he had a glorious future, he would not disabuse them.

'Does the sachem always do what his dreams tell him?'

Moses looked surprised. 'It is through dreams that the ancestors speak to us and guide us.'

'What does your priest think of that?'

Moses touched the cross he wore around his neck. 'There are many spirits in this world. If they speak to us, how can we say they do not exist?'

• • •

For days, they made slow progress through the wilderness. There was no plan that Theo ever saw, no map or schedule. To an outsider, it would have looked like random meandering. But Theo could sense an unhurried purpose in their route. The Abenaki understood the landscape as intimately as their own thoughts. They rarely discussed where they were going next: they simply knew, or perhaps felt it. These were paths and rhythms from deep in the tribal memory.

Much of the time they travelled on water. Sometimes they would strike out overland, and carry the canoe for miles before they reached another river. Even when they halted, they did not leave it in the river but carried it to their campsite. There, they overturned it and propped it up on sticks to make a shelter. It was cramped underneath, but its watertight hull was protection against rain.

On occasion they made a more lasting camp and stayed several days. The men would fill their pouches with cured venison and dried corn, gather their bows and rifles, and head out hunting. Game was plentiful. There were deer, far larger than the swamp deer Theo had occasionally seen in India.

There were huge, ox-like creatures with shaggy brown coats and long horns, which grazed on the long grass in wild meadows. Moses told Theo that the French called them 'buffaloes'.

Theo was not given a gun. He followed behind, watching how the hunters tracked their prey with the faintest spoor. He learned how to skin the animals they killed, and how to dress and pack the meat to waste as little as possible. His main purpose was as a beast of burden. When it came to carry the spoils back to camp, Malsum always gave him the heaviest load.

'Why does Malsum hate me?' Theo asked, struggling under a haunch of venison. Blood ran out of the meat and trickled down the back of his neck. 'Is it because I am English?'

Moses looked surprised. 'The blood of the white man has been washed from your veins. You are adopted into our tribe, now.'

'Yes, I know. But I sometimes wonder if Malsum remembers it.'

'Malsum does not hate you because you were English,' Moses explained. 'He hates you because of Mgeso.'

Theo waited for him to explain.

'Malsum was in love with her. But when it came time to marry, she chose another man – the man who was killed by your friend. It is said that Malsum still loves her, that when her husband died he thought he would have his chance at last. Then the sachem declared that you should take her husband's place.'

Theo pondered. 'And what does Mgeso think?'

Moses shrugged. 'Even the ancestors cannot say what is in a woman's heart.'

At the front of the line, a tomahawk flashed. Malsum reached down and lifted up a long brown snake, writhing in his grip. Theo could not believe he would pick it up so casually. Then he saw blood gushing from its neck where the head had been hacked off.

Malsum bit off a lump of squirming snake flesh and chewed it heartily. He tossed it over his shoulder to Theo. 'Hungry?'

Theo gaped at the creature, still in its death throes. The raw meat glistened pearly white, smeared with blood. His stomach turned. 'Is it poisonous?'

'It is a rattlesnake,' Moses informed him. 'One bite will kill you. But the poison is all in the head.'

The men were watching, Malsum most keenly of all. Theo took the dead snake in both hands, opened his mouth, and bit down hard.

The flesh was tough and leathery. Theo chewed it to a pulp and swallowed, then took another bite.

The others laughed and cheered. Theo handed the snake to Moses, who bit through the flesh and passed it on. Theo felt light-headed, but warm with the glow of triumph.

Malsum turned away without a word.

• • •

After the first night, Theo didn't touch Mgeso. When they went to bed, she lay beside him, but separated by a handspan. If Theo rolled over, she moved away. It was always the same distance, a warm chasm of air between their bodies.

He knew that if he tried to take her, she wouldn't resist. She was his wife, and she would not fail in her obligations. But he would feel her hatred, every second a rebuke. He did not want her like that.

He had no idea what he wanted. Chance had thrown him into circumstances he had no control over. He had to trust his intuition, his innate survival instincts.

He thought of Abigail, their night by the waterfall. But that seemed to belong to a different life. The man he saw when he glimpsed his reflection – shaved head, painted face, pierced ears – had nothing in common with the youth who had arrived in Bethel. The longer he roamed the forest with the Abenaki, the more he felt his old life slipping away. He did not think he would ever see Abigail again. Was she married now? Or had her intended spurned her because of their transgression?

Some nights he dreamed of her. But in those dreams she often became Mgeso, writhing on top of him while he thrust into her. He would wake smeared with his own fluid, filled with a confusion of guilt and desire.

They were in camp one afternoon, on the edge of open grassland, when Malsum approached Theo. He pointed to a thicket on the far side of the meadow. 'There is a bees' nest there. Are you brave enough to fetch the honey?'

He smiled as he said it. His eyes sidled past Theo to where Mgeso sat on a log mending a blanket.

Her face betrayed nothing, but Theo felt her gaze like hot coals on his skin.

Malsum laughed. 'I can go – if Ahoma is so frightened of a bee sting.'

Ahoma was the nickname he had given Theo. It meant 'chicken'.

Mgeso was bent over her blanket, pretending not to have heard. He stood. 'I will go.'

Theo was dressed in the Abenaki style, barefoot and bare-chested, wearing a loincloth, buckskin breeches and his knife belt. It no longer struck him as foreign dress. In the forest, he moved more like the Indians, long loose strides that avoided his flesh snagging on the undergrowth. His feet, once so used to stout leather shoes, had adapted to the soft moccasins they wore. Even the face he sometimes glimpsed in still water, or on his knife blade, did not seem so alien.

Theo moved easily through the tall brown grass, enjoying its touch against his bare stomach. As he neared the thicket Malsum had shown him, he heard the hum of bees. He could see them flying out from the trees and swarming angrily. At least Malsum hadn't lied about the nest. Theo had suspected it might be a prank to make him look ridiculous.

The trees swayed. If Theo had been paying more attention, he might have thought it strange on that still day. He was too busy thinking about how to remove the honey from the nest. No doubt the Abenaki had a method, but Theo had been too proud to ask in front of Mgeso. He had seen beekeepers in India using smoke to drive off the bees, but he had no flint, and he could not lose face by going back to the camp to fetch a brand from the fire.

He ducked under a bough and entered the thicket. He became more aware of the noise, not just the furious buzzing of bees, but a crashing of branches as if a gale was blowing through. Ahead, through the leaves, he saw a dark shape halfway up a tree.

The tree was moving and so was the nest. Theo pushed through the undergrowth and came out at the foot of the trunk. The nest was surrounded by a cloud of bees. It sat in a fork of the tree trunk, which was bent almost double by the weight on it and shaking violently.

Theo wasn't the only one who wanted the honey. The dark shape he had seen wasn't the nest.

It was a bear.

The trunk wasn't thick. Theo could hardly believe such a big animal could have hauled itself so high up it. It reminded him of the monkeys he'd seen in India, hanging off the end of the slenderest branches to get to the fruit.

The bear was almost as big as Theo. He saw long, sharp claws digging into the tree trunk, while a paw the size of a cannonball swatted at the nest. Every movement made the tree sway like a topmast in a storm.

Suddenly the trunk snapped. Bear, nest and bough fell to the ground. The nest bounced and rolled across the ground. The bear let out an angry roar.

Theo was rooted to the spot.

The bear looked up and saw Theo. In an instant, its posture changed. It lowered its head and spread its paws, rocking on its haunches. The fur on its back rippled with menace.

A stinging pain shot through Theo's foot. He looked down. A bee had stung him: three more were crawling over his bare skin.

The bees' nest lay where it had landed, near his legs. It had smashed open, splashing a brown trickle of honey over his feet.

The bear sprang at him.

Theo stepped away from the nest and instead of taking the weight of the bear's charge full-on, he caught a glancing blow. It knocked the wind out of his lungs and sent him sprawling onto the forest floor.

He rolled over, wincing at the pain in his ribs. He was some distance from the nest, but the bear reared up on its hind legs, snarling at Theo and baring its teeth.

Theo's hand went to the knife in his belt. It wasn't there. It must have fallen when he was knocked over. He was defenceless.

The bear dropped onto all fours and loped towards Theo. The gaping jaws lunged for him. Theo grabbed a stick and swung it with all his might at the bear's head. He caught it on the nose, an instant before its teeth would have sunk into his thigh.

The bear recoiled. Theo jumped to his feet, brandishing the stick, forcing himself to advance, despite his terror. The bear rocked from side to side, a prizefighter looking for an opening. Its claws glinted, sickeningly sharp. If they touched him, they would rip his skin to ribbons. Its close-set eyes were like two black stones.

It reared up again and, with one swipe, knocked the stick from his hands. Theo did the only thing he could think of.

He threw himself at the bear.

Its vast bulk barely moved as Theo hit it with his full force. It wrapped its forelegs around him, flailing with its paws. The jaws snapped and bit inches away from his head. Theo held on to its matted fur, pressing himself so close that the teeth and claws couldn't reach him.

It took all his strength to cling on, as the bear bucked and writhed to tear him off. The claws caught him, carving bloody stripes down his back. The pain was agony. Soon he would tire. The bear would toss him aside like a doll. He swung his fists, but they made no impact. He tried to gouge its nose or its eyes.

The bear swung around, slamming Theo into a tree. Theo lost his grip. He dropped to the forest floor. The bear roared, so loudly that Theo felt the ground shaking beneath him.

There was an explosion and suddenly the beast went silent. It toppled forward on top of Theo. If the tree hadn't broken its fall, it might have crushed him. He was pinned beneath its weight.

All he could do was move his head. He twisted round, trying to see what had happened.

Mgeso stood ten paces away. White smoke drifted from the mouth of the musket she held at her shoulder.

With a crashing of undergrowth, three more Abenaki appeared. Malsum was in the lead. His face lit up when he saw Theo lying under the carcass – until he realised Theo was alive.

Theo had managed to pull one arm out from under the bear. It was scratched and bleeding, so sore he wondered if the bear had broken it. He forced himself to extend it towards the broken bees' nest lying a distance away. 'There is your honey.'

• • •

Theo avoided Mgeso for the rest of that day – and most of the following week. Her face was like a thundercloud. No doubt she despised Theo for being so careless in harvesting the honey. Perhaps she regretted saving him.

Winter approached. The campfires burned all day and night, curing the meat that the hunters brought back. The hides were rubbed with elm bark and dried on wooden frames beside the fires. The canoes were buried underground to preserve them for spring. They made a longhouse, with walls of stacked logs plugged with moss, and a pitched roof of lynn bark. Moses assured Theo it would stay watertight all through the winter. They floored it with more bark and spread bearskins for sleeping. With a fire burning in its centre, and the tribe crowded inside, it was warm and would ensure their survival.

Game was scarce. Theo could not see how the meat they had preserved would last the winter, but the Abenaki seemed untroubled. They lived with the rhythm of the seasons: they accepted that winter meant empty bellies and hard rations.

One day, probably in early December, Theo was in the forest looking for more lynn trees from which to strip the bark. He was alone. The Abenaki no longer feared he would flee. There was nowhere for him to escape to.

He ranged easily through the woods, far from the camp. Solitude was the one thing he lacked among the Abenaki. He prized those moments when he could be alone, away from Mgeso's scorn and Malsum's hostility.

He saw a flash of movement through the trees. It was a deer, grazing on a young sapling. She was upwind, and his movements had not alerted her.

He had no gun, but he never left camp without a bow and arrow in case he sighted game. He threw off the blanket he wore over his shoulders, unslung the bow, nocked an arrow and aimed. The deer paused, sensing the danger. She turned her head. Theo stayed absolutely still.

A bird fluttered out of a bush. The deer took fright and bounded away. Theo loosed his arrow, but too late. It embedded itself into a tree.

He should have let it go. But his blood was up, and his stomach was empty. He ran after the deer, moving gracefully through the cold forest. He vaulted over fallen logs and ducked under low boughs. He hurdled briars and dodged between thickets. His bare feet were as fleet on the hard ground as the deer's.

He lost her. She forded a stream and disappeared into a thick stand of bushes. He knew that if he got his feet wet, they would freeze. And he could not penetrate the thicket.

The sky had darkened. A bitter wind had risen, whistling through the trees. Trudging back, the gale hit him hard in the face. He wished he hadn't discarded his blanket.

The dim, flat light distorted everything. Fixated on the deer, he hadn't paid attention to the way he came. The frozen ground yielded few hoofprints, while the wind blew up the leaves and destroyed any trails.

'Are you lost?' said a voice behind him.

He spun around, hand on his tomahawk. Mgeso was watching him, so close she could have put a knife through his shoulders. He hadn't seen or heard her.

'You were lucky I was not an Iroquois,' she said. 'Your spirit would have joined the ancestors. They sometimes range this far in winter, in search of food or animals.'

Theo shivered. 'Did you follow me?'

'They sent me to find you. You have gone far from the longhouse.'

Was she accusing him? 'I was tracking a deer.'

Mgeso gave a look at the forest, and then at Theo's empty hands. Theo felt a rush of shame and frustration at being mocked again. But he thought he saw the corners of her mouth rise. Almost a smile, though only for a moment. Her face reverted to its inscrutability. 'You should not have gone so far,' she said. 'A storm is coming.'

'I can find my own way back,' Theo insisted.

Mgeso raised an eyebrow. Again, something like a smile seemed to hover near her lips. 'Show me.'

He began to retrace his tracks through the trees, conscious of her eyes on him. Sometimes he found a snapped twig, or a bent frond that gave him hope it was the way he had come. The wind blew stronger. Above the trees, the sky was the colour of gunpowder.

He reached a rocky outcrop and paused. Even before he saw the look Mgeso was giving him, he knew he had been there before.

'We've gone in a circle.'

Something stung his skin. A feathery piece of down had drifted from the sky and landed on the back of his hand. But why was it so cold? It melted as soon as he touched it.

Mgeso giggled.

'Is this snow?' he said in wonder. More of it was falling, swirling down between the trees, like blossoms.

'Have you never seen it before?' said Mgeso.

'I have read about it in books, and heard men speak of it.' He marvelled at the sight. 'It's magical.'

'You will get used to it.' But she was no longer laughing. 'We must get to shelter soon.'

He let her lead the way. The wind rose. The snow was falling fast. Fat flakes settled quickly on the cold ground. Soon it was completely covered.

'Are you sure you know the way?' Theo asked.

Mgeso glared at him. 'I can—'

She broke off with a yelp of pain and sank to the ground clutching her ankle. The snow had hidden a rabbit hole, and she had stepped into it. She tried to stand, but the moment she put weight on her foot she collapsed again.

'Let me carry you,' Theo offered.

She didn't argue. But, light though she was, it was hard work. The wind cut against his face, blinding him with snow. He had to bend double to make progress, blundering into branches and trees. On his back, he could feel the heat seeping out of Mgeso. Her weight became heavier as she lost strength.

He began to be afraid. Theo had no blankets, and only a few kernels of dried corn in his pouch for food. Mgeso's head slumped on his shoulder. She paid no attention to where they were going, though it would have made little difference. He had lost all sense of direction.

If they continued they would get more lost. But walking was keeping Theo warm. If he stopped moving in the blizzard, they could freeze to death.

In the chaos of the storm, he almost missed it. But living with the Abenaki had heightened his awareness of the forest: he noticed things he barely saw. There was a tree, split open at the bottom, the trunk peeling apart to reveal a hollow inside.

The gap was wide enough for a person to enter. Theo pushed Mgeso through, then gathered twigs and branches. He squeezed in after her and reached out to pile up the wood over the entrance. The wind still cut through like a knife against his skin. Mgeso, pressed against him, was ice cold.

'Take off your dress,' he said.

Bending almost double in the confined space, she took off her buckskin tunic. Theo wrapped her in his jacket, then wove her tunic through the sticks over the opening. The wind pressed it taut. He chopped away rotten wood from the inside of the tree and stopped up the cracks around the edges. When he had finished, the hollow was almost weatherproof.

Theo cradled Mgeso against him, letting his bare skin warm hers. She didn't protest. After the maelstrom, the warmth and stillness had a strange serenity. The wind howled outside, the tree groaned, like a ship on a high sea, but Theo felt safe.

'What do you think of the snow now?' Mgeso asked.

'I am not sure I care for it,' Theo admitted.

'It is a gift to the earth,' said Mgeso. 'In the ancient times, the frost giants held the whole world in their icy grip. Our ancestor, Koluskap, travelled north to the kingdom of the frost giants. He fought them. Most, he wrestled to death, but a few he left alive. They venture forth again in winter, spreading their blanket over the land so that the earth can rest.'

'I would like it better if the earth didn't try to kill me while it was resting.'

'Because you try to fight it. It is the way of your people, the Bastaniak. They fell the trees. They hunt the animals until there are none left, and then they complain they are hungry. They take more than any man needs to live. That is why the earth fights back.'

'The Bastaniak are not my people.' Theo touched the lock of hair on his shaved head. 'I am Abenaki now.'

'Yes.'

She snuggled against him. Theo was glad to feel heat returning to her body.

'Tell me about where you come from,' she said. 'Is it a hot land?'

'So hot, I once saw a brass door handle melt.'

'What is a door handle?'

He laughed. Lying in the dark, he conjured up visions of India. The women in their vivid saris going down to the ghats to wash. The smell of curry, arrack and spices. The call of monkeys and peacocks. The airy palaces that Mughals and merchants built for themselves, and the bright chaos of the bazaar. He told her about the elephants. He expected she would disbelieve him, but she grew animated, asking questions.

'Our ancestors knew these creatures,' she declared. 'In the first days, they roamed these forests like the bear and the deer. We hunted them.'

Theo wondered if it could be true. The chill forest seemed a world away from the dusty plains of India. Surely any elephant would have frozen to death, like Hannibal's crossing the Alps. Yet when Mgeso said it, she sounded as if she had seen them herself.

Her head nestled against his shoulder. Her glossy black hair was so close, he started stroking it. He leaned forward to kiss it.

Mgeso tipped her head back, so that his mouth met her lips.

She was the first woman he had kissed since the night with Abigail. The memory brought a stab of guilt, but only for a moment. Warmth and desire drove out the thought. At last he accepted that Abigail was gone for ever.

The old tree creaked. The wind whistled through the branches. A dim glow showed around the edges of the entrance, where the last traces of daylight reflected off the snow. Inside the tree it was almost pitch dark. They held the kiss for what seemed an eternity. Her tongue pushed his lips apart, seeking his mouth. He responded, pulling her closer against him, thrilling to the touch of her bare breasts against his skin. She gave a moan of pleasure.

Eventually they broke apart. Her face was close, her breath brushed his cheek.

'You did not have to do that,' Theo murmured.

'I wanted to. And more.'

She felt for his hand in the dark and guided it down to her buttocks. Fumbling in the cramped space, she angled herself so he could lift her onto him. His body was firm and eager, galvanised by the kiss. She gasped as he slid inside her.

Mgeso used the same expert movements she had that first night in the village, throbbing around him while barely seeming to move. But there was tenderness, this time. She was not trying to control him, but to please him: bringing him to the brink, letting him go, then bringing him back to even greater heights of pleasure.

At last he poured himself into her with shudders of delight that seemed rooted in the deepest parts of his being. But she had not finished with him. She kept him in her grip, working him against her body until, with cries so loud they drowned out even the storm, she climaxed.

'I thought you hated me,' Theo said afterwards. They lay entwined, sticky with each other's sweat.

Mgeso laughed. A soft, seductive sound. Theo could have listened to it for ever.

'At first, yes. But then . . .' She traced her fingers through the hairs that were growing thick on his chest. 'I watched you. I saw what kind of man you are. You take the hardest work and do not complain. You give the children the choicest sweetmeats from the animals you hunt. Your strength when you fought the bear.'

'I thought you were furious with me. That you despised me for making you save me.'

She shook her head. 'I was angry with Malsum. He knew the bear was in the thicket – he boasted of it afterwards. It was a cruel trick. As soon as I knew, I came running to rescue you. But if you had not held off the bear so long, you would have died.'

She nibbled his earlobe. 'You are kind and brave.'

'But Moses told me . . . You and Malsum . . .'

'I do not love Malsum,' she said. 'I love you.'

'And I love you.' He hadn't thought it until that moment, but as he said it he knew beyond doubt it was true.

She felt between his legs again. He needed no coaxing: his body was ready.

'The storm may last for hours,' she murmured in his ear.

'Then we had best make sure we keep warm.'

• • •

When sunlight broke through the next morning, the snow in front of the entrance was two feet deep. Mgeso's dress, which they had used to cover the door, was frozen solid. It took a long time to thaw and eventually they dug their way out. Into a different world.

Everything was white. Snow clung to the trees and layered the branches, which bent, as if they were laden with fruit. The forest floor was a single smooth carpet, softly contoured where the snow folded over a rock or a fallen log. The sun shone strongly out of a clear sky, and the sleeping earth glowed with dazzling light.

Theo remembered Nathan's words: *So clean and pure, when the snow's just fallen, you think it's wiped away every bad thing in the world.* At last he understood.

He took a step forward, and sank up to his thigh in snow.

'You look like a moose in a swamp,' Mgeso said.

'How will we get back to the camp?' Theo asked. Mgeso's ankle had swollen, with violent bruising. It would be impossible for her to walk. They had eaten the last corn from his pouch hours earlier, and his stomach was clenched with hunger.

He began to worry.

Mgeso sat up. 'What is that noise?'

He listened. Snow had changed the forest, deadening the sound so that everything became very still, punctuated by the occasional crack of a branch breaking under the weight of snow. There was a new noise. A rhythmic crunch, like footsteps walking on gravel. But no one could walk so fast through that snow.

Theo craned his head out of the opening of the tree trunk, and almost bumped heads with Moses stooping to peer in. Four more Abenaki stood behind him. They wore bearskins, and soft hide shoes with the fur turned inward. They had sticks tied to their feet.

Moses took in the sight of Theo and Mgeso, wrapped up together. 'I was worried about you in the storm. But I see you have found a resting place, Ahoma.'

• • •

The moon beat the tempo of the seasons.

At the Greeting Moon, they welcomed the turning of the sun with feasting, singing and dancing. Days were dark and short. For Theo, raised in the tropics where one day ran much the same length as another, it was a strange and disconcerting time. For the Abenaki, it was a season of rest. They spent many hours in the longhouse, sitting around the fire telling stories. Theo struggled to understand, for they spoke of the deeds of their distant ancestors and those of their parents with the same familiarity, as if they had witnessed them all.

More snow came with the Moose-hunting Moon. The Abenaki showed Theo how to make the strange snowshoes they used, bending green branches into circles and strapping them with crosspieces, so they could fasten them to their feet. In that way, they could skim over the thickest snow without sinking. The moose, mired in the snow, were easy prey. They picked cranberries, bright red and bullet-hard; they trapped beaver in the frozen ponds. Even in the depths of winter, they never went hungry.

'The Bastaniak call this moon the "Hunger Moon",' said the sachem. 'But that is because they do not know how to live with the forest.'

The days began to lengthen with the Sugar Moon, though snow still lay on the ground. The sap ran high in the trees, making their bark loose and supple. The Abenaki stripped it away in great sheets for their canoes and huts, always remembering to leave a small offering of tobacco among the roots as a token of thanks.

But one tree in particular was the focus of their labour. This was the maple tree, whose sap they tapped for its sugar. They made a V-shaped cut in it with their tomahawks and drove in a wooden spike. The sap ran out down the spike and dripped into a birch-bark bucket below.

'In the ancient times, the syrup flowed from the trees like water, all year round,' Moses told Theo. 'It made the people fat and lazy. So the trickster god made the sap thin and watery, except in winter. Then, when the crops are dead and the game is scarce, it flows as it did before.'

On freezing nights, they left the sap out in shallow trays. In the mornings, they picked off the crust of ice that had formed and were left with thick syrup: amber and deliciously sweet. When they mixed it with bear fat and dipped their meat in it, Theo licked every drop from his fingers.

Theo said a prayer for Nathan, the friend whose dying wish had brought him here. It also made him think of Abigail. What had become of her? How far away was she? The Abenaki had no maps, and their names for the mountains and rivers meant nothing to Theo. She might be twenty miles away or two hundred: it would make no difference. She might as well be in India. He wondered again if she had married the farmer her parents had chosen for her. He hoped she was happy.

He was content with Mgeso. A change had come over her that he did not understand, an inner peace. Sometimes he caught her smiling to herself. But if he woke late at night under a full moon, his mind would drift back to the pool by the waterfall at Bethel. And wonder.

As the Planting Moon approached, they left their winter camp and returned to the village they had left in the autumn. The sachem forbade storytelling, for the tribe needed all their energies focused on sowing the new season's crops. Days lengthened. It was a time of buds and sunshine. Mgeso had never seemed so radiant.

One day, when they were planting corn on the bottomland near the river, she took his hand and put it on her belly. Her eyes met his, bright and alive, answering his question before he had begun to ask it.

'Yes,' she said. 'Our child.'

That night, Theo sat with her on the clifftops overlooking the village, pondering the strange currents of the world. His grandfather had been born in England, the son of a famous privateer. His father had been born in Africa to an Omani princess. He himself had been born in India, and now his son would grow up as an Abenaki.

'Your heart is beating faster,' Mgeso said. Her head snuggled against his chest. 'Are you worried?'

'No.'

'Happy?'

Theo stroked her cheek. 'Very happy.'

Mgeso's belly swelled as the corn ripened. Theo's feelings swung between paternal pride, and anxiety about Mgeso's wellbeing. If she so much as cracked a fingernail he was consumed with worry for the baby. He tried not to let it show.

He could not always be with her. When the Blueberry Moon rose, the men left the women in the fields and went back to the forests. Malsum led the hunting party. Theo had avoided him all winter, but now the sachem insisted that they must travel together.

'There is no quarrel between you now,' he said. 'You must fight together, not against each other.' But Theo remembered the bear in the thicket and was not so sure.

They ranged across the land, further and further as spring edged into summer. They smeared themselves with fat to keep off the clouds of insects that fed on them voraciously. The game was plentiful, the forest abounding in fruits and berries. Malsum kept his distance.

They were not the only people on the move that summer. They often encountered war bands from other tribes, armed and painted for battle, heading west. Some greeted the Abenaki warmly and shared food and news. Others passed with hurried steps and suspicious glares. A few had fresh scalps already tied to their belts. Theo could feel violence permeating the forest.

One day the Abenaki came into some lowlands, where the river had spread into the forest and made dense marshes. Bubbles broke the black water, emitting an evil-smelling stench that reminded Theo of the slums of Black Town in Calcutta. The swamp was too shallow and tangled for their canoes. They carried the boats, keeping to the ridges that made a network of paths through the mire. In some places, even Malsum could not find a way, and they would have to wade waist-deep through the stinking mud and water. Flies clustered around them, more than Theo had ever seen.

They camped on a muddy island in the marsh. Moses made an attempt to fish, but without luck. Theo wasn't sure he wanted to eat anything that came out of those foul waters. Damp wood made their fire spit and throw off a noxious black smoke.

Theo could not sleep. He sat on a rotting stump, talking with Moses.

'Hard choices are coming,' Moses said. 'The King of the Bastaniak and the King of the Blaumonak have made a great war.'

'You mean the English and the French,' Theo said. Though it seemed natural to use Abenaki words for life in the forest, he could not get used to their names for European matters.

'That is why so many tribes are on the move. The kings have summoned their allies to battle.' Moses picked away fragments of rotten wood and threw them into the water. 'You know the Abenaki fight alongside the Blaumonak.' He cleared his throat to make the unfamiliar sound. 'The French.'

'I know.'

'There is a man named Bichot. We are going to meet him. After we have traded for our furs, he will summon us to war. We will sing the war song, and raise the hatchet, and we will go.'

'Is it far?'

'Across the mountains there is a great lake. The French have a mighty fortress there. The English have gathered a great army to attack it. They say the war for all this land will be decided there.'

Theo marvelled that he could have come halfway round the world, and still find England and France trading blows on his doorstep. Was there nowhere on Earth you could escape?

Moses watched him, his eyes pale circles in the night. 'I know you are Abenaki now, Ahoma. But will you be able to fight against the people of your birth?'

Theo thought of his parents. He thought of Constance. Fighting with the French would betray every vow he had made to avenge them. Refusing would be to reject Mgeso and his unborn child.

A light flashed in the darkness. Not the magic green of the fireflies, which he had grown used to, but a burst of flame. Theo threw himself to the ground, expecting a shot to fly overhead. But there had been no bang and no smoke: only a soft belching sound, and the smell of gas.

The flame came again, this time in a different place. It seemed to be coming out of the ground itself.

'What is that?' Theo breathed.

'They are the ghost fires,' said Moses. 'The souls of the dead who have not found peace. They lurk in these places to prey on the living.'

Theo shivered. Though he had taken on many of the Abenaki customs, he had remained respectfully agnostic towards their spiritual beliefs. In that place, watching the eerie fires flare in the darkness, he felt he had lifted the curtain on another world.

A chill went down his spine. He thought of the people he had loved, who had died too soon. His parents. Constance. Nathan. Were their spirits out there too, flickering in restless torment?

They left the swamp the next day and entered a thick pine forest. Hardly any light penetrated the canopy; the air was damp and dim.

Around mid-morning, Theo paused.

'What is it?' Moses asked.

'I smell something.' He sniffed the air, orienting himself to the scent as effortlessly as breathing. A year with the Abenaki had realigned his senses. In the dense forest, sound and smell were as important as sight.

'An animal?'

'No.'

It was a smell he had known every day of his childhood – and now it was so alien he had almost not recognised it. He laughed out loud to find this echo of Madras suddenly in the American wilderness, then turned sombre. It reminded him of his father.

'I think it is coffee.'

Unstrapping his tomahawk, he followed the scent. He heard the trickle of water, and the sound of raised voices. He crouched lower, using the woodcraft the Abenaki had taught him to make himself almost invisible as he followed the slope down towards a sluggish river.

Half a dozen men sat around a campfire. A skinned rabbit roasted on a spit, and a kettle bubbled on a hot stone in the embers. Theo could feel the danger, like entering a den of wild animals. The men were dressed in furs and leather strapped with knives and hatchets. They had scarred skin, calloused fists, and faces that had been rearranged many times by violence. They kept their long-barrelled rifles leaning against the trees in easy reach. They could not have seen him. If they had, he would be dead.

They were speaking in French, though a rough, crude dialect far removed from what Theo's tutor had taught him in Madras. One – a huge man in a bearskin cloak – was telling a story about a prostitute who had tried to cheat him. The men laughed as he described how he had taken his revenge.

Suddenly the laughing stopped and the men had guns in their hands. Theo froze, but the guns were not pointing at him. Malsum had appeared. He walked out into the clearing. The Frenchmen did not seem surprised to see him. The guns were lowered. The big man rose and came to greet him.

Theo slipped in with the rest of the Abenaki as they emerged from the forest behind Malsum. Now he could see the big Frenchman clearly. The black bearskin cloak clung to him with an aura of darkness, and he wore a string of sharp claws around his neck. There was a dreadful asymmetry about his face. Between the top of his head and the bottom, it looked like two halves of an orange that had been squashed carelessly back together. The lank, greasy hair combed over his scalp did not hide the livid bald patch beneath. There was blood on his hands from skinning the rabbit.

He stank of death. Thinking of Moses' story of the ghost fires, Theo considered that one of those vengeful spirits had come alive.

'That is Bichot,' Moses whispered.

Malsum embraced the Frenchman. Seeing the two together was like looking at a pair of wolves. Theo kept a safe distance and put his hand on the shaft of his tomahawk. Every man in the clearing had a weapon ready. The mistrust was almost palpable.

The Frenchman's gaze swept over the Abenaki. With his dark skin, piercings and shaved head, Theo looked no different from any of the others. Yet, by some base instinct, the trapper's eyes settled on him.

'*Qui est-ce?*' he snarled.

'Bastaniak,' said Malsum.

A skinning knife flashed in Bichot's hand. With two strides, faster than blinking, he was in front of Theo with the blade moving towards his throat.

Theo was faster. Metal clashed as his tomahawk caught Bichot's knife so hard it was knocked out of the Frenchman's hand. Arm extended, Theo held the tomahawk blade an inch from Bichot's neck.

'I am Abenaki,' said Theo, softly.

He held his weapon poised for what seemed an eternity. His senses were so alive, he fancied he could hear a single pine needle dropping to the forest floor. He was aware of every man in the clearing:

if his gun was loaded, if his finger was on the trigger, if his heart was beating faster in preparation for an attack. If Bichot had so much as blinked, he would have taken his head off.

'He is Abenaki,' said Malsum, at last. 'We have no quarrel.'

The French trapper stepped back with a growl. From the smell of his breath, Theo guessed there was something stronger than coffee in his cup.

'What is your name?' said Bichot. He spoke the Abenaki language like a native.

'Ahoma of the Abenaki. Remember it.'

Bichot bared his teeth. 'One day, I will make you tell me your real name. You will scream it out as you beg me to kill you.'

Theo smiled. 'I will whisper it in your ear as the tip of my knife slides into your heart.'

'Enough!' called Moses. 'Did you come to trade insults with us or furs?'

It broke the tension. The Frenchmen made space around their fire, and produced bottles of brandy from their baggage. Still, Theo kept a wary distance from Bichot as they settled down to business. The hides that the Abenaki had gathered during spring were presented, examined and haggled over. Despite himself, Theo found himself drawn in. The skills he had honed with the cotton-weavers and spice-merchants of Calcutta returned effortlessly as he bluffed, cajoled and persuaded the Frenchmen. It was harder than it had been in Bengal. The Frenchmen shared their food and pressed drink upon the Abenaki – who were not used to strong liquor – but every word and gesture betrayed the contempt they felt for the natives.

Is this what I was like? Theo wondered, thinking about the English in India. It was hard to barter with a man who thought you little better than a dog. And the goods the French had brought to trade were derisory. Beads, which the Abenaki women prized, and little mirrors they could sew onto their clothes. There was tradecloth, which had started to replace the flax shirts that the Abenaki used to wear.

Examining one parcel, Theo gave a cry of surprise. There was a weaver's mark stamped in the corner of the cloth, a swirling Bengali letter, like an elephant's tusk. He recognised it. It belonged to a weaver in Kasim Bazar, a stooped old man with thirteen children and a moustache that almost reached his chin. If Theo closed his eyes, he could see the house and the two tamarind trees outside. Perhaps he himself had purchased this very bale of cloth on one of his trips with Deegan, and it had moved through the trade arteries of the world to arrive in this remote place.

Was there nowhere he could go to escape his past?

• • •

Most of the pelts were traded for brandy. Theo tried to dissuade the Abenaki, but even Moses would not listen. They could not resist the lure of spirits. When the haggling was over, they got blind drunk. Theo, feeling Bichot's presence, did not dare drink. He spent a miserable night clutching his tomahawk, pondering all the animals that had died so the Indians could have one night of dissolution.

The next morning they set out together downriver. The Abenaki travelled in their bark canoes, nursing sore heads and wretched stomachs. The French followed in their *bateaux*, wide-bottomed craft made of white pine with sharp raised ends. They were good for transporting the furs they had acquired, but cumbersome and awkward to carry around the rapids. By the time they reached the village, four days later, the men were bruised and bad-tempered.

The tribe came down to the river to greet them. Theo vaulted out of the canoe and splashed through the water to greet Mgeso.

'You have grown,' he exclaimed. Her belly protruded so far he could hardly get his arms around her. He gave her a long, deep kiss. 'I have missed you. Are you well?'

'Everything is well.' She placed his hand on her stomach, as she had all those moons ago. Then it had been flat, with only the faintest swelling to betray the life growing inside. Now the bulging skin was swollen, like a ripe berry.

A tremor went through his hand. Theo stared. 'Was that . . . the child?'

She nodded. 'He is pleased to see his father.'

'*He?*'

'Only a boy could kick so hard.'

He followed her back to the village. They sat side by side, while the tribe feasted and danced.

But Theo could not forget his cares. Bichot and Malsum sat apart with the sachem and some of his other warriors, talking earnestly. Theo guessed they were discussing the coming war.

Mgeso saw how his gaze kept drifting towards their fire. She knew what it meant. 'Where do you stand? Are you still certain you are Abenaki?'

'My loyalties are with you,' Theo reassured her. 'And with our son.'

When the dancing had finished, she took him to their bed. As he undressed, Mgeso reached between his legs and began stroking him intimately. After weeks away, Theo's body responded eagerly – but he held himself back. 'Is it safe? For the baby?'

Mgeso smiled. 'Even with your great manhood, you will not disturb him.'

She rolled over. Theo entered her from behind, nestling into the curves of her body, like a nut in its shell. He reached around her, cupping the full-grown breasts and squeezing her engorged nipples until she moaned. 'You were gone too long,' she gasped.

'Then let me show you what you were missing.'

• • •

Theo was cold when he woke. Mgeso had gone. He pulled the blanket tighter, smelling her musk on the fur. Perhaps she had taken a trip to the river to wash.

He wondered if their activity the night before had stirred the baby into coming. Surely she would have woken him if that was happening. But would

she? Abenaki women gave birth in the forest, surrounded by other women. She would have known
that telling Theo would only make him worry.

He rose. Dawn had broken early. Most of the
Abenaki were resting after the night's feast, though
a few of the children were digging with sticks in the
soft earth by the river. Theo watched them playing,
imagining his own son among them one day.

Mgeso was not there.

He returned to the stockade. Birds circled in the
sky. He felt the same unease as he had watching the
ghost fires in the swamp, of an evil spirit stalking
him. He tried to shake off the dread.

He heard someone behind him. But it was not
Mgeso: it was Moses. He was limping, clutching a
gash that bled down his thigh.

'What happened?'

'Bichot and Malsum have taken Mgeso,' the
Abenaki gasped. 'I tried to stop them, but they
were too strong.'

'Where did they go?'

'To the cliffs.'

Theo was naked, apart from his loincloth. He
did not even have his knife. He should have gone
back and fetched his tomahawk, or a gun. But fear
for Mgeso – and the child inside her – drove out all
reason.

He ran up the path to the cliffs that overlooked
the village. Footprints showed on the dew-damp
ground. Theo thought he registered Mgeso's
bare feet, pressed deeper into the soil by the extra
weight she was carrying, Malsum's splayed toes,
and Bichot's hobnailed boots. He ran on, vaulting

over rocks, bounding up the slope like a mountain lion. Moses, barely able to walk, was left far behind.

Theo came onto the open ground at the top of the cliffs. The rocks there were broken and uneven, riven by frost and rain. Holes and cracks made the going treacherous. One wrong step could have broken his leg.

The stones showed no displacement by footprints, but something glittered on the ground ahead. It was a glass bead from one of Mgeso's necklaces. Theo picked it up, panic mounting. He saw another, and another beyond, at the opening to a crack in the cliff that made a dark, narrow cave.

Theo ran to the cave. Was Mgeso in there? Perhaps she had escaped Malsum and Bichot – breaking her necklace – and hidden in the cave.

He called her name. All he heard was echoes – and a strange noise, like a saw scraping a metal pipe. It reverberated off the walls so he could not tell where it came from.

He should have brought a knife. Any weapon. Dread rose from the pit of his stomach as he squeezed into the crack. The rock closed over him. Inside the cave, the light faded behind him. The rasping noise grew louder.

There was movement on the floor at the back of the cave. Was it Mgeso? Theo shook with rage as he imagined what Malsum and Bichot might have done to her. He edged closer, deeper into the cave. His eyes were adjusting to the dim light. He could see a dappled pattern, like fabric, maybe limbs or the folds of a dress. The noise was almost deafening.

And suddenly he saw what it was.

It was an enormous rattlesnake. Its colour was dark as molasses, its tail blazed with many buttons showing all the skins it had shed over its long life. It stood up erect, its angular head feinting and darting at him. Uncoiled, it would be as long as a man.

He remembered Moses' words from many moons ago. *One bite will kill you.*

The snake's movements became more hostile. Its tail vibrated so fast it was a blur. The noise of its rattle filled the cave with menace.

If Theo had hesitated for a second, he would have been dead. But he was Abenaki now, and he breathed with the animals. He felt the snake's muscles contract to strike as if they were his own. He stepped back, and as the snake lunged past him he stamped down on its head, pinning it to the floor. Its scaly skin writhed and twisted against his bare foot. Before it could free itself, he grabbed it behind the neck and yanked it away. He had a momentary vision of a flared mouth, a forked tongue and long, venomous fangs. He hurled it as hard as he could out of the cave and onto the open ground outside.

He heard shouts of fear and consternation, then a short scream and a blade ringing on stone.

His heart stopped. He recognised the scream.

He saw them the moment he squeezed out of the cave. Bichot held Mgeso with her arms pinned behind her back. She was struggling, but he was too strong. Malsum stood in front of them, blood dripping from the blade of his tomahawk. The decapitated snake lay twisted at his feet, still twitching.

'Let her go,' said Theo. He spoke to Malsum, but he could not take his eyes off Mgeso. 'Let her go and I will forget this madness.'

Malsum's lip curled in a sneer. 'Mgeso is mine. But I will give you this one chance. Go back to your own people. Run away into the forest. Never set foot on Abenaki land again, and I will let you live.'

Theo's eyes locked with Mgeso's, burning with defiance, and he knew what he had to do.

'She is my wife,' he said. 'I will not allow her to be dishonoured.'

Malsum looked surprised. He swung the tom-ahawk in a lazy loop. 'The snakebite would have been a quick death. I will not be so gentle.'

He came at Theo. The tomahawk blade danced in the air, like a hummingbird, so fast Theo could barely keep track of it. Mgeso cried out, but Bichot crooked his arm around her neck and choked her into silence.

Theo had no illusions about his chances. Malsum was older, taller, and as strong as a bull. A hundred times on the hunt, Theo had seen him perform feats of strength he would have thought impossible. Theo had no weapon except his anger. He moved backwards, circling to try to keep distance between him and Malsum.

Malsum went on the attack, swinging the tom-ahawk at Theo's head. Theo threw out his hand to wrest the weapon from Malsum's grip. He missed, but if his forearm had collided with the shaft it would have snapped. Malsum followed in hard, launching a string of quick attacks, and only Theo's reflexes saved him from being carved into pieces.

From across the clearing, Bichot laughed. He was enjoying the sport.

Malsum feinted towards Theo's head, then pivoted around and brought the tomahawk in low. The flat of the blade struck Theo with a crack on the kneecap. Theo's leg buckled. Malsum punched him in the stomach, and as Theo doubled over the Abenaki swept his legs from under him. Theo fell on his back.

It was over. Malsum stood over him. He had won. He tossed the tomahawk aside on to the rocks and drew the knife from his belt. He was going to scalp Theo alive. Theo heard a choking sob from Mgeso. He tried to see her face one last time, but Malsum blocked his view.

From the corner of his eye, he saw something moving on the ground beside him. It was the snake, still twitching even in death.

Malsum stooped with the knife. At the same moment, Theo grabbed the snake's tail and swung it with all his might. The dead reptile uncoiled like a bullwhip. It smacked Malsum's face with a spray of blood that so startled him he dropped the knife.

Theo scrabbled on the ground for the weapon, feeling the blade with his fingers. With a jerk of his wrist, he drove it pommel-first into his enemy's face. A savage joy coursed through him as he felt Malsum's nose break under the impact.

Malsum reeled away. Theo leaped to his feet and sent him sprawling with a couple of vicious kicks, followed by a punch to the head with the butt of the knife handle that knocked the Abenaki unconscious. Theo tucked the knife into his belt and retrieved the tomahawk that Malsum had discarded.

He could have killed Malsum with a single blow. But he hesitated. Killing in cold blood revolted him, and Malsum was Abenaki, his tribe. He looked towards Mgeso. Bichot still had his muscular arms wrapped around her, and he was holding a knife at her throat. He would surely sever her windpipe.

'Let her go,' Theo ordered. 'This was Malsum's fight, not yours. You have nothing to gain now.'

'Stay back,' Bichot warned. 'Or I'll kill her.' It was a stand-off. Brutal though he was, he could see the fire in Theo's eyes.

'If I tell the sachem what you tried to do, he will carve open your skull and fill it with hot coals,' Theo shouted. 'But I will give you this one chance, the same that Malsum gave me. Let her go and run from here as fast as you can. I will not follow you.'

Bichot jerked his head. The string of claws around his neck rattled. 'I will take the girl with me. I will release her when I am safe.'

'Let her go now!' Theo screamed. He stared at Mgeso. Though she could not move with the knife at her neck, her eyes blazed with the message. *Fight.*

Without warning, Bichot flung his arms wide and thrust Mgeso away. She stumbled forward and sprawled on the ground, falling on her pregnant belly. Bichot fled.

Theo ran to her. As he put his arms around her, he felt a hard object protruding from her side. She was moaning, a deep guttural despair: a hot, sticky liquid was oozing over his fingers.

He turned her over and let out a cry as if his heart had been ripped from him. Bichot had driven the blade of his knife deep in her side. Theo tried to extract it but pulling the handle only opened the wound. Blood gushed and Mgeso screamed in agony.

Theo could tell the stab would be fatal. He tried to staunch the bleeding but the escaping blood bubbled with air seeping from her lungs.

Bichot had disappeared into the forest, but Theo had no thought of giving chase. He cradled Mgeso in his arms. He felt her heart against his chest, faint and failing. Her eyes were clouded with pain.

'I am sorry,' he whispered. Tears flowed down his face, weeping for Mgeso and the child he would never see. 'I would have crossed oceans and fought armies to save you. But I could not.'

She lifted a weak hand to brush away his tears. 'I will wait for you with the ancestors. And in winter, when the snow is deep, go to the hollow tree and remember me.'

'I will.'

'Siumo,' she murmured. Her voice was no more than a whisper. Theo's desolation was all-consuming, as it had been when he had lost his father. She and the child were slipping away, and there was nothing he could do. 'Hold me, Siumo.'

'I am Ahoma,' he reminded her.

'You are not Ahoma,' she said. A distant look had come into her eyes. 'You are Siumo, the hawk. You will fly far from this place and fight many battles.

You will swoop on your enemies and tear them to pieces. You will avenge me.' Her hand closed around his. 'Do this for me.'

'I will,' Theo promised. But the light had gone out of her eyes, and she did not hear him.

He gently laid Mgeso on the ground and as he did so he saw Malsum stir. Theo picked up the tomahawk and with a rage that shook his whole body he lunged at him. Malsum was quick to see the attack and kicked viciously into Theo's stomach, winding him. Malsum was dazed and his nose was still gouting blood. Instinctively he scrambled to his feet and ran into the forest, leaving Theo on his side, bent double, clutching his midriff, gasping desperately for air and weeping uncontrollably.

• • •

After they had buried Mgeso and the child inside her, the sachem came to console Theo. He looked old and careworn. Mgeso's death had shaken the tribe. Malsum was nowhere to be found. He had not been seen since running from Theo. Theo knew there were many in the tribe who resented that their kinsman was a fugitive while Theo, the outsider, was still among them.

'I had a dream last night,' the sachem said, 'like the one I had the day you came. The child sat in the clearing and the wolf came to menace it. This time, the hawk did not fight the wolf. He flew into the forest, drawing the wolf away.'

He searched Theo's face. 'It means you will leave us.'

Theo wondered if there had been a dream, or if this was the old man's way of telling him to go. It made little difference. With Mgeso, he had felt at home among the Abenaki. If their child had been born, he would have belonged with them. Now he had nothing – except a burning hunger for revenge.

'I had a dream too,' Theo told him. It had come in the depths of the night, lying in an empty bed that felt as cold as a tomb. 'Mgeso was lying underwater in a dark pool. She was not dead, but it was as if the surface was covered with clear ice and she could not break out. When she tried to speak, all that came from her mouth was a snake as long as a house. It coiled around her body and throttled her.'

The sachem sucked his teeth. 'She died unjustly. Her soul is not at peace.'

Theo thought of the black swamp, and the wicked flames of the ghost fires burning there. He told himself it was superstition and he didn't believe it.

'Malsum and Bichot did this,' he said. 'I will find them and make them pay.'

'If you follow that path, you will no longer be Abenaki,' the sachem warned. 'The Blaumonak are our allies, and they will protect Bichot. Malsum is one of our fiercest warriors. If you fight them, you will do it alone.'

'Then that is what I must do.'

The sachem nodded. 'We do not do as we choose, but as the ancestors command.'

A warning cry sounded from the lookouts on the cliff. Someone was coming. The women and children melted away into the forest, while the men gathered their weapons. The war had not touched them that summer, but they knew it was not far off, like a fire burning in the forest. A simple change in the wind could bring it to them in a heartbeat.

A man wandered down the cliff path and entered the village, just as Theo had a year earlier. He wore brown buckskin trousers and a short green jacket, like the trappers, but also the white cross belts and haversack of a soldier. He had a powder horn and a shot bag, but no rifle.

The Abenaki watched him, weapons ready.

'I come for a parley,' the newcomer announced. It was the first time Theo had heard any man speak English since the day he was taken prisoner. The language sounded strange and jarring on his ears. 'My name is Lieutenant Trent, from the Company of Rangers.' He looked uncertainly around the village, scanning the watching faces. 'Is there an Englishman in your tribe?'

The ranger's gaze passed over Theo without a second thought. None of the Abenaki glanced at him to give him away. They understood that this was his choice to make, and his alone. Was he Abenaki, or Bastaniak?

A long silence held the clearing. The ranger hesitated. He could feel that something was amiss, but the Indians' impassive faces betrayed nothing. Eventually, impatience won over curiosity. He touched his hat. 'It seems I was misinformed. Good day to you.' He turned to go.

'Wait!' Theo called.

The word echoed around the silent clearing. The ranger paused and looked back. Even then, he did not know who had spoken. All he saw was Abenaki.

Theo stepped forward.

'My name is Theo Courtney.'

The Paris gossips lingered on the fringes of the ballroom, among the marble columns that lined the dance floor. Once, these women would have been out in full view, dancing and flirting and toying with men's hearts, but that was a young girl's sport. Now, they wore so much powder on their faces that the exertions of dancing would have ruined their complexions. They sat on the sidelines and watched the dancers over the tops of their fans and hands of cards.

One dancer, in particular, was the subject of their interest – of many conversations, in fact, all over the room. She had long fair hair elaborately braided, wide green eyes and a breathtaking figure that drew jealous looks from the other women – and covetous stares from men. The bodice of her dress was cut so low that her every move risked embarrassment, yet she spun and danced with rare abandon – as if she were alone in her boudoir, not being judged by a hundred pairs of eyes.

'Who is she?' demanded the first gossip. She was the Marquise de Sologne, an elderly woman whose affairs had been legendary in her youth. She prided herself on knowing all of the eligible young women in Paris. A word from her, and a woman might find the door of every respectable salon closed to her without knowing why. And yet the girl on the dance floor was unknown to her.

'She is Madame Constance de Courtenay,' said her friend, eager to show off this crumb of knowledge. 'Recently arrived from India.'

'Does her husband know she is here?' said the marquise, to widespread laughter.

'She is widowed.' The friend lowered her voice, forcing her companions to lean in closer. In their circle, rumour was gold. She wanted full credit for this nugget.

'It is a most romantic tale. She is an English-woman, from India. She was at the fall of Calcutta, and was captured. The nawab, who is a kind of king in India, threw her into his dungeons. Who knows what indignities he may have inflicted upon her there?'

The women around the table shivered as they imagined it. All had vivid ideas of the debauchery of the Orient.

'Mercifully, she was rescued. Her husband was a captain with our army in India, a gentleman named Capitaine de Courtenay. He released her from the nawab's dungeon. Naturally, she fell in love with her gallant saviour. She married him. But no sooner had she obtained this happiness than trag-edy struck again. Her husband fell overboard on the voyage home and drowned. She embarked as a bride and landed a widow.'

The women considered this momentous trove of information.

'She does not look unduly burdened by her loss,' said the marquise, archly. On the floor, Constance was dancing a particularly energetic gavotte. 'That poor young man can hardly keep up.'

'That *poor young man* is worth ten thousand livres a year,' noted one of her companions.

There was a sigh of understanding. Exotic she might be, this Indian-born Englishwoman who had arrived in Paris, but her motives were as familiar as the bells of Notre-Dame.

'In a few months, she will limp back to some provincial village, and eke out a living on whatever her late husband's pension affords her,' declared one of the gossips. 'Some men may find a passing distraction in the charms of youth, but in the end, they will always opt for fortune and pedigree.'

'How lucky for you that that is so,' said the marquise. 'If men always chose beauty over fortune, you would be a spinster still. But I am not so certain about this one,' she added, turning her attention to Constance. 'She has survived an Indian dungeon and an inconvenient husband. I do not think she will be so easily brushed aside.'

On the dance floor, Constance was aware of the attention she was attracting. She would have been offended if she had been unnoticed. She had spent hours preparing herself. She had applied make-up so her eyes seemed wider and her mouth more girlish. She had arranged every strand of her hair to affect an artless innocence. Lacking the funds to pay either a maid or a seamstress, she had sewn and re-sewn her dress until the effect was perfect.

She knew the old women would be gossiping about her behind their fans. Let them. She was well versed in the art of gossip from Calcutta: it was the last consolation of women who had lost their beauty and had no other advantage. No longer interesting to men, they spent their energies tearing down those who had supplanted them.

And even gossip had its uses. If those women made catty remarks to their husbands, it would make the husbands look more lasciviously at Constance. If they invited her to their homes so they could sneer at her – who knew whom she might meet once she was through the front door?

The women were looking at her because men were looking at her – and that was what mattered. She sensed their gazes, even though she pretended to ignore them, soaked up their regard and drew strength from it. She wasn't complacent. Like her dress, straining against her bosom, her life was one stitch from disaster. But it gave her a delicious energy. On the coach journey from Lorient she had promised herself two things: that she would survive, and that she would never be as bored again as she had been by Lascaux.

The dance ended. She curtsied to her partner and he bowed, stealing a surreptitious glance at the tops of her breasts. 'May I have the privilege of the next dance, madame?' he enquired.

She assumed an expression of deep regret. 'Alas, I am already spoken for. And the next five dances, as well.'

She saw his crestfallen look. 'We will surely dance again before the night is over, monsieur. I will seek you out.'

But she could not keep her word. The throng of men around her – young, eligible, ardent – kept her busy all night.

It was nearly eleven o'clock, and supper was about to be served, when the door to the assembly room opened. Even the musicians seemed to skip a note as the new arrival marched in. He took a glass of wine from a servant on a tray and tossed it down in a single gulp, surveying the room.

'Major General de Corbeil,' the footman announced.

Constance had been dancing with her back to him. At the sound of his name, she almost trod on her partner's foot – but she resisted the impulse to stare. The name was burned into her memory along with every other detail of that terrible siege. He had been there only for an instant, one moment in the sweep of a mighty campaign. Surely he would not recognise her.

But what if he did? What if he remembered that she had married Captain Lascaux? What if he knew that Lascaux was not lost at sea, but living with his fat wife somewhere in Bordeaux? Constance would be ruined.

She glanced over her shoulder. Discreetly – but not discreetly enough. Their eyes met. Corbeil's face, already pale, went deathly white. His lips looked blood red, like those of an animal that had been feasting on a carcass. He flinched as if someone had kicked him.

Constance and Corbeil made to turn away at the same time, but one of the bystanders had already noticed their eyes meeting. Oblivious to the undercurrents, eager to make introductions, she said, 'You know Madame de Courtenay, General?'

Corbeil shook his head. 'No.'

Constance did not contradict him. He looked as if he wanted to murder her, though she had no idea why she should provoke such a reaction. All she felt was the rush of relief that he had not betrayed her secret.

With a curt nod, Corbeil spun on his heel and walked away. Watching from the card tables, the old women lowered their heads and conferred behind their fans.

'There is history there, you mark my words.'

'Who knows what may have happened in India?'

'You do not think there could have been a *liaison*?'

'It cannot have been a happy affair. Did you see the look he gave her?'

'It is because she is half English. General Corbeil hates the English to the very depths of his heart.'

They all concluded that must be the reason. Only the old marquise disagreed. She knew more of men than anyone else in the room. Over the course of her life she had studied them, probed them and amassed a considerable collection. She understood their ways and their motives. To her eye, it was not hatred that animated Corbeil, but something quite the opposite.

She kept her thoughts to herself.

• • •

After the marquise's ball, Constance received more invitations than she had hours in her days. Lunches, dinners, walks, picnics, races: there was no occasion at which she was not welcome. She sat in private boxes at the Comédie Française and the Opéra. She was taken for rides in the Bois de Boulogne. She visited grand townhouses, and vast châteaux in the country. All her hosts commented on her impeccable manners, her charming conversation and her vivacious company.

It was true that not everyone finished with so favourable an opinion. A wealthy merchant from Poitiers declared she had a heart of stone. The son of the Comte d'Artois spent three days weeping in his bedroom when she returned his letters. There was a minor scandal when, at a château near Rheims, her hostess's husband was found in Constance's bedroom at three o'clock in the morning in a state of undress. He claimed he had been sleepwalking. The invitations Constance received redoubled.

The Courtney family had always had a genius for trade. Constance applied this talent to her own chosen field. She was a speculator in men, and her adventures were – in their way – every bit as successful as those of her privateer ancestors. She received many gifts, which she reinvested to considerable profit once the giver was no longer around. A pair of diamond earrings bought her a maid so she did not have to spend so many hours grooming and preparing herself. A necklace enabled her to secure better lodgings on the rue de Varenne, with a discreet landlady who allowed her to receive visitors without embarrassment. Even then, she never had enough money. Her endless round of social engagements required ever-changing costumes, and the number of dresses in her wardrobe proliferated like spring flowers. As fast as she made her profits, she had to reinvest the proceeds in the future of her enterprise.

Sometimes she lay awake, naked under the moonlight, after her lover had left. In those small hours, she wondered how long this could last. But then she would remember the thrill when a man caught her gaze, the comforting power she felt as she allowed him to kiss her hand. The wretch who had been locked in the Black Hole was dead. Here, in this new land, she was mistress of her own destiny.

And there were still other, richer, worlds for her to conquer.

. . .

It seemed half of Paris society wanted to make her acquaintance. But Constance had few friends, and almost none she could confide in. The exception was a much older woman, the Marquise de Sologne, who had sought her out after her introduction to society at the ball. She had fine, angular features that hinted at the beauty she had once been. She was the only woman with whom Constance did not feel in competition. She could be honest with the marquise. The older woman was so astute, it was impossible to deceive her.

They were walking down the Grande Allée of the Jardin des Tuileries one afternoon when the marquise asked suddenly, 'How long do you think you can keep up your little game?'

Constance smiled. She had spent hours in front of a mirror practising her best smile. Sometimes she would even prick herself with a needle, forcing herself to keep smiling through the pain. 'I'm sure I don't know what you mean.'

'I am sure you do,' said the marquise. 'You are climbing a ladder, my dear, and the higher you go, the more it threatens to topple you. The only question is whether you will stop before you fall.'

Constance continued to smile – but, inside, she was in turmoil. She knew how precarious her position was. She had lived in Paris for almost a year with no income. Her admirers' gifts had been useful, but life was expensive and she always needed more funds. She had pushed her credit to breaking point. That morning, her landlady had given her one week to pay what she owed or leave.

The marquise fixed her with shrewd eyes. 'When will you stop? When you have snared a count? A duke? When you are presented at Versailles? When the King of France himself takes you into his bed – will that be enough?'

Constance's smile faltered. She looked around, terrified that someone might have heard. 'I need security. I want to be safe.'

'And you think one more rung on your ladder will achieve it?' The marquise laughed. 'I know the temptation, when the game is running high and one more card can make the difference between fortune and poverty. But that is the way to bankruptcy.'

'Do you doubt my skill at this game?'

'For a time, you had Paris at your feet because you were a beautiful novelty. But beauty fades, and novelty wears off. I have not seen you at the Opéra this past fortnight.'

'I have been feeling under the weather.'

'You are so charming when you lie. The truth is, you have not been invited. Your star is waning – I tell you this as a friend. The whiff of scandal already follows you. I have done what I can to dismiss the rumours, but people will talk. I am sure you can imagine what they are saying. A little notoriety is no bad thing, but one day you will step too far. You have no family and no estate to support you. You have a long way to fall.'

They reached a corner, where three brazenly dressed prostitutes were laughing together. Constance was still smiling, but her eyes were moist with tears she would not let go. She felt naked, as exposed as she had been on the nawab's bed. 'Why are you telling me this?'

'Because I am your friend. And I admire your bravery.'

That much was true. It was also true that she had wagered a hundred livres with one of her friends that Constance would find a husband before she was disgraced, but she did not mention that. The poor girl was under enough pressure.

They walked on, the gravel crunching beneath their feet. Constance knew the marquise was right. But it was not only the danger to her reputation she feared. If she married – if she called time on the game and stepped away from the table – what then? A tedious life as a respectable matron, closeted in a château in the country where she could deliver heirs for some minor noble? Was this what she had escaped the Black Hole and the nawab's attempted rape for?

'What about him?' she said suddenly. A man was approaching down the path, dressed in the splendid uniform of the hussars. A colonel's epaulettes gleamed on his shoulder.

The marquise shuddered. 'Stay away! That man is more dangerous than a nest of vipers.'

But he had seen them. He veered towards them and swept off his hat in such a theatrical manner that Constance could not help giggling.

'Madame,' he greeted the marquise.

'Monsieur de Mauvières,' she answered coolly.

He turned his gaze on Constance and she felt emotions stir. He was much older than her, in his forties, but it suited him. The little lines that creased the corners of his eyes gave him a knowing look, while a scar on his cheek made it seem that his mouth was drawn into a permanent sardonic grin.

'Have you raided a convent again to find this vision of beauty?' he asked the marquise. 'How is it I have never seen her before?'

'I understood raiding convents was your speciality,' the marquise returned. 'This is Constance de Courtenay, a respectable widow. She has been in Paris this past year.'

Mauvières took Constance's hands between his and fixed his stare on her. It was a long time since she had blushed, but a tinge of pink rose to her cheeks at the intensity of his attention. 'So this is the famous Constance de Courtenay,' he breathed. 'Even in the front lines of the war with Prussia, your name is a byword for charm and accomplishment.'

Constance could feel the marquise radiating disapproval. But Mauvières had an energy that was irresistible. 'Have you been in the war?'

'I was at Hamelin. But beauty should not speak of such ugly matters. Now I am in Paris, I insist on only joy and pleasure. In fact, I have tickets for the Opéra on Friday. Perhaps you would do me the honour of attending with me.'

The look that accompanied his invitation was so intense that Constance almost said yes. A dig in the ribs from the marquise's elbow said otherwise.

'Alas, I cannot . . .'

His face fell. 'Perhaps there will be another occasion.'

'I should like that.'

'Until then – *au revoir*.' He doffed his hat again and kissed her hand. Constance followed him with a lingering look as he strode jauntily away.

'He seemed very pleasant,' she murmured. 'I cannot understand why you called him "dangerous".'

'That man has many faces, and he calculates which to show with a cunning you cannot fathom,' said the marquise, darkly. 'Stay away from him, if you value your future.'

But when Friday evening came, Constance was at the Hôtel de Bourgogne, wearing her most daring dress. She had begged the ticket from a friend whose mother was ill and unable to go – Constance could not afford to buy one for herself. She had one more night before she would be evicted from her home.

'That man over there is paying you a great deal of attention,' said her friend, pointing to a box on the far side of the theatre while the orchestra tuned up.

Constance pretended not to notice. 'I am sure he is looking at you, my dear Sophie.'

'Do you think so?' Sophie surreptitiously adjusted the bodice of her dress. 'Do you know who he is?'

'Should I?'

'That is Colonel de Mauvières. They say he is worth fifty thousand a year, but Maman has forbidden me to speak to him. He has a wicked reputation.'

'Your mother is very wise,' Constance said. But after the performance, when Sophie had gone to powder her face, she heard a familiar voice behind her in the salon.

'So you have come, after all.'

The press in the salon was tight. The air was thick with wig powder and candle wax. Mauvières leaned in close, his face inches from hers. Again, Constance felt herself flush. She told herself it was the heat.

'I had hoped the opera would be about India,' said Constance. 'I so looked forward to seeing what Paris would make of the country where I grew up.'

The opera was *Les Indes galantes* – 'the seductive Indies' – by the ageing composer Rameau. In fact, the opera turned out to be about the Indians of North America, a subject in which Constance had little interest.

'Alas, America is all the fashion now,' said Mauvières. 'Soon everyone will be wearing bearskins and painting their faces. The king is assembling a great army to invade the British colonies there and take possession once and for all. I myself have been granted a command.'

'And will you seduce a poor Indian princess, and make her choose between you and her native lover, like the opera?' Constance's eyes sparkled.

Mauvières pretended to consider it. 'Perhaps. I hear that the Indian women dress with a scandalous lack of modesty and are liberal with their favours.' He ran his eyes over the neck of Constance's dress. 'Happily, you Parisian women are models of propriety and virtue. Give me a *femme galante* over an *Inde galante* any day.'

It was a pun – and more than a little risqué. A *femme galante* was a prostitute.

The theatregoers were starting to disperse as their carriages were called. Mauvières moved so close she felt his breath warming her neck. His hand rested lightly against her back. 'Come to my house tonight. I will send my coachman. No one will see.'

Before Constance could reply, he pirouetted away with feline grace and disappeared into the crowd.

• • •

Sophie had invited Constance for supper afterwards, but Constance claimed she was feeling a little faint and cried off. She returned to her apartments on the rue de Varenne and sat by the window, watching rain patter on the damp streets. She waited so long, she convinced herself he would not come. But still she sat there.

It was nearly midnight when she heard the rattle of wheels on the slick cobbles. She flitted from the house to the carriage door so fast she was sure she could not have been seen. The coachman cracked the whip. The carriage pulled away.

He drove quickly. Paris after midnight was not a safe place, particularly once they'd left the protection of the city walls. Constance knew from the bloodcurdling stories she'd heard that highwaymen and brigands lurked in dark places. They drove on through the Bois de Vincennes. All she saw in the light of the carriage lamps was tight clusters of branches, sometimes so close they brushed the doors of the coach, like fur. She wrapped her shawl closer around her bare shoulders.

At last the bumpy road gave way to a firm drive. The coach pulled up outside a huge château. She glimpsed massive old stones and stern towers, before a liveried servant led her inside.

Most of the house was dark, but a large fire burned in the salon. The servant brought her a glass of spiced wine and withdrew. She stood beside the fire, warming herself.

'You came.'

Mauvières's voice was so unexpected in the mournful house it made Constance jump. Wine spilled over her fingers. He stood in the doorway with a bottle in his hand. He wore no coat or cravat, and his shirt was unbuttoned to his navel.

He advanced towards her. The flames threw long shadows behind him, while hunting trophies watched from the wall. Constance felt a flicker of fear.

He took her hand and licked the wine off her fingers. His teeth grazed her flesh. She felt disoriented. She was no stranger to seduction – but always on her own terms. It frightened her to have lost control so quickly. 'The Marquise de Sologne tells me you are a wicked and dangerous man,' she murmured.

Mauvières threw back his head in mock horror. 'In her youth, the marquise was a noted coquette. Once, she misread my attitude – which was only good manners – and threw herself at me. I was a model of discretion, but word got out. I fear she has never forgiven me for the embarrassment.'

He lowered his voice. 'I can tell you, I would rather face Prussian cavalry than have to fend off that woman again. Her bosoms alone are like siege guns. Pity the man she trains them on. '

They both laughed. Mauvières refilled her glass and took a swig from the bottle.

Constance was uneasy. She wanted to step away, to reassert control, but Mauvières had a magnetism that would not let her move. It reminded her of Gerard Courtney, a charming confidence so sure you could not resist it.

With an effort, she turned to the picture over the mantelpiece. It showed a dark castle surrounded by storm clouds. 'This is very pretty. Do—?'

'I did not bring you here to discuss art.' Without warning, Mauvières pushed her forward. She dropped her glass and it smashed on the hearthstones. His hand reached around, squeezing her breast so hard she cried out.

'Monsieur!'

The full weight of his body pressed her against the wall. He bent over her neck, kissing and biting. He pulled her hair loose – not gently – and wrapped her long tresses around his fingers. 'You like that?'

Constance did not know what to think. Among all the men she had slept with in Paris, she had never encountered anyone like him. He overwhelmed her, an animal urgency that she could not resist.

She had to regain control. She had to use her strength, touch him in particular places and whisper in his ear all the things she could do to him, as she had with so many men before. To fill his head with promises until he would do anything for her.

Mauvières backed away a little to unbutton his breeches. Constance turned. She reached out to touch him, but he was not interested. He caught her wrists and held them with one hand, while the other hand tore open the front of her dress and tugged it down to her waist so that the sleeves pinned her arms by her sides.

This was all wrong. Her body was her power, the one weapon she could wield over men. Mauvières had taken it from her and left her helpless. She wanted to scream.

And yet she did not resist. After the arch fops and dainty aristocrats she was used to, Mauvières's passion was like an ocean wave that carried her along in its force. A part of her was frightened by it, but another part longed to succumb, to silence the voice in her mind that was always calculating in the bedroom, counting the profit and loss of every kiss, and simply surrender to the force of his desire.

He spun her around against the wall. 'You want this?'

She told herself it was only for one night. She told herself that once he had satisfied his desire, he would become more reasonable. She would let him have his way, and in the morning she would tame him, just as she had tamed the others.

'Yes,' she whispered.

He lifted the skirts of her dress. His hands grasped her buttocks and spread them apart. He entered her roughly from behind, thrusting deep and hard. Experienced as she was, Constance winced with the pain.

There was violence in him. Every thrust slammed her against the wall, as if he wanted to obliterate her. He had the stamina of a bull. Again and again he came into her, until she hardly felt it any more.

With a final thrust that almost knocked her unconscious, Mauvières emptied himself into her. He slumped over her for a moment, his head lolling on her shoulder, breathing hard. The smell of sour wine enveloped her.

He pulled away. Constance shuddered and sank to the floor. Mauvières buttoned his clothes and rang a bell. A servant arrived and cleared away the broken glass, sweeping up around Constance as if she wasn't there. Constance stared at the wall, clutching her torn dress, and waited for the servant to go.

Mauvières helped Constance to her feet – surprisingly gently – and led her to a chaise longue. The footman had left two fresh goblets of wine. Mauvières handed her one. Constance drained it in a single gulp. It calmed her nerves, though it could not numb the burning between her legs.

'Did you enjoy that?' Mauvières asked.

Constance did not answer. She hurt too much to know what to think.

Mauvières misread her silence. 'Do not play the ravished ingénue with me. You may be blushing, but you are very far from a virgin. If you stammer and cry after a little fun, I may not invite you back.'

Constance rose. It hurt to walk, but she managed to reach the bottle of wine Mauvières had left on the mantelpiece. She uncorked it, splashed a full measure into her empty glass, and drank it down. Tomorrow, she promised herself. Tomorrow she would tame him. 'I would like to come again.'

Mauvières smiled. 'Good. But no one must hear of our little arrangement. It will be our secret.'

'Of course.'

The coachman brought her back to the house on the rue de Varenne before dawn. Constance drew the curtains and went to bed, but she could not sleep. Memories of the night crowded her mind. A thousand emotions she could not untangle. Mauvières's touch was like a burning iron, so intense she could not tell if it was hot or cold. Certainly, he had been brutal with her. But perhaps that was only proof of his passion.

She refused to admit there was a man she could not bend to her will. She wanted to see him again, if only to prove her power.

At last, her memories lapsed into dreams – but it seemed she had barely been asleep when a banging at the door woke her. She waited for the maid to answer, until she remembered she had dismissed her.

With a lurch of horror, she realised this was the day she had to vacate her apartment. In the shocks of the night before, she had forgotten why she needed Mauvières in the first place. Now she had nothing.

The knocking had not stopped. She wrapped herself in a gown and opened the door. As she had feared, her landlady was waiting, a note in her hand. Before she could speak, Constance began, 'I am sorry, madame. But, please, give me just one more week. My prospects are improving. I am certain I can find the money I owe you soon.'

The landlady looked at her in astonishment. 'But that is what I came to tell you. Your debts have been cleared and your rent is paid for the next six months. A coachman brought the money this morning.'

Fear turned to wonder on Constance's face. A widow herself, the landlady pitied the young woman. She was a good tenant, and she had not wanted to be rid of her. 'It seems your prospects have already improved, madame. You have a kind friend.'

• • •

Constance congratulated herself. She had survived again. When disaster and ruin had loomed, she had found a way out. She lacked for nothing. Mauvières showered her with gifts: new clothes, books, seats at the theatre, though never jewels or anything she could convert into money of her own. It did not matter. She was welcome in all the great houses again, a regular guest at lunches and soirées. But she was always at home before midnight, sitting by the window and listening for the sound of the coach.

She saw Mauvières often. In public, he was as charming as ever: handsome, vivacious, always the centre of attention. He had a sharp and subtle wit, ever ready with a quip or a riposte. He was merciless in ridiculing the pretensions of his companions, though in such oblique ways that they frequently found themselves laughing along with the joke. Only later, if at all, did they realise the vicious edge in his humour.

But in the bedroom, he was a different man. Constance had come of age in India and refined her skills in Paris. She had thought she had nothing to learn about how to pleasure a man. But none of it worked on Mauvières. At first, she thought it was her fault, and she tried every trick and innovation she had ever heard of to please him. He remained unimpressed: indeed, her attentions only seemed to make him angrier. Eventually, she realised he did not care what she did. He would not be tamed. He wanted to dominate her, to debase her. All he demanded of her was submission.

They did not reveal their affair. Mauvières said it was for her own good. 'Your reputation would be ruined, my dear, if people found out. It would be the end of us.' In company, he paid her little attention. Sometimes he could be deliberately cruel. 'Only to throw them off the scent,' he would tell her afterwards. 'Those infernal gossips are like bloodhounds. One sniff of weakness, and they will tear you to pieces.'

Constance was not so sure. She noticed the way people looked at her. She hardly saw her old friends any more, and she wondered if they were avoiding her. Even the marquise rarely replied to her letters. What if they were all laughing at her? Was she another of Mauvières's victims who had not yet realised that the joke was on her?

But what could she do?

• • •

The first time he hit her was in the bedroom. He had always liked rough coupling, and she had taken to wearing long-sleeved, high-necked dresses to hide the bites and scratches left by their lovemaking. So when he hit her in the face, she assumed he had got carried away. It left her with a bruise around her mouth and she could not go out for a week. She pretended she was ill.

The second time, there was no doubting his intention. They were in his dining room taking breakfast – she was less fastidious about returning home now – when he said casually, 'Who was that man you were speaking to on the Pont Neuf yesterday afternoon?'

Constance looked surprised. 'Which man?'

'In the blue striped coat.'

'That was the Chevalier de Montfort.'

'You were very familiar with him. At one point, I saw you laughing quite uncontrollably.'

'He had told a joke. I was being polite.'

'I saw you touch his arm.'

'Perhaps.' She frowned. 'It can only have been for a moment. I'm surprised you noticed. You barely paid me any attention.'

His chair fell back with a crash as he sprang out of it. In two strides, he was standing over her.

'I see everything,' he hissed. 'Do you think you can flirt and simper without me knowing? Do you think you can make a mockery of me?'

'I only—'

He hit her so hard the blow knocked her out of her chair. She fell to the floor, landing on her arm with such force she thought she must have broken it. Mauvières came around and kicked her in the ribs. She screamed and curled into a ball, waiting for the next blow.

It didn't come. Mauvières stood over her, breathing hard, his body twitching with the effort of self-control. That was the most frightening thing of all. He wanted to hit her again.

'Go to your room,' he ordered. His voice shook with the effort. 'I was going to take you hunting today, but you have ruined my plans. If I cannot trust you in company, you will stay here until you learn better manners.'

She fled to her room. She heard the key turn in the lock from outside.

A week later, a chest appeared in her room in the mansion with all of her belongings from her apartments. 'There was no point in paying your rent when you were never there,' Mauvières explained carelessly. 'This is your home now.'

• • •

She rarely left the house. One day, the marquise came to see her. She arrived unannounced, while

Mauvières was in town: otherwise, she would certainly have been turned away. The servants tried to deter her. It was only when Constance heard her voice in the hall, and came to see, that the servants gave up pretending she was not at home.

Constance and the marquise went for a walk in the garden. It had been raining, and the overgrown foliage dripped on the unkempt paths.

'How did you know to find me here?' Constance asked.

The marquise eyed her with something close to contempt. 'All Paris knows you are Colonel de Mauvières's mistress.'

Constance flinched at the word. 'No one has said anything to me.'

'Of course not. They play along with the charade because it amuses them to see you so oblivious, so eager to pretend.'

'But you must help me, madame. He keeps me a virtual prisoner. He beats me.' She pulled up the sleeve of her dress, revealing the livid bruise where Mauvières had almost broken her arm. 'I fear one day he will kill me.'

The marquise gave a chill laugh. 'He will not kill you. He has a crueller fate in mind. When he is bored with you, he will find the most public and humiliating way to expose your affair. You will be finished.'

'Why would he do that?'

The marquise shrugged. 'Does cruelty need a reason? I told you he was dangerous. You should have taken my advice.' She did not add that it had cost her a hundred livres in a lost wager, which she had already paid.

'What can I do?'

'We are women, my dear. The weaker sex. A man may make a hundred conquests without rebuke, but if we drop our guard just once we are finished.'

She saw the despair in Constance's eyes, but she had seen young women ruined before, and doubtless she would see it again. She could not pity Constance any more than she pitied the opponent who had lost her fortune at the card table. It was a rule of all games that somebody had to lose.

They walked on in silence.

'You must go,' Constance said at last. 'If he returns and finds you here, he will be very cross with me.'

Her voice was so empty, so filled with fear and desolation, that even the marquise felt her heart slip a little. She tried to find some crumb of comfort to offer the girl. 'The only way to defeat a man is with another man,' she said. And, because she could not help herself, she continued, 'But I do not think you will find one.'

Constance was terrified that the servants would tell their master about the marquise's visit. She knew he would beat her if he found out. But the servants knew he would punish them too, for letting the guest in, so they said nothing.

When Mauvières returned that evening, he was in a playful mood. He had brought a present for Constance. She unwrapped it in her bedroom.

It was a dress. Scarlet, with the bodice cut so low it might as well not have been there. She caught her breath.

'Try it on,' Mauvières said, lounging on the bed.

She stripped to her stays, feeling his eyes raking over her. She tried not to look at the mess of bruises and cuts that the mirror reflected back at her. It took three maids to pinch, prod and squeeze her into the dress.

When she glimpsed herself in the mirror, she almost burst into tears. The effect was stunning, the message unmistakable. Even the prostitutes in the back alleys around the Opéra would have blanched at such a dress. She looked a perfect Jezebel.

'Don't you like it?' His tone was sharp and dangerous.

'It is the most beautiful dress I have ever worn,' Constance said, with a shudder. 'But why—?'

'There is to be a ball next week at the Palais Royal. All society will be there. You will accompany me. I wish you to wear this dress.'

Words the marquise had said echoed in her mind, stony and final. *When he is bored with you, he will find the most public and humiliating way to expose your affair.* To arrive at the ball with a man who was not her husband, dressed as a shameful harlot: Paris would speak of nothing else for months. Constance would be cut off, treated like the whore she had become.

Mauvières saw her despair and smiled. 'Do you have another engagement?'

'Of course not.' She had become better at lying and smiling those past few months, desperate to avoid giving him any excuse to hit her.

'Good. Now turn round.'

• • •

The ballroom of the Palais Royal was smoky from the thousands of candles. Their flames shone on a glittering array of magnificence: gold braid, gold thread, gold buttons and gold medals. If the war for the world could have been decided with brilliance in the ballrooms of Europe, France would have won already.

Constance and Mauvières arrived late. He wanted everyone to be there to witness her presentation, and Constance had obliged by taking an age with her *toilette*. She had grown so irritable with her maids that they were glad to be sent away from her boudoir. Mauvières was waiting for her in the coach when she came down. It was not a cold night, but she wore a long cloak that reached to her ankles, giving no hint of what was beneath.

In the entrance hall of the ballroom, Mauvières threw his hat and coat to a footman. He had been drinking all afternoon and was in an ebullient mood. 'Will you not remove your cloak, my dear?'

'I am not ready,' she answered. 'I will wait until we are in the ballroom.'

She skipped through, before she had been announced. The air inside was hot and close from so many bodies and candles. She could feel every eye in the room turning to her. The crowd parted to let her through.

Mauvières trailed behind her. When she reached the middle of the room, under the great chandelier, he said loudly, 'You look warm, my dear. Let me take your cloak.'

Constance turned. She forced her most charming smile that she had practised in front of the mirror and tried to calm the shaking in her bones. There would be no way back after this. 'Of course.'

Her trembling hands fumbled with the buttons. Mauvières tried to hide his impatience. From above, tiny drops of wax dripped from the chandelier like snow.

She shrugged off the cloak and let it drop to the floor.

Mauvières stared at Constance with undisguised fury. 'What's this?' he spluttered.

She gave a little twirl, so that the skirts flared around her. 'Do you like it?'

She was not wearing the red harlot's dress he had given her. It was a different gown, long-sleeved and high-necked to hide the bruises he had inflicted. A patch of lace over the bodice was the only decoration. Constance had sewn it herself, late at night when Mauvières and the servants had gone to bed.

Every inch of fabric – the cloth, the lace, the buttons and the chemise beneath – was pure, virginal white.

Constance curtsied to Mauvières. 'Would you care to dance, monsieur?'

For a brief moment, she hoped he might drop dead of a seizure. His face had gone purple with rage, and his neck throbbed against the collar of his shirt. His hands balled into fists, shaking at his sides. She knew he wanted to hit her. She smiled, encouraging him. Let everyone see him for the brute he was.

But Mauvières was no fool. He would not strike a woman with the cream of Paris society watching.

Mastering his anger, he leaned in to her and whispered in her ear, 'You will pay for this.'

He turned on his heel and left the room. Titters and murmurs followed him out. No one watching understood what had happened, but gossip would not be slow to fill the void.

A footman gathered the fallen cloak from the floor. The orchestra started playing again. Ignoring the stares, Constance made her way to the edge of the hall. She felt empty. She had gambled everything on making Mauvières hit her and failed.

If she went back to his château, he would kill her. But where else could she go?

She couldn't dance. It had taken so much powder to make her battered face presentable, a drop of perspiration would ruin the effect. She had so little dignity left, she had to hoard every last scrap.

'You do not dance, madame?'

She turned to the man who had spoken. It was General Corbeil. He wore a splendid uniform, covered with medals, yet he stood alone and awkward. The overall effect would have been rather sad – if she'd had room in her heart for pity.

'Constance de Courtenay,' she introduced herself. She wondered why he had sought her out. Was fate taunting her by bringing all her enemies to one place? 'We met once before, at the Marquise de Sologne's ball.'

'I know who you are.' There was a strange intensity in his voice, so different from the hollow charm that the rest of the *beau monde* affected. Constance could not remember the last time she had heard someone speak with so little artifice. 'And we have met twice before, if memory serves. At the ball . . . and in Calcutta.'

Constance eyed him warily. 'I did not think you would remember.'

'It is not easily forgotten.'

That was true: she had been face down, naked and tied to the nawab's bed. Yet Corbeil did not give the impression of a man bent on raking over scandals. Though it was hard to be sure in the dim candlelight, he seemed to be blushing.

An idea grew in Constance's mind. 'I never had a chance to thank you,' she murmured.

'It was nothing,' he said brusquely. 'I could not let the nawab give orders to a Frenchman.'

'You were very gallant,' she insisted.

Corbeil frowned. He might be a general of France, but there was an awkwardness about him. She feared he might retreat from sheer embarrassment.

She took his arm. He flinched, but she did not let go. She steered him into a corner.

'The man I am with is a monster,' she said urgently. 'He keeps me a prisoner in his château and beats me like a dog. You saved me once. Please can you save me again?'

Corbeil stared at her. A seemingly bloodless man, she could see him writhing with discomfort. 'But what is this to do with me?'

'He is one of your officers – Colonel de Mauvières.'

Corbeil's cold face registered no surprise. 'I have heard rumours of his tastes. But he is one of my finest commanders. If all my officers were saints, I would never win a battle.'

Constance sensed her hopes fading. She took Corbeil's hands between hers and looked imploringly into his eyes. 'He is a brute.'

'The king has just asked me to appoint him to my staff for the American campaign.'

The news that Mauvières was leaving Paris should have been a relief to Constance. But it was too little, too late. She had defied his wishes, and he would make her pay.

She reached up and unbuttoned the high collar of her dress, turning her back to the room so that no one else could see. Corbeil tried to look away but she would not let him. She pulled the fabric apart, revealing pale skin and the tops of her breasts.

'Look at me, General. This is what Colonel de Mauvières has done.'

A livid bruise spread over her collarbone. She tugged down the top of her stays to reveal another red welt in the flawless skin of her breast. Corbeil stared, rapt.

'Please, monsieur. If you could help me in this matter, I would do anything to repay you.'

• • •

Mauvières arrived at the army's headquarters in a foul temper, still hung-over from the night before. He had stayed in town, so he had not had the opportunity to punish Constance. He still could not believe that the little whore had defied him. The pent-up fury was like a black beast eating away at his heart.

He was kept waiting for more than an hour, which did not improve his mood. He sat in an anteroom, imagining what he would do to Constance when he found her, until he was eventually summoned.

Major General Corbeil sat behind a broad desk, beneath a life-size portrait of King Louis XV. There was no chair for Mauvières: he had to stand.

'You have forgotten to salute,' Corbeil observed.

Mauvières flushed. 'I expected an interview with the secretary of state for war.'

'He is indisposed.'

Corbeil looked through his papers, ignoring Mauvières. The colonel's patience frayed. Eventually he blurted out, 'Why did you summon me?'

Corbeil pursed his lips in disapproval. 'I have orders for you to go overseas.'

Mauvières did not try to hide his exasperation. The general might outrank him, but he was from a minor provincial family of no reputation. In breeding, fortune and reputation – everything that mattered – Mauvières was infinitely superior.

'I fear you are behind the times, monsieur,' he said condescendingly. 'My regiment is already prepared to embark for Québec.'

Corbeil did not take offence at his tone. His thin mouth tightened into a smile. 'Those were your old orders, monsieur. They have been superseded.'

Mauvières didn't grasp his meaning. He took a step forward, looming over Corbeil. 'The king himself wishes me to go to Canada.'

Corbeil looked at his papers, unwilling to meet the colonel's eye. *Good*, thought Mauvières. That would teach this bourgeois nobody to have ideas above his station.

When Corbeil looked up, there was neither fear nor humility in his bearing. His grey eyes were steel as he handed Mauvières a paper. 'These are your new orders. The king signed them this morning.'

The blood drained from Mauvières's face as he read the paper. His skin went grey. He stared at the heavy wax of the royal seal attached to the orders.

'What is this?' he stammered.

'What it says. You have been posted to the West Indies.'

Mauvières stared at him in horror. The West Indies were tantamount to a death sentence: fever islands where a man might be lucky to live six months. 'But . . . why?'

'The king has need of your talents in the territory. There are runaway slaves who need to be caught, and smugglers to be brought to justice. And I hear the climate is delightful.'

'There has been some mistake. I must speak to the king in person.'

'I fear there is no time. You must ride for Brest tonight. Your ship sails on Friday.'

Corbeil stood to indicate the interview had ended. Mauvières did not move. Only when Corbeil rang a bell, and an aide appeared, did the colonel consent to be led out.

'*Bon chance*,' Corbeil called after him. 'And *adieu*. I do not think we will see each other again.'

Mauvières returned to his château in a fury. Confusion and horror swirled in his mind, but one thought trumped them all. *He would kill the bitch*.

He did not know how or why, but he was certain she was behind this calamity. She was duplicitous. He would make her pay. He would do such things to her that exile in the fever islands would seem tame by comparison.

He threw open the front door. The servants, familiar with his moods, scattered. Mauvières went up the stairs to Constance's bedroom, kicking open the door.

The room was empty. All her possessions had gone.

It was as if she had never been there.

Lieutenant Trent did not speak as he led Theo up the trail. The shock of finding a white man so indistinguishable from the natives had silenced him. He moved quickly – almost as fast as an Abenaki.

They had not gone far when Theo heard footsteps running behind them. The lieutenant drew his pistol, but Theo put his hand across the barrel. He could tell the difference between the hoofbeats of a doe and a buck so he was quite sure he could recognise *these* footprints.

It was Moses. The wound in his leg was healing well, but he still walked with a limp.

'Did I leave something behind?' Theo asked.

The Abenaki looked determined and pointed to himself. 'I will come with you.'

Theo shook his head. 'You should stay with the tribe.'

'No.'

'If you come with me, you may have to fight against your brothers.'

'If I stay, I will have to fight against *you*.' His face grew serious. 'Please, Siumo. I owe you a debt for Mgeso and your child. I should have stopped Malsum taking her. If I do not pay it, the ancestors will be angry with me.'

'You did all you could,' Theo assured him.

'Soon the tribe will go to war alongside the Blaumonak – the French. Bichot will be there.' He spat on the ground. 'I will not fight alongside such a man.'

Theo could have argued longer, but he knew it would be futile. Moses would not relent. And Theo was glad. Once again, he was leaving behind a life that had been everything to him. This time, at least, he had a friend.

'I am honoured to have you with me.'

Lieutenant Trent raised his voice. Theo and Moses had been speaking in Abenaki, and he had not understood a word. 'What does the Indian want?'

'He is coming with us,' Theo told him.

'I had no orders to bring an Indian.'

'When we reach your camp, they will think you brought two.'

• • •

It did not take long to reach the rangers' camp. Theo was surprised that they had dared come so far onto Abenaki land. But everything about these soldiers seemed different from the band of raw recruits he had joined in Bethel. The men – even the youngest of them – had the seasoned look of soldiers who knew their business. Instead of red coats, their uniform was a brown shirt dyed to the colour of dried leaves, with a short green hunter's coat and tanned buckskin breeches. They were well armed.

A tall man in a dark green greatcoat strode to meet the new arrivals. He had a green cockade in his tricorn hat, and a handkerchief tied loosely around his neck. Theo noted the way his men looked at him. Though he wore no badge of rank, it was obvious he was their captain.

He studied Theo and Moses, and turned to the lieutenant who'd brought them. 'I told you to fetch me an Englishman.' He spoke with a laconic drawl, confident and easy.

Theo answered before the lieutenant could do so. 'He did. My name is Theo Courtney.'

'Where are you from?'

A line from Theo's favourite author came into his head. 'Fate jumbled me together, God knows how; Whate'er I was, I'm true-born English now.'

The captain studied him. 'An Englishman who dresses like an Abenaki and can quote Daniel Defoe, no less. What a curiosity you have turned up, Lieutenant.' He looked at Moses. 'Does this one recite Chaucer?'

'He is an Abenaki,' said Theo. 'He is my brother.'

The captain accepted it without comment. 'No doubt it makes quite a tale.'

'How did you know to come and look for me?' Theo asked.

'We captured a French trapper.'

Theo stiffened. 'Bichot?'

The captain gave him another keen look. 'I guess by your tone you have met that gentleman. No – not Bichot. It would take the devil's own luck to capture that monster. But we caught one of his gang. While we were interrogating him, he let slip that there was an Englishman living with the Abenaki. I sent Trent to investigate, in case it was one of our own. It has happened before that we lost men we thought dead, only to find years later that the Indians had adopted them.'

'I am glad you found me.'

'Where were you bound when the Indians captured you?' said the captain.

'To Albany. I had just enlisted.'

'Then we will have to delay your arrival a little longer. We have an appointment with the French near Fort Royal, and we are already late.'

He turned away. 'Wait,' Theo called. 'May I at least know who has rescued me?'

'Captain William Gilyard.' He touched his hat with an ironic bow. 'My men are His Majesty's First Independent Company of Rangers.'

'What is a ranger? Are you the regular army?'

'Indeed not. We are decidedly *irregular*. The ghosts of the forest. Men who have grown up in this country and learned how to fight here. We travel far into enemy territory and hit them where they least expect it.'

While he'd been speaking, his men had been striking their camp. By now, there was barely a trace they had ever been there. There were no pack animals or wagons: they carried their supplies in haversacks on their backs.

Gilyard looked Theo up and down. 'I trust you will not slow us.'

'I believe I will be able to keep up.'

The rangers marched in single file, with Theo and Moses close to the front. Gilyard interrogated Theo about what he had learned from the Abenaki. He was particularly interested to learn what Theo knew of Bichot.

'He set an ambush that killed seven of my rangers in April,' he muttered. 'What I would give for the chance to pay him back. How long since he left you?'

'Two days,' said Theo. The hours since Mgeso's death had been a dark blur of grief. 'Bichot also stole from me someone I loved deeply. If the time comes for you to take your revenge, I would gladly be at your side.'

Gilyard gave him a sober look. 'I admire your spirit, Mr Courtney, but General Abercromby will want to be sure of your allegiance before he lets you take up arms for England.'

Theo knew Gilyard meant no malice, but it caused a stab of pain in his heart. He had spent a year as a foreigner among the Abenaki. Now he was a foreigner to his own people.

They left Abenaki land and entered unfamiliar terrain. All the time, they had been climbing higher into the mountains – where the Indians did not go for fear of the evil spirits that lived there. It was weary work even for rangers. They often had to cut their own trails, and the steep slopes sapped the strength from their legs. Every time Theo thought he saw the top, it turned out to be a false summit that brought yet more climbing.

But on the third day they came out on a rocky crag to see the far side of the mountain. It sloped away beneath them, in the shadow of a long spur that ran west towards a blue lake gleaming in the distance.

'That is our destination,' said Gilyard.

Theo squinted. The trees ran up against the lake shore, but on one promontory the forest had been cleared. A fort stood, a splayed star, like some primeval pattern in the earth. Its walls were stone, topped with timber parapets of heavy oak. The main redoubt was an octagonal tower, three storeys high, dominating the lake. A web of trenches, bastions and ravelins surrounded the walls with an almost impossible ring of defences.

Gilyard swept his hand across the scene. 'You are looking at the axis of the whole war, and that lake is the centre point. From its southern end, a short march will bring you to the Hudson River, which flows all the way to New York. To the north, the St Francis River leads to the French strongholds of Montréal and Québec. Control the lake, and you control the rivers. Control the rivers, and you control the continent.'

Theo surveyed the scene. To the north, a ship was tacking its way up the lake. It reminded him of the East India ships beating up the Hooghly, seen from the guard towers of Calcutta. Another continent and another battlefield in the endless war between Britain and France.

'That fort – Fort Royal – is the key to the campaign. If we can pick the lock, it will open the door to an invasion of Canada,' said Gilyard.

'It looks a stout lock,' said Theo.

'That is why General Abercromby has asked us to reconnoitre it.'

It took another day and a half to descend from the mountains. Their progress slowed as they neared the lake, spreading out among the trees for fear of encountering the French or their allies. For the first time, Theo saw the forest through European eyes: unmapped and unknowable.

Yet Gilyard could read it as well as an Indian. On the second afternoon, Theo saw a light sparkling through the trees. He hurried through the undergrowth and came out on the shore of the wide lake he had seen from the mountain. The sun burnished the placid water, which stretched for miles in every direction.

But that was not the most extraordinary thing. In front of him, within musket range, was a ship under sail. This was no canoe or *bateau*, but a square-rigged sloop fit for an ocean voyage. She sat low in the water, with cannon poking from the ports in her side. The white flag of France snapped from her masthead.

Theo ducked behind some reeds and watched her stately progress. Moses crouched beside him.

'That is a mighty canoe,' the Abenaki marvelled. 'Who are the men who can build such things?'

'It is not so very big,' said Theo. 'I have sailed on ships that would dwarf that vessel, and over oceans that make this lake look like a drop in a bucket.'

He saw the incredulous look his friend was giving him. 'It is true.'

Moses laughed. 'How can you expect me to believe such tales. Siumo, when you mock me if I talk of the spirits who speak to us every day?'

Theo didn't argue. He watched the sloop glide past, around the point towards the fort. 'She is heavy laden,' Theo mused. 'She must be bringing supplies to the fort.'

Later that afternoon they came to a small cove where the sloop lay at anchor. A landing stage had been built out into the lake, protected by a wooden guardhouse. A rough track led through the forest towards the fortress, whose flagstaff was visible above the trees.

Gilyard surveyed the cove from behind a fallen log. There were pickets on the landing stage, and doubtless more in the guardhouse.

'You and your Indian friend will wait here,' he told Theo. 'I will take my men to the fort to scout it out. General Abercromby will want a full report of their strength.'

Theo nodded. He felt again the ache of not being trusted, but he knew he would have done the same in Gilyard's shoes. A scouting expedition was no time to discover a man's loyalties.

Gilyard was watching him. For once, his supreme confidence was afflicted with doubt.

'I would be considered remiss in my duty if I left two strangers – including an Indian from an enemy tribe – unsupervised while operating deep in French territory.'

Theo gave a nod. He should have expected this.

'But I do not wish to waste good rangers guarding you here, when they could be with me scouting out the French.' Gilyard hesitated. 'I do not understand your past, Mr Courtney, but I am rarely wrong about men. If you give me your word that you and the Abenaki will not try to escape, or betray us to the French, you may stay here without a guard.'

It was a generous concession and Theo was grateful. 'Thank you, sir.'

'We will be back at dawn tomorrow.' Gilyard handed Theo a pistol. 'I will give you this in case of trouble, though I do not expect you to use it.' He gave another keen-eyed stare. 'If I am wrong, you will find that it is not only the Indians who can scalp a man.'

'You may rely on my honour.'

• • •

The day passed slowly after the rangers had gone. Theo and Moses stayed hidden in a thicket with the company's packs and baggage. They listened to bird calls and practised imitating them. Theo tried to teach Moses chess, using pebbles scratched with symbols, but his heart was not in it. He could not be at ease, knowing there were Frenchmen only a few hundred yards away. The memory of what Bichot and Malsum had done to Mgeso was too raw. He burned for revenge.

At last, impatience overtook him. He jumped up.

Moses saw the intent on his face. 'You promised the captain you would not go anywhere,' he said.

'I promised not to betray him,' Theo retorted. 'And I am only going for a look.'

They crept down to a place where they could spy out the landing stage. Theo watched the sloop carefully. There was little activity on board: he guessed they would wait until the following morning to unload the cargo.

'See how the crew put on felt slippers every time they go below,' he observed to Moses.

'Why is that?'

'They are afraid of striking sparks. I will wager you a golden guinea the ship is packed to the gunwales with powder for the garrison.'

He caught Moses' eye. 'Gilyard was sent to scout out the enemy's strength. It would be useful intelligence to know what is on that ship.'

'It would,' Moses agreed. He saw the look in Theo's eyes, a blood lust he had seen many times in warriors preparing for battle. 'And we are only going to scout?'

Theo shrugged. 'Gilyard will not be back until morning.'

'If he does not find out, he cannot be angry,' said the Abenaki.

• • •

They made their preparations and took up watch. Theo had removed the jacket and shirt the rangers had given him and was wearing only a loincloth and leggings. He had squeezed blueberry juice to make war paint, and Moses had shaved the stubble from his scalp with his knife. Once again, Theo had transformed himself into an Abenaki.

He and Moses crawled forward on their bellies to the edge of the clearing around the cove. They did not make a sound. Peering through the long grass, Theo observed the harbour with the concentration of a hunter. As well as the sloop at anchor, a dozen *battoe* and canoes were drawn up on the shore or moored to the landing stage. Men came and went along the road from the fort. Every two hours, one set of sentries returned to the guardhouse and was relieved by another. Theo watched and counted, until he was confident there were no more than eight men in total.

A stone jutted into his hip. He hadn't noticed it when he lay down, but the longer he lay there the more he felt it. He gritted his teeth and tried to ignore the pain.

Towards evening, the sloop lowered one of her boats and sent it ashore. A man in a lieutenant's uniform sat in the stern: the commander, no doubt. A dozen men accompanied him. From the size of the vessel, Theo guessed there could hardly be anyone left aboard. The crew disappeared up the track, perhaps to enjoy a good evening's hospitality in the fort.

Shadows lengthened in the long summer evening. The stone digging into Theo's hip was almost unbearable. He was about to move, when the guardhouse door opened. One of the sentries came out and scanned the area.

Theo went still. He flexed his muscles one at a time, like the Abenaki did when stalking game.

Moses, lying beside him, rolled his eyes to warn him to be quiet.

The Frenchman lit a pipe and wandered across the clearing. He did not seem concerned. But he was coming closer to Theo and Moses.

Theo lifted himself up on his hands and knees to relieve the pain in his thigh. Surely the sentry would not have seen anything.

But dusk had heightened the Frenchman's hearing. He heard the rustle in the grass. He halted, staring at the place where Theo was hiding.

Theo held his breath, one hand on the pistol Gilyard had given him and the other on his knife. He prayed the guard would go back inside. The sound he had made could have been a breath of wind, or a bird or an animal. Surely the guard would not investigate.

The Frenchman unshouldered his musket and walked warily towards Theo. In the silent evening, Theo could not cock the pistol for fear of confirming his presence. And if he fired, it would bring every Frenchman in the fort down on him. There would be no chance of escape – for him, or for Gilyard's company.

The footsteps approached. He listened for the telltale sounds that would reveal he had been seen. He braced himself to leap at the man with his knife and hoped he could close the distance before the man fired.

The footsteps stopped.

'*Qui va?*' barked the guard. But not in Theo's direction. A second set of footsteps had entered the clearing away to his right.

'*Ami, ami,*' said a voice. It was Moses. Theo risked a glance. While the guard was distracted, the Abenaki had walked into the clearing as if he had nothing to hide. He smiled at the guard and raised his palms in peace.

Theo took his chance. He crawled to his left, then stood and strode out through the grass. To the astonished guard, it was as if he had appeared from thin air. He jerked his musket between Theo and Moses and shouted something to the guardhouse.

Theo's heart raced. Now was the time to find out how truly convincing he could be as an Abenaki.

A red-faced sergeant emerged from the guardhouse and lumbered up the slope to join them. He stared at the two arrivals. He saw two Abenaki Indians.

'I found them hiding in the forest,' the sentry explained.

Theo put his hands on his hips. 'No,' he said in French. 'We let you see us. If we were English, you would be dead already.'

The private looked to his sergeant for instructions. The sergeant shrugged. 'Do they know the watchword?'

'Of course not,' said Theo. 'We have just come. Our sachem sent us ahead to tell you our war band is approaching.'

The sergeant considered it. Theo could see he was not convinced.

'We march all day. Very thirsty.' Theo cupped his hands and mimed drinking. 'You have brandy?'

It was almost dark. The sloop on the lake was little more than a shadow.

'Take them to the fort,' the sergeant decided. 'They can tell their story to the commandant.'

Theo nodded, but behind his smile his mind raced. If he went inside the fort, there might be other Indians who would see through his disguise. If they did, he would never get out alive. He could not let himself be taken there.

He raised his pistol. The private's musket jerked towards him, but Theo reversed the grip to show it to the sergeant.

'I trade you for brandy,' he said. 'Worth money.'

'This is an English pistol,' said the sergeant. 'Where did you get it?'

Theo drew a finger around the top of his scalp and mimed slicing it off. 'English officer.' He made the drinking gesture again. 'Please. Very thirsty.'

Greed got the better of the sergeant. The pistol was a handsome weapon, with silver chasing and a pleasing balance. He could get a good price for it in Québec. There were not many opportunities to make a profit on this godforsaken frontier.

'If you give me your knife as well, we have a bargain.'

Theo, Moses and the private followed the sergeant to the guardhouse. Theo walked slowly, noting every detail. He knew there were eight guards. Two were on the landing stage, and one was on the roof of the guardhouse. Allowing for the sergeant and the private, that left three inside the guardhouse.

The guardhouse was built of thick logs, two storeys high. There were no windows, only narrow loopholes for muskets. The upper level was larger, overhanging the ground floor by a couple of feet to create a porch around the building. Once they were under it, they would be invisible to the guard on the roof.

The sergeant was about to open the door. The private stood to one side. Theo nodded to Moses.

The sergeant had taken Theo's knife, but not Moses'. With a single fluid motion, the Abenaki whipped it from his belt and drew it across the sergeant's neck. The sergeant tried to scream, but the air rushed out through the gash in his throat and he made no sound.

At the same moment, Theo grabbed the bayonet from the private's belt and rammed it through his eye. He dropped to the ground without a murmur.

But the sergeant was still flailing in his death throes. He broke free from Moses' grip and toppled against the door. It crashed open under his weight.

The guardhouse was a single room with an earth floor. Bunks lined the wall; a ladder led to the upper storey. In the warm yellow lamplight, three men sat around a table playing cards. They had been drinking – brandy vapours filled the room, and an empty bottle stood on the table.

The three men stared at the body of their sergeant as it collapsed through the doorway, blood pooling around it, and the two Indians behind him. They lunged for their weapons.

Alcohol slowed their reactions. By the time they moved, Theo and Moses were in the room. One man went down with a bayonet in his belly, another clutching his throat where Moses had carved it wide open.

The third was harder to dispatch. The table was between him and the door, and he had a fraction more time. He grabbed his musket from a hook on the wall and swung it around. Theo's world seemed to pause as the Frenchman's finger tightened on the trigger. He stared down the black muzzle.

But the gun was not loaded. Using it as a club, the Frenchman knocked the bayonet out of Theo's hand. Theo sprang at him and tried to wrestle away the gun. His opponent was strong and wiry. Locked together, the two men stumbled across the room, knocking over the stools and the table. Glasses smashed.

Suddenly the man's grip loosened. A drop of blood appeared on his shirt, spreading in a broad circle around the tip of Moses' knife that was protruding from between his ribs.

The noise of the fight had carried to the man on the roof. A head appeared through the hole in the ceiling that led to the upper storey. '*Qu'est-ce qui se passe?*'

Perhaps the soldier had assumed his comrades were having a drunken brawl over cards. Perhaps it had happened before. Whatever the case, he didn't have his gun ready.

Theo grabbed Gilyard's pistol that the sergeant had dropped, and fired. The explosion was deafening in the cramped room. The Frenchman toppled through the hatch and landed hard on the floor. If the bullet hadn't killed him, the fall would have broken his back. He lay with his neck askew as the sound of the shot echoed.

'That was unwise, Siumo,' said Moses. 'The other guards will have heard.'

Theo nodded. In the still night, the sound might even have carried to the fort. With luck, the garrison would think it nothing more than a musket discharged accidentally, or a soldier taking a pot shot at some game.

But Theo had learned never to trust to luck. And there were still the two men down by the landing stage. As his ears recovered from the pistol discharge, he heard urgent voices outside.

A figure appeared at the door, a young man with a wispy beard staring in horror at the carnage. Unlike the other soldiers, he was expecting trouble. He saw his companions strewn around the room, the broken furniture and two blood-smeared Indians standing over them. He followed his instincts.

He ran.

Theo swore and gave pursuit. Moses was faster. He pulled his knife from the dead man's ribs, and whipped it hard after the fleeing soldier. It struck the man between the shoulder blades. He collapsed with a cry.

There was one left. Out in the darkness Theo heard footsteps running up the track to the fort. He seized the musket from the fallen soldier. It was loaded, but the priming had spilled, and Theo wasted precious seconds adding more powder to the pan. He put the gun to his shoulder.

It was too late. The night had swallowed the fleeing guard. Theo could barely see him against the trees. Moses put his hand on the barrel.

'It will take him time to reach the fort and raise the alarm. One shot may have been an accident. If they hear another, they will come at once.'

'Then let us be quick.'

All the guards were accounted for. Theo and Moses pulled on the coats and hats that the dead Frenchmen had left and hurried down to the lake shore.

Voices drifted across the water. The sloop's crew had heard the commotion and had gathered at the rail.

There was no way Theo could approach unseen. He didn't attempt it. He fetched the lantern from the guardhouse, holding it low so he would be in silhouette. He hoped the borrowed clothes would be enough disguise.

They launched one of the smaller *battoe*s. Theo took the oars. Moses, facing him, kept his hat pulled low over his face.

'What are they doing?' Theo murmured. He pulled the oars with strong, confident strokes, but inside he was nervous. Rowing into danger, his back to the enemy, required all his courage and concentration.

'They have guns, Siumo.'

'They won't fire,' Theo said. 'That ship is a powder keg. If a piece of wadding fell between the decks, they would be blown to pieces.'

They came under the lee of the sloop. Theo, trained by the East India Company, shipped his oars with a practised flourish and brought the boat against the side with barely a sound.

The sailors above shouted questions, frightened and suspicious. 'What has happened? What were those shots?'

'English soldiers,' Theo answered, in guttural French. 'We chased them away. The sergeant sent me to make sure the ship was safe.'

As he spoke, he had already started climbing the ladder. He could feel the crew's hostile gaze on him, but he did not look up for fear of revealing himself. He kept talking. 'Your captain will be here soon to take command. Meanwhile, load your guns and—'

Shots interrupted him – a volley of musketry from somewhere on shore. Gunfire flashed among the trees like lightning. The crew looked out in alarm.

That gave Theo precious seconds. In two quick steps he reached the top of the ladder and vaulted onto the deck.

He swung an uppercut into the nearest sailor's face. As the man reeled backwards, Theo charged across to the far side of the deck, scattering buckets and coils of rope to make as much noise as possible.

The crew cornered him against the far rail. Some had muskets, which they would not dare to fire, but others carried cutlasses, and they were ready to use them.

While the crew were distracted, Moses had gained the deck. Now he let out his war cry, a bloodcurdling whoop that must have carried all the way to the fort. The sailors turned in horror.

Moses threw off the French coat he had worn. He stood on the grating in the middle of the deck in the hostile attitude of an Abenaki warrior. He held the lantern high in the air, casting ghoulish shadows over his face.

'Put down your weapons,' Theo warned, 'or he will drop that lantern into the hold.'

The crew were hard men, no strangers to violence. They had brawled and fought their way through half the world's ports. But Moses' threat left them helpless. There was nothing sailors feared so much as fire, even without the presence of a hundred tons of gunpowder. Watching Moses – naked to the waist, covered with blood and war paint – none of them doubted he was crazy enough to blow up the ship.

The Frenchmen were mariners, far from home and from the sea. None of them wanted to die in this wilderness.

They threw down their weapons. Theo found rope and bound their hands, while Moses watched them with the musket. The lamp flickered dangerously on top of the capstan.

Moses surveyed the ship they had won. 'An easy victory this time, but I wonder what the Bastaniak captain will say?'

• • •

Gilyard was furious. He had been watching the fort all day, carefully monitoring its strength. A little after dusk, they had heard a shot fired from the cove. A few minutes later, a man had come running up the track from the harbour.

Gilyard did not know what it meant, but he could guess the reason. He cursed himself for having left Courtney and the Indian alone. His company would have to fight their way back – fifty miles through the wilderness. At the very least, he could expect to lose a third of his men.

Already, the fort was alive with the sounds of soldiers being roused for battle. Gilyard whispered the order to withdraw. Like ghosts, the rangers slipped out of their hiding places and retreated through the forest. Gilyard would have preferred to detour well away from the lake, but his men had left their packs there and they could not march without supplies.

Moving at a brisk pace, they retraced their steps to the cove. As Gilyard had suspected, Theo and the Indian were gone.

There were no sounds from the guardhouse. No light, either. A sixth sense that he had learned to trust prompted him. He crawled forwards into the dark clearing, until he was close enough to see by the starlight.

There were no guards. A corpse wedged open the blockhouse door; two others lay nearby. Gilyard didn't understand what had happened, but he knew better than to reject good fortune when she presented herself.

He beckoned his men. 'Down to the lake,' he ordered. 'We'll make our escape in those *battoes*.'

'What about the sloop?' asked Lieutenant Trent. A lantern burned on her deck, revealing dark figures moving. They seemed to be loading a cannon.

At that moment, the moon came from behind a cloud. There was nowhere to hide. Gilyard and his men were lit up in the clearing, like actors on a stage. But the men on the sloop did not train their gun. Instead, one ran to the mast and started hauling on a halyard.

Three of the rangers dropped to their knees and sighted their rifles. Even in the dark, against a target bobbing in the water, Gilyard would have backed them to hit the mark.

They looked to him for the order. Gilyard considered. 'Hold your fire.'

A flag broke from the masthead, pale in the moonlight. It was the white banner of France – but it had been altered. Over the white fabric, someone had taken black tar and painted a round skull and a pair of crossed bones.

Trent stared. 'It looks like the Jolly Roger.'

Despite the tension, Gilyard couldn't suppress a grin. 'They are men after our own hearts. Get to the boats.'

Pausing only to smash holes in the thin bark canoes, the rangers loaded themselves in the *battoe* and rowed out to the sloop. They had taken barely three strokes when suddenly the cove was lit up by the light of many torches. A company of Frenchmen rushed down from the track. It did not take them long to work out what was happening. They formed a line along the shore and raised their muskets.

There was nothing Gilyard and his men could do. At that range, even the notoriously inaccurate muskets could not miss.

For a second, the lake seemed to explode in a clap of lightning. A cannonball flew over Gilyard's head and ploughed into the French line. It carved through the men, showering their companions with blood and limbs and spreading panic through the ranks. They had not expected to face cannon fire from their own ship. The line buckled.

'Pull!' Gilyard shouted. The men on the oars redoubled their strokes, making the *battoes* leap through the water. On shore, the French officers shouted orders and beat their men with the flats of their swords to get them into line. A few managed to let off a ragged volley. But the shots fell harmlessly into the water.

Some of the Frenchmen ran to the landing stage. But the *battoe* were gone, and the canoes were scuttled. They could only watch impotently as the rangers came alongside the sloop and climbed aboard.

'We will find out what manner of pirates these are,' said Gilyard, as he clambered over the side. By the lantern light, he saw a quartet of sailors bound and gagged in the fo'c'sle. Two more men were standing by the cannon, sluicing down the deck with buckets of water to drown any stray sparks. Theo and Moses had gambled their lives by firing the cannon on the deck of the gunpowder-laden ship.

Theo came over and saluted. 'Welcome aboard, sir.'

'I ordered you to remain in your place.'

'Yes, sir.'

'Nonetheless, I cannot deny you seem to have done a useful night's work.' He turned to Trent. 'Set fuses, Lieutenant. We will destroy this vessel and make our escape in the *battoes* before the French can give chase.'

He saw the expression on Theo's face. 'You disagree?'

'With respect, sir, it seems a shame to blow up a serviceable ship. I'll wager your General Abercromby would be glad of the cargo she carries.'

'And if I had wings to fly, I would be home for breakfast.' Gilyard was getting impatient. 'We are rangers, Mr Courtney, not sailors. And we are losing precious time.'

'I can sail her.'

Gilyard stared.

'I worked my passage from Calcutta to Boston. If your men can haul a rope, I fancy I can navigate this vessel to safe harbour.' He glanced at the shore, where the French had started to organise themselves. Soon they would bring up artillery or find other boats. 'But we had best be quick.'

Gilyard tried to maintain his air of command – but he could not help the roar of laughter that erupted.

The men stopped their work: they had never seen their captain so cheerful. Gilyard clapped Theo on the shoulder. 'Mr Courtney, I think you are the most remarkable man I have ever met.'

• • •

The British fort at the far end of the lake looked familiar. The plain walls and star-pointed corners were of a model that had been reproduced all over the globe. If the fir trees were replaced with palms, and the grey waters of the lake with the blue of the Indian Ocean, the building could have been any one of the trading forts that Theo had seen in India. It was the mark of empire, stamped wherever Britain planted her flag.

Theo moored the sloop under the fort's guns. The rangers disembarked in good spirits, ready to spend the prize money they had earned from capturing the ship. But a sombre mood met them on land. The taverns were empty; the surgeons' tents were full.

It did not take them long to find out why.

'General Abercromby has been routed,' Gilyard reported. 'He had eighteen thousand men, and four thousand Frenchmen drove him off with heavy casualties. The summer's campaigning has been wasted.'

The elation that had carried Theo from Fort Royal dissipated, leaving him empty and desolate. He had thought that by taking the fight to the French, he might dull the pain of Mgeso's murder. But the void opened inside him, leaving him gasping and tearful.

Gilyard saw the distress on his face, though he did not understand it. 'Where will you go?'

Theo had no answer. Every home and family he had known had been taken from him. He had no one. A memory of Abigail Claypole flitted across his mind, but she would be long since married to her farmer. No doubt she would have forgotten Theo, though perhaps she still bore the scars of the beating her father would have given her on his account. She was another woman Theo had loved and failed.

'You would make a fine ranger,' said Gilyard.

Theo accepted the compliment. 'I fear I might have problems with military discipline. I do not have a knack for obeying orders.'

'If you gave them, I hazard men would follow you. In the rangers, we prize initiative over slavish obedience. "Every man's reason and judgement must be his guide," as the Rules of Ranging have it.'

Theo considered. 'It need be for just a few months,' Gilyard urged. 'The enlistments expire with the year's end. We founded the rangers because we knew we needed a different method of fighting. We wanted to combine British discipline with the craft and tactics of the Indians. You know the Indian ways better than any white man, and you fought in the East India Company's armies at Calcutta. I do not say this lightly, but I would give my eye teeth for a hundred men such as you.'

'I thought the army was withdrawing,' said Theo.

'The *regular* army may be in retreat. The rangers will be needed more than ever. Through the autumn and over the winter, we will sabotage the French.

We will spy on their positions and capture their correspondence. We will disrupt their supplies and strike such terror into them that they will hardly dare venture out of doors.' Gilyard fixed Theo with his vivid blue eyes. 'The French have invoked their treaty with the Abenaki. The man who killed your wife and the Indian who helped him will be active in the mountains. Perchance we will run into them.'

Theo remembered his dream: Mgeso drowning in the black water as the snake coiled around her. He did not know if he would ever lay her spirit to rest, or assuage the emptiness he felt constantly, but at least he could fight to avenge her. 'It will be an honour to serve with you.'

· · ·

That autumn, the French came to believe that devils haunted the woods.

Gilyard's rangers harried their enemies everywhere they could. They took canoes and *battoes* up the lake into French territory. They burned outposts, laid ambushes, captured supplies and slaughtered livestock. They killed Frenchmen. Theo was astonished to see the rangers scalping their victims with as much bloody enthusiasm as the Abenaki.

'The army offered our Indian allies a bounty for every French scalp they brought in,' Gilyard explained. 'It did not take our men long to demand the same terms. If there is profit in a custom, men will adopt it no matter how barbarous it may seem.'

For all the savagery, Theo enjoyed those months more than any other time in his life. The soldiers, with their rough camaraderie, became his family. The danger was constant, but he thrived on it: the battle of wits with the French, the knowledge that one mistake could cost not just his life but the lives of the men he fought beside. He embraced the responsibility. Soon Gilyard commissioned him as a lieutenant.

Days in the forest had a simple clarity: kill or be killed. But at night, Theo was haunted by the demons of his past. Sometimes he dreamed that Mgeso was on a mountain top, with crows circling; more often she was submerged in the swamp, hair swimming around her face. She was trying to tell him something, but all that ever came out of her mouth was the snake.

One night, Theo woke covered with sweat and felt hands on his shoulders. It was Moses, crouching over him. The loyal Abenaki had enlisted with the rangers at the same time as Theo, and had saved his life more than once in the subsequent months.

'You cried out in your sleep,' said Moses. 'Was it Mgeso again?'

Theo nodded.

'Her ghost fire burns fierce,' said the Abenaki. 'You will never find peace until she does.'

'And how will that happen?' Theo asked, though he already knew the answer.

'You must kill the man who killed her.'

After every skirmish, Theo examined the dead to see if Bichot or Malsum was among them. He fought with a savagery that shocked even the rangers. He volunteered for the most dangerous assignments, and pressed Gilyard to go further into enemy territory.

'You cannot shoot every Frenchman in North America yourself,' Gilyard warned him, one day in the forest. 'And if you count your own life cheap, at least have a thought for your friend's.' He gestured to Moses. 'He follows you like a shadow. Beware you do not get him killed.'

Winter drew on. One morning, Theo woke to find the lake unnaturally still. When he went to wash, a thin film of ice covered the water. A bitter north wind blew in flurries of snow, bringing memories of Mgeso and the storm they had spent trapped in the hollow tree. The ice on the lake grew stronger.

Theo's mood worsened. There would be no more campaigning that year, no chance of finding Malsum and Bichot. The British army had retreated to its winter quarters in Albany and would not emerge until spring.

But one day in early December, Gilyard came to Theo with a grim smile. Theo noted the fresh gold stripe on his cuff that showed he had been promoted to major.

'Your wish has been granted,' Gilyard said. 'The general has given you an early Christmas present.'

'I thought General Abercromby had called a halt to the fighting.'

'Abercromby has been recalled to London. His successor, General Williams, is a great improvement. He intends to prosecute the war with vigour. But the French have not been idle. They have replaced their commander, too. By all reports,

General Corbeil is a talented soldier and an unyielding foe.'

Gilyard spread a map on the table in the mess tent. 'It is vital we keep abreast of their movements over the winter. Some say the French may abandon Fort Royal, others that they are reinforcing. The general has ordered us to take a scouting party north to find out.'

He lowered his voice. 'We captured a French trapper two nights ago. He revealed that Bichot is leading a company of irregulars based in Fort Royal. Among their number, he says, is a terrifying Abenaki with battle scars and a wolfskin cloak.'

'Malsum,' said Theo. His pulse quickened.

'This will be a hard scout,' Gilyard warned, 'marching through snow and ice, up against the enemy's fortress in the grip of winter. Even if the French do not kill us, I fear the weather will. I am taking only volunteers.'

Theo's eye ran over the map, noting the length of the lake and the small star at the top that marked Fort Royal. He tried to imagine crossing that great distance in winter. 'When do we set out?'

'It will take ten days to prepare our equipment. Take a week's leave – enjoy the delights of Albany – then rendezvous with me at the lake.'

• • •

Albany was smaller than Theo had expected – though still the largest settlement he had seen since landing in Boston. Some of the streets were paved, and the grander houses were built of brick, with long eaves and square gables in the Dutch style. The town stretched some two miles along the Hudson River, where small craft dodged the huge blocks of ice that bobbed in the water like floating boulders. Taverns were plentiful, though lodgings hard to find. The town was busy with English soldiers, German mercenaries, Indian scouts and volunteers from all over the colonies – as well as profiteers, speculators and whores who had attached themselves to the army. Theo was just one more piece of human jetsam washed up by the tides of war.

It was a gloomy, overcast day. A bitter wind blew down the Hudson and brought stinging hail showers that emptied the streets. The low roofs of the houses sent water streaming down Theo's collar as he sought a boarding house. In an unfamiliar town, his mind churning and head bowed to keep the hail out of his eyes, Theo lost his way. He tried to find a church spire to orient himself, but the high houses hemmed him in.

Across the road, he saw a woman in a blue shawl. She was carrying a basket of laundry, attempting to keep it away from the mud that splashed up around her. Hail and sleet had soaked the cloth and made it heavy: she struggled under the weight. Her plight was pitiful, and instinctively Theo crossed the road.

'Let me help you,' he said, taking the basket from her hands.

She looked up in fright. 'Go away,' she said. 'I have nothing for you to steal.'

Their eyes met.

Theo's grip slackened. The basket tipped from his hands, spilling clean linen over the filthy street. It was a face he had almost forgotten, that he had not expected to see again: but the moment he saw her it was as if they had never parted. He felt the same shock in his heart as he had the first time, when he had found her picking mushrooms in the woods.

'Abigail Claypole?' he breathed.

'Theo Courtney?'

The last time he had seen her she had been in the crowd of villagers, waiting for her father to take his vengeance. Did she blame him for what had happened that night? For leaving her to a cruel future?

Abigail let out a gasp. She threw herself into his arms and hugged him hard enough to crack his ribs. 'I never thought to see you again.'

The wind had blown off her bonnet. Sleet soaked her raven hair and ran down her cheeks like tears. Theo wiped it away and cupped her head in his hands. She had grown up in the time they had been apart: she was even more beautiful than he remembered.

'What miracle . . .?'

He took her to a tavern and ordered hot wine. They held hands across the table and stared into each other's eyes in wonder.

'I heard your company was ambushed by Indians,' she said. 'They said you were dead.'

Theo told her about his capture and adoption by the Abenaki. There was one uncomfortable fact he could not ignore and would not lie about. 'They made me take a wife.'

Her eyes widened in something close to terror. 'You are married?'

'She died.'

Abigail's face softened. 'Did you love her?'

'Yes,' Theo answered honestly.

She pondered a while. 'Then I am sorry.'

'I thought I would never see you again, that you would be long since married to the man your father chose.' Theo felt his cheeks colouring: he was protesting too much. In truth, his mind was in turmoil. First in marriage, then in death, Mgeso had been the guiding flame of his life. Anything that took him away from her felt like a betrayal of his deepest self. Yet, looking at Abigail across the table, he felt a passion rising in him that was impossible to deny.

'How did you come to be in Albany?' he asked.

'Father would not let me stay in Bethel. He beat me until I thought I would die, then drummed me out of the house with nothing except the dress I was wearing. No one in Bethel would take me in. They feared Father too much. And they hated me for what I had done.'

Her voice was calm, her hand steady as she took another sip of her drink. Theo could only marvel at the strength in her.

'I'd heard the militia captain say he was taking you to Albany,' she continued, 'so that was where I went. Then I heard about the ambush, and that you were dead. But I had nowhere to go. And then there was Caleb.'

Theo's chest tightened. He should have known. She was young, beautiful and alone. It was foolish to think she would have waited a year for the memory of a man she thought was dead.

'Caleb?' He could hardly utter the name. He told himself it was for the best if she was married. He could force back the feelings that had erupted so unexpectedly and devote himself to avenging Mgeso as he had sworn.

Abigail smiled. 'It is not what you think. Come and see.'

Leaving the tavern, she led him to a neat, shingled house near the top of the hill at the edge of town. Theo followed, carrying the basket of muddy laundry. Hens pecked the ground by the front door, while steam billowed from a small shed at the side of the house.

Without knocking, Abigail entered straight into a small parlour. A cat was curled in front of the fire burning in the grate. An old woman sat in a rocking chair, holding a bundle of knitting against her chest.

'This is Mrs Jacobs,' said Abigail. 'She looks after Caleb while I am working.'

The bundle that Theo had taken for knitting began to move. It uncurled itself, revealing two small hands and a tiny head, almost as bald as an Indian's.

The baby was wrapped in a woollen shawl. Its nose twitched, its mouth opened and closed. It began to wail. Mrs Jacobs handed it to Abigail, who cradled it to her breast until the crying stopped.

She held out the baby to Theo. 'Take him.'

Confronting the nawab's rampaging army at Calcutta was nothing compared to the terror Theo felt now. His hands had turned to blocks of wood. 'Is it safe?'

Abigail's eyes sparkled. 'He is only a baby. He will not hurt you.'

'That is not what I meant,' Theo mumbled.

Abigail put the boy in his arms. Theo clutched him awkwardly. The child was so delicate, he feared that one twitch of his muscles might shatter him, like porcelain.

'You will not break him.' Abigail read his thoughts. 'He is made of strong stuff. Like his father.'

The baby had found the crook of Theo's arm and was nuzzling his face into it. He was soft and warm, and Theo found himself relaxing, his arms knowing instinctively what to do. He met Abigail's gaze. 'Is he . . .?'

'Yours – and mine. Together. He was born two months ago.'

She kissed him. 'I thank God I have found you, Theo Courtney.'

The rage of conflicting emotions still burned in him as fiercely as ever. But holding the child – *his son* – he tried to forget it all. The baby's brown eyes stared at him, a mirror of his own, and spoke to his heart. For the first time in many months, he could begin to feel at peace.

He kissed Abigail. 'I thank God I have found you too.'

• • •

The next day, they went to the Dutch church and were married. The priest officiated and Mrs Jacobs was the witness. Caleb wore a gown that Mrs Jacobs had knitted. He slept through the entire service, oblivious to the ceremony around him. A few days later Moses arrived in Albany and gave Caleb a bear-claw amulet.

Theo had married Abigail quickly to legitimise his son. There was another reason that he did not voice. If he died in battle, he wanted to leave Abigail with a widow's pension.

They spent their wedding night at Mrs Jacobs's house, whispering and fumbling in the dark while Caleb slept in his cradle. When Theo laid his hand on Abigail's bare skin, he flinched as if he'd been burned. He felt he was betraying Mgeso. But Abigail was patient. She lay beside him, soothing his nerves with soft touches. 'I know what you have lost. We do not have to do this if you are not ready,' she murmured.

'No.' He was ashamed of himself. 'You are my wife now.'

It was a long time since he had been with a woman but eventually his body relaxed. This time when he caressed her, he felt desire spark inside him. A sudden urgency overtook him, driving out all guilt and memory. He rolled on top of her, thrusting himself between her eager thighs. When they climaxed, together, he felt they were the only people who existed in the world.

Later, Theo was woken by screaming.

'Is something wrong with the baby?' he said, in a panic. Leading men into battle was one thing. Having responsibility for this tiny, fragile life terrified him.

Abigail gave him a strange look. 'Caleb is fine. It was you who were crying out in your sleep.'

The noise had woken the baby: Abigail brought him into bed and gave him a nipple to suck. 'You sounded distressed.'

'It was a bad dream,' Theo said.

For a moment he thought he would tell her everything. But when he tried, the words stuck like stones in his throat. He hated himself for it. He should not be keeping secrets from his wife on the first day of their marriage.

But could he really tell his bride that he had been dreaming of another woman on their wedding night?

'I was thinking of the future,' he told her, half truthfully. 'My company has been sent north against the French. I must leave at the end of this week.'

He saw the pain on Abigail's face, though she tried to conceal it. 'So soon?'

'They are my orders.'

That was also a lie. He had volunteered. He told himself he could not abandon Gilyard: he owed it to his men to fight. The truth was, he could not pass up the chance to kill Bichot and Malsum.

Theo looked at Abigail nursing the baby. *I will not orphan you*, he promised silently. *I will not widow you.*

The baby, contented, had fallen asleep again. Abigail carefully laid him back in his cradle. 'Then let us enjoy the time we have.'

• • •

From the moment Theo first met Abigail, he felt he'd known her for ever: but there was still so much to learn about his new bride. She had a quick mind, a kind heart and a sense of humour that had thrived despite the flinty soil of her upbringing. Sometimes her laughter was so hearty it woke the baby.

The more he delighted in her company, the more his decision to go north weighed on him. On their last morning together, he sat in Mrs Jacobs's parlour, staring into the fire. He was carving a piece of antler with a knife, but he had not touched it for ten minutes.

'I wish I was not leaving you,' he said at last.

'So do I,' said Abigail. 'Is there any way you can avoid it?'

Theo stared at the piece of bone in his hands, his thoughts travelling back across years and oceans. 'My father always said only a fool seeks a battle. He saw what war did to his own family.'

He had never spoken of his father to Abigail before. She listened in silence – but in the cradle, the baby stirred. Theo lifted Caleb and held him against his chest, stroking the fine fair hair until the child settled. 'Did I ever tell you my grandfather was the Sultan of Oman?'

Abigail laughed, thinking it was a joke. Her eyes widened as she saw he was serious.

'As a boy, my grandfather Dorian was adopted by the Prince of Muscat. Later, he won the Elephant Throne for himself. But when he went away, a usurper named Zayn took his place. Dorian killed him in Africa, but there were many men still loyal to Zayn – and my grandfather had sustained a grievous wound in battle with him.'

The baby had begun to grumble again. Theo put his knuckle in the boy's mouth for him to suck, feeling the strength in the toothless gums.

'Dorian and my father returned to Oman to claim the throne, though their family tried to dissuade them. The wound was festering, but Dorian would not reveal it for fear of losing face with the desert sheikhs. They fought a terrible battle. In the thick of the fighting, Dorian fell from his horse and could not remount. The Arabs dragged him away and hacked him to pieces.

'Their army was defeated. My father left Oman and sailed for India. He never forgave his family for refusing to come to their aid, and I think he never forgave his own father for having chosen to give battle.' He stared at the fire. 'When the French came to Madras, my father ran before them – and died anyway.'

Abigail leaned across the settle and stroked his face. 'If fate was predictable, we would all know our futures. We can only do as we think best at the time.'

'I do not want to be like my father,' said Theo. 'But the French have taken away too many of those I loved.'

A knock sounded from outside. Moses' face appeared in the doorway. 'It is time, Siumo.'

Theo stood. The baby started to cry again when Theo handed him to Abigail, the tiny red face screwed up in a picture of misery. Theo put on his heavy coat and wound the muffler around his neck. He felt like a condemned man stepping into the noose.

Moses saw the pain in his eyes. 'Are you sure this is right?' he asked in Abenaki.

Snow swirled in the street outside. Standing on the threshold, Theo felt torn in two. Behind him were Abigail and Caleb, love and the warmth of home. Ahead, only ice and revenge. He considered going to Gilyard to resign his commission.

But he could not. Not while Malsum and Bichot were alive.

Abigail came forward and kissed him. Theo embraced her awkwardly, trying not to squash the baby in her arms. He wanted never to let them go.

'I know you must do as you must,' she whispered. She was weeping. 'But you are not your father. And, whatever the future holds, you know I will always love you.'

• • •

Theo rendezvoused with his company by the lake. It was a week before Christmas, and snow lay thick on the ground.

'Did you enjoy your leave?' Gilyard asked. 'Did any fine Albany ladies catch your eye?'

Theo nodded. 'In fact, I got married.'

Even Gilyard looked astonished. 'By God, you are a constant fount of surprises. My congratulations to Mrs Courtney. I hope she knows what she has let herself in for.'

'And we have a son.'

Gilyard gaped. 'I trust there is a story behind this miracle.'

'Indeed, sir. Also, I have this for you.' Theo felt in his pocket and pulled out a knife with an antler handle. Working his passage from India, he had learned the seaman's art of scrimshaw. He had used all his skill on the weapon, decorating the hilt with intricate pictures of deer, canoes, muskets and tomahawks. He gave it to Gilyard. 'It is for you,' Theo said. 'A token of thanks for retrieving me from the Abenaki.'

Gilyard turned it over. On the reverse of the handle was carved, 'To Major Gilyard from Theo Courtney, in gratitude.'

'This is not necessary.'

'If you had not brought me back, I would never have seen my wife again, and never have known my son. You gave me new hope in life.'

Gilyard slipped the knife into his belt. 'Thank you. Maybe one day it will give me new hope in life, too.' He grinned. 'Now, are you ready to march?'

They mustered the rangers. There were fifty men dressed in warm beaver hats jammed low over their ears, woollen mittens and fur-lined white smocks. They carried their supplies on sledges and wore metal skates fitted to their moccasins so they could travel swiftly across the ice.

Theo had never been on skates before. He fell over several times within the first ten yards, much to the amusement of his companions. He rubbed his elbow and glared at them. Even Moses seemed to be faring better.

But gradually he found his balance. Soon he grew used to the strange gait, swaying easily as he pushed himself forward. It was a joyful and liberating motion, as if being freed from some of the burden of gravity. Unlike the tramp of a march, the only sound was ice hissing under the metal blades, and the wind gusting around him. The effort warmed his blood, inducing such a sense of euphoria that for a time he forgot the dangers ahead, and the confused emotions of leaving Abigail.

The cold returned with a vengeance when they stopped on shore for the night. The sweat he had built up skating turned to ice against his skin. Their food had frozen solid, and Gilyard would not let them light fires for fear of giving themselves away. Theo had to hack off each morsel of meat, then suck it in his mouth until it thawed enough to chew. They had brought bearskins as blankets, but even wrapped in the thick fur Theo could not get warm enough to sleep. At dawn, they were off again.

The first day had been difficult; the second was agonising. The wind howled down the lake, driving snow into their faces so hard that Theo could barely see where he was going. His cheeks and nose went numb. Even in their mittens, his fingers began to lose feeling. The sledge harness bit into his shoulders. He felt exhausted, sick and dizzy.

The short winter day ended early, but Gilyard did not call a halt. The moon appeared, reflecting on the snow so that the world became bright and eerie.

Suddenly, flames broke the night on an ice-bound island where the lake narrowed. The rangers threw themselves onto the ice in an instant. Theo thought he saw dim figures moving around a fire among the trees. He held his breath. It could be Indians, or the French, or even a party of fur traders. It might be they were warming themselves in the bitter night – or it might be a signal.

No answering fires showed from the shore. No one ventured out from the island. How long would they wait? Lying against the ice, Theo felt the cold creeping into his bones. Much longer, and he might never get up.

'What shall we do?' he whispered.

'We cannot risk going past that island,' Gilyard decided. 'The lake is too narrow – we would pass too close. We will have to make for land.'

They hauled their sledges back to shore and passed a restless night, keeping a wary eye on the island. Had they been seen? The fire burned lower, a dull orange glow among the dark trees, then went out. Theo started to wonder if they had imagined it.

Next morning, Gilyard sent out scouts. They were gone most of the day and returned with disquieting news. The forest was crawling with the French. They had found fresh tracks in the snow everywhere they went, criss-crossing the forest like a net. Once, they had nearly blundered into an enemy patrol.

'And even if we could slip past them, we would have them at our backs, cutting off our retreat,' said Lieutenant Trent. 'There is no way we can reach the fort.'

Gilyard sucked his teeth. 'I've never known these woods so full of Frenchmen in winter. Usually they remain safe and warm close to the fort.' He reached into his pouch and withdrew a roughly sketched map, staring at it like an astronomer scanning the skies. 'There must be another way.'

Moses leaned in. He squinted at the paper as he tried to reconcile the bare lines with the vivid pictures he held in his mind. He tapped a heavy, jagged line drawn across the centre of the map.

'That is a spur of the mountains that comes down from the north-east,' said Gilyard. 'It runs all the way back to the lake. But there is no way over it.'

Moses shook his head. 'There is a pass.'

Trent eyed him sceptically. 'I have never heard of it.'

Gilyard ignored him. 'If we could gain the top of the ridge, we could follow it to Fort Royal. We could look down into the fort and see what the commandant was having for breakfast. And that far west, there won't be any patrols.'

'Because they know there's no way through,' Trent persisted.

Gilyard turned to Theo. 'What do you think, Lieutenant Courtney?'

Theo was torn. Part of him wanted to side with Trent, to give up the expedition and return to Abigail and Caleb. But he looked at the map, at the fort and the forest and the mountains around it. Malsum and Bichot were somewhere in that wilderness.

'I trust Moses,' he said.

Gilyard cracked a smile. 'There can be no harm in taking a look.'

They hid their sledges under snow and brush on the lake shore, taking only what they could carry on their backs. In the thick snow, extra weight would slow them down, even with the snowshoes they tied on to their moccasins. They set out on foot.

The further they travelled, the more Theo doubted the wisdom of the expedition. He had begun to lose feeling in his face. If it came to a battle, he was not sure his frozen hands would be able to take the wrapping off his rifle, let alone pull the trigger. He tried to distract himself with thoughts of revenge, but often he found his mind drifting back to Albany and Abigail, of the life they could build together.

The next day they came up against the mountain range. The long, high ridge soared across the landscape, barricading them in. All morning, they skirted along its foot. The cliffs above were high and forbidding, so steep even the snow did not settle on them. Clouds lowered. The air felt warmer than it had in weeks.

'The frost giants are retreating,' Moses worried. 'A thaw is coming. We should get back to our sledges before the lake ice melts.'

'We must press on,' Theo insisted. Every time he glanced up at the mountain, he felt a dread in his stomach he could not explain. Yet he could not look away. The icy heights exerted a strange pull on him. Somewhere up there, he felt certain, he would find Malsum and Bichot.

Perhaps it was nervous exhaustion. All the men were on edge. The cliffs echoed with the sound of melting ice falling and shattering. Unable any longer to bear the weight of wet snow, tree branches snapped, each one like a musket shot that kept the rangers anxiously peering into the forest shadows. What if the French had patrols this far north? What if they had found the rangers' tracks?

Tempers frayed. The cliffs seemed as high and impassable as ever. Theo no longer looked up in hopes of finding the pass. He walked with his head bowed, staring wearily at the ground. 'What is that?' he said suddenly.

If it wasn't for the thaw, he would never have seen it. Earlier, and the snow would have smoothed it over. Later, and the ground would have softened to a mire. The rangers' boots had tramped the snow to slush, while the ground below remained solid. Captured in the frozen soil, Theo saw the unmistakable gouge of a wheel rut.

He summoned Moses and Gilyard. 'It must have been a heavy load,' said Gilyard. 'See how deep it sank into the earth.'

'Who could have brought a cart this far into the wilderness?' Theo wondered. 'There is no road, and nowhere to go.'

'There is a path.' Moses pointed back. It took Theo a good while to see what he meant among the thick foliage. There was a gap between the trees, so narrow it might have been a buffalo trail. The rangers had walked several hundred yards along it and not realised it was there.

'Where does it go?'

Probing the snow with sticks, they followed the track the wheel ruts had made. The marks hugged the base of the mountain, then swung inwards towards a sheer cliff.

'Did they fly away?' Theo wondered.

Moses disappeared.

He seemed to have vanished into the rock. Theo stared at the place where he had been, his fatigued mind struggling to make sense of it. He was still staring when Moses' head reappeared. 'Come.' He beckoned.

Theo followed him. Although the cliff looked like a solid wall, it was an illusion. A rocky spur made a narrow ravine leading up and into the mountain. Until they were inside it, the entrance was invisible.

'It seems these mountains were not as impassable as we thought,' said Gilyard.

'And we are not the first people to find it.' Moses pointed to a clear patch of ground. A campfire had melted the snow, leaving a blackened circle of ash and cinder on the bare earth. It must have been recent. No snow had fallen to cover the ashes. Gilyard swore. 'Everywhere we go, the French have been there first.'

Theo stared up the ravine. It was long and narrow, strewn with boulders and hemmed in on both sides by high walls. 'I would not want to get trapped in there. A dozen men with the advantage of height could hold it against an army.'

Gilyard nodded. 'Then we had best be on our guard. Ready your weapons.'

They made a cairn to mark the pass, then entered the ravine. Rifles loaded, they scanned the heights for any sign of an enemy. The snow was thicker there, where the sun had not penetrated, but soft and sticky. It clung to their snowshoes in heavy clumps, making progress even harder. Struggling with the weight of his pack, Theo pulled off his furs to avoid overheating. For the first time in days, he had feeling in his fingers.

He knew he ought to feel elated. Every step took him closer to his enemies and the chance for revenge. Instead he felt mounting dread, as if some dark and terrible animal was sniffing at his trail.

'I do not like this place,' said Moses, beside him.

'More evil spirits?'

Moses frowned. 'I do not need the spirits to tell me this place is bad.' He gestured at the high walls of the ravine. 'If our enemies are up there, we will be trapped, like beavers in a frozen pond.'

Theo glanced upwards, checking the skyline for any hint of movement. Moses was right: a few marksmen on the heights would be able to pour fire into the ravine.

'Ouch.'

Theo had stumbled on a smooth rock under the snow. He swore and rubbed his foot.

'The mouse who only watches for the hawk may not see the snake behind him,' said Moses, amused.

Theo was about to move on, when something about the stone he had kicked made him pause. Under the scuffed snow, he could see a shape that was too smooth and regular to have been fashioned by nature. He crouched and started to clear away the snow. Moses joined in. The object was much bigger than he'd thought, as thick as a tree trunk and ten feet long, a cylinder tapering towards one end. It was neither stone nor wood, but cold, hard bronze.

There was a stamp in the metal. Theo brushed away the last of the snow and saw it was the royal crest of King Louis XV of France.

It was a twelve-pounder cannon.

Theo called Gilyard.

'That is why they have so many patrols,' Gilyard breathed. 'They did not want us to see the truth of what they are planning.'

'But what would they do with a cannon in this desolate place?' Theo asked. Excavating deeper in the snow, he found the splintered remains of a gun carriage. The wheels must have snapped on the broken ground as the French tried to haul it up the ravine, and they had not been able to lift it out.

'I'll wager a bottle of General Williams's finest brandy that this was not the only gun,' said Gilyard. 'The ridge ends in a high eminence above the fort. If they can get guns up there, they will have an impregnable battery commanding all the approaches. It would make the fort unassailable.'

Theo tried to imagine the effort it must have taken. They were miles from the fort. The French must have dragged the guns all the way to this ravine, up the treacherous slope and then along the ridge. What sort of a man would drive his troops to such lengths?

Something rose from the cliff above. Quicker than thought, one of the rangers trained his rifle and fired. The others dived for cover behind boulders, weapons bristling. The sound of the shot echoed like thunder between the rocks, so loud Theo thought it would bring an avalanche down on them.

A crow fell dead to the ground.

'Who was that man?' Gilyard demanded. He found the unfortunate soldier and snatched the rifle from his hands. 'Do you want every Frenchman from here to Québec to know where we are?'

'We should return to Albany,' said Trent. 'General Williams must have this intelligence at once.'

What he said was true. Theo knew it; so did Gilyard. The major nodded, though reluctantly. Theo could see his eagerness for battle chafing against his sense of duty.

But if they left now they would never find Bichot.

'One broken gun is proof of nothing,' said Theo. 'We should go further and see if there are more.'

Theo saw Gilyard hesitate.

'The general needs to know what we have found,' Trent insisted.

'The general needs complete information,' Theo countered. 'Are we so afraid of the French that we will not complete our scout?'

Gilyard thought for a moment. But Theo's barb about being afraid had hit its mark.

'Ready the men,' Gilyard said. 'We will continue up to the ridge and see what the French have up there.'

'A warm welcome, perhaps,' muttered Trent. But he could not disobey an order.

They kept climbing. They were now so high Theo was sure they must be near the summit. Yet still the path wound upwards, as tight and steep as ever.

They came to a fork where the ravine split in two. A tributary stream flowed in from the right. In spring, it might be a roaring torrent, but now the streambed was a shallow thread of ice.

'Which way?' said Gilyard.

Moses pointed to the left. 'This goes to the ridge. The other—' He had heard a sound, coming from around the corner of the right-hand fork. The sound of voices. 'They are singing,' he said. The words were indistinct but the tune carried. It sounded like a marching song, sung by tired soldiers near the end of their patrol.

Ten Frenchmen came into view. They were dressed like the rangers, in fur capes and hats, with snowshoes slung over their backs and muskets on their shoulders. They could not have expected to find Gilyard's men there, but they were not slow to react. They turned and ran.

The rangers were in no mood to let them escape. Before Gilyard could give an order his men charged after the fleeing Frenchmen, hungry for action at last.

Theo was as eager for battle as any of them. He was about to follow, when a firm hand on his arm stopped him.

It was Moses. 'Something is not right,' said the Abenaki. 'You would not find so few men far from their fortress, with little thought for their safety.'

'They would never have reckoned on rangers in French territory,' Theo argued. His blood was up: he wanted to kill Frenchmen. Maybe Bichot himself was near.

'Did you see how quickly they turned and ran? They knew they would find us.' Moses' grip tightened on his arm. 'They *want* us to follow them.'

While they spoke, the rest of the company had disappeared around a bend in the gully. Shots were fired, snatched and sporadic, the sound of men taking aim at running targets.

'This is no time—' Theo broke off. The tenor of the battle had changed. From down the gully came the sound not of rifles but of musketry:

the massed blast of disciplined troops firing in unison.

Excitement turned to horror. 'It is an ambush,' he realised. In an instant, he saw it all. The French had men on the steep slopes above, able to pour fire down on the rangers in the gully.

Moses pointed down the hill. 'We should escape while we can and take the news to your general.'

'No.' Theo did not even consider it. His loyalty was to his company. 'We must save the men.'

'Then we need to get up that slope.'

The walls were steep, but Theo found a place where a rockslide made a path he could scramble up. Crouching low, he crept through the trees that lined the top of the gully. The sound of gunfire told him where to go, growing ever louder as he increased his pace.

The gully dead-ended in a rocky hollow, where a frozen waterfall dropped down a cliff into a pool of black water and jagged ice. The trap had been well executed. The rangers were trapped like rats while the French rained fire down from three sides. More Frenchmen filled the entrance, blocking any escape.

The rangers were being slaughtered. Their blood ran over the broken ice and stained the snow crimson. But they would not surrender. A knot of them had formed around Gilyard, pinned against the side of the hollow, as they fired desperately through the choking smoke.

There was no time to plan. Every second Theo delayed meant more of his friends would die. Some of the Frenchmen were ahead, clearly visible through the trees. They had their backs to him. With a glance at Moses, to check he understood, Theo raised his rifle and fired.

It was a good shot. A remarkable shot, considering his freezing hands and the chaos of the situation. It hit the Frenchman on the nape of his neck, shattering his spinal cord in an instant. The man slumped to the ground. To his left, another man was felled by Moses' bullet.

With the noise of battle, pouring their fire into the hollow, the other Frenchmen were slow to realise the danger. Theo and Moses had time to reload and fire again. Two more men went down.

This time, their comrades were alerted to the new direction of fire. They had not expected an attack from the rear, but they were quick to respond. While Theo fumbled to reload, their guns were already primed. He ducked behind a tree as a hail of bullets came at him. Some flew past. Others struck the trunk. He felt the vibrations ripple through the branches.

He rolled out from his cover, trained his gun on the first man he saw and fired. The man stumbled back and disappeared over the lip of the gully. His companions retaliated, but their bullets struck snow. Theo was already back behind the tree.

Caught between the rangers below and Theo and Moses behind them, the French soldiers scattered in confusion.

Theo let off another shot, then fixed his bayonet and charged forward. A Frenchman stepped out from behind a tree, ready to fire, but Theo's bayonet impaled him through his belly before he could pull the trigger. He doubled over. Theo took the Frenchman's musket, reversed it and shot him in the face. He withdrew his rifle and bayonet and kept running. Another man appeared and was felled by a shot from over Theo's shoulder where Moses was covering him.

Theo was at the lip of the slope, looking down into the hollow around the waterfall. There were no Frenchmen in this area, though a group of them kept up a steady fire from the far side and the mouth of the ravine. Below, the rangers were trying to climb the slope, clutching at exposed tree roots as they skidded on the thawing earth. They were easy targets.

Theo took off his cross belts, looped one end around a tree stump and let the other hang down as a handhold. He turned his rifle towards the Frenchmen at the mouth of the gorge.

Now he had the advantage of the terrain, with height and trees to shield him, while the French troops were exposed in the valley. When Theo opened fire, they could not see it was just one man. All they knew was that bullets were coming at them from above. Their discipline broke and they ran for cover. It gave the rangers enough time to scramble up to join Theo, adding their firepower to his.

Gilyard was last. He brushed the mud from his coat, discharged his pistol towards a Frenchman who had shown himself, and crouched beside Theo. 'Once again, Mr Courtney, I find you where you are most needed.' He touched his hat, which had miraculously stayed on throughout the fight. 'Now

I need you for another task. I have decided we must make sure that news of what we have found gets back to General Williams. Take six men and make your way to the sledges we cached at the lake. I will hold off the French as long as possible, and then I will follow, but *do not wait for me*.'

Theo stared. 'With respect, sir, is it wise to divide our forces?'

Gilyard bit off the end of a paper cartridge and tipped the powder into his pistol. 'With respect, Mr Courtney, you will obey my orders. Now *go*.'

The only way down the mountain was through the ravine, which was blocked by the French.

The clouds were lowering: a grey mist drifted down from the slopes above. Theo pointed upwards. 'We will make for the ridge and see if we can lose our enemies in the fog.'

He found Moses, and five other men and struck out up the mountain.

• • •

Theo put the men in pairs, one firing while the other ran and reloaded. Running, firing, ducking for cover and then running again. Meltwater turned the slope into a mire that sucked at their feet. The damp soaked the powder and made the rifles misfire.

The battle had become a series of skirmishes, fought in the mud and snow. Theo did not know what had happened to Gilyard's detachment, but they had not kept the French at bay for long. One by one, his men fell.

The mist thickened. It hid them from their pursuers. Theo kept climbing. They had to be near the summit now. The ground grew rocky; the trees thinned. The shooting became sporadic. Gunfire sounded distant and muffled.

Theo ran to a tree stump, crouched, reloaded – and waited.

'Moses?' he called.

There was no reply. He tried again, calling the names of all the men he had last seen alive. His only answer was silence.

He was alone.

A fine commander I make, he thought bitterly. *I have lost all my men.*

He wondered whether to wait for them, but he was disoriented. He offered a quick prayer that they were safe and continued through the fog and snow, which lay thicker at that elevation. He supposed he was very high up, though there was no way of telling. He wished he had not discarded his snowshoes.

Through the fog, he heard raised voices, a shot and a cry. He stumbled on in the snow towards the sound.

A warm wind blew against his face. The mist parted, showing snatches of his surroundings. He was on the top of the ridge, on an exposed knoll that ended in a sheer cliff. He was lucky he had not gone over it.

The splash of blood was like a crimson flower on the snow. There were footprints, too. Theo followed them. Every few feet he saw more blood-stains, marking the trail until it ended in a dark body sprawled on the ground. Theo ran to the man and rolled him over.

It was Gilyard. His eyes fluttered open.

'You were supposed to escape,' he grunted.

'So were you,' replied Theo, fighting back the despair that threatened to overwhelm him. Gilyard had given him one task, to get away, and now they had blundered straight back into each other. Blood was seeping from Gilyard's belly, spreading across his white smock. Theo tore off a strip of cloth and pressed it against the wound to staunch the bleeding. 'I must get you down from here.'

Gilyard shook his head. 'No time. Save yourself.'

'I will not.'

Gilyard balled his hand into a fist and grabbed Theo's coat. He pulled Theo close, his face scarlet with the effort of speaking. '*Go.*'

Footsteps crunched in the snow behind Theo. Too late, he realised that the blood spilling from Gilyard's guts was fresh and bright, the wound recently inflicted. He turned.

Dark shapes glided out of the fog. A dozen men, all armed, fanning out so that Theo was trapped against the cliff. Wrapped in their furs, they looked like a pack of black bears.

Their leader unwrapped the scarf that covered his face. He pulled off his hat and threw it on the ground. Lank hair spilled down around his scarred face, and the patch of bare red skin on the crown of his head seemed to pulse with anger. He smiled, showing yellow teeth as sharp as the wolf claws strung around his neck.

It was a face from Theo's nightmares, the man he had sworn to kill a thousand times in all those nights mourning Mgeso. And now that he was face to face with Bichot, he was on his knees and unarmed. The gods had deserted him.

Theo's eye drifted to the pistol in Gilyard's belt. Was it loaded?

There was only one way to find out. In a single motion, he drew it and levelled it at Bichot.

The Frenchman stopped in his tracks. Theo stood. His legs trembled, but the pistol in his hand didn't waver.

'Don't you recognise me?' he said in French.

Bichot shrugged. Theo was dressed in his uniform. With his hair grown out and his piercings removed, he was very different from the Indian warrior he had been the last time they met.

'I am Siumo, sometimes called Ahoma, of the Abenaki.' Theo spoke it loud and clear. 'My wife was Mgeso, whom you killed.'

Bichot's eyes widened a fraction, before his face settled in a cold grimace. 'I wonder – will you die as easily as she did?'

Theo didn't bother to answer. He pulled the trigger.

The gun was loaded. The pan was primed. Bichot was barely ten feet away. Before he could react, the flint snapped forward and struck a spray of sparks. The powder in the pan ignited with a flash and a puff of smoke.

Nothing else happened. Either the charge in the barrel was wet, or the touch-hole had been clogged with grit. The gun did not fire.

A leer spread across Bichot's face. His hunting knife was already bloody from the battle. He wiped the blade clean with his hand, and sucked blood off his finger.

'You will not die as quickly as your wife,' he promised. 'I will take my time and do the things to you I would have liked to do with her.'

Theo stepped back. His heels felt the cliff edge. Beyond it was only cloud. There was nowhere for him to go. He glanced at Gilyard, but the major was lying still and cold in the snow. He was beyond help.

Bichot loomed towards him. He sliced the air with his knife, laughing as he saw Theo flinch. Theo tensed himself to spring, but Bichot's eyes betrayed him. He wanted Theo to attack. He was waiting for it.

Theo could not fight him. All he could do was deny him the satisfaction of the kill.

He stepped backwards off the cliff.

Constance had never known she could be so cold. February in Paris had been bitter. Crossing the Atlantic in October, while gales battered the ship and breaking waves soaked everything, had made her blood freeze. But winter in Québec made those look like fond memories. The draughty houses could not keep out the shrill north winds, while the snow that clogged the streets made stepping outdoors an excruciating ordeal. She had spent so long huddled close to the smoky fires, she feared she would turn into a haunch of ham.

This was the place her new husband had brought her.

They had married in haste, at his family home in Normandy, en route to join the fleet at Brest. On their wedding night, Constance had put on her most revealing *négligé* and steeled her body for what was to come. Mauvières's brutality had left more than physical bruises on her.

But Corbeil had been a cautious lover – so tentative, in fact, that she had had to coax him into her to bring him to his climax. Afterwards, he had lain over her, shuddering with such deep breaths she feared he might have suffered a seizure.

'I have desired you since the moment I saw you in Calcutta,' he murmured in her ear. 'When I saw you at the marquise's ball in Paris, I thought God had answered my prayers. And when you came to see me and begged my help against Mauvierès,

I believed that all your adventures had been ordained by Providence to bring us together.'

'And now you possess me,' she had whispered to him. 'You are all I want and all I need.'

She had lain awake, long after he had fallen sleep, pondering the implications of what he had said.

The honeymoon had been short-lived. She did not doubt that Corbeil adored her, but the needs of the army occupied his every waking moment. Aboard ship, he spent hours with his aides in the great cabin, reviewing the details of the coming campaign. When they arrived in New France, the demands on him had doubled.

'I do not see anything heroic in your work,' Constance said, one evening. 'All I hear about are supplies, commissaries, rations and ammunition.'

'The British outnumber us,' Corbeil explained. 'Pitt, their prime minister, is sending ten battalions to America, but our king's ministers will not commit the men I need to face them on the battlefield. Our best strength is our forts. So long as those hold firm, the British cannot advance. That is why I must do everything I can to ensure that they are well supplied, and that their defences are in good order. I will seek to lure the British on to our guns, then destroy their proud army.'

The passion in his voice made her shiver. 'Why do you hate the British so much?' she asked. She had been married to him for six months, but she had never dared ask the question before. It had stood like an invisible obstacle between them, never acknowledged but always present. In his behaviour towards Constance, Corbeil was courtesy itself, attentive and loving. But when he spoke of the English, he reminded her of the caged tigers she had seen in the merchants' gardens in Calcutta.

'I don't hate you, and you are from that infernal island.'

Corbeil stared out of the window at the frozen St Lawrence River. 'When I was growing up, there was a girl in our town called Julie. Her father owned the estate. My father was merely a clerk. But we were friends. We played together barefoot in the orchards around her house. She had fair hair, like you, and skin as pale as milk. I was in love with her. She said she loved me too. But of course I had no fortune.'

'What happened?'

'I joined the army. It was the only way I could use my talents to gain the rank that would satisfy her father. It turned out I had a talent for soldiering: I prospered. When I was promoted to major, I asked for her hand in marriage and her father agreed.

'But soldiering took me far from home. I could not bear to be separated from my bride, so I took her with me. She lived with me in my quarters at a village near the Rhine, called Dettingen.' He said the name with special emphasis, as if Constance should recognise it. 'You have heard of it?'

'No.'

'There was a battle there. A British army had marched down the Rhine to invade France, but we outmanoeuvred them. We cut their supply lines, blocked their line of retreat and lured them to a place where our army was waiting. We called it "the mousetrap", and they walked straight into it.'

He had a distant look in his eyes, as if he could see it in front of him.

'Everything was arranged for a glorious victory. King George II himself led the British forces. Imagine if we had captured him. We would have won the war that day, and Britain would have been at our mercy.'

'What happened?'

'Our fool of a commander attacked too soon. His haste meant we could not bring our cannons to bear. The British counter-attacked into the gap he had left, and our line broke. Our army was routed. The village where we had our headquarters was overrun.'

His voice shook. The memories brought anguish flooding to his face, but he went on: 'Julie should have retreated with the army. In the confusion, she did not know what to do, and I was not there to tell her. She waited for me to come and rescue her. But I was too late.

'By the time I got there, the British soldiers had been through the village. I am sure Julie begged them for mercy, but they did not give it to her. When I found her, I barely recognised her. The things they had done . . .'

Constance tried not to shudder. 'And that is why you hate the English?'

'The English believe they are born to rule. They want to own the world. They do not have romance in their heart, only rapaciousness and greed.'

Constance looked away.

'The first time I killed an Englishman in battle, I thought of Julie.' A rare smile spread over his face. 'I think it is the happiest I have ever been.'

'And now you have an English wife.' She laughed, trying to make light of it. Otherwise, she would have wanted to scream.

'Our hearts have a way of making fools of us,' mused Corbeil. He stroked her hair, pressing it against his face. 'When I first saw you, you reminded me so much of Julie that I knew I had to possess you. I look back at how destiny brought us together, first in India, then on the other side of the world, and I tremble. However much I despise the English, I love you. But, like two sides of a sword, when I think of your countrymen, all I want to do is murder them.'

'You sound like my brother,' said Constance. 'He was desperate for revenge. But when his chance came, he fled like a coward.'

A dangerous shadow clouded Corbeil's eyes. 'I promise you, I will never flee the battlefield. Not while there is one Englishman left to kill.' He turned to the window again. A horse-drawn sledge was gliding up the frozen river, towards the harbour. The animals' feet were muffled against the cold, while a closed cabin had been built on the runners to protect the passenger. A squadron of dragoons trotted behind.

'Our new master,' announced Corbeil. 'The Comte de Bercheny, the governor general of New France. He has just arrived from Paris.'

Constance rose. 'He will want to see you at once. I will leave you to your meeting.'

'Stay.' A lifetime in the military meant every word that came out of Corbeil's mouth sounded like a command. 'I would like you to be here.'

'Must I? I am sure you and he will speak of nothing but enfilades and Monsieur Vauban's principles of fortification.'

Corbeil frowned. 'He is the governor general of New France. My future prospects – to say nothing of the coming campaign – depend on his good opinion of me. He will appreciate a woman's company after the rigours of his journey.'

'Then I shall be charm personified,' Constance promised. 'If only it will help you get a posting back in Paris.'

Corbeil looked surprised. 'Why would I want that?'

'You have spent half your career in these far-flung outposts of our empire. India, Canada . . . Is it not time to lead a more comfortable life, somewhere more civilised?'

'But this is where the war must be won. The English know that, even if our own king's ministers cannot see it. If we defeat the English in their colonies, we will throttle their trade and bring them to their knees.'

Anger flecked his voice. Constance knew better than to argue.

Corbeil kissed the top of her head. 'I know you would prefer the lights and gaiety of Paris. But this is my duty. This is what you were given when you married me, for better or for worse.'

'For better, always for better,' Constance murmured. But she did not meet his eye.

• • •

On first impression, the Comte de Bercheny confirmed all of Constance's misgivings. He was the wrong side of sixty, with sagging jowls and a bright red nose. The buttons on his waistcoat were fighting a losing battle to contain his massive belly. He walked with a limp, which Constance identified as the symptom of gout.

Corbeil saluted. 'May I present my wife, Madame Constance de Corbeil?'

Constance extended her hand. Bercheny took it in his pale paw and raised it to his lips. '*Enchanté*,' he breathed. He bowed low, still holding her hand and staring into her eyes. The effect was of an overgrown gargoyle. 'Believe me, madame, in Paris they still speak of your beauty.'

Constance giggled. 'Monsieur, I am sure you exaggerate.'

'I assure you, I do not.' He still hadn't let go of her hand. 'You must find colonial life very dull after France.'

'I grew up in India. I am used to the far reaches of the world – though not, I must confess, to this cold.'

Bercheny's deep-set eyes widened in delight. 'Then we have something in common. I grew up on Île de France – Mauritius, as the English call it. This damnable cold – forgive my language, madame, but it is necessary – will be the death of me.'

'We must suffer it for the glory of France,' said Constance, dutifully. A smile played at the edge of her lips.

Reluctantly, Bercheny let go of her hand and turned to Corbeil. 'You are neglecting your wife,' he scolded him. Corbeil flushed. 'As governor, I cannot allow such a crime. Bring us wine and let us talk of hot places to warm our spirits.'

'Alas, my wife has an engagement,' said Corbeil, brusquely. He ushered Bercheny towards a table strewn with maps. 'Soldiers' talk bores her, and I have much to explain to you about how I plan to trap the English.'

'Of course,' said Bercheny. 'We will have our conversation another time, madame.'

Constance curtsied. 'I shall look forward to it.'

As she left the room, she noticed Bercheny's eyes followed her.

• • •

Theo fell through the clouds longer than he had thought possible. Wind whistled in his ears, his body accelerating at a terrifying rate. He could not see the ground approaching.

But when he hit, it was softer than he had expected.

By some miracle, he had missed the jagged rocks that protruded at the bottom of the cliff and landed in a hollow between them. Wind-blown snow had filled it to the brim, while the high rock walls had kept it shaded and cold. Theo sank into almost six feet of snow and still did not touch the bottom.

He had a split second to rejoice that he was alive. Then the hole he had made in the snow began to collapse in on itself. Snow cascaded over him, freezing and suffocating. He would be buried alive.

Lunging and crawling, flinging his arms wide to distribute his weight, he floundered out of his cocoon. The snow was like quicksand: with every movement he seemed to sink deeper. Snow filled his mouth and nose.

At last his flailing hand touched something solid. He was so numb with cold he barely felt it, but he managed to bend his frozen fingers and get a purchase. He hauled himself onto solid ground and lay there for a moment, dazed and hardly able to believe he had survived.

His body ached all over, he had no food or weapons, and he had not eaten since the morning. But there was no time to rest. Shouts sounded from the clifftop, distant and hidden in fog. The French could not have seen what happened – but they might come looking for his body.

Theo set off down the mountainside.

Finding his bearings in the fog was impossible. He stumbled downhill, veering as much as he could towards the brightest part of the mist. If he headed south and west, he might eventually get back to the sledges they had left at the creek.

For the first time that day, luck favoured him. He had reached the bottom of the slope when he saw a small pile of stones. It was the cairn they had made to mark the entrance to the pass. From there, he found the trail they had followed from the lake.

Hope gave him new strength, but he had many miles to cover. His clothes were soaked from the snow, and his limbs felt soft and heavy as lead. Night fell. Unable to see the way, and terrified of getting lost, he made a rough shelter from branches and curled up inside. The night lasted an eternity, but he barely slept. When dawn came, his body was stiff and bruised. He forced himself onwards.

Theo walked all day. Staggering forward, unable to see further than the next step, he didn't realise he had reached the lake until he noticed sand underfoot. He collapsed on the ground, listening to the ice cracking and groaning.

Men emerged from the trees and ran to him. Theo did not know if they were friend or foe, until he saw Moses' anxious face leaning over him. 'Praise God and all the ancestors that you are alive,' said the Abenaki. 'We feared there was no hope.'

Theo reached up and embraced his friend. 'I feared the same for you.'

Later, they might dwell on what they had lost. Now there was no time. 'How many men have we?' Theo asked.

'Those you see.' Moses pointed to the bedraggled group huddled at the edge of the creek. There were seven – four who had escaped with Moses, and three who had stayed behind with the sledges because they were too weak for the march. It was a wretched return on the fifty brave men who had marched out of Albany.

'Were you followed?' Theo asked.

'No,' said Moses. 'But they will come looking for us.'

Theo didn't doubt it was true. He had cheated Bichot of his prey, and the Frenchman would not forgive him. He would find where Theo had fallen and realise he had escaped alive.

He was in no condition to move. 'We will lie up until dark,' he decided. 'Gather our strength and wait for the moon to rise.'

'The ice is thin, Siumo,' Moses warned.

'Then it is lucky we are thinner.'

• • •

Bichot peered over the edge of the cliff. The fog hid the bottom and hushed any sound of impact. The Abenaki-Englishman named Siumo had vanished.

A less cautious man would have assumed he was dead. But Bichot had not survived so long in the wilderness by leaving anything to chance. The scar on his head was a reminder of what happened if you dropped your guard, even for an instant.

He knew these mountains well, every notch and groove. He knew the cliff was not as high as it might appear, and that snow sometimes filled the hollow at its base. He reckoned a man might survive the leap.

He would not attempt it himself. There were other ways of catching his prey. If the Englishman or any of the rangers had survived, they would have to navigate the long trek back to the lake.

The hunt was up. Bichot would follow them, corner them, and spit them like deer. He would skin them alive and take the hides back to his masters in Canada. They would shudder, but they would pay good solid gold. Bichot would enjoy seeing those French gentlemen squirm at the knowledge of their hypocrisy. They depended on men like him to keep the frontier safe from the

English, even as they kept the blood from their own hands.

He lingered a moment on the edge of the cliff, searching the mist for clues. He was unsettled that this one-time Abenaki warrior had suddenly been reincarnated as a ranger. He remembered what the young man had said to him the first time they met. There had been purpose in those words that rang with the truth of destiny.

I will whisper it into your ear as the tip of my knife slides into your heart.

He shook off the thought. Fate was good to Bichot, and putting Ahoma in his power was one of her little gifts. It would add spice to the hunt.

'Gather our forces,' he ordered. There was no point in giving the English too generous a head start.

He heard a sound from the corpse on the ground. One of his men knelt beside the fallen ranger and put an ear to his mouth.

'He is alive.'

Bichot stared at the ranger. He kicked him hard with the toe of his moccasin, drawing a grunt of pain. The eyes flickered open. 'So he is.'

'What shall we do with him?'

Bichot crouched. He stroked his knife over the man's forehead. 'What is your name, worm?'

The prisoner gritted his teeth, gathering his strength to spit out the words: 'Major William Gilyard, of His Majesty's First Independent Company of Rangers.'

Bichot swore. He stood.

'Send him to Québec.' The new general from France had given orders that any captured officer ranked major or higher was to be interrogated by him personally. It deprived Bichot of his prize, and of the pleasure he'd have had in flaying the man's secrets out of him. He felt cheated.

It did not matter. He would soon have other prisoners to entertain him.

• • •

Moses made a meal with the supplies they had left on the sledges. Theo had not eaten in two days, but he forced himself to chew slowly and take modest portions. He could not afford to make himself sick. Then he curled up in a bearskin. He did not think he could sleep – his body was coursing with danger and urgency – but the next thing he knew Moses was shaking him awake. Stars were out, and a thin moon lit the sky.

'It is time.'

They strapped on their skates and left all but one of the sledges. One of the men, a Connecticut farmer named Judd, had suffered such severe frostbite in his toes he could not walk, so they lashed him to the sledge with their remaining provisions. Even the cool of the night hadn't stopped the thaw. Meltwater pooled on top of the ice, spraying up behind their skates in thin streams. The ice creaked and shifted under their weight. With every stride, Theo feared it would break.

Then he forgot that danger. Glancing back, he saw lights by the creek where they had left the sledges. There were many men carrying pine resin torches.

Shouts told him they had seen the fleeing rangers. Soon the torches ventured out on the ice. Theo tried to skate faster, but he was exhausted, and his pursuers were strong. Sleek as wolves, they glided down the moonlit lake after him. However hard Theo pushed himself, they were gaining on him.

'Leave the sledge!' shouted one of the rangers. 'We cannot outrun them if we are laden down.'

'We will not leave Judd behind.' Theo knew what Bichot would do to anyone who fell into his hands. 'I would rather die on the ice.'

'Then you may get your wish, Siumo,' said Moses. He pointed ahead and to their left. More torches had appeared. Men were running along the shore, heading to a point that protruded far into the lake – within rifle range. Theo and the rangers would be caught in a pincer between the men on shore and those behind.

'Head further out!' Theo shouted.

They changed to a course that took them clear of the point, but it shortened the distance to the men behind. Their pursuers redoubled their efforts, racing to reach the place where their paths would intersect. Theo and Moses hauled the sledge between them, but it made cumbersome progress on the wet ice.

The layer of meltwater on top of the ice grew deeper. They were far out, near the middle of the lake, and the ice had come alive, splitting and groaning. Theo felt it flex under his weight. To his horror, he saw cracks spreading around his feet. But he could not turn back towards the shore, only skate on and pray the ice held.

The hard report of a rifle drowned out the sounds of the ice. Theo saw the ball strike the surface behind him with a spray of ice fragments and water. But the next shot was closer, and the third closer still.

He shrugged off the sledge harness. The French were a hundred yards behind and closing quickly. The ice stretched far in every direction with no cover – except, some distance away, where the branches of a fallen tree waved from the ice. It looked incongruous, so far from land. It must have been washed away in an autumn storm and trapped in the ice when the lake froze.

It could serve as a barricade defence, but they would never reach it in time.

'We cannot run any more,' Theo decided. He slit the straps that held Judd to the sledge and rolled him off. The man screamed, thinking he was being abandoned, but that wasn't Theo's plan. He tipped the sledge up on its side, creating a makeshift shelter. It was hardly big enough for three men to crouch behind – but it was better than nothing.

He could see the enemy clearly. Twenty men, their winter furs streaming behind them. Theo's heart skipped as he recognised Bichot at the front. In his bearskin cloak, his face seemed to float out of a cloud of darkness against the moonlit ice.

A shot slammed into the sledge, fracturing the wood. Their barrier would not last long. Theo felt the hopelessness of the situation pressing in on him. Thoughts of Caleb and Abigail clawed at his mind, but he fought off the despair. While he breathed, he would fight. If he died, he could at least pay a debt on his way.

He loaded his rifle. But when he tipped powder into the pan, it stuck and caked. Drops of water appeared on the barrel. A soft rain had begun to fall. The guns were useless.

The French changed their tactics. Some fixed bayonets, while others threw down their rifles, drawing axes and tomahawks. They would finish this at close quarters.

They spread out in a broad circle, surrounding the knot of rangers clustered around the sledge. The pine resin in their torches hissed and spat.

'Is that you, Ahoma the Englishman?' called Bichot. The rain flattened his hair against his scalp, showing the scarred skin beneath. 'You should have known I always find my prey.'

'We will not surrender,' Theo warned.

'That is not your choice.' Bichot revealed his teeth in a wide grin. 'By the time I have finished with you, you will beg me to let you surrender. But I will not. Do you remember the way your wife's blood flowed when I stuck her like a pig? That was an easy death compared to what I'll do to you.'

Theo breathed hard and did not rise to the provocation. Beside him, Moses was crouching, rummaging in the bundle they had tied to the sledge.

'Unless you have a gun that does not need powder, and shoots twenty bullets at once, I do not think you will find anything to help us,' Theo muttered. He hefted his tomahawk, his eyes darting, keeping his enemies in sight. The odds were impossible: they were all around him.

Moses stood. Moonlight gleamed on the weapon in his hands. It was the axe they had brought for chopping firewood.

Moses raised it above his head. With all his strength, he swung it down and struck a mighty blow on the ice. Glistening shards flew in the air. Dark cracks raced out from the point of impact.

The Frenchmen stopped moving. Moses landed another blow. This time, he hacked and hacked like a man possessed until he had cut through the ice to the dark lake beneath. Water slopped up through the hole. The cracks in the ice lengthened.

'Are you mad?' said the wounded ranger. 'We'll all drown.'

Theo saw the desperate logic of Moses' plan. He stamped on the ice and hammered it with the butt of his rifle. Some of the Frenchmen edged back, but that was a mistake. Their movements put more stress on the fracturing ice. The cracks began to run together, forming islands of ice that broke away as the water lapped their edges.

Gaps opened in the circle of Frenchmen around the rangers.

'To the tree, Siumo!' Moses yelled in Abenaki. Theo was already moving. Dropping the rifle, he hoisted the wounded Judd over his shoulder and started towards the tree trunk still frozen in the ice. Half stumbling, half sliding, he slipped across the unsteady surface.

Suddenly, a rift tore through the ice in front of him. Theo had no time to react. The toe of his skate snagged in the gap and pitched him forwards. Judd was jolted off his shoulder and thrown in a heap as Theo landed flat on his belly.

For a moment, he thought the ice had held. Then it gave way with a snap, and he dropped into the water.

The shock of the freezing water almost stopped his heart. His head pounded; his limbs burned; he couldn't move. The weight of the thick furs pulled him down. If he went under, he would slip beneath the ice and drown.

A vision of Mgeso, trapped underwater, flashed through his mind. It gave him the strength to start moving again. He reached out of the water and scrabbled on the ice, trying to pull himself out. It was too slick. His fingers scraped and slid but could not grip. The water sucked him down.

Theo reached into his belt and felt his knife. He drew it, raised it over his head and drove the blade into the ice. He feared the steel would snap, or crack the ice, but both held. The blade dug in.

Using the hilt as a handhold, Theo hauled himself out of the water. Getting to his feet almost tipped him back in. Ignoring the cold that seized his bones, he began leaping from slab to slab towards the tree. The ice was rupturing in earnest, breaking into an archipelago of floes. It was like being caught in a giant game of chess, where all the pieces were moving at once. Everything was chaos. Some of the Frenchmen had fled to the thicker ice nearer shore; others, trapped in the fissures, splashed and floundered.

Theo could see the tree. He leaped like a madman to reach it. He skidded the last few feet and came up against the trunk. He reached for a knot in the wood to pull himself upwards.

A hand grabbed the scruff of his neck and spun him around. A snarling face loomed towards him. It was Bichot. A knife glittered in his hand. He swung it at Theo who ducked, but with the tree at his back he had little room to manoeuvre. The blade sliced his cheek open. He tried to kick Bichot away, aiming his skates at the Frenchman's legs.

With a groaning sound, like a gate slowly swinging open, the frozen tree broke free of the ice and rolled over. Its branches whipped viciously with terrifying speed, all the energy that had been trapped in the ice suddenly unleashed with tremendous force. One branch nearly toppled Theo. He just had time to jerk out of the way or it would have broken his back.

Bichot was not so lucky. The branch that missed Theo hit the Frenchman in the face. It knocked him into the water and pushed him under. He tried to escape, but it battered him down relentlessly, like the paddles of a water wheel as the trunk spun round.

The flailing tree had shattered the ice that Theo was standing on. He leaped into the churning water as another branch lashed past his head. Fighting for air, he swam up and grabbed one of the branches, letting it whip him around as the tree slowly settled.

At last it came to rest. Theo hauled himself onto its trunk, riding it like a panicked horse as it floated down the newly opened channel in the ice, carrying them away. Further down the trunk, he saw Moses and three other rangers clinging on. Even Judd had somehow managed to get aboard.

Theo looked back, but Bichot had disappeared into the dark lake.

• • •

General Corbeil was in a foul mood. 'Your finance minister is a criminal!' he raged. 'He has made himself a millionaire, while my men go cold and hungry. I demand he be recalled to Paris immediately, and tried at Versailles for his corruption and embezzlement.'

The governor general, the Comte de Bercheny, stared at Corbeil over his glass of wine. 'The finance minister is doing a splendid job. It is not easy, keeping your troops supplied through winter in this godforsaken country.'

'How can you not see it?' Corbeil raged. 'He charges me twice the price for meat I could get on the waterfront and pockets the difference himself.'

It was true. Bercheny knew it perfectly well. How else could the finance minister afford the generous bribes that the governor general insisted on? 'At least you cannot claim that I have short-changed you on your fort,' said Bercheny. 'You have lavished more on its defences than King Louis spends on his mistresses.'

'That fort is the key to all of New France,' Corbeil retorted. 'If it falls, then in a very short time you will see English ships anchored off Québec, and English guns firing through these windows into your salon.'

There was a knock at the door. An aide poked his head in. 'A messenger has arrived from Fort Royal, *mon général*.'

'Show him in.'

The man who entered seemed to have walked straight out of the forest. He was a *coureur des bois*, one of the irregular soldiers who lived wild, trapping, trading and fighting on the frontiers. He smelt of smoke and bear fat. He placed his beaver-skin hat on the table and did not salute. 'Capitaine Bichot sends his regards. He wishes to inform you that two weeks ago he surprised a patrol of English rangers on the slopes above Fort Royal.'

Corbeil went very still. 'Did they see the new defences?'

'We do not think so – but it is a possibility.'

'And did they escape?'

'A few. Bichot followed them. He had not returned when I set out, but I am sure they did not escape him.'

'*A few?*' Corbeil rose from his chair and slammed his fist on the table, so hard that the beaver hat flew into the air. 'His orders were to make sure that no English patrols came within ten miles of the fort.'

Bercheny stood. 'I will leave you to your soldiers' business,' he said smoothly. 'No doubt you have much to discuss.' He turned in the doorway and added, 'My compliments to your wife, General. I look forward to seeing her at the dance the regimental wives are holding.'

Corbeil didn't hear him. He was glaring at the courier with icy fury. 'How many of the English escaped?'

The courier shrugged. He had the natural insolence of a man who lived by his wits. 'Why don't you ask the prisoner?'

Corbeil paused. 'What prisoner?'

Gilyard was almost indistinguishable from the men who had brought him. His beard had grown wild, his clothes were ragged and filthy. Dark blood stained his shirt where it had seeped through the bandages. But fire still burned in his grey eyes, and though he was limping, he refused the chair Corbeil offered him by the fire.

The *coureur* left. Corbeil poured two glasses of wine and offered one to the prisoner. Gilyard did not touch it.

'I hope your journey was not too arduous, Major Gilyard,' Corbeil said courteously. He spoke in English, to Gilyard's surprise.

'You cannot understand your enemy unless you understand his language,' Corbeil explained. 'And I have an English wife.'

'Life is full of ironies,' said Gilyard.

Corbeil was silent. He tapped his fingernail against the side of his wineglass, studying the prisoner. He had long fingernails, Gilyard noticed. Added to his hooked nose and close-set eyes, it made him look like a bird of prey, studying a mouse.

'What should I do with you?' Corbeil mused aloud.

'I am an officer and a prisoner of war,' Gilyard answered. 'Shouldn't you offer me parole?'

Corbeil laughed, as if the idea had not occurred to him. 'If I offered you liberty, in exchange for your promise not to attempt escape, would you accept?'

'Of course not.'

'Then I shall not waste my breath. I have a different fate in mind for you.'

A gust of wind rattled the window panes, blowing icy air through the loose-fitting frame. Despite his best efforts, Gilyard flinched. After his brutal journey, standing so long was sapping what little strength he had left. But he would not break.

'I need you to tell me everything you know of your general's plans,' Corbeil said abruptly. 'His forces, their strength and dispositions. When and where he will attack this summer. Everything.'

For all the pain racking his body, Gilyard forced his face into a grin. 'I see you have mastered the English sense of humour.'

Lightning fast, Corbeil lashed out with his boot. It struck Gilyard on the kneecap. Something cracked. Gilyard's leg twisted and he dropped to the floor with a grunt of pain. He tried to rise, but Corbeil landed another kick in the side of his ribs that made him curl into a ball.

Corbeil stared down at him. 'However strong you think you are, however brave, you will not resist me.'

Gilyard moaned and cowered. Corbeil kicked out again.

But this time, his boot didn't strike. Gilyard's arms were instantly wrapped around his foot, hauling backwards with surprising strength. Corbeil sprawled on his back. Before he could get up, Gilyard was kneeling over him with a small bone-handled knife against his throat. 'Never count a ranger out,' he hissed. Putting his weight on his good leg, he dragged himself to his feet, coaxing Corbeil up. Though he clenched his teeth with the pain, the blade at the general's neck never wavered.

'Are you going to kill me?' Corbeil hissed. 'You will never escape this fortress alive.'

'I fancy my chances. I will lead your men a merry dance all the way to Boston, if need be.'

'And where will you find a way out?'

Gilyard shrugged. 'You tell me.'

He shifted his grip, keeping one hand around Corbeil's throat while the other held the knife pressed against the general's back. 'The point is between your third and fourth ribs,' he said. 'If you call for help, it'll slide clean through into your heart before you can make a sound.'

'I do not wish to die a hero's death,' Corbeil assured him. 'I will lead you to the water gate. The river is frozen. You will be able to escape that way.' He started towards the door.

Gilyard tightened his grip on Corbeil's neck, pulling him back on to the knife so that the point penetrated the fabric of his coat. 'Do you take me for a fool? There is a sentry outside that door, and I do not care to meet him.' He nudged Corbeil round towards the back of the room. In the corner a small door was set in an arch. 'Where does that lead?'

'My private apartments.'

'Guarded?'

'No.'

'Servants?'

'They will be in their quarters.'

'If you're lying, you will die before I do.'

'I am not lying,' said Corbeil.

Could Gilyard trust him? He had no choice. When they stepped through the door, they found a small salon with a chaise longue, an ottoman and a fire dying in the grate. More doors opened to left and right.

Gilyard surveyed his options. 'Which way is the river?'

Corbeil jerked his head left. It led into a woman's boudoir, also unoccupied. The candles were lit, and the scent of expensive perfume was heavy in the air. Through the window, Gilyard could see the white expanse of the St Lawrence River and the lights of the warehouses on the far shore.

Under Gilyard's orders, Corbeil stripped the sheets from the bed and tied them together, then fastened them to the bedpost. He opened the window and dropped the daisy-chained sheets down. The wall fell sheer to the frozen river below.

'I am sorry to leave you,' said Gilyard. 'General Williams would have paid me a large sum of money if I brought you back alive. But it is a long journey, and I do not think you and I would make good travelling companions. And Williams will still pay thirty shillings for your scalp.'

Without warning, Gilyard clenched his arm around Corbeil's throat again. Holding him fast, he pulled off Corbeil's wig and put the knife against his scalp. Corbeil tried to scream, but Gilyard's grip was crushing his windpipe and no sound emerged. This could not be happening. He was a major general of France, in his own headquarters. To die like this, at the hands of the vermin he had dedicated his life to destroying, was insupportable.

'Maybe only twenty shillings,' Gilyard muttered. 'This blade is a little small for the task. But it will serve if I . . .'

Suddenly, the arm around Corbeil's throat loosened. The blade fell away from his scalp. That was all the opening he needed. He fought his way free, quick as a leopard, ready to throttle the life out of the ranger who had nearly humiliated him.

Gilyard writhed on the floor, clutching his backside. A small penknife stuck out from his buttock, which was bleeding heavily. Constance stood over him, wearing a blood-spattered *négligé*.

A marble wig-stand stood on her dresser. Corbeil snatched it and smashed it into Gilyard's face with such force that it shattered his nose. The ranger collapsed, blood and bone fragments covering his face. Corbeil knelt over him. He raised the block of marble, ready to strike again. His fury was boundless. He would smash this man's skull until it was nothing but a pulp of bloody flesh.

A voice from behind him stayed his arm. 'What has happened here?'

Governor general Bercheny was at the doorway. Two soldiers waited in the corridor outside, though Corbeil had not heard anyone call for help.

'The prisoner tried to escape. I . . .' Corbeil dropped the wig-stand and struggled to his feet, burning with frustrated blood lust. 'I prevented him.'

He realised blood was dripping from the cut on his scalp that Gilyard had begun. He would have a scar across his forehead for the rest of his life. A wig would hide it, but Corbeil would always feel the shame.

'It seems you had some help,' said Bercheny. 'Happy the man who can call upon his wife in his hour of need. You are lucky, General.'

He was mocking him. Corbeil felt the anger swell inside him again, fixing irrationally on Constance. How demeaning to be saved by a woman wielding a penknife from her writing desk.

Gilyard groaned. He was a hard man to kill, but Corbeil would enjoy finding out what it took. The guards carried him away to the cells.

'I will make you pay for everything you did to me!' Corbeil shouted after him.

By the window, Constance had picked up Gilyard's knife. It trembled in her hands – her body was shaking. The shock of what had occurred caught up with her.

She saw Corbeil watching and made to offer him the knife. 'Keep it,' Corbeil said brusquely. 'I will show you how to use it so that next time, when you stab a man in the back, you do it properly.'

Constance slipped the knife into the drawer of her dressing-table. 'I look forward to the lesson.'

• • •

Fifty rangers had set out on the scout. Five returned, four making their way over the slushy ground, dragging a fifth on a makeshift stretcher of saplings. A bell was tolling from the small village that clung to the lake shore. It was nearly midnight, but as Theo approached he saw lights inside the church. The doors opened, and a throng of people in their Sunday best spilled out onto the muddy road.

'What are they doing?' Theo wondered.

Some of the congregation were still singing a hymn: 'Hark how all the welkin rings,/ Glory to the King of Kings.'

'It is Christmas!' Moses exclaimed.

With his Abenaki appearance and dress, it was easy to forget he had been taught in a mission school. Theo would have sensed the irony if he hadn't been so exhausted.

The parishioners were alarmed to see five filthy, bloody vagabonds staggering into their village. Some of the men from the outlying farms carried pistols as protection against wild animals. They drew them and might well have fired if Theo had not managed to cry out, 'God save the King! We are English.'

Then he collapsed. The last sound he remembered hearing was children singing, 'Born to raise the sons of Earth,/ Born to give them second birth.'

A week later, he presented himself at the headquarters in Albany. His arm was in a sling, his face bandaged from Bichot's cut, and he walked with a limp. The first thing he had done on reaching the town was to visit his wife and son. Abigail was tearful at how broken her man appeared, but she hugged him first tentatively and then more closely as she felt his full warmth against her skin, and for a moment she was whole again. Caleb cried, too, but more with hunger than surprise. Theo knew the world stopped spinning when he was embraced by his family. He wanted never to leave them again.

Although it was the depths of winter, the headquarters were filled with bustle and activity. He expected a long wait, but instead he was ushered straight up the stairs, and into General Williams's office.

Theo saluted. The general regarded him with keen eyes. He had an aquiline face, with salt-and-pepper hair and the easy command of a born patrician. Pictures of hunting and horses adorned the walls. From appearances, it would be easy to dismiss him as another English aristocrat, given an army to play with by his friends at court. In fact, he was the son of a Kentish lawyer, who had earned every promotion on the battlefield. Theo could tell at once that he was a born soldier.

'My condolences on your unit,' the general said. 'No doubt you lost many friends – and Major Gilyard was a fine soldier.'

Theo nodded.

'His absence is a grievous blow.' Williams leaned forward. 'This must be the year we defeat the French in America or concede the fight. There are powerful voices in London, whose owners insist we should be concentrating our war efforts in Europe, not some far-flung wilderness. We cannot afford another defeat like last year.'

Theo gestured his assent.

'When spring comes, I shall attack Fort Royal.'

Theo knew he had to speak. 'With respect, sir, we found evidence the French have taken guns up onto the ridge that commands the fort. They have made it impregnable.'

'I have read your report,' snapped Williams. 'One rusting gun does not make a battery, and no fort is impregnable. If we cannot take Fort Royal, the war fails. I will break their resistance if I must level the mountain and drain the lake to do it.'

'Yes, sir.'

'The task will be harder without Major Gilyard,' Williams conceded. 'The French fear the rangers like the pox. I need your men guarding our flanks, keeping the French pinned behind their walls and out of the woods.'

Theo blinked. 'My men, sir?'

'You are now the senior officer in the company.' He passed a paper across the table. 'I signed the order for your promotion this morning. Congratulations, Captain Courtney.'

Theo didn't touch the paper. 'It is a great honour, sir, but I fear to tell you, I mean to quit the army.'

Williams stared at him, as though he had uttered the most arrant nonsense imaginable.

'Today is New Year's Eve,' Theo persisted. 'My enlistment expires at midnight tonight.'

'You do not know what you are saying,' said Williams. 'You have suffered a great deal of hardship these past weeks. Take two weeks' leave, then return to your unit.'

Theo felt the full weight of the general's stare, the power of a man who had broken fortresses and directed armies with the force of his will. Yet he did not waver. He had thought of little else since he returned, talking long into the night with Abigail. It was time to look to his future.

'My father died too young, and his father before him. I want to see my son grow up.'

Williams held his gaze. Perhaps he saw something of his own strength in Theo's eyes, for the outrage on his face softened to something like respect. He folded the commission and pressed it into Theo's hand. 'It is undated. If you think again, there is always a place in my army for you.'

'Thank you, sir. But my mind is made up. We will buy a wagon and settle new land in the Ohio country.'

'A pity. Word of your exploits is getting out, Mr Courtney. After what you have achieved, your men would do anything for you.'

Theo left the room, disquieted. Something inside him sat uneasy with abandoning the fight, and what remained of his men. He also considered his higher purpose, his revenge for the death of his loved ones. But he forgot his doubts the moment he saw Abigail and Caleb waiting on the street outside.

Abigail ran to him, scanning his features anxiously. 'Did he try to dissuade you?'

Theo showed her Williams's paper. 'He offered me a commission as captain.'

Her face fell. 'I told you they would try to tempt you.'

'And I told him no.' Theo took the paper in both hands and ripped it up until the pieces were so small they blew out of his grip. He watched them float down the street. They settled in the mud and were soon ground underfoot.

He took Caleb from Abigail's arms and held him aloft, delighting in the baby's squeals of excitement.

'From now on, I belong only to you.'

• • •

Corporal Pierre Duchambon had not seen daylight in a fortnight. For the minor infraction of stealing a few *sous* from his messmates – only to pay money he owed a pimp – he had been punished with two weeks' prison duty. The dungeon lay beneath the fortress of Québec, deep within the insurmountable promontory of Cap Diamant that commanded the St Lawrence River. For eight hours a day, Pierre stood guard on the solitary prisoner who occupied it. Down before dawn, up after sunset on the infernally short winter days, he lived every hour by the light of a single lamp that was forever threatening to sputter out. He was sick of solitude, and sick of the dark.

When he heard footsteps descending the long spiral stair, he was pathetically grateful at the prospect of company. He heard soft footsteps, not the heavy tread of soldiers' boots. An officer?

Pierre stiffened to attention but hunched with surprise when he saw who it was. A beautiful woman with shining golden hair, wrapped in a fur stole, came towards him with an attractive maid-servant carrying a lantern.

He saluted. 'Are you lost, madame?'

'I wish to see the prisoner,' she said, in a voice that brooked little argument.

Pierre shifted uneasily. 'I have orders from the captain that no one is to be admitted.'

'My husband is the general.' She stared at him, her cool green eyes adamant. 'All I am asking is that you leave us for ten minutes.'

'I cannot desert my post.' He could not face the prospect of more punishment, more weeks in darkness.

'If anyone finds you, tell them I fainted and you went to fetch water. My maid will go with you and support your story.' Her face softened into a warm, willing smile. 'No one will know. And I'm sure you would be glad of a few minutes of my maid's company. It must be lonely for you down here all by yourself.'

To have the sympathy of such a beautiful, noble woman after all his hours of misery – Pierre would have done anything for her. Her maid was not unattractive either. 'You will not help him escape?' he asked.

'He tried to kill my husband. He will die in that cell before I see him released.'

Her tone was so chilling, Pierre could not doubt she meant it. He unlocked the door and retreated up the stairs with the maid.

The moment Constance stepped into the cell she felt the darkness and the confinement smother her. The stench of decay and waste and despair washed over her. Memories she had forced deep inside herself burst out, flooding her with the shock of revelation. She put a hand against the slick wall to steady herself and almost shrieked. It was like touching the past, the desperation of the Black Hole in Calcutta. A vision of Deegan swam before her eyes, the fat old sot's face sliding down her stomach as she trampled him to death.

The memory gave her strength. She closed her eyes, counting her breaths. 'You survived that. You can survive anything,' she told herself.

The panic passed. She mastered herself. She opened her eyes again. When she lifted the lamp to study the man she'd come to see, she saw only a wretched prisoner in her power.

'Did you come to finish your work?' croaked Gilyard. He was chained against the wall, his face wrapped in black blood-soaked bandages. Small holes had been cut for his nose and lips, while his one remaining eye gazed at her through a narrow slit.

She reached in her purse and pulled out the small knife she had taken from Gilyard in the fight. She crouched in front of him, out of his reach, so he could see the Indian totems and wild animals carved into the antler handle. She turned it over to show him the writing on the reverse.

To Major Gilyard from Theo Courtney, in gratitude.

'The Theo Courtney who gave you this knife: is he about my age? Does he have red hair, and brown eyes?'

Gilyard would not speak. She leaned closer, wondering if he could smell her perfume through what was left of his nose. She let her hair brush his face as she whispered in his ear, 'Theo Courtney is my brother.'

Gilyard could not hide his surprise. He craned his head round, trying to read Constance's face for any hint of a trick or a lie. All he saw were her green eyes gazing back. A hard stare, like he used to see in Theo's determined glare.

She saw the truth in Gilyard's one, unblinking eye. 'Where is he?'

Gilyard tried to speak but was consumed by a fit of choking. 'How?'

'We were separated by tragedy almost three years ago. I did not know he was alive.'

He watched her, making grim soughing sounds through his nose. 'Help me,' he whispered.

Memories of the Black Hole swirled around her in the noxious air, ghosts waiting to tear her mind apart. She could not hold them off much longer. 'What do you want of me?'

He bobbed his head towards the knife in her hands. It shone with lethal promise in the lamplight. 'Release me.'

'Where can I find my brother?'

Under the bandages, Gilyard's face was unreadable. Constance feared he might slip into unconsciousness. 'Albany,' he breathed at last.

'Thank you.'

She offered him the knife, but he pushed it back into her hand. 'I am too weak. You must do it.'

She nodded. She felt no guilt. If she did not do this, Gilyard would suffer either an agonising death from gangrene, or an even slower, more painful death at the hands of Corbeil's torturers. And a dead man could not reveal her connection with Theo.

'Show me where.'

He raised his left arm and pointed to a place under the armpit. 'Here. Slide it in flat, between the ribs.'

It was the second time in her life that Constance killed a man. The first had been frenzied, the instinct of a panicked animal. This was almost serene. She sat beside Gilyard, putting one arm around his shoulders to brace him. She moved the blade, probing for the right spot until he nodded. Then she rammed it through the skin. It was easier than she'd expected.

The little blade was long enough to reach the heart. She watched him die. The shudder that went through the body, the momentary tension, then the slump as his muscles relaxed for the last time. A life, gone.

A noise in the passage announced the guard's return. She pulled out the knife, wiped the blade and returned it to her purse. Blood welled from the wound, soaking into the bandages, but they were so filthy it barely showed. No one would examine this rotting corpse too closely.

She swept out of the room and closed the door before the guard could look in.

'Thank you,' she said. 'Did anyone challenge you?'

'No, madame.' Curiosity got the better of Pierre. 'What were you doing in there?'

'I prayed with him,' she said. 'I do not think he has long to live.'

Pierre nodded, relieved. With her golden hair and alabaster skin, she looked the perfect angel of mercy.

'And if you tell anyone I was here, I will make sure my husband assigns you the furthest, coldest outpost on the frontier.'

His jaw dropped.

She smiled sweetly. 'The best charity is done in secret.'

Her fixed smile disappeared the moment she returned to her boudoir. First the dungeon, now Theo: her body was shaking with the release of emotions she'd thought she had locked away for ever.

She stank of the dungeon. She had her maid fill a hot bath and undress her, then sent the girl away to launder the clothes in case any blood had stained them. Constance settled into the steaming water, letting the water lap over her breasts. The heat opened her pores and let out the filth of the prison. She soaped it away.

That Theo should be so close, barely two hundred miles away, beggared belief. Did he know she was alive? Impossible. She had been carried out of the Black Hole as a corpse: everyone in India would have believed her dead.

Should she try to find him? What would she say?

Another image from the past returned to her. Theo as she had last seen him, caught in the spyglass as his ship sailed from Calcutta. Abandoning her, breaking every promise he had ever made to protect her.

But he was all the family she had.

She was still pondering it when Corbeil arrived. He threw his hat and coat into a corner and sank onto the chaise without taking his boots off. They left dark dirty streaks on the upholstery.

The sight of it – the black mud oozing over the blue silk – changed something inside her. She hated it here: the snow, the mud, the cold, having to make small talk with the garrison wives, their fashions five years out of date, and bumptious merchants who talked only of money. Paris was where she belonged: the only place she had approached true happiness.

'Please do not put your dirty boots on my chaise,' she said. 'I had the fabric imported from Paris.'

Corbeil gave her a dismissive look and didn't move his feet.

'I want to go back,' Constance announced. 'As soon as the ice melts, I will take the first ship for France.'

'You belong with me.'

'I belong to no one.' Constance stepped out of the bath. She stood for a moment, dripping and naked. She knew she was beautiful, and the power she had over men. She enjoyed seeing the conflicting emotions play out on Corbeil's face. 'You cannot keep me here,' she said.

'Of course I can. You are my wife.'

She dried herself, arching her back so that her breasts pushed forward, letting her hand linger in intimate places. A bulge was rising in Corbeil's breeches, and it delighted her to see the effect she had on him.

'Come back with me,' she said, advancing towards him. 'Let us leave this frozen wilderness and go somewhere we can be warm.'

Corbeil shook his head. 'You know I cannot. The English are advancing on three fronts. They are over-extended. This summer we will destroy them utterly.'

He swung his legs off the chaise, spreading the mud wider over the fabric, and stood. 'I do not care for this mood of yours. All day I have that idiot governor general undermining me and questioning my orders. Half my supplies have disappeared, I cannot feed my men, and the finance minister is growing fat on the pickings. A wife should be a solace to her husband, not a scold.'

He noticed that Constance was staring past him, her eyes fixed on the streaks of mud on her chaise. He grabbed her shoulders. 'Are you listening to me?'

'I am leaving.' She shook his hands off her and went to her dresser, pulling out clothes. 'I am sick of it all – this fort, this country. I am sick of *you*.'

She had meant to wound him. But she had not expected to strike so deep. Corbeil crossed the room and clamped his hands on her shoulders. She struggled, clawing him away; her nails caught his cheek. He threw up his arms – whether to block her or to retaliate, she didn't know.

His fist struck the middle of her face in a quick rabbit punch. Blood erupted from her nose and ran down her naked skin. She shrieked with pain but more with shock, transported in an instant back to Mauvières's château.

Corbeil stepped back, breathing hard, his features hard as stone. He adjusted his neck-cloth. 'You will not leave New France until I have finished. Do I make myself clear?'

From the corner of her eye, Constance saw the marble wig-stand back in its usual position on the dresser. For a moment, she imagined seizing it, doing to Corbeil what he had done to Gilyard. She imagined how his face would look staved in, like a barrel.

But he was strong and she was weak. She did not want to be hit again. She bowed her head, letting more blood drip over her breasts. 'I will obey my husband.'

• • •

Constance did not cry. She sat in her chair with her head held upwards until the bleeding stopped, then let the maid sponge the blood off her face. The bruising could have been worse. Corbeil hadn't driven through with his punch and her nose was not broken. She painted the skin that was beginning to colour with heavy make-up.

She dressed in her finest gown and sent the maid with a message. 'Convey my compliments to the governor general, the Comte de Bercheny, and inform him I would be delighted to receive him in my salon. He may come alone.'

Bercheny arrived half an hour later, strutting through the door like a cockerel. He had dressed in silk stockings, and a fine coat the colour of Burgundy. He sat close beside her, and she turned her head away to hide the caked powder that covered her bruises.

'You afford me a rare honour, receiving me so late.'

Constance bit her lip. She played with her skirts, twisting the fabric in her hands in obvious distress. 'I had to see a friendly soul.'

Bercheny patted her hand. 'Do not fret, my dear. Tell me what troubles you.'

'You are very kind. Sometimes I think you are the only true companion I have in this colony.' She sniffed, then cried out, 'Oh, monsieur, if only I could tell you what is in my breast. But no – there are some secrets a married woman must never breathe aloud, even if hiding them breaks her heart.'

Bercheny nodded sympathetically. He took her hand between his and stroked it, edging closer so that their thighs pressed together. 'If I may presume to read a woman's heart, madame, I think I know the source of your troubles.'

'Pray tell.'

'I will show you.'

He leaned over, closed his eyes and kissed her – at first tentatively, but rapidly gaining confidence when she did not resist. She let him slip his tongue into her mouth. It had the tart taste of red wine and tobacco.

His hand pawed at her bodice. She drew away with a little gasp. 'Monsieur, I cannot,' she breathed. 'I am a married woman.'

Bercheny wrinkled his nose. 'What of it? You know as well as I do that marriage is no barrier to the occasional *liaison*. My friend, the Marquise de Sologne, tells me that in Paris you were quite renowned for your conquests.'

'That is not very gallant of you,' Constance reproached him. 'I was a widow then. I left that life behind when I married General de Corbeil.'

'He is a fine commander. But is he everything you wanted in a husband? I have seen the candles in his office burning long into the night. Does he give you all the affection a husband owes his wife?'

Constance averted her eyes. 'He saved me from ruin in Paris. I owe him everything. Please do not persist in this conversation, monsieur. It dishonours both of us.'

Bercheny's hand had wormed onto her leg again. It drifted between her thighs, rubbing against her. Constance let herself enjoy the feeling for a moment, then firmly lifted the hand away. 'I cannot.'

'Perhaps I have been too clumsy. But, if so, it is only because love impels me.'

'Love?' she cried. 'Do not speak that word. I am a married woman. I am forbidden love.'

'Please, madame,' he implored. 'Your husband need never know.'

'No,' she said determinedly.

'I thought – I flattered myself – you harboured certain feelings for me. Feelings I most ardently reciprocate.'

She blushed. 'Do not mistake duty for lack of feeling. If I were a widow again, everything would be so different.'

She met Bercheny's gaze and held it until he could not miss her meaning. His eyes widened, then narrowed into cold calculation.

'Anything can happen on the battlefield,' he said. 'Even generals lose their lives.'

'Do not say such things. I tremble even to think of something befalling my husband.'

'Of course. I was speaking in general terms. Your husband is a hero of France, and his loss would be catastrophic.'

'Where will the fighting be fiercest?' Constance asked.

'Fort Royal. That is where the British are concentrating their forces, and where we must resist them.'

'You would need your greatest commander there.'

Constance leaned so close towards him that he could feel her breath on his lips when she spoke. His ardour left him blind to the imperfections she knew she displayed on her face. 'Believe me when I tell you, sir, there are feelings in my breast that no married woman could admit. I know it is a silly thing: a woman must subordinate her desires to duty. But if only circumstances allowed, monsieur, I would give you . . . everything.'

•   •   •

As soon as he had gone, Constance went to her *secrétaire* and wrote a letter.

> *The man who took Calcutta, General de Corbeil, will be commanding at Fort Royal. He is responsible for the deaths of many you held dear. If you loved your sister, do not miss this chance to avenge her fate.*

I dare not identify myself, but I assure you we share a common purpose. I enclose this knife, which belonged to a mutual friend, as proof that you may trust me.

She wrapped the letter around the knife and sealed it. Then she enclosed the package in oilcloth, tied it with string and sealed it again. Finally, she took a fur shawl, slit the lining and hid the packet inside. When she had sewn it shut, she gave it to her maid, along with a purse of gold.

'Go down to the low town. There must be trappers or furriers who trade with the British. Find one who can take this to Albany.'

The maid curtsied. She was a sly girl, but utterly loyal since Constance had rescued her from an unfortunate pregnancy.

Constance stared out of the window at the falling snow with a glass of wine. She had killed one man today, and perhaps signed a death warrant for another. Yet when she lifted the glass to her blood-red lips, her hand was as steady as the marble wig-stand.

• • •

Winter turned to spring and Theo and Abigail made their preparations. Abigail, who had grown up working on the frontier, knew what they needed, and everything they could do without or make for themselves. In the evenings, she knitted clothes for the growing baby, while Theo carved utensils and tool handles. They stockpiled flour, oats, dried peas and all the other foodstuffs they might need on their journey. Theo still possessed his rifle, though it was difficult to find powder or lead for shot when the army's quartermasters were patrolling.

The wagon and the ox team they needed were even harder to come by. It seemed that General Williams had commandeered every vehicle and draught animal in the thirteen colonies. The town was filled with soldiers passing through to the lakes, as the army massed for the coming campaign. One day, Theo saw a company of rangers marching by, tall and cocksure in their new green jackets.

'Do you miss it, Siumo?' asked Moses. When Theo had told him he was quitting the army, the Abenaki had not blinked. It had never been discussed but it was understood he would accompany them to their new home. His loyalty ran deeper than that of any other man Theo had known.

'No,' said Theo. 'That life is behind me now.'

Moses burst out laughing. 'What is so amusing?' said Theo.

'You are lying and you do not even know it.'

'I insist I am not,' Theo protested.

'Does the hawk stay at home to feather his nest? Does he brood over the eggs?' Moses tipped back his head in mirth. 'Mgeso named you well. You are Siumo, the hawk. The hunt is in your blood.'

'You're wrong,' said Theo. 'My ancestors chased glory and died young.'

Moses nodded, as if Theo had only confirmed his point. 'And when you speak to your ancestors, do they say they regret it?'

It seemed they might never leave Albany. One evening, Theo met a Dutchman in a tavern with a wagon to sell. Theo bought it on the spot for an eye-watering price. After the purchase, the days disappeared in a frantic blur of last-minute preparations.

The morning they were to depart dawned clear and bright. Everything was bustle as they stowed their last supplies and harnessed the ox team. There were numerous delays. As they were about to set off, young Caleb decided he was hungry, and commenced such a howling that they had to pause for Abigail to nurse him. The child soiled himself and needed changing. Abigail remembered she had forgotten a set of her favourite combs in her dresser drawer.

At last they began their journey. Theo took a final look at Albany. He had thought this would be a triumphant moment, the start of a new chapter in his life. But something inside nagged at him. The night before he had dreamed of Mgeso again.

Abigail gave him a keen look. 'No regrets?'

'None.'

He cracked the whip. The wagon lumbered into motion. The going was slow: the roads were rutted and deeply scored by the military traffic. The wagon swayed and bounced with every bump in the road. Caleb, who had fallen asleep, was jolted awake, and made his displeasure known with a great wailing that frightened the birds from the trees.

'Now I know why the Dutchman was so eager to sell you this wagon,' said Abigail. 'It seems to be a contraption for transporting us at the slowest pace, with the greatest effort, in the least possible comfort. The whole thing sounds as if it is about to fly into pieces.'

No sooner had she spoken than there was a tremendous crack. The wagon lurched and tipped over, spilling sacks and baggage onto the ground.

Theo leaped from the driver's box and ran to the back. He swore. The axle had split, and one of the wheels had snapped. It would take hours to move the wagon, let alone find a wheelwright to make a repair.

'Stay with Abigail,' he told Moses. 'I will return to Albany for help.'

On his way through the town, he passed their old house. A greasy-haired man in buckskin leggings and a hunting shirt was outside, looking through the windows. He had a strange air about him, furtive and dangerous, and a bundle tucked under his arm. It would probably have been wise to avoid him.

But Theo was curious. 'Can I help you?'

The man turned. Theo noticed how his hand instinctively went towards the sheathed knife in his belt.

'I am looking for Theo Courtney,' he said. He had a strong, guttural accent that sounded French.

Theo rested his hand on the hilt of his own knife, though he smiled. 'Then you are a lucky man. An hour ago, I had quit this town for good, but now I find myself returned.' And then, seeing the man had not understood: 'I am Theo Courtney.'

'I have to give you this.'

The man tossed Theo the bundle. Expecting a trap, Theo let it drop in front of him. But the

Frenchman made no move to attack. He tucked his thumbs into his belt, watching Theo with an insolent expression.

Theo picked up the package and slit the cloth wrapper with his knife. Inside was a soft, beaver-fur shawl. 'Who sent me this?' he demanded. But when he looked up, the man had disappeared.

He stared at the shawl, wondering what it could possibly mean. The man had been clear about whom he should give it to. But there was no note, no explanation. And it was a woman's garment. If he held it close, he could still smell traces of perfume.

Who was she?

Absently, he stroked his hand over it. The fur was soft – it must have been expensive – but near the nape of the neck, he touched something solid.

He cut the lining, felt around and found a package, wrapped in oilskin.

He opened it.

• • •

Abigail sensed a turn of events the moment she saw Theo stride around the bend in the road. 'Where have you been? Where are the men? What is that look on your face?'

Wordlessly, Theo passed her the note. He held Caleb while she read it. The baby babbled happily as he snuggled into his father's chest, unaware of what was happening.

'What does this mean?' said Abigail. 'What is this token he talks about?'

Theo gave her the knife. Abigail gasped as she recognised it. 'The gift you carved for Major Gilyard.'

'They must have found it on his body. How it came to me, like this . . .' Theo shook his head. He had thought of nothing else as he made his return, and still could not fathom it.

'Can it be true?'

'What she says—'

Abigail gave him a sharp look. 'Why do you think it is a "she"?'

'The letter came hidden in a woman's shawl. Also, there is an aspect to the handwriting that is . . .' Theo stared at it. The word 'familiar' had been on the tip of his tongue, but that was impossible. '. . . feminine.'

'But how could she be so knowledgeable about you? About Calcutta, your sister, Gilyard . . .'

'I do not know.'

Abigail glared at him. The hope in her face heated to anger as she saw his intentions. Behind her, Moses had already started unloading the rifles and ammunition boxes from the wagon. 'You promised, Theo. A new beginning.'

Theo hugged Caleb. He wanted so badly to agree, to make her happy and honour his promise. But he could think only of the ghost fires burning in the swamp, the restless spirits of the unavenged dead. So many he had left behind. Would they find peace, if he killed Corbeil? Would he?

'You will regret it,' Abigail warned. But he hardly heard her. A voice sang in his head, and at last he recognised it for what it was. His ancestors were speaking to him.

He knew what he had to do.

• • •

The salon door slammed open. Constance looked up from the book she was reading to see Corbeil striding across the room. He was wearing his dress uniform, with a face like thunder.

She raised an eyebrow. 'From the noise you made, I thought the English must have overrun our defences. I quite feared for my virtue.'

Corbeil paid no attention. 'Do you know what stupidity our illustrious governor general has concocted now?'

'I cannot imagine.'

'He has ordered me to supervise the defence of Fort Royal in person.'

Constance closed her book. 'But surely that is a great compliment. You said yourself it is the most important theatre of the war. The governor does you a great honour by insisting you take personal command.'

Corbeil shook his head impatiently. 'You understand it no better than he does – though at least *you* have the excuse of your sex. It is madness. I have to direct our war against the English on three fronts. If I commit myself to one, how can I supervise the others?'

'The governor general is your superior,' said Constance. 'You must defer to him – as a wife defers to her husband.'

A sly tone entered her voice with those last words. Corbeil heard it: his head jerked up. He stared at her, and she made no effort to hide the contempt or delight she felt. Understanding dawned across his face. 'This is your doing, isn't it?' he said slowly. 'You think this will be revenge for our quarrel, that you can gamble the future of France in a fit of spite?'

Constance smiled. Corbeil laughed bitterly. 'Why not? It worked with poor Colonel de Mauvières. I was your willing executioner. And now you have tired of me, you think that fat fool Bercheny will do the same to me.'

He leaned down and held her chin, raking her face with his eyes. 'What did you offer him? The same as you promised me? It no longer satisfies you to be a general's wife. You feel a count would be more appropriate to your station.'

'I wish to be with a man who honours me.'

Corbeil shook his head. 'You want a man you can twist around your finger. But you will find me a worthier adversary than Mauvières. If I am to perish, I will bring you down with me. You will accompany me to Fort Royal.'

'The governor general will forbid it,' she answered.

'The governor general has departed on business to Montréal. By the time he returns, you and I will be happily settled in our quarters at Fort Royal. In summer it is a stinking, fly-ridden swamp – but that should not trouble you. It is where a creature like you belongs.'

She did not flinch. Even as he hated her, he had to admire her self-control.

'Bercheny is finished,' he told her. 'I have written to the king of how his corruption and avarice threaten our campaign. You want to go to Paris? When I have defeated the English, I will return to France a hero.' He stroked a lock of hair back from her cheek. 'When the king receives me at Versailles, you will accompany me. And if you so much as smile at another man . . .'

'What?' she challenged him. 'Will you hit me again – brave General Corbeil who makes war on women?'

'I will lock you in a convent for the rest of your life.'

He opened her dressing chest and pulled a pile of clothes onto the floor. 'Come, *dear wife*. We should prepare for our journey.'

Obediently, she called her maids to start folding her clothes. She knew when to yield.

'But who will you find waiting for you?' she said, under her breath.

D appled sunlight painted the forest floor. The May air was noisy with the chirrup of birdsong and the hum of insects. In the treetops, branches thrashed where a woodpecker was pursuing its mate. Below, the three men stalking through the trees barely stirred a leaf.

They were covered with earth and broken twigs. Their beards were like birds' nests, their faces streaked with mud. The brasswork on their rifles had been scorched black so it would not gleam in the light. They moved in a low crouch, taking slow, exaggerated steps.

They crossed a narrow stream, taking care not to let their powder get wet.

'You can stop right there,' said a voice behind them. 'I have been watching you these past ten minutes.'

The three men stood and looked around sheepishly. They saw nothing.

Theo dropped from the branch where he had been sitting. He wore a moss-green ranger's jacket and brown breeches, which had blended with the tree trunk. He landed lightly on his feet and strode towards them. 'I trust you were more discreet around the French.'

The leader of the patrol saluted. 'We finished our scout without being seen. Nothing to report, Captain Courtney.'

Theo nodded. His new rank was a novelty that hadn't worn off. Every time he heard it, he had to resist the urge to swell with pride. He took his status seriously. He was responsible for the well-being of two hundred men, most of them new recruits, and he felt the weight of their lives as keenly as his own. 'You returned the way you came,' he admonished them. 'Today it was me waiting for you. Another day, you may not be so lucky.'

The men nodded, contrite. They were raw and had much to learn. Theo would not accept excuses. He had the same high expectations of all his men, from the hardest veteran to the youngest greenhorn, but they did not grudge it. They knew it was because he cared for them. Behind his back, and around the campfires, the stories they told of his exploits grew so tall that Theo would have blushed if he'd heard them.

'Go back to camp and clean up,' he told them.

They saluted again and hurried away. Theo lingered, leaning against a tree, peeling bark off a twig. These snatched moments of solitude were a tonic.

'You can come out,' he said, to no one in particular.

Moses rose from a patch of sassafras. He looked wounded. 'Did you know I was there?'

'No,' Theo admitted. 'But I knew you must be close. How did they do?'

'Not well enough to know I had followed them.'

'Did anyone follow you?'

Moses bared his teeth in a smile. 'If anyone had dared, I would have brought you his scalp.'

'We will lose a man if we're not careful,' Theo fretted. 'The French know this terrain better than we do, and they have many allies. What did you find?'

'As they told you. There is no way through.'

Theo swore. The army had marched up the lake a month ago. It had been painstaking progress: fifteen thousand men trying to cut a road through impenetrable forest. They had ground to a halt before the defences the French had put in place. On their left flank was the lake, on their right the impassable heights of the bluffs. They were so steep, Theo still did not know if guns were mounted on top of them. But he knew the French had men up there, for he had seen the smoke of their campfires.

The only approach to the fort was between the lake and the heights. The British faced a labyrinth of the most devious and sadistic defences that military engineers had ever devised. The French had flooded land, felled trees, dug trenches and raised every sort of obstacle, so that the forest became a nightmare of navigation. The rangers were the only men who dared enter it – and even they could not find a safe route through.

'We will not last long if we cannot negotiate the impediments,' Theo predicted. 'The first cases of fever have already set in. Our supply lines are long, and we are horribly exposed if the French bring reinforcements. We cannot afford to wait them out.'

He did not admit it was more personal than that. *He* could not afford to wait. The last night with Abigail had been the hardest of all. She had wept and beaten his chest with her fists, while the baby slept unaware in his crib. In the end, she had accepted Theo must go. 'But I will not wait for you for ever,' she warned. 'I need a husband who thinks of his children, not the ghost of a dead woman.'

He wasn't sure if she meant Constance or Mgeso. He had never told her about his dream, but he wondered if she had guessed. The thought was like a piece of ice in his heart. Every morning, he woke wondering, *Have I chosen right?*

Moses looked at him, reading his thoughts as usual. 'What do your ancestors say?'

Theo laughed. 'They say I will find nothing if I send other men to do my work. I will reconnoitre the terrain myself.'

'The French hate the rangers above all others,' Moses reminded him. 'If they catch you, it will be a slow and savage death.'

'Then you had better come, too, to make sure they do not find us.'

• • •

That evening, two men slipped away from the British camp. To all appearances, they were Abenaki, dressed and painted for war. If they had been sighted by the sentries, they would surely have been shot on sight.

But no one saw them.

Theo had shaved his scalp and painted it red. He had put the rings in his ears, forcing open the holes that had healed, and a porcupine quill through his nose. He was bare-chested down to his buckskin leggings and moccasins. He had not told his companions, for he did not want his men to see him like that. They knew he had lived as an Abenaki for a year – it was part of his legend – but this was still the army. It would not do for the men to think their captain had gone native.

'How will we find a way through?' Theo asked.

'When you are seeking eggs, how do you find the nest?' Moses replied. 'You follow the bird.'

He led Theo into the woods, flitting silently between the trees like a moth. The moon was out, though little light penetrated the forest canopy. But Moses seemed able to see in the dark. He stopped. He had felt a tremor in the earth, the vibrations of a sentry stamping his feet to keep his blood moving. He followed it to a place where they could peer from behind a bush to see a pair of French soldiers standing behind a wooden palisade.

Theo glanced at Moses and mimed slitting his throat. Moses shook his head. They waited, listening to the soldiers gossiping and grumbling. Soon, a light appeared in the forest. A second pair of soldiers arrived, carrying a lantern.

Relieved, the first pair headed back to the fort. But they did not go alone. Theo and Moses followed, as close and dark as shadows. They crossed trenches on log bridges, skirted around earth embankments that had been thrown up, and navigated a maze of felled trees. Once, Theo nearly fell into a pit filled with sharpened stakes. If they had not been tracking the sentries, they would never have found their way through.

The obstacles ended near the edge of the forest. The lights of the fort were clear beyond the trees, but Moses and Theo didn't take that route. Parting ways with the sentries, they climbed the slope to the higher ground under the cliffs, from where they could survey the terrain.

The lake gleamed in the moonlight. The fort, with its intricate arrangement of bastions and revetments, looked like a spider perched at the water's edge. From their position, the slope ran gently down to the fort on its promontory, a few hundred yards away. The land in between had been cleared. Some trees must have been felled in the fort's construction, or for firewood; others had been ring-barked and burned, leaving blackened stumps that pocked the ground, like gravestones.

The burned area made a wide ring around the fort, open ground where the defenders' muskets and cannon could tear through any attackers, who would have no cover. Closer in, trenches and earth ramparts, lined with sharp-pointed sticks, made formidable outworks.

Theo observed his surroundings. Somewhere behind those sharp-pointed walls, lit by the glow of watch fires, was the man who had been the author of all his misfortunes, the man who had shaped Theo's fate one death at a time. He had to resist the temptation to forget his army and his mission, scale those walls and hunt down General Corbeil in his bed.

Beyond the fort, a creek cut in from the lake, running up against the rear of the bluffs. Theo knew that General Williams had considered forcing the channel but rejected the idea. It was too shallow for any vessel except canoes and *battoes*, while the fort's guns gave the French total mastery of its entrance.

Theo saw a wide-bottomed boat pushing off from a landing stage near the fort. Another followed, then a third, their oars making white splashes in the moonlight. From their profile, they seemed to sit low in the water.

'What cargo are they carrying up that backwater?' Theo wondered. 'Is there a river that empties into the creek?'

'Only streams,' said Moses. 'It goes nowhere.'

The boats disappeared behind the shoulder of the mountain ridge. Theo kept his eyes on the area, waiting for them to reappear where the creek snaked back into view. Ten minutes passed, twenty, then an hour. Still the boats hadn't emerged.

'Where have they gone?' Theo's blood quickened, the pulse of a hunter picking up the first trace of the spoor. He did not know where the trail would lead, but he knew it was worth following. 'We must go and see.'

'We will have to cross this open ground,' Moses reminded him. 'If there's something they do not want us to find, they will surely keep it well guarded.'

Theo nodded. There was no cover, and no hope of passing unseen in the moonlight. He straightened, touching the unfamiliar hairless skin on his head. 'This is why we came in disguise.'

'*You* came in disguise,' Moses corrected him. 'I am myself.'

'Then you have nothing to fear.'

Theo took out a small flask of brandy. He took a quick sip, then poured a good measure over his face, letting it dribble down onto his shirt. Moses did the same. The two of them strode out from the trees.

They were well within rifle range. Theo tensed himself for sounds of alarm, any sign that they had been recognised. If they were lucky, the French might challenge them before they opened fire. If not . . .

'Walk slowly,' Moses counselled.

'I am,' Theo hissed.

'But you walk like a man who *wants* to run. Relax.'

Theo did his best to follow his friend's advice. The breeze was coming down off the mountain, towards the lake, so they could not hear what might be happening inside the fort.

No one sounded the alarm. They passed by the defences and reached the shelter of the forest on the far side. From there, they could see moonlit water sparkling through the trees. A well-trodden path led away along the creek in the direction the boats had gone.

The metallic squeak of oars in rowlocks made them duck down. Peering through the trees, Theo saw boats gliding over the water towards the fort. The boats rode much higher than they had when they set out.

As soon as they had passed, Theo and Moses continued on their way. The path led on for a mile, then emerged from the trees by a small stony cove. Scored lines in the beach showed where boats had been dragged up on shore. They must have been unloaded. But whatever their cargo was, there was no trace on the beach. It had disappeared.

Cliffs rose high into the night above. Theo gazed up at them. 'If they have guns at the top of that cliff, there must be a path they use to send supplies and ammunition.'

'It would have to be narrow,' said Moses, doubtfully. Even his eagle eyes could not make out anything in the steep rock face. 'Impossible to take by force.'

'Let us see.'

Theo knew he ought to return, but the thrill of opportunity overcame all caution. He had passed the fort without being challenged: he felt invincible.

He ran out onto the beach and started searching the tangled bushes around the base of the cliff for a way up.

'It must be here somewhere.' Theo cursed. The moon had disappeared behind a cloud, making the landscape all but pitch. He did not dare kindle a light.

'We should go, Siumo,' Moses warned.

The cloud drew away, like a curtain in the theatre, leaving Theo and Moses exposed to the full glare of the moon. By its light, in the far corner of the beach, Theo saw a flat stone sill, like a stair leading up towards the cliffs. He took a step towards it.

'Halt!' called a voice in French.

Theo's first instinct was to grab his tomahawk, but he held back. Going for his weapon would have been the last move he ever made, an invitation to the French to open fire.

He raised his hands and turned slowly. '*Ami, ami!*' he shouted, slipping naturally into the pidgin French of the Abenaki.

Six soldiers stared back. All had muskets raised, trained on him and Moses.

'What are you doing here?' said their sergeant.

Moses affected a haughty innocence. 'Chief send us here. Say there are boats need protecting.'

The sergeant relaxed a fraction. He could smell the brandy on the Indians' clothes and guessed they had got drunk and abandoned their posts. 'The supply convoy left half an hour ago. Which tribe are you? Ottawa?'

'Abenaki.'

'What is the password?'

Theo felt the soldiers' eyes on them. Hesitation would be fatal. '*Vive le roi!*' he shouted enthusiastically. Moses joined in.

The sergeant nodded. 'And your chief sent you here?'

'Yes.'

The sergeant nodded again. Then suddenly: 'Seize them!'

Four of the soldiers advanced. Two stayed behind, muskets aimed at Theo's and Moses's hearts.

Theo had an instant to make his decision. The soldiers looked tough, seasoned veterans of the harsh frontier. But he and Moses were warriors: in a fair fight, Theo would have backed them even at three to one.

It wouldn't be a fair fight. The guns made sure of that. The weapons were too far away for Theo to wrest aside, too close to miss. Even if he used one of the soldiers as a shield, that still left the second musket.

A flicker of doubt on the sergeant's face convinced Theo. They didn't *know*. On the one hand, they had found two men skulking about behind their defences. On the other, they seemed to be Abenaki Indians who spoke French and smelt of brandy. It was confusing – too complicated for a mere sergeant to decide.

And if they took him to the fort, who knew what Theo might discover? He would keep his eyes peeled for gun emplacements, and hope he could escape.

Theo protested but did not resist. The soldiers surrounded him and marched him away at bayonet point.

● ● ●

Constance couldn't sleep. Every nightmare from her past seemed to have come alive. The fort reminded her of Calcutta: those last days trapped by the besiegers with no way out. She was alone. In Corbeil, she had found a new Mauvières, a jealous brute who kept her locked in her quarters every hour of the day.

All her life she had wanted to be free but, several times now, she had exchanged one prison for another.

She wondered if Theo had received her message. Was he in the British camp beyond the forest? What would he be like? She tried to imagine her brother's hands carving the intricate designs on the knife she had found but could not reconcile that with the shy boy she had known. How he must have changed.

But what good would it do? She knew the siege was going badly for the British. They had come to take the fort, but it was they who were trapped in their camp. They could not bring their guns into range because of Corbeil's devious traps. Every day Constance heard her husband gloating over the reports he had from his spies. There were outbreaks of fever; supplies were running short. The British soldiers were mutinous, and the politicians in London would soon lose patience. Victory was only a matter of time.

She could not let that happen. She would not let Corbeil win.

The fort was not so big that Constance could have her own bedroom. She had to share with her husband. He was beside her now, a great dark lump under the sheets. The demands of his work meant he slept only for a few hours each night, but in that short time he was dead to anything.

Constance rose. Wrapping her gown around her, she stole to the door. The sentry started. 'At ease, Corporal,' she whispered. 'It is only me.'

He was the soldier she had met guarding Gilyard in Québec. Pierre Duchambon had kept silent about Constance's visit to the prison and did not raise the alarm when faced with the strange coincidence of Gilyard's passing away after her meeting with him. Recognising his potential, she had subtly arranged for him to be assigned as the guard to her apartments. Grateful to be released from prison duty, and rewarded with regular visits from Constance's maid, he was a useful ally.

Constance descended the steep stairs and let herself into Corbeil's office. She lit a lamp. Every surface was strewn with papers. 'The fort's defences are stone and iron,' Corbeil liked to say, 'but its foundation is all paperwork.'

There were hundreds of pages, and she didn't know what she was looking for. But she trusted her instincts. She could sniff out weakness, like a jackal. And she knew her husband. He would keep his most important papers secure, but always ready to hand.

The top drawer of the desk had a lock. It needed a small brass key, one that Corbeil kept on a chain around his neck even when he slept. Constance had made a duplicate, pressing the key into a wad of wax while he was sleeping. She had given the mould to Pierre, instructing him to produce a second key in case the original was lost. She unlocked the drawer and lifted out the pile of papers inside.

It was dauntingly thick. Again, she trusted to instinct. Four pages from the top, she found a thick document folded in quarters. One glance inside told her it was what she needed.

It was a map, the key to the battle, right there in her hand. She recognised the fort, with its arrowhead corners and octagonal tower, and the defences around it. Everything was laid out in precise drawings: the hidden paths through the obstacles in the forest; the guns on the ridge; the positions and strengths of the units Corbeil had deployed.

Patiently, quickly, Constance copied the map on to a fresh piece of paper. She worked diligently with the quill, transferring as much detail as possible. This was treason. Corbeil would have her shot, or hanged, if he found out. Her heart beat fast, but her hand didn't tremble. She would rather die fighting than let him win.

A noise from outside made her catch her breath. How could she explain herself? But she had not been discovered. The sound came from below, outside by the gate. Curious, she looked out of the window.

The postern gate stood open. Through the glassless window, she saw a platoon of soldiers usher two Indians inside and across the courtyard. This was not unusual – the French army's Indian allies were everywhere. But it was past midnight, and the Indians' hands were bound.

Could they be spies?

As she watched the soldiers take the prisoners to the gaol, an idea began to form. Fearful of being found out, she hastily completed the salient details of the map, replaced the original where she had found it, locked the drawer, folded her copy tightly and tucked it into her bodice.

'Come with me,' she ordered Pierre, when she reached her quarters.

The corporal rubbed his eyes. 'I am ordered to guard the general's bedchamber, madame. With you in it,' he added.

'The general will not wake for another three hours.' Like everything else he did, Corbeil slept with clockwork discipline. 'And I need you.' She lowered her voice. 'My maid Pascale will be waiting for you when you go off duty. I have heard she will do things for you that would make even the prostitutes of Les Halles blush.'

Pierre's eyes bulged to hear a noblewoman speak of such things. By the time he recovered his wits, Constance was already halfway down the stairs. He had to hurry to catch up.

The guard at the gaol was in a surly mood. It was already past the end of his watch and he had been on duty all night. Now he would be there until dawn. The sergeant had gone to fetch the Abenaki chieftain, but who knew how long he would be? And for what? It was obvious the two men were Indians who had lost their way – probably drunk, judging by the stink of brandy on them.

When Corporal Duchambon came to relieve him, the guard did not question it. He returned to his bed, grateful for a few hours' sleep. As soon as he had gone, Constance emerged from the shadows. She had borrowed Corbeil's hat, which she wore pulled low over her face.

'Wait here,' she said. 'Do not let anyone in.'

'Will the prisoners still be alive when you come out?' Pierre Duchambon said quietly, under his breath.

She had already gone in and didn't hear.

Again, stepping into the prison, Constance felt the shiver of memory. She would suffer it for the rest of her life. But this was nothing like the Black Hole, or even the cell in Québec. The walls were clean and whitewashed, with a barred window to the outside and a beaten-earth floor. The two prisoners sat on stools in the corner, talking in their own language.

They looked up as she entered. They were undeniably savage: heads shaved but for a single lock of hair, faces bristling with quills and ornaments, their bare skin painted with cabalistic designs. Both were strongly built, muscles rippling through their arms as they moved. In other circumstances, Constance might have enjoyed the sight.

She hesitated. She had seen Indians in camp and around the fort, but always from a distance. Corbeil disdained them as primitives, even as he recognised he needed them against the British. She had never been so close before.

Was she safe? Or would they lunge at her and tear her apart?

'Why are you imprisoned? Are you spying for the British?'

She spoke in English, abruptly and without preamble. At the same time, she moved forward so she could see the reactions on their faces.

Neither man would be a fool, and both must be able to control their emotions, but to hear a woman's voice speaking perfectly accented English, in a French fortress in the middle of the night, was too much of a surprise even for them. Their expressions rapidly turned defensive, their eyes widening. One of the men, Constance noticed, had deep brown eyes and features that startled her.

A tremor went through her. It was like looking into a mirror, or at a portrait of an ancestor. Surely . . .

She took another step forward. Fixed on the Indian's face, she knew she had nothing to lose. Throwing caution to the wind she removed her hat. The fair hair she had piled up beneath it spilled out, framing a face that was no longer in shadow.

The brown-eyed Indian was staring at her as if he'd seen a ghost. 'Connie?'

• • •

Constance almost fainted with shock. The inner resolve she had spent her life cultivating, her strength of will, her remarkable ability to dissemble and her practised skill at facing up to the most hostile of situations, all fell away: nothing had prepared her for this.

The brown-eyed Abenaki leaped up from the stool and embraced her. She stared up into his face, so strange and foreign, yet so familiar. There was everything she remembered – his eyes sparkled, like a glimpse of precious childhood innocence.

'When I saw that knife, I could not believe it. I thought you were in India,' she whispered.

'I thought you were dead.'

She straightened and stood, stepping away so she could see him properly. Suddenly, she burst out into uncontrollable laughter. 'Oh, Theo! However did you come to be a Red Indian?'

'How did you come to be walking free in a French fort?'

'It is a long story.'

'So is mine.'

They fell silent again, staring at each other in wonder. They had so much to say that they did not know where to begin.

Constance collected herself. She reached inside her dress and pulled out a small folded piece of paper, which she pressed into his hands.

'You must take this to the British general. It lays out the plans for the fort's defences.'

Theo didn't look at it. 'You can bring it yourself. If you let us out, we can all escape together.'

Constance hesitated. Nothing was as she expected, and everything was happening too quickly. She knew she ought to be thanking God for reuniting her with her brother against all odds and reason. She looked into his eyes and wanted there to be nothing between them.

And yet . . . something deep in her soul warned her to move carefully. She told herself it was shock, but that was not the whole truth. The reunion of long-lost siblings might be cause for joy, but it was not easy or straightforward. He was not who he had been and neither was she. She could not simply throw herself into his arms as if the past three years had not happened and trust her destiny to him.

'If I go with you, the French will know I have betrayed them,' she said.

'It does not matter.' Theo tugged her arm, pulling her towards the door. 'All I care about is that we are reunited. I am married now, Connie. I have a son. Abigail and Caleb. I want you to meet them, to complete our family.'

'Do you not wish to revenge yourself on General Corbeil?'

Theo stared at her, hardly capable of surprise any longer. 'You sent me the letter?' He thought quickly. 'Is he here?'

'Asleep in his bed.'

'Then let us go now. We will kill him and make our escape before anyone raises the alarm.'

Constance felt that the night was moving in ways that did not suit her purpose. She wondered how she could feel so detached from her own brother, the boy she had grown up with. But she had run out of excuses.

She followed Theo towards the door.

'Wait!' called Moses. While Constance and Theo had been speaking, Moses had been keeping watch out of the window into the courtyard. 'The guards are coming.'

Theo moved to the side of the door. 'We will take them when they enter.'

'No,' pleaded Constance. 'You are locked in a fort with five thousand French soldiers. One shot would bring them all down on us. They will kill you as a spy and me as a traitor. We would never avenge ourselves on Corbeil.'

Theo paused. He was struck by indecision. Every instinct said he should fight. But he could not ignore the beseeching look his sister was giving him.

Voices sounded outside the door. Constance could hear the corporal greeting the guards, and insisting they go no further. A bolt slid open.

'What do you suggest?'

• • •

Sergeant Bartier had a nose for trouble. If men were shirking duty, if a soldier was taking more than his share of the rations, if the quartermaster tried to cheat the company, Bartier could tell. It was why his superior officers relied on him, and his subordinates feared him.

He knew something was wrong when he entered the prison. The door had been bolted; the two prisoners sat where he had left them, on their stools at the far end of the room. But why was the general's wife present? Why had the guard on the door been replaced by Corporal Duchambon, a notorious troublemaker? The hairs on the nape of the sergeant's neck were prickling in a most uncomfortable way.

'You should not be in here, madame,' he said to Constance.

She turned on him with an imperious glare. 'Perhaps you would like to share your opinion with the general. He thought they might be English spies and asked me to see if they spoke that language.'

There were a number of reasons for Bartier to doubt this. He performed a quick mental calculation and concluded none of those reasons was worth disturbing the general for in the middle of the night. 'What did you learn from them?'

Constance gave her most dismissive shrug. 'They are savages. They are no more English spies than I am. You should let them go.'

Bartier felt a prickle of mistrust. 'The Abenaki chief is coming. He will be able to vouch for them – or not.'

He tipped back his head, eyeing Constance with the expression he used for particularly stupid officers. Challenging her to defy him.

Did he imagine it, or did a look pass between her and the prisoners? Did one give a subtle nod?

'As you wish.'

Constance swept out, leaving Bartier alone with the two Indians. He gestured them to their feet. 'Up.'

Theo stood. Events were out of his control. He felt dazed. Almost as soon as Constance had left the room, he began wondering if he had dreamed the encounter. How else could they have been reunited? She was dead.

The door opened again. An Indian entered, dressed like Theo and Moses with the marks of the Abenaki. He was strong and broad-shouldered, so tall that he had to duck under the lintel. For a moment, his face was hidden.

When he straightened up, Theo had his second shock of the evening.

If he had thought he was dreaming before, now he was sure of it. There was no other explanation. First Constance, now—

Malsum walked towards them with casual steps. He had not changed, except for a few more scars. His nose was crooked, probably from when he and Theo had fought the day Mgeso died. He carried the same aura of menace. The French guards gave him a wide berth.

'These are the men we found,' said the sergeant.

Malsum nodded. He circled Theo and Moses, studying them like prey. Theo had not felt so helpless since his first day in the Abenaki village. He remembered how Malsum had tortured his companion, Gibbs, and how long it had taken the unfortunate victim to die. Now it was Theo's turn.

Malsum turned to the sergeant. 'Leave these men to me,' he said curtly, in French.

Bartier fought back his misgivings. But his orders had been to check with the Abenaki chief, and that was what he had done. It was a soldier's duty to obey orders.

Even so, he wanted certainty. 'Are they your men? We found them loitering on the beach below the bluffs.'

Malsum jerked his head contemptuously. 'They are Abenaki. They are under my authority.'

Bartier gave in. With a salute, he left the three Indians alone in the prison.

Malsum put his hands on his hips and studied the two prisoners. The expression on his face was impossible to read.

'So,' he said slowly, to Theo. 'I know you. I can see through to your gibbering soul. Ahoma the chicken has become Siumo the hawk.'

Theo said nothing. He should have expected Malsum to be there. The tribe had always been allies of the French. And Theo had delivered himself up, right into his enemy's power. He would have wept with frustration, if he had not been too busy thinking of how to save his life.

'And you.' Malsum turned to Moses. 'Siumo is Bastaniak. But you deserted our tribe to fight with our enemies.'

'Siumo is my brother,' Moses answered.

Malsum grunted. 'Come.'

He led them across the courtyard, a thick rope attached to their bound hands, as if he was leading dogs to slaughter. A sentry challenged them, but Malsum growled so fiercely at the man that he opened the gate without further question.

Theo and Moses followed him out between the great bastions of the corner towers and onto the burned land in front of the fort. The killing ground.

Malsum halted.

He was alone and outnumbered. But Malsum had a tomahawk in one hand, and a sharp knife in his belt. Theo and Moses had their hands tied behind their backs.

Malsum grasped the knife and thumbed the blade. It took a sharp knife to scalp a man, and his was always ready. 'Last time we met, you might have killed me,' he said.

'If I'd known we would meet again like this, maybe I would have,' said Theo.

Malsum spat onto the ground. 'You should listen to the ancestors. They always told me we would meet again. I have waited for this day.'

He walked behind Theo.

'You look like an Abenaki,' he said, 'but you were always Bastaniak. I never understood how Mgeso could love you.' He ran his hand over Theo's bare scalp, stroking the single lock of hair Theo had left at the front.

'She loved me because I loved her,' said Theo.

'So did I.'

'You killed her.'

'I did not kill her, you fool. It was Bichot. Your mind is playing tricks on you. But she was never meant to die.' A sudden change had come over Malsum – Theo had never heard him sound so raw. The words came out like a howl of pain: 'I would rather have died a thousand times than live one day with the thought of Mgeso's death. It was you I wanted dead.'

Theo said nothing. Bichot and Malsum had abducted Mgeso, subjecting her to the terror of their groping hands and, he was sure, worse violations to her person. Then she had been brutally murdered. For months, his plans for revenge on Malsum and Bichot had been braided into the deepest strands of his being. Yet he saw his adversary's pain, a despair that came from Malsum's deepest self. Could this brute know the agonies of loss? Feel the keen, blade-sharp incision of true love? Perhaps there was humanity in his soul . . . or was it all an elaborate performance?

'Now is the time to finish this,' said Malsum. He rubbed the flat of the blade over Theo's scalp. With a quick cut, he sliced through the cords that bound Theo's wrists. Theo was so surprised, his hands stayed in place behind his back even after the rope had fallen to the ground.

'You spared my life,' said Malsum. 'You could have killed me with my tomahawk as I lay unconscious. For that moment, you deemed me worthy to continue living. Now I have returned the favour. And more.' He cut Moses free as well. 'Mgeso's spirit will not haunt me any longer.'

Theo turned to look into Malsum's eyes. He was suspicious and tried to divine the Indian's motives. Could it be true? Was he really free? In the rush of relief and gratitude, he almost wanted to embrace his old enemy. But it would be like embracing a wolf.

'Come with me,' Theo urged. 'The Bastaniak will win this war. They will be generous to their friends, but cruel to those who helped the French. For the sake of all the Abenaki, join us.'

For a moment, he dared hope Malsum might agree. Then the Abenaki's face hardened. 'I cannot. I must stay with my men.' Malsum pointed into the woods. 'The way to your camp is there. Go. Tonight I have spared your life, but if we meet on the battlefield, there will be no mercy.'

'Then, for both our sakes, I pray we do not meet there.'

Malsum bared his teeth. 'You may pray, but the ancestors will guide us to their own purposes. You know and I know it is inevitable.'

$$\bullet \quad \bullet \quad \bullet$$

Three canoes glided over the lake making barely a ripple. The weather was clement. Under the new moon, they navigated by starlight, while a southwest wind was steady at their backs.

It was ten days since Theo and Moses had reconnoitred the fort: a week of frantic preparation, and three days' waiting for the right conditions. The plan of the defences that Theo had brought had stirred the general into high excitement. 'We have them now, by God,' he had exclaimed.

But the problem remained of the guns on the heights. 'If the French have a battery up there, they will make mincemeat of our men,' Theo fretted.

The general studied the map. 'It is not marked here.'

'It must have been copied in haste.' Theo leaned forward. 'I know it is there. Send me with my men and I will prove it, sir.'

'But you cannot scale those cliffs. The only way on to that ridge is the ravine you found in the winter, and the French will surely have it guarded. You said yourself a dozen men could stop an army.'

'I believe there is another way,' Theo insisted. 'A path up the rear side of the mountain from the creek. If I can force it with a company of rangers, we will fall upon the French without warning.'

'Have you seen this path?'

'No.'

'Even if it exists, forcing the heights will be a perilous mission.'

'I am willing to try it, sir.' Theo knew the danger. But if he was to have any chance of rescuing Constance, they had to embrace it.

Williams clasped his fingers together and cracked his knuckles. His face was pinched in thought. 'If you are willing to hazard your life, then it is worth the gamble,' he said at last. 'If the French have guns up there, the fort will withstand us and the war will fail.' He stood and clasped Theo's hand, holding it fast. 'I pray you are wrong, Captain Courtney, but I fear you may be right. If so, fifteen thousand lives depend on you.'

Theo knew his duty to his comrades. But right now, one life above all obsessed him. Constance's. She was alive. She was *here*. At all costs, he must avoid a bloody siege that would see the general's howitzers launching shells indiscriminately into the fort. Taking the guns was his only hope. Then the French would surrender, and he would be reunited with his sister. I could not save you in Calcutta, he thought. I will not fail you this time.

He said it again to himself, now, in the canoe, digging his paddle into the water. He forced himself to relax. If he paddled too hard, he would make splashes that might be seen by the watchers in the fort.

They were close. To enter the creek that ran up behind the bluffs, they would have to pass close to the fort's ramparts. On his expedition inside the fort when he had been imprisoned, Theo had carefully noted where the guns were positioned. Though most faced landward, towards the besieging army, a few had been left aimed at the lake, in case the British attempted an amphibious assault.

In the thin bark canoes, it would take only one hit. Even a musket ball could pierce those fragile hulls.

The men in the boat lay flat. The paddlers bent double, high enough to reach over the side.

'Stop paddling.' They were at the mouth of the creek, under the fort's guns. Theo saw a light blink on the walls. Probably a soldier lighting his pipe – but what if it was the match being applied to the touch-hole?

Theo kept so still he hardly breathed. The canoes drifted agonisingly slowly with only the wind to drive them. Every time he risked a glance, they seemed barely to have moved.

At last they were past. Theo relaxed a little. Trees came down to the bank again, hiding them from anyone inland, but they also acted as a barrier to the wind. Without the extra force it gave them, they had to paddle more vigorously.

Theo glanced at the moon, now dipping towards the horizon. It had taken longer than he had expected to reach this point, and he did not know the distance to the cove. 'Faster,' he said. General Williams would begin the main assault on the fort at dawn. If there were guns on the cliff, Theo would have to discover and disable them or the army would be slaughtered.

He heard water rippling along the side as they gathered speed. The canoes behind followed their lead.

'There,' Theo hissed. They had come around a bend. In the faint starlight he saw the massive cliffs, and a break in the trees where the shingle beach sloped to the water.

There were men on the beach. Whether that was a normal precaution, or whether Theo's scouting expedition had put them on their guard, he had not expected it.

The rangers had to get rid of them – but if the men at the top heard shots, they would be prepared, and all the soldiers in the world would not be able to scale those cliffs against determined defenders.

'We will go further upriver,' Theo decided, 'see if we can find a landing place and circle back.' It would mean going past the men on the beach, but it was too late to change course. The canoes were travelling at speed: turning them would create wake and noise. All they could do was hold fast and hope the French didn't see them.

The rangers stared at the men on the beach and fingered their weapons. They were twenty yards away. It was impossible not to be seen – at that distance even the whites of their eyes might give them away.

A shudder tore through Theo's boat. The canoe's progress was halted so suddenly that the men inside were thrown off balance. They had been closely observing the land, and did not see the submerged tree dead ahead.

It ripped open the hull. Water flooded in. Men shouted and splashed, careless of the danger. Answering shouts rose from the beach as the French heard their cries. A lantern was lit, and soldiers rushed to the shore, training their guns on the creek.

The men in the canoes behind saw what had happened. They could not rescue the men in the water – their own craft were already overloaded – but they recognised the danger from the shore. They opened fire. A volley of deadly accurate rifle bullets tore through the unsuspecting French. Some went down, others firing wildly into the darkness.

Theo, treading water, could only watch helplessly as the plan unravelled. He could not order his men to stop firing. Now that the battle had begun, they had to see it through. He was a sitting target in the water.

He swam for shore. Muskets and rifles were going off all around him. Some balls landed so close he heard the hiss as the hot lead met the cold water. Screams rent the air between the explosions of the guns. He could not tell which side they came from.

The men in the canoes outnumbered the men on the beach – and they had been shooting since they were old enough to hold a rifle. They could hit a rat in the dark at two hundred yards. In a short time, the French defenders were pushed back and cut down.

But at what cost?

Theo scrambled onto the beach, dripping, like a dog. His rifle, ammunition pouch and powder horn were all lost or useless, though that was the least of his problems. He made a quick count as his men came ashore. One was wounded in the thigh, and another's arm was bleeding. Otherwise, there were no casualties.

'Take two men and follow the path back to the fort,' he told Moses. 'If any of the French got away, kill them before they can raise the alarm. Quietly,' he added. They were downwind from the fort, and a good mile distant. Theo still dared to hope that the sounds of their skirmish might not have carried.

He looked up and saw lights glowing at the top of the cliff. The men camped up there must have heard or seen the muzzle flashes. They could not know the outcome of the battle, but they would prepare for the worst.

Speed and confusion were Theo's only advantages.

'Take what weapons you can,' he ordered. The rangers stripped the dead French of their muskets and ammunition, while Theo searched the fringes of the beach. He found the stone sill he had discovered the night he was captured – and there, rising away up the sheer cliff, was a path.

By now, Moses had returned.

'Did any get away?' Theo asked.

'Yes – and no.' Moses held up two bleeding scalps. 'They will not raise the alarm.'

'Then let us press the attack while we still have hope.'

The path wound between boulders, then climbed steeply up the cliff. Theo marvelled at the men who had made it, let alone managed to haul supplies up it. In some places it was little more than a ledge. Elsewhere, gaps were filled with loose rocks that looked as if they might collapse at any moment. Sometimes Theo had to drop to all fours and scramble up a slope so sheer he feared he might fall off. And always the terror nagged of shots from the heights above.

He looked down. The rangers were strung out behind him, like a knotted rope, trailing across the cliff. There was no space, and no cover. A single marksman at the top could have picked them off at leisure.

So far no one had challenged them. Below, Theo saw the ribbon of the creek, the dark mass of the forest and the lights of the fort in the distance. Somewhere beyond that, Williams's army would be priming their muskets and touching their lucky charms. Some of the scout companies would already have started their advance towards the French lines. He pushed on faster, ignoring the pain in his weary legs.

'*Qui va?*' called a voice from the darkness.

Theo froze. He scanned the path ahead, trying to see where the voice had come from. '*C'est Jacques,*' he said, as casually as he could manage.

'What happened? We heard shots.'

'A boatload of English soldiers tried to come up the creek. We gave them a warm welcome.' Theo reached into his coat and pulled out the small flask of brandy he carried. He shook it, so that the sentry could hear the liquid sloshing inside. 'I came to toast our victory.'

The sentry stayed hidden. But he must be cold and frightened, and the promise of liquor was too much to resist. He raised his head. A small movement, barely perceptible in the darkness. Enough to give away his position.

Moses' tomahawk sailed through the air and split the Frenchman's skull between the eyes. Theo ran forward and slit his throat before he had time to cry out.

'Perhaps he was the only one,' whispered Theo, hopefully. The eastern horizon was hidden behind the bulk of the mountain, but dawn could not be far off.

Stone splinters erupted from the rock next to his face. They peppered his cheek and sliced his forehead; one just missed his right eye. He threw himself to the ground. A second bullet flew through the space where he had been and hit the cliff, raining more shards of rock on him.

'They have seen us,' said Moses.

There was nowhere to hide. The cliff was their only protection. Theo ran a few paces to a hollow in the rock, where a small overhang offered a modicum of safety. He flattened himself against the cliff face.

He was trapped. If he went down, he would expose himself to fire from the soldiers above. If he tried to carry on up the path, he would walk into a volley of lead.

Below, the rangers had begun a brisk exchange of fire. A few had found rocks or crags to shelter behind, from where they could take aim at the French defenders. But too many were exposed in the open, where their only hope was the inaccuracy of the French muskets. Some lived. More died.

'We cannot stay here!' Theo shouted to Moses, squeezed into the hollow beside him.

Moses raised an eyebrow. 'Does Siumo the hawk think he can fly?'

'I can climb.'

Theo turned, hugging the rock desperately. He reached up, feeling for places where he could find a grip. One hand closed around a knob of rock; his fingers wormed into a crack. He probed with his foot and found a solid foothold.

Moses looked at him in wonder. 'When you meet the ancestors, tell them I said you are crazy.'

The Abenaki ducked out from behind the hollow, dropped to his knee and cracked off a quick shot to cover Theo's ascent. There was a scream, but Theo didn't hear it. He had started to climb.

The rock was hard and almost sheer. But an aeon of winters had taken their toll. Ice had cracked it; meltwater had created tiny, almost imperceptible contours. It was enough for his desperate fingers to cling to.

He could feel the endless emptiness below, like a weight around his ankles. The cliff at this point bulged out from the mountainside, overhanging the path. If he fell, it would be a long drop all the way to the beach.

He closed his mind to the danger. He did not notice the bullets flying past. His total concentration was fixed on the climb, on the four small points where his hands and feet met the rock. They were all that anchored him to the world. The wind tugged at him. The void seemed to suck him backwards, as if gravity itself was offended by his presumption. Every move risked disaster; every decision was an act of faith. He could not tell if a hold would bear his weight until he lunged for it.

He did not know how far he'd climbed. He was aware that the rangers' fire had eased off, but he could not tell if it was because they were winning or dying. He looked up. What he saw struck more fear into his heart than bullets or the cliff or anything else that night. The sky was lightening. It had turned from black to purple, while a band of dark blue advanced over the mountain. Dawn was breaking.

The cannons on the ridge opened fire. Theo felt the vibrations through the rock, before the sound rolled down from the heights. He had been right about the guns, about the danger, about the trap General Corbeil had laid for the advancing British army. But he was too late.

Despair coursed through him. He imagined the cannon-balls that had been fired, the arc as they descended towards their targets. How long would it take them to strike home? Ten seconds? Twenty? They would strike the ordered ranks of British troops as they emerged from the trees into the killing ground around the fort. A direct hit would shatter a man's head. Even bouncing along the ground, a ball might smash a body in two.

The horrors flashed through his mind only for a fraction of a second. But his concentration had lapsed. His grip loosened. His foot slipped from the crack where he had lodged it, just as he reached for the next handhold. He tried to cling to it, but his fingers closed on thin air.

• • •

In the fort, General Corbeil surveyed the battlefield from the top of the octagonal tower. He had not heard the first skirmish when Theo and the rangers landed on the beach, but he had seen the flashes of the gunfight on the cliffs. He was not concerned. The attackers had not come close to the summit, and five men could hold that path against five hundred.

A deeper roar sounded from the mountain. The great guns opened fire. That was what he had been waiting for, months of effort leading to this moment. He had ordered the guns to be hauled up in the depths of winter, against the advice of his engineers. Fifty men had died in the effort, crushed when the cannon slipped their tackles on the ice, or freezing from cold on the exposed mountain top. Every life lost had been worth it for this. The end justified the means as in all wars. Winning was everything.

He turned to Constance. He had ordered her to join him, to witness the destruction and to punish her for her wavering loyalty. Two soldiers hovered behind her, with orders to arrest her if she attacked her husband. Corbeil had seen the look in her eyes. They smouldered with hatred, like those of a cornered animal.

He knew he should not provoke her further, but he could not resist twisting the knife. 'Will you toast my victory?' he asked. 'The plan you cooked up with your lover Bercheny has failed. The victory, and the glory, will be mine.' Corbeil was incandescent with rage, but he contained it with the self-control of a born killer.

Across the cleared ground in front of the fort, where the forest started again, he saw flashes of red among the trees. He did not know how the British vanguard had come so quickly through the traps and trenches he had placed in the forest, but it did not matter. Now they had halted, thrown into disarray by the cannon fire on their flank. He had not expected to have to use his guns so soon, but as long as his men kept up their fire, the enemy was cornered.

A pine tree exploded in a spray of wood as a cannonball struck it. The British soldiers around it scattered, some clutching their faces where splinters had lacerated their eyes. The tree tottered, then fell, crushing half a dozen beneath it. Corbeil felt euphoria spread through his veins.

Soon the victory would be complete.

• • •

Theo was falling. The cliff receded. He flung out his arms, flailing for a grip. His fingers scraped

over the smooth stone, scrabbling at every imper-
fection as he gathered pace.

Suddenly he halted so abruptly that the jolt almost
pulled his arm out of its socket. He had managed to
grab on to a lip in the rock. It was a precarious grip.
His full weight drew down on his hand, trying to
loosen the hold. He squeezed tighter, hanging on
with every ounce of his strength.

The strain was intolerable. The cannons fired
again. In extremity his mind conjured images of
Constance, Abigail, Caleb, and all the soldiers under
those guns. He could not fail them.

Drawing on strength he did not know he possessed, he hauled himself up one-handed. His
muscles screamed with pain. His body felt as heavy
as stone. Sweat stung his skin and seeped painfully
into his eyes. His hand couldn't take the strain. He
felt it begin to slip.

With a final heave, he lunged up. His left hand
grabbed the ledge, just as his right could bear it no
more.

Now he was hanging two-handed. He felt some
relief, but that would not last long. The only way
out was to climb.

He reached up with his left hand and felt a knot
in the stone, no bigger than a crab apple. It was
all he needed. He found a foothold, then another.
His heart was beating hard enough to shake the
mountain. All he wanted was to rest and recover
his strength, but momentum was essential. He
kept climbing, oblivious to the rifles and muskets
spraying fire below and the rumble of the great
guns.

The mountain yielded. His hands reached over a ledge and he felt flat ground at last. He scrambled over it and sprawled in relief. His arms and legs ached as if they'd been stretched on a rack.

There was no time to rest. He had come out on another section of the path, far above where he had started, higher than the French soldiers. He observed them below, spread out across the mountainside in their foxholes and hides. They had not seen him climb, and they were unaware of him as he bore down on them from behind. Having survived the climb, Theo found new strength. He killed one, severing his spinal cord with his tomahawk, then a second with a knife between the ribs. A third he threw off the cliff.

The soldier had just loaded his gun. Theo took it, trained it on another marksman he could see ten yards away, and fired. He bellowed the Abenaki war cry, a deep howl that echoed off the cliffs and froze the hearts of all who heard it.

Moses knew what it meant. He burst from his cover and charged up the slope, firing his pistols as he ran. The surviving rangers cheered and came up behind, while the French on the heights above, confused by Theo's attack on their rear, hesitated.

Theo fired again. And again. The French did not know where to aim, and their indecision was all the rangers needed. They swarmed over the French positions, butchering them on the points of their knives and bayonets. The French reserves saw the slaughter and panicked. They turned and fled back up the cliff.

'Do not let them regroup!' Theo shouted. By now, Moses had reached him. They ran on together, racing their enemies for the summit. A straggling Frenchman blocked their way, limping from a wound in his leg. Theo grabbed his shoulders and hurled him off the edge.

Around the next bend he reached the top of the cliff. He prayed he was not too late.

• • •

The British were suffering terrible losses. They had tried to sally out of the woods and paid a heavy price. The burned ground in front of the fort was filled with mangled corpses and the screams of dying men. Caught between the guns from the fort and the guns on the cliff, they had been pulverised. Those who had survived lurked in the woods, waiting for respite that would not come. Soon they would break.

Corbeil had kept a battalion of men in reserve for this outcome. When the British fled, their retreat would become a rout. He could pursue them all the way to Albany – maybe even New York. A defensive campaign would become a glorious conquest. He imagined how he would mark his victory, perhaps like the Roman generals of old: impaling the defeated army's severed heads at the roadside, one every mile from Québec to New York. He closed his eyes and smiled as he imagined the sight.

'Take a message to the reserves,' he ordered one of his aides. 'Tell them to prepare for pursuit.'

The aide saluted and set off. The guns on the heights had gone quiet. Perhaps the British had retreated and his men no longer had any targets. Corbeil looked up at the mountain. The fighting seemed to be over, though a few puffs of powder smoke lingered, like cloud, around the cliffs.

He saw a yellow flash as one of the cannons fired again. At that distance, it took several seconds for the sound to reach him. The British soldiers in the woods heard it and looked up in terror. It would take a few moments longer for the ball to complete its long arc: moments when the men in its path could pray, or soil themselves. They were powerless.

Corbeil closed his fists around the parapet. He waited for the thud of the impact, and the screams.

But when the sounds came, they were much closer than he expected. Below him, on the fort's outer bastion, two of his gunners lay dead. The cannon they serviced had been blown off its trucks, pinning a third man beneath its two-and-a-half-ton weight. He was bellowing in pain.

Corbeil stared in fury. How could it have happened? The guns on the heights had been ranged and aimed meticulously. Why would one have misfired now?

More muzzles flashed from the clifftop. Now it was Corbeil who endured the excruciating delay, every second weighing like a death sentence. Surely these shots would be back on target and smash the British.

The balls struck the fort's rampart with hammer blows, four in quick succession. Men were torn apart, cannons upended and great gouges were blasted out of the stone.

Constance turned to him, her eyes alight. 'It is the British. They have taken the heights. They have turned your own guns on you.'

Corbeil felt as if one of the cannons had been fired through his guts. With a cry of fury, he slapped Constance across her face. He grabbed her wrist. 'I am not finished yet,' he hissed.

• • •

Theo stood on the heights and surveyed the battle-field. Huge holes had been blasted out of the walls of the fort, while men and cannons lay scattered.

By the parapet, Theo's men serviced the artillery, loading and firing with lethal efficiency. They were not gunners, but they had trained for this battle all week, and they were in a brutal humour after losing so many of their friends on the cliff.

Behind them, several rangers kept watch on the miserable huddle of prisoners they had taken. Many of the captives must have been regretting not fighting with more spirit. Even when Theo gained the summit, the French could have held it. They had more soldiers and the rangers were exhausted. But the defenders had been so shocked to see the British mounting the impassable cliff that they had surrendered before they could ascertain how few there were.

The guns roared again. Each time they fired, Theo worried about Constance under the bombardment. He had ordered his men to aim for the outer defences. But the rangers were novices with artillery and could not guarantee accuracy at that range. Theo had seen more than one ball strike the octagonal tower.

On the battlefield, red-coated soldiers were swarming out of the forest towards the walls. This time, they had nothing to fear from the French guns above them.

Theo gestured to one of his lieutenants. 'Has Moses returned?'

He had sent the Abenaki along the ridge to scout the French rear. He did not want to fall victim to a last-minute counter-attack. They had the upper hand, but the battle was not yet won. Corbeil was ruthless and as cunning as a snake. He might yet make one last roll of the dice.

And what if he sought revenge on Constance?

• • •

Corbeil had planned for victory. But he had also made certain contingencies for defeat. Now that was his only consolation. However furiously his troops fought, they could only prolong the inevitable. Eventually, they would be pushed back. The British would take the fort.

But they would not live to enjoy it.

He led Constance inside and down the steps. He passed an aide hurrying in the other direction and grabbed his arm.

'Find Captain Bichot. Tell him to meet me in the powder magazine. Then give my compliments to the garrison commander and tell him he is to fight to the last man. There will be no surrender to these British sons-of-whores.'

The aide looked anxious. 'No surrender?'

'It is not the French way.'

He saluted sharply. '*Oui, mon général.*'

Dragging Constance behind him, Corbeil continued down the steps. They hurried past his living quarters, his office, and the mess on the ground floor, which had been turned into a makeshift hospital. He opened another door, where the staircase continued into darkness.

'You first, my dear.' He pushed Constance so hard she almost fell and broke her neck. She stumbled down the twisting stair and emerged in a low, brick-vaulted chamber. Dim light seeped in through grilles in the ceiling. Constance supposed they were in the foundations of the tower, but the space seemed to stretch the whole width of the fort.

'Where are we?'

'The vaults,' Corbeil said. He had to admire the men who had built this fort. They had brought supplies where there were no roads and found stone where there were no quarries. They had created a military masterpiece, right down to its foundations. They had dug through the mud and chiselled the rock to create a huge space beneath the fort, big enough to store provisions for a year-long siege.

Dust shook from the ceiling as more cannon-balls struck the walls above. As Constance's eyes adapted to the gloom, she saw that almost the whole space was piled high with small barrels.

A man came out of the shadows with a match glowing in his hand. He trailed a rope behind him, like a serpent's tail.

He didn't salute. 'Everything is prepared as you ordered.'

Constance recognised him. It was Bichot, the fur trapper who served the French Army. He held the rank of captain, though he never wore a uniform. The only men Constance had seen him command looked like condemned murderers. He should have died many times – that winter it had been rumoured he had drowned chasing rangers across breaking ice – but each time he had returned from the dead. Many of the men believed he was indestructible. Some, especially the Indians, whispered it was because he was a fiend returned from Hell. Constance could believe it.

Corbeil studied the stacked barrels. 'Is it enough?'

Bichot smiled, showing yellow teeth. 'There is enough gunpowder here to level a mountain.'

Constance turned on Corbeil in horror. 'You are going to blow up the fort? With all your men in it?'

'Not all my men,' Corbeil corrected. 'You and I and Captain Bichot will be well away when the powder goes up.'

'To coincide with the English moment of triumph,' said Bichot. His eyes widened, savouring the thought.

Theo might be among them, Constance realised. If Corbeil destroyed the British army in the explosion, he might be able to claim the battle as a victory, a tactical masterstroke. He would *win*.

She would not go back to Paris as his prize, to be paraded at Versailles, then locked away in a convent. She would rather die.

Bichot knelt beside the rope he had dragged out and touched the flame to the end. The cord sputtered and began to glow. It was a fuse, snaking its way to the heart of the pile of gunpowder barrels.

How long would it take to burn?

Footsteps hurried down the stairs. A young lieutenant appeared, the aide they had seen earlier. 'All your orders are delivered, monsieur.' He looked uncertainly at the barrels, and the burning match on the floor. 'Is that . . .?'

'It does not concern you,' Corbeil snapped. He thought about killing the man – with the bombardment going on overhead, no one would hear – then reconsidered. He had not made good his escape yet. An extra man might be useful.

He tossed the aide a ring of keys and pointed to a small door set in the outer wall. 'Unlock that.' He turned to Constance and Bichot. 'Come.'

As they moved towards the door, Constance pretended to catch her foot on the floor. She stumbled forward and knocked into the aide in front of her in a most unladylike way. Instinctively, he caught her, taking her weight in his arms until she could regain her balance.

'For Christ's sake, do not delay us.' There was a hysterical edge in Corbeil's voice. His gaze darted to the burning matchcord. 'Do you want to see us all killed?'

The lieutenant was more chivalrous. He steadied Constance onto her feet. 'Are you all right, madame? I hope you did not . . .'

The words trailed off as he saw the pistol in her hands. She had removed it from his belt when she collided with him. She raised it, cocked it and pointed it at General Corbeil before anyone could react.

'You will surrender this fort,' she told him.

Corbeil stared at her down his hooked nose. 'Or what?'

'I will shoot you.'

From the corner of her eye, she saw Bichot edging around behind her. She stepped backwards so she could keep a clear view of him and ground out the burning match-cord under her shoe.

'You cannot shoot us all,' Corbeil pointed out. 'Even if I die, my men will avenge me.'

'Then I will die with a smile on my lips.' Constance knew there was not much time. The rattle of musketry echoing through the walls was growing closer and more sustained. The British must have reached the inner defences. All she had to do was keep the pistol aimed at Corbeil. In a few minutes, the British would surely break through those doors. Corbeil would be defeated, a prisoner to be paraded by the victors. His humiliation would be complete.

Corbeil's thoughts had run the same course. He laughed – an uncomfortable sound that resonated among the vaults, like a dragon's snarl.

'This is a pretty impasse we have reached. You think you can beat me by pointing a gun at me?' He turned to Bichot. 'Fire the magazine now.'

Even Bichot gaped at the command. 'But that is suicide.'

'Do it,' Corbeil insisted. He met Constance's gaze. 'You underestimated me, my dear. I would happily die in the inferno – as long as you are beside me.'

He was deadly serious. Constance saw it in his eyes. She had no alternative: he had called her bluff.

Except she had not been bluffing. She pulled the trigger.

In the dark vaults, the flash of the pistol almost blinded her. She saw Corbeil thrown backwards before the smoke closed over her. Her eyes wept; her ears rang from the blast.

Something heavy collided with her and knocked her to the floor. She struggled but it pinned her to the ground, crushing her with its weight.

As the smoke cleared, she saw it was Bichot. He was far too strong for her. She stopped resisting as she saw Corbeil laid out flat on the floor a few feet away. Blood seeped through his shirt and pooled around him.

The aide was still on his feet, looking on in bewildered shock.

'What shall we do?' he asked uncertainly.

'Prepare to fire the magazine, you idiot,' growled a voice. 'And, for God's sake, keep my wife under control.'

Corbeil sat up, clutching his arm. Constance stared in horror as his eyes narrowed in rage. 'I am surprised at you,' he said. 'I have never known you to miss a man's heart before.' He held his bleeding arm and grimaced.

'Shall we leave her here?' asked the aide.

'Of course not.' Corbeil sounded outraged at the suggestion. 'She is my wife. I will not let her off so easily.'

He stood. 'Tie her hands and bring her with us.'

While the lieutenant bound Constance's wrists, Bichot struck a light and touched it to the match-cord again. It caught quickly this time, the flame eating its way eagerly towards the nearest cask. Corbeil unlocked the door. A dark tunnel stretched out beyond.

Constance was disoriented, but she guessed it must lead under the walls and out into the forest. She should have known Corbeil would have an escape plan. She cursed herself for not killing him with her shot. Her last chance – and she had failed.

Shouts came through the open door above. The British must have gained the walls. Corbeil hurried into the tunnel, the lieutenant dragging Constance after him. Bichot followed behind, his knife pricking at the small of her back.

In the vaults, the match burned down.

• • •

Flame flashed from the cannon's mouth and was swallowed in a great cloud of smoke. The gun rocked back with the recoil. Theo smiled.

Down below, the fort was a wreck. The captured guns had made short work of it. The walls had been smashed open, and the defenders driven from their positions. A sea of redcoats surged around it. Through his spyglass, Theo could see scaling ladders being raised to the ramparts.

'Cease fire,' he ordered, 'or we will hit our own men. The infantry can take it from here.'

The rangers around the guns cheered. Their faces were black with powder marks, their clothes scorched and torn. They were covered with cuts and bruises. Later, they would have to go back down the cliffs to collect their dead and wounded. But for now they could enjoy their victory.

The French were still defending desperately. Smoke from their muskets filled the courtyard, obscuring the ebb and flow of battle.

'Why don't they surrender?' Theo fretted. Constance must be in danger. He ought to be down there now: if the victorious redcoats found a woman in the fort . . .

'I have news, Siumo.' Moses had returned, slipping out from the trees unnoticed. His face was grave. 'The French have men in the forest below. I think they are making for the pass.'

'How many?'

'Five hundred? More?'

'But that is a whole battalion.' Theo tried to process this new intelligence. 'It must be Corbeil's reserve. Do you think they are coming to retake the guns?'

'They would be too late. Now the battle is lost, they are retreating.'

'Where can they go?'

'Other paths lead on from that pass. If they get over the mountain, there is a road that would take them all the way back to Québec.'

Theo's thoughts raced. 'We have an army under General Wolfe approaching Québec. If that battalion gets through, they will cut off Wolfe's supply lines. It would turn victory in this battle to defeat in the war.'

'Then we must—'

If Moses finished his sentence, or if he was simply lost for words, Theo never knew. Whatever he meant to say was obliterated by the noise that roared over them. Theo had never conceived of a sound so vast, like a hundred thunderclaps rolled together and fired out of the biggest cannon imaginable. It shook the mountain itself. Moments later, a hot wind swept across the heights. Trees rocked and swayed as if in a hurricane; branches cracked and shook loose. A section of the cliff collapsed, sending three of the guns tumbling down the slope. The rangers around them leaped back in time.

Down by the lake, a dirty-brown column of dust and smoke rose into the sky. It had engulfed the fort. At the edge of the forest, trees lay strewn and snapped, like trampled dry grass. If the blast had done that to solid wood, what would it have done to flesh and bone?

Within a radius of almost a quarter of a mile, everything was still. Further out, men crawled in the earth like ants: the remnants of General Williams's army.

'They fired the magazine,' said Theo. His ears were ringing. He felt sick to his stomach, though he didn't know if that was the force of the explosion, or the knowledge that Constance had been there.

Dust rained down over the battlefield. Wind started to disperse the smoke. Theo rubbed his eyes.

The fortress had disappeared. All that remained was a giant crater in the ground, surrounded by rubble, slowly filling with water as the lake seeped into it.

'Did we do that?' asked one of the rangers. He was as hard a man as any, but at that moment he sounded like a frightened child.

'The French.'

'But they were still fighting.'

Theo could not fathom it. It was hard to believe an explosion so sudden and instantaneous could have been an accident. But who would blow up a fort with thousands of their own men inside?

'Corbeil,' he whispered. Only the general could have ordered it. Theo tried to imagine the hatred that would make a man sacrifice so many of his men, purely to spite his enemy.

Would he have sacrificed himself with them? Theo doubted it. The general would have had an escape plan. Maybe he had taken Constance. If nothing else, she would be a useful hostage. He grabbed Moses. 'That battalion you saw. Where is it heading?'

'If they are retreating north, there is only one place they can go. To the pass on the ridge.'

'We must stop them.'

• • •

Constance stumbled through the forest. The land was one long swamp, but there were paths that only Bichot knew. They were not obvious, but firm enough that a whole battalion of crack French troops could move at speed.

It was an ordeal. Often, the track sank into stretches of mire. Water filled her shoes, and stinking mud caked her ankles. Flies the size of musket balls buzzed in clouds around her. With her hands bound, there was nothing she could do when they settled on her skin except shake herself. Soon she lost the will even to do that.

Corbeil was glancing around anxiously.

'We have not been followed,' Bichot drawled. He spoke casually, without any deference to rank. 'If any of the British survived, they will be picking through the ruins of that fort for days before they realise we are gone.'

'It is the men on the heights who worry me,' Corbeil answered. He stared up, though the cliff was so steep they could not see the summit. 'They gained the heights when you said it was impossible. If they follow the ridge, they will be able to attack us at the pass.'

'I sent our Indian allies to scout the way.' Bichot snapped a branch that had grown across the path and threw it into the swamp. 'If there are any Englishmen waiting for us, the Abenaki will bring you their scalps.'

They hurried on. Constance had never walked so far in her life. Her legs felt like straws, her feet had blistered in her wet shoes, her dress was torn by the briars and spiked plants that she had to push her way through.

What would Bercheny think if she returned to him? Would he rescue her from Corbeil? Or would he calculate there was no gain in antagonising his victorious general, and leave her to her fate?

You must survive. That simple imperative had seen her through the Black Hole, and it would see her through this. She whispered it to herself with every step, over and over, until it contracted into a single vital mantra.

They left the swamp and started to climb. There was no respite, only trading one kind of hell for another. The stony ground was as sharp as saw teeth, shredding her damp shoes and cutting her blistered skin. Each step was agony.

Bichot drew level with her. His eyes stripped her bare and he smiled, in a way that revealed exactly what he was thinking. Constance shivered. What if Corbeil tossed her to *him*, a morsel for his faithful hound? There were whole worlds of misery worse than sore feet.

The path rose steeply past a cairn and funnelled into a narrow ravine. From below, it was invisible. Constance's hopes faded. There was no way the British would discover this hidden route.

Confirmation came an hour later when the advance scouts returned. 'The pass is clear,' they reported. 'No sign of the British.'

Corbeil clapped his hands together in triumph. 'Then we are home and free. We have destroyed one army. Now we shall fall upon Québec and destroy another. The victory will be total.'

The men cheered. All morning they had marched in sullen silence, stunned by Corbeil's brutal *coup de force* at the fort. Many of the men who had died had been their friends. But the shock was passing. They were alive, and the British were beaten. They knew Corbeil was an uncompromising tyrant. That was why he would win.

They reached the top of the ravine in good spirits. If there was going to be an ambush that would have been the place for it. Now the ground opened out. The summit of the ridge was only a hundred yards away, up a shallow incline.

The major who commanded the battalion sought out Corbeil. 'We should call a halt. The men have been marching for hours without rest.'

'Not until we are down the other side.'

The major was loyal to his men, but the look on Corbeil's face brooked no argument. The major saluted.

'Why not rest here?' The voice came from an unexpected source. Constance had wandered out of the main column, wincing with every step, and was staring at the forest. A stream babbled out of the trees, its banks lined with blueberry bushes. 'There is water for the men, and fruit. If you march them into the ground, they will never reach Québec.'

The soldiers glanced uncertainly between their commander and his wife. Some gazed longingly at the cool water flowing by. Others wondered why the wife was bound and being led, like a prisoner. Even in her distress, she was undeniably beautiful.

Corbeil did not hesitate. He strode across to Constance and, open-handed, slapped her across her face. 'You think you can manipulate my men against me, the way you manipulated Bercheny? You think you can delay me so the British can catch up? Say one more word and I will gag you.'

Blood oozed from the corner of Constance's mouth. Five hundred men had witnessed her humiliation. And still she smiled.

Corbeil saw it. He paused. There was nothing she could do to him now. He was safe, victorious. So why was she smiling like that?

He knew she was provoking him to ask. He did not want to give her the satisfaction. But he had to know.

'What is it?' he said, despite himself.

She glanced again at the forest. 'My brother.'

• • •

Theo's lungs were bursting. His legs screamed with pain, and his eyes were red with sweat. He had run along the mountain, knowing that nothing less would give him a chance. He had almost made it in time.

But he was too late.

He saw the French column through the trees. They had come out of the ravine, where he might have been able to block them, and were marching over the open ground towards the ridge. He made a quick calculation. There was no way he would be able to get ahead of them before they reached the summit.

Theo saw a flash of golden hair among the uniforms. He almost cried out in frustration and despair. He pushed back the branch that hid him and leaned forward. He could see Constance, and whether she had noticed his movement, or was scanning the forest in hope of salvation, she was looking straight at him.

Their eyes met. Theo almost sprang out of the forest, but that would have been certain death. There was nothing he could do.

And then the column stopped.

Theo didn't have time to wonder at his good fortune. He waved to Moses and the men behind him. Only two dozen rangers had made it this far, against five hundred Frenchmen. They couldn't hope to win. But he had to try.

'We must climb to the top of the slope,' he whispered. That would give them the higher ground and a modicum of cover. 'It is our only chance.'

Moses nodded. 'Go. I will gain you time.'

There was no other option. The French soldiers were readying themselves to move again. Theo had to get ahead of them.

A shot rang out from behind him. Moses had opened fire, throwing the French into confusion. It was a brave effort. The French did not take long to collect their senses. They unshouldered their weapons and poured a volley of musketry into the bushes where Moses had hidden.

Theo broke from the trees and sprinted the last few yards over open ground to the rise of the ridge. Not all the French had been distracted by Moses' diversion. Some had seen Theo. Musket balls ploughed into the ground around his feet.

Theo was too quick. He crested the ridge and slid down on the loose gravel behind it. In a single motion, he unslung his rifle, sighted it on Corbeil and fired.

He shouldn't have missed from that distance. But he had fired in haste: the shot went wide, hitting the officer next to Corbeil. He could see Constance, her fair hair blowing loose in the mountain breeze.

'Connie!' he shouted.

Corbeil was holding her. More musket balls peppered the ground around Theo. He ducked. By the time he had reloaded, Corbeil and Constance had disappeared behind cover.

The rest of the rangers had managed to reach the ridge. There was no sign of Moses. Theo hoped he was safe. The rangers made a loose line along the rear side of the ridge and began a furious barrage of fire.

The French battalion was caught in confusion. Theo had killed the major who commanded them, and Corbeil had vanished. Instinctively, they retreated from the rangers' attack, backing towards the ravine where the end of the column was still coming up. Panic threatened to take hold.

It would not last long. Theo could hear their sergeants shouting, whipping their men into order. On open ground, the rangers wouldn't stand a chance. They had to force the French down into the ravine.

'Reload and then fix bayonets,' Theo barked.

The command was passed along the line. If the men were alarmed, they didn't let it show. Theo had instilled ferocious discipline in them.

'Charge!'

This was the true test of leadership: telling two dozen men to follow you against a whole battalion. No one hesitated.

A cloud of white powder smoke choked the ridge. All that the French saw was green-jacketed devils storming out of the fog behind a wall of bayonets. They did not stop to count, or to wonder how many men the British might actually have. It did not occur to them that so few men would recklessly charge a greater force. They had not reckoned on British fighting spirit.

The rangers discharged their weapons, almost at point-blank range, and kept running. The sight was too much for the weary, leaderless French infantry. They broke, fleeing down the ravine with little thought of defence. The few who hesitated felt the full force of the rangers' bayonets.

'Find cover!' Theo shouted. The press of men in the narrow ravine was so tight that the French could not physically flee any further. Some slipped on the loose stones and were trampled underfoot.

The rangers spread out around the mouth of the gully. They were still dangerously exposed, especially if the French realised their true numbers.

Theo knelt behind a fallen log, reloaded and fired into the fleeing throng. It did not matter where he aimed: he could not miss.

Perhaps they might win.

• • •

Corbeil observed the rout in furious disbelief. How had the British arrived so quickly? How could they have turned the tide with so few men? He had seen them scurrying over the ridge: there could not have been more than two score of them.

His soldiers streamed down the ravine in flight. The crush of bodies between the narrow walls was all that slowed them: otherwise, they'd be halfway down the mountainside.

Corbeil stood in their midst like a rock in a torrent. 'Stand and fight!' he yelled. 'Stand and fight!'

Men pushed past him, heedless of his rank. But Corbeil would not be defeated.

'I will execute any man who does not fight!' he bellowed. 'I will rip out your hearts and make you eat them. I will slaughter your children and let my dogs take your wives. Stand your ground!'

His reputation was hard won. The men who heard the threats heeded them. Some slowed and turned, even as the rangers poured more volleys into their rear.

Bichot fought his way towards Corbeil, beating men to return to the fight with the handle of his axe. Others – many of them evil-faced veterans of Bichot's marauders – joined him. Screaming, threatening, striking and cursing, they forced their soldiers up the slope.

The tide turned. The unstoppable force that had sucked the men down now reversed itself, pushing up the hill in spite of the fire coming against them.

But they were still stuck in the ravine.

Bichot had organised the front ranks into some semblance of order, using the cliffs and boulders as shelter while they engaged the rangers above. The rate of fire slowed now that the rangers lacked easy targets. The rhythm of battle fell to a steady exchange of sporadic shots, keeping the other side pinned down. It was a stalemate.

'Form up the men!' Corbeil shouted. 'Ten abreast, in one column.'

With the major dead, the battalion's senior officer now was a fresh-faced captain from Bourgogne. He looked anxiously at Corbeil. 'Monsieur?'

'We must break out of this hole. Those rangers are too few to resist us if we concentrate our numbers.'

The captain gestured to the sides of the ravine. 'But we cannot make it happen while we are in this deathtrap.'

'Then we will march up this slope and force our way out.'

The captain stared. 'They will inflict terrible casualties on us.'

'Not fast enough to save themselves.'

There was a dangerous madness in Corbeil's eyes. The captain saluted and began shouting orders that were repeated down the gully. The weary men formed up as best they could.

'The first ten ranks will load. The remainder, fix bayonets.'

Corbeil hung back as the men advanced up the slope. He could not see the rangers, but he sensed his soldiers' panic as the column came into view. The rate of fire increased to a desperate pitch. The men in the front ranks would be torn apart.

But always there were more to take their place. It was a human battering ram, driven forward by the weight of men behind. The shooting rose to a frenzied crescendo, then ceased almost at once. The French soldiers had broken out. The rangers must be retreating, running too fast to reload.

Corbeil broke cover to witness his victory. Everything had happened as he designed. French bodies lay strewn around the mouth of the ravine, but the column had advanced. They had over-whelmed the rangers, who were attempting to make a fighting retreat up the slope.

They had no chance. The French army fanned out, bringing all their numbers to bear. And as they began the charge, Corbeil saw the final proof of his triumph.

Men had appeared from the trees behind the rangers. Their single locks of hair blew in the wind. They were the Abenaki Indian scouts he had sent ahead to spy out the road to Québec. They must have heard the battle and returned. The rangers were cut off, caught between the Abenaki at their backs and the army pushing out of the ravine.

Corbeil smiled.

• • •

For a time, Theo thought he might be winning the battle. The French had recovered their discipline, but they showed little appetite for attack. They sheltered in the ravine, firing at a desultory rate that did not much trouble the rangers.

Through the smoke, Theo searched for Con-stance. She must be down the slope. The thought of her in the midst of the fighting knotted his guts.

She survived Calcutta while you were floating away on a ship, he reminded himself. *She can survive this.* It was little consolation.

Moses had not appeared. He was concerned for his friend, but for now Theo put it out of his mind.

He felt as if he had been fighting for hours. It could not go on for ever.

If the main British army had heard the battle raging on the mountainside, how many of them had survived the fort's explosion and would be able to come to support them? Theo could expect no help from that quarter.

He reached into his ammunition pouch to grab another ball and felt the leather at the bottom. He was down to his last few shots.

He heard a different sound from the ravine: the tramp of many boots in unison, marching. A line of men appeared through the smoke, muskets in their hands.

They were walking towards him, lined up like straw targets on a shooting range. What were they thinking? Theo fired, and saw one collapse clutching his bleeding chest.

No gap appeared in the line. Another man went down, and another, as the rangers took advantage of their opportunity. Each time, the French closed up and kept moving. Theo could see the line behind the front rank – and the line behind. The French had thrown their entire weight into this offensive manoeuvre. They suffered terrible casualties. But they were advancing, carried forward by the momentum of the men behind.

The rangers fired as rapidly as they could. There was no time now to wrap their balls in the greased leather patches that gripped the rifling. Accuracy was not a priority: speed was everything. They bit cartridges, poured powder, rammed balls and loosed their shots in a blur. At that range, they could not miss. But they could not halt the advance.

The bodies of the dead were a gruesome sight at the mouth of the ravine. Trampling over them, the front line of the column came out from the rocky defile. They started to spread out, giving Theo's men more targets to aim at.

But it was desperate. In a few minutes, their positions would be overrun and they would be slaughtered.

'Retreat,' he ordered. 'Keep formation.'

Crouching low, the rangers fell back towards the trees. It was their only hope. In the forest, they might hold off the French, or escape altogether. But they might not make it that far. Coming out on the mountain top, the French had formed a triple line emptying volley after volley of musket fire at the rangers. Theo's men could not move without braving a hailstorm of lead. The withdrawal would become a deathtrap.

Theo's hand scrabbled in the pouch and felt the last ball. One by one, the rangers were cut down. Men Theo had known since the day he had left the Abenaki village, men he had led out of Bichot's winter trap: he watched them die and could do nothing to protect them. The safety of the forest was far away.

And then the firing ceased.

Theo knew he should run. It might be his only chance. But he stayed where he was, crouched behind a boulder. Why had they stopped shooting? Had they run out of ammunition too? Or did Corbeil mean to take him alive?

His eye caught a movement behind him. He hardly dared take his gaze off the wall of Frenchmen to his front, but he risked the briefest of glances.

A war band of the Abenaki had come out of the forest. Malsum stood at their head, his painted chest glistening with sweat. The porcupine quills on his leggings gleamed like knives in the sunlight. The French had stopped firing so they would not hit their allies.

Theo's spirits sank even lower. Standing beside Malsum, and a little behind, was Moses. They must have captured him.

Malsum bellowed the Abenaki war cry, more chilling and fearsome than Theo had ever heard. The men along the line took up the call, so that it echoed across the mountain, like a wild wind. It was the sound of death.

The Abenaki charged. There was nothing the rangers could do to resist. They were out of ammunition, and most had lost their bayonets. Some drew their knives; others gripped their rifles like clubs. It would make little difference.

Moses came with the Abenaki as they swept forward. He was wielding a tomahawk. Was it possible he had betrayed the rangers? Or had he seen that the British were doomed, and chosen to rejoin his people?

How could Theo blame him?

Theo felt in his belt for a knife. It would be a hopeless weapon. He saw a pistol on the ground, dropped by one of his men. His hand closed on the butt of the gun. It was loaded. One shot left. The gods were giving him a final chance.

Should he save the bullet for himself, or try to take Malsum with him? He had seconds to decide. The Abenaki were almost upon him. Their war cries were deafening. Moses was shouting at him, gesticulating, shaking his head wildly, but Theo could not hear. He trained the pistol on Malsum, but once again he hesitated. He had him in his sights, he could blow him away in an instant – but what were the words Moses was screaming?

It was too late. The Abenaki fell upon the rangers with savage howls. Theo threw himself flat on the ground, still searching for Malsum. If he was to die, he could at least avenge Mgeso for his complicity in her death.

But Malsum was gone. All the Abenaki passed by. They had run straight through the rangers as if they weren't there.

Theo turned. It was no trick. The Abenaki were sprinting, yelling their war cry as they raced towards the French line. Some of the French put up their muskets, but most held fast, dumbfounded. Like Theo, they could not understand what was happening.

The Abenaki tore into the French, like wolves into a flock of deer. A few shots were fired, but most in such panic that the French hit only their own men. The slaughter began.

This time, there was hardly any resistance. The French had been marching and fighting all day. They had suffered terrible casualties. Now, betrayed by their allies in their hour of triumph, they caved in. The line collapsed. Abandoning their wounded, their weapons, even the coats on their backs, they fled down the mountain.

The rangers charged in behind the Abenaki, fighting alongside them with the frenzied energy of dead men offered a last reprieve. Theo found Moses peeling the scalp off a dying French lieutenant. He embraced his friend. 'I thought you were dead.'

Moses gave a smile that was more relief than joy. 'I found their trail in the forest. I persuaded them to come back.'

'But how—?'

Malsum emerged through the smoke obscuring the ravine. 'After I let you go from the fort, I was troubled,' he said. 'Deep spiritual blackness came over me, like I had never encountered before. I spoke to the sachem, who reminded me of the dream he had the night before you arrived in our village. That you are the hawk who would save our children from the wolf.'

Theo felt the world had spun from its axis. So much had happened, he could hardly understand.

'The sachem said the French would lose this battle,' Malsum continued. 'He said that the British would be cruel victors to those who fought with the French, but that those who aided them would be treated with honour. The British are the way of the light. The sachem said he has a strong soul connection with your people, that your values of humanity and compassion are as deep as the earth. You are on the side of the ancestors. I felt the darkness lift from inside me when I listened to his words. He said you would speak for us to the British general. Now we fight with you as allies.'

Theo had no idea if this talk of dreams and destiny, light and darkness was sincere, or merely justification for switching allegiances when it appeared the Abenaki had picked the losing side. Right now it didn't matter. The battle was decided, and Theo had his own decision to make. Malsum would always be responsible for Mgeso's death. But Malsum had loved her, maybe almost as much as Theo, and he would carry that guilt for the rest of his life. Nothing Theo could do would relieve that burden. Malsum had tried to kill him, but twice he had saved him. He had paid his debt. It was time to put their quarrel aside.

They embraced. Two blood-soaked warriors, victorious in battle.

'Mgeso named you well,' said Malsum. 'Truly you are Siumo the hawk, the hunter who falls like lightning from the sky.'

But Theo only half heard him. Already, he was scanning the battlefield.

Where was his sister?

• • •

Corbeil watched the carnage in disbelief. He did not care about the men – they were expendable – but the destruction of his hopes cut him to the bone. How could he have lost the battle?

What mattered now was saving his skin. When the line broke, he had been quick to leap into the gully. Before he could get very far, he was over-taken by the mass of soldiers fleeing down the mountain. It was chaos. Men slipped on the loose rocks and broke their legs: they begged their comrades for help, but no one would waste a second on the wounded. They were left where they fell.

Soon only the dying remained. And there was Constance. Corbeil had left her when the battle started, in a shallow depression a little way down the ravine. The guard he had set over her had fled, but Constance remained. She was bent over the rope that tied her to a tree, trying to sever it with her teeth.

She saw Corbeil arrive and spat out a mouthful of fibres. 'You have lost,' she said. 'Everything.'

'Not everything.' Her spite gave him strength, a reason to keep fighting. 'I still have my wife.'

He cut the rope with his sword and jerked her forward so that she fell on her knees.

'I am not finished yet,' he told her. 'I will drag you all the way back to Québec if I have to.'

Swift footsteps crunched on the stones. Corbeil put up his sword, then lowered it when he saw Bichot approach. The trapper had been in the thick of battle. His hair was matted, and the scalping scar throbbed like a giant boil. Blood dripped from a wound at his wrist.

'We must escape at once,' Corbeil said. 'You know the paths. Find one that will get us over this mountain.'

Bichot spat on his hands. He combed his greasy hair with his fingers, so that it covered his scar again. 'I know a path over the mountain,' he said. 'But what is it worth to you?'

Corbeil stared. 'Worth? It is worth both of our lives, you fool.'

'I do not need anyone to show me the path. And you will only slow me down. I need compensation.'

Screams echoed down the ravine from the ridge above. The Abenaki were scalping their victims. Before long, they would descend to pick off any survivors in the ravine.

'What do you want?' Corbeil asked.

Bichot's black eyes travelled across to Constance. 'Her. For myself.'

Corbeil did not hesitate. 'When we reach safety, I promise you can do whatever you want with her.'

Bichot scratched his armpit. Spittle dripped from his yellow teeth and ran down his chin. He slipped his hand inside Constance's dress, and squeezed her breast until she gasped. He ripped the sleeve off her dress and put it to his face before throwing it to the ground. He traced his fingers over her bare shoulder.

'I will look forward to it,' he murmured.

He pulled her to her feet and beckoned Corbeil. 'Come.'

• • •

Theo searched the piles of dead. He could not believe there were so many. The cries and sobs of the wounded followed him everywhere, but he could not help. The Abenaki trailed him, stripping scalps from the corpses.

Constance would have been behind the lines. He plunged down into the ravine. The bodies lay thick on the ground: though the fighting had not been so frenzied here, many had been trampled and crushed underfoot.

It was almost too much to take in, too much to believe that Constance might have survived. He kept going, checking every corpse until their faces swam before his eyes, like a living nightmare.

'Siumo.'

Moses' voice broke into Theo's despair. The Abenaki beckoned Theo to a tree growing in a hollow in the wall of the ravine. A loop of rope was tied around the trunk, its blunt end showing where it had been cut. There was blood on it. Moses pointed to a strip of white cloth on the ground. Theo picked it up, felt its softness in his hands. It was the sleeve of a dress. He lifted it to his nose. It had a feminine scent.

'Who else would have been tied up in the middle of the battle?' said Moses.

'And who cut the rope?'

Moses fingered the rope end. 'See how clean it is? No fraying. This was done with a long, sharp blade.'

'Where could they have gone?'

'They will try to find another way across the mountain.'

And suddenly Theo knew exactly their destination. He turned and ran.

'Wait!' Moses called.

Theo was impelled by what some might deem a sort of madness. He was exhausted, terrified. He'd witnessed and been responsible for so much death and destruction that he had to find his sister to assuage the demons eating away at his soul. His life had been a series of abandonments, his loved ones killed or murdered. Rescuing Constance would be his salvation. She needed him. He didn't listen to Moses. He scampered down the ravine, nimble as a goat, hurdling the bodies of the dead and dying. Everything looked different than it had in the snow, but he remembered the geography from that terrible winter's day. He rounded a corner, and there was the fork where the gully joined the ravine. It was the place where Bichot had ambushed them all those months ago.

Moses ran down the slope behind him, struggling to keep pace. 'You should let the others catch up. If the general has your sister, who knows how many men may be with him?'

'I will not let them escape this time.'

Observing with the eyes of an Abenaki, Theo missed nothing as he ran up the other fork. A smear of blood on a rock where a cut hand had pulled itself up. A snapped twig and scuffed leaves. A long strand of golden hair caught on a branch.

Theo held it up to Moses. 'You see? We must be close.'

• • •

Constance was doing everything she could to slow Corbeil's progress. If they didn't get too far ahead, she was convinced Theo would rescue her. But now she was so tired, she could hardly keep upright. Rocks grazed her knee; branches snagged her hair.

They climbed out of the gully by a waterfall and entered forest again. She could not see a path, but

Bichot led the way unerringly. Corbeil followed, using the rope that bound her hands as a halter to tug her always forwards.

She fell painfully, forced herself up and fell again. This time, she was finished. She could not get up.

Corbeil jerked the rope. He swore and kicked her, but she remained motionless. He dragged her on her stomach, like an animal carcass, through the mud. She tasted earth in her mouth.

Constance was slim and light. Corbeil had the strength of the devil. But even he could not pull her far. 'We should leave her,' he said.

Bichot was breathing hard. 'You promised me I would have her as my prize.'

'She'll be no use to you if you are dead. When we reach Québec, I will give you enough gold to buy so many women your cock will fall off,' Corbeil promised.

'But none of them will be like her.'

Corbeil rolled his eyes. 'If you want to stay and screw her until the Indians scalp you, that is your affair. Otherwise, finish it.'

Reluctantly, Bichot drew his scalping knife. He grabbed a fistful of Constance's hair, wrapped it around his hand and yanked her onto her knees. He pulled her head back, exposing her pale throat. She seemed to have lost consciousness.

'I would so much have enjoyed taking more time with you,' he murmured in her ear. 'But *c'est la guerre.*'

He stroked his knuckles across her face, then pulled away, screaming. The knife fell to the ground. Blood poured from his hand.

Constance spat out a fat lump of flesh she had bitten off. Blood dribbled down her chin.

'You bitch!' Bichot shouted. 'You'll regret that as I inflict slow pain before you die. You will truly suffer.' He slapped her face so hard she fell to the ground. Still sucking his wound, he pushed up her skirts to expose her creamy thighs. He cut the ties around her wrists to spread her body and held her hands above her head. Bichot undid his belt and pulled down his breeches, revealing a great tangle of dark hair.

'Put away your manhood. There is no time,' said Corbeil, angrily. 'The enemy will be on our trail.'

'The British could never follow us, and the Indians will be too busy scalping the dead.'

The point of Corbeil's sword pricked the back of his neck. 'If you waste one more second on her, I will run you through.'

Bichot scooped the knife off the floor and turned to face him. 'Do not threaten me, monsieur. Without me, you will never find your way off this mountain.'

'If you plan on tarrying until the English take us, neither of us will get out alive. Make yourself decent and let us be away.'

Bichot buttoned his breeches. He cut a strip off Constance's dress and bound his bleeding hand.

'Death is too kind for you,' he hissed, as he raised the knife again.

• • •

The trees were thinner at this altitude. Theo saw his quarry from a hundred yards away, the flash of

Constance's white dress among the brown of the forest.

He was still running, pushing himself to physical extremes he hadn't known existed. Cramp tormented his side, like an open wound. Every step was agony. Still he forged ahead. Moses was lagging behind. If he was lost, or simply exhausted, Theo didn't know. He had no time to find out. If he stopped moving, even for a moment, he knew he would never have the strength to pick himself up again.

He had no plan. The woodcraft he had learned from the Abenaki was useless in his current state. He felt as if he was blundering through the forest as noisily as a buffalo. His enemies would surely hear him coming.

Except – for some reason they did not. Perhaps his Abenaki instincts made him quieter than he thought. He could see them plainly in a clearing where the trees opened out. There was General Corbeil, and also a man Theo had never expected to see again. A man he thought he had consigned to the depths of a frozen lake. Bichot.

It was as if all his enemies had been summoned from his nightmares, but Theo had no time to wonder how Bichot had survived. The trapper and Corbeil faced each other, blades drawn. Constance lay on the ground beside them, unmoving.

Was she dead?

Theo still had the pistol in his belt loaded with the single bullet. Otherwise, he was unarmed. He did not stop to think about it. He burst into the clearing so suddenly that – for a moment – Corbeil and Bichot could only stare in horror.

Then Bichot reacted. He sprang at Theo, knife raised. Theo jerked up the pistol he carried, though he had no powder for it. Bichot's blade struck the barrel with an angry ring of metal that sent shock waves down to the hilt.

With his bandaged hand still bleeding, the impact jarred the knife from Bichot's grip. It fell to the ground. Theo moved in and smashed him in the face with the pistol. Blood sprayed from the trapper's mouth.

But Bichot had been brawling all his life. He punched Theo in the stomach, then kicked his shins. Theo stepped back. Out of the corner of his eye he could see Corbeil lifting his sword to strike. Against two adversaries Theo wouldn't stand a chance.

But the blow never came. Theo raised his pistol to strike Bichot again, but he was slow and the Frenchman was quicker. Bichot grabbed Theo's arm and, with a practised movement, snapped his wrist.

Theo gritted his teeth against the pain. He brought up his knee, aiming for Bichot's groin, but the Frenchman dodged the blow. While Theo was off balance, Bichot delivered two sharp punches that sent Theo reeling. He caught his foot on a branch and fell.

Bichot was on him in an instant. He straddled Theo, pinning him to the ground and raining blows all over his body. All Theo could see was Bichot's open mouth, the yellow teeth flecked with blood, drooling over him.

Bichot spat out a tooth that Theo must have knocked loose. 'I will send you to meet your Indian whore,' he hissed. 'You thought you had drowned me? You can never kill me.' His knife lay a few feet away, but he did not go for it. He meant to beat Theo to death with his bare hands.

Theo's vision blurred. Sweat and blood mixed in his eyes. A white nimbus seemed to surround Bichot, and Theo wondered if it was the ancestors coming to claim him. He thought of all the times he had laughed at Moses when he spoke of them.

I will not feel ashamed in their company now, he thought.

Perhaps he was already dead. He could no longer feel Bichot's blows. The weight that pinned him down had lifted. Was his soul drifting away?

He tried to move his arm. Pain stabbed through his wrist. Surely the dead did not feel pain. Holding his limp hand as best he could, he wiped his eyes.

Bichot still straddled him, but he was lifeless. A cascade of blood poured down his face, gushing from the open wound where a tomahawk had split his skull. The weapon was buried in the bone up to its hilt.

Bichot collapsed to his side. Theo scrambled out from underneath the dead weight of the body.

'You fly fast, Siumo. Maybe too fast.' Moses put his foot on Bichot's back and levered out the tomahawk. 'A pity. I have ruined his scalp.'

Theo was speechless, almost tearful with gratitude. He glanced around the clearing. 'Where is Constance?'

She had vanished. So had Corbeil.

'I saw them go that way.' Moses pointed to a gap, where Theo could see open sky beyond the trees.

He felt barely alive. He felt agony in places he had not known could hurt. His right hand was useless, his left arm numb, and stabbing pains shot through his leg each time he moved it.

He tucked Bichot's knife in his belt and found a long stick. He leaned on it for balance as he staggered towards the clearing. Moses had already gone ahead.

The forest ended abruptly at a great shelf of rock that protruded from the mountainside. A cliff fell away below, giving immense views of the great wilderness beyond. Moses stood beyond the trees, while Constance and Corbeil faced him with their backs to the cliff.

Moses had dropped his tomahawk and put his arms at his sides. Theo could not understand why – until he saw Corbeil's sword at Constance's throat.

'One step closer and I will kill your sister!' the general shouted.

Theo didn't move. He thought he was hallucinating. Figures merged, so that he did not know if he saw Constance and Corbeil, or Bichot and Mgeso. It was as if his nightmares from the past had come to life.

'Put down your weapon!' Corbeil called.

'Don't, Theo!' Constance cried. The wind whipped at her golden hair. 'I'd rather die than let him take me away. My life will be worse than death.'

Theo believed her. The despair in her voice was all too real. He turned the knife in his hands, stricken by the choice he had to make. He stared at

Corbeil, at the hooked nose, and small black eyes that sneered at the world. Across continents and oceans, the general had taken from Theo almost everything he held dear.

'Release her,' Theo said. 'Your fort is destroyed and your army is lost. Hand over your sword and, under the proper terms of surrender, the British will treat you with the respect deserving of your conduct and rank.'

Corbeil laughed and tightened his grip. A thin drop of blood ran down Constance's flawless white neck. 'Do you take me for a fool? Even if I could trust you, I would not let myself be taken in chains back to London, to be paraded as a captive.'

'If Constance dies, you will not live one second longer,' Theo said.

'If she dies, your life will not be worth living.'

And that was not far from the truth. With his black heart, his unerring instinct for human weakness, Corbeil had recognised it. Theo had left Constance for dead once before. He could not do it again.

A wave of desolation and exhaustion broke over him. He had found his sister halfway around the world, but now he could not keep her safe.

He dropped the knife. The look Constance gave him almost split his heart in two.

'I promised I would always protect you,' he said.

Corbeil jerked his head. 'Enough. It is almost dusk, and we have far to go. Do not try to follow us. You can be sure I will see you coming.'

Every muscle in Theo's body ached from his ordeals, but he did not feel it. He was numb. He tried to catch Constance's eye, to beg her forgiveness for his decision, but she would not look at him.

'*Adieu*,' said Corbeil, his tone jeering.

Theo didn't answer. Tears ran down his face. He doubled over in a paroxysm of grief, clutching his boot, then straightened.

'Connie!' he called.

This time, she heard the urgency in his voice. She looked back.

'A last souvenir to remember me by.'

He tossed her the object he had pulled from his boot – it was the knife he had carved for Gilyard. Her wrists were unbound, and it was a perfectly weighted throw. She caught it hilt first.

She did not hesitate. Before Corbeil could react, she drove the blade into his belly.

He screamed. But Constance hadn't finished. With all her strength, she dragged the knife up through Corbeil's flesh, widening the cut beyond hope of healing. His guts slithered from the gaping wound. He dropped his sword and clutched his stomach, trying to hold in his intestines.

Constance pulled out the knife and stepped back, defiance and rage distorting her face. 'No man will own me.'

She raised her leg and lashed out, planting her foot into his chest. He staggered backwards towards the cliff edge.

'You whore!' he cried. He teetered on the precipice, flinging out his arms to keep his balance.

With the last desperate lunge of a dying man his fingers managed to close around Constance's dress. He fell back, pulling her after him. Caught off balance, she dropped the knife. There was nothing to grab on to. His weight and momentum were irresistible. She felt herself going over.

Strong arms closed around her waist from behind. For a moment she was suspended, hanging between the two men who had hold of her. Corbeil's face snarled up at her, dangling over thin air, while Theo roared with pain as his broken wrist took the full strain of Constance's and Corbeil's weight. They were all about to go over the cliff.

With a tear of fabric, Constance's thin dress ripped. A fistful of cloth came away in Corbeil's hand. His face turned to horror. He flailed with his other arm, but he was falling too fast. All he clutched was air.

He tumbled and somersaulted as he bounced off the cliff face, his dying scream echoing over the forest. Then there was silence.

Theo pulled Constance from the edge and hugged her to him. He felt her heart beating through his chest. He stroked her golden hair.

Far below, on the jagged rocks at the foot of the cliff, a turkey vulture swooped down to peck at Corbeil's broken body.

• • •

The patrons of the Red Lion Tavern in Albany were in a merry mood that September evening. The harvest had been gathered, the weather had been as fair as anyone could remember, and the heat of summer had not yet given way to the chill of winter.

But those were not the only reasons why the men and women drank so freely. The threat that had stalked the frontier since the first settlers arrived had been lifted. Word had come on that day of a great victory. Far to the north, an army under General Wolfe had stormed the Heights of Abraham and routed the French from Québec. All Canada now belonged to Britain. Meanwhile, news travelled from India that General Clive had recaptured Calcutta and broken the Indian Army in battle at a place called Plassey. The nawab, Siraj-ud-daula, had fled on a camel. Later, he had been captured and executed.

The men in the tavern passed around the newspapers, eagerly reading articles aloud.

'Clive defeated sixty thousand Indians for the loss of twenty-two men.'

'Wolfe lost fifty-eight.'

'It says here that General Clive would not have won his campaign without the heroic efforts of Major Gerard Courtney.' A militia lieutenant with elaborate sideburns peered over the top of the paper at Theo. 'A relation of yours?'

Theo grimaced. 'Never heard of him.'

'Better watch out. Soon he'll be more famous than you.'

The men around the table laughed. Reports of Theo's exploits at the battle of Fort Royal had travelled extensively. With half of the French army slaughtered in the explosion, the public had needed a hero to make the victory seem real. Theo could not enter a tavern without every man offering to stand him a drink.

'Perhaps General Wolfe will get all the attention,' he said hopefully.

'I doubt that. It says he died in the battle.'

A momentary quiet came over the table.

'But so did the French general. And the governor, de Bercheny, has fled to Paris with his mistress.'

The men cheered, their spirits restored. No one noticed that Theo did not join in, though Abigail gave him a keen look.

Later, he excused himself from the company and walked to the river. He stared at the fast-flowing current. Some of those drops of water would have begun their journey in the mountain pass above Fort Royal. They would flow down the river all the way into the Atlantic Ocean. Maybe one day they would wash up on the white beach under the walls of Madras or mingle with the brown Hooghly as it met the Bay of Bengal.

Who can say where the tides will take us? he thought.

He heard a rustle of skirts. Abigail came and sat beside him, Caleb asleep in her arms. She passed the child to Theo. 'He is getting too heavy for me,' she said. 'And I will soon have my arms full with the next one.'

She had told him the news when he returned from the campaign. The new baby was growing even faster than the first: she had already let out her dresses twice. Theo was convinced it would be a girl this time.

Abigail slipped off her shoes and stockings and let her feet dangle in the water, as she had that night at Shaw's Pond so many moons ago. She took Theo's hand.

'Were you thinking about Constance?'

'No,' Theo protested. It was a lie. Every day for the past two months, he had revisited those last moments on the clifftop, holding Constance to him, reunited at last, as happy as he had ever been. For a fleeting moment, he felt his family was whole again, that his father's and mother's spirits were with them, embracing them all. His childhood had come alive to him in the most vivid, overwhelming way, and then the vision dispersed, like a mist clearing, and he had returned to the cold, hard present.

When he had made sure Constance was safe and away from the cliff's edge, he had relaxed his grip. 'We had best get back.'

Constance had pulled away from him. 'Back where?'

'To my men – and then to Albany. You will live with us – with me and Abigail and Caleb. We will be a family again.'

'And what will I do?' She spoke with a bitterness Theo had never heard in her before. 'Marry a farmer? Live as some frontier wife, sweeping pig dung off the mud floor?'

Theo stared at her, almost speechless. 'Where else can you go?'

'I want to return to Paris. It's where I left my heart and soul. I will live as a countess and dance, wear fine gowns, visit the Opéra and be received at Versailles.' She gave a joyless laugh, the most chilling of all the terrible things Theo had heard that day. 'Living in a wilderness playing at soldiers and Indians may be your life, Theo. It is not mine.'

'But you would not be safe. Men will exploit you, use you, discard you when they have had their fill of your beauty and charm. It is the way of the world. I will look after you, cherish you and make sure no harm comes to you. You are too easily hurt, my dear sister. Please, Constance, I beg you.'

There were tears in Constance's eyes. 'I know you mean well, my little brother, but I want to be free, to sing like a bird, to love myself and not always be in thrall to another person's idea of who I am, how I must conduct myself, to behave like a lady or a wife or, God forbid, a miserable spinster, bitter at the choices I never made, the roads I never travelled, shrivelled by lovelessness, ugly stares, loneliness.'

She touched his cheek. 'You are my brother and I love you. But if I had to live here with you, in this godforsaken wilderness, I would come to hate you as much as I ever hated Corbeil.'

They had talked until Theo was close to tears. But Constance would not yield, and Theo was too weak to compel her. Eventually, Moses had agreed to take her with a band of Abenaki as far as the French mission village at St Francis. From there, she could find an escort to Québec and Bercheny, thence to Paris.

She embraced him and held him as if she would never let him go. She was sobbing, and Theo knew deep in his heart that he could never protect her from the hurt that would inevitably come her way. The sun was setting; her lips were cold. She started to shiver.

'*Adieu*,' she said. 'I do not think we will meet again. Although,' she added, 'who can say where the tides will take us?'

The last Theo saw of her was as a dim shadow, descending the eastern flank of the mountain towards the oncoming night.

• • •

On the banks of the Hudson, Caleb stirred in Theo's arms. Theo stroked the boy's hair, and murmured in his ear until he settled again. The child was warm against him.

Abigail watched him closely. 'With the French gone, I worry life here will be a little quiet for your tastes.'

Theo thought of all he had witnessed, the savagery of the frontier, and the lengths to which men would go to destroy their fellows.

'Perhaps,' he said. Already he had heard men in the tavern complaining that the government in London was taxing the colonies too heavily to pay for the war they had won. As long as there were riches in the world, and women and guns, men would find things to fight over.

At least Mgeso would be at peace. Theo had not had his dream since the battle at Fort Royal. She was avenged. Deep in the swamps, her ghost fire would have turned to smoke and blown away in the wind.

Abigail misread his thoughts. 'We do not have to stay. I had never left Bethel until I met you, but now I would follow you to the ends of the earth.'

'And the children?'

'They have your blood in them – and I must share at least a little of my brother Nathan's. I am sure they will grow up to be great adventurers.'

'They will,' Theo agreed. 'You and I will see to that.'

'So should I be packing my bags for England? Or India? Or Africa or China?'

Theo shook his head and kissed her forehead. He drew her in close to him, so that all his family – Abigail, Caleb and the unborn child – were wrapped tight in his arms.

He could feel a natural harmony emanate from within him, as if he'd reached the end of an arduous journey. His life had been in danger more times than he could count, and no doubt there would be further battles to test his resolve, betrayals to endure, hostilities to overcome. But now he was at home, and at peace, with his family.

'We do not need to go anywhere. This is where I belong now.'

BOUND BY LOVE. DRIVEN BY REVENGE.

CALL OF THE RAVEN

The son of a wealthy plantation owner and a doting mother, Mungo St John is accustomed to the wealth and luxuries his privilege has afforded him. That is until he returns from university to discover his family ruined, his inheritance stolen and his childhood sweetheart, Camilla, taken by the conniving Chester Marion. Fuelled by anger, and love, Mungo swears vengeance and devotes his life to saving Camilla – and destroying Chester.

Camilla, trapped in New Orleans, powerless to her position as a kept slave and suffering at the hands of Chester's brutish behaviour, must learn to do whatever it takes to survive.

As Mungo battles his own fate and misfortune to achieve the revenge that drives him, and regain his power in the world, he must question what it takes for a man to survive when he has nothing, and what he is willing to do in order to get what he wants.

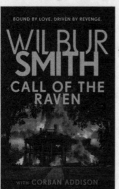

An action-packed and gripping adventure about one man's quest for revenge, the brutality of slavery in America and the imbalance between humans that can drive – or defeat – us.

AVAILABLE NOW

The chamber was packed. Young men in evening dress squeezed ten-to-a-row on the benches; more stood around the edges of the room, bodies pressed together. The lamplit air hung heavy with sweat and alcohol and excitement, like a prize fight at a county fair.

Butnobloodwouldbespilledtonight.Thiswasthe Cambridge Union Society: the oldest debating club in the country and the proving ground for the nation's future rulers. The only sparring would be verbal, the only wounds to pride. At least, those were the rules.

The front of the room was set up like a miniature parliament. The two sides faced each other from opposing benches, divided by the length of two swords. A young man named Fairchild, with sandy hair and fine features, was addressing the audience from the despatch box.

'The motion before you tonight is: "This house believes that slavery should be abolished from the face of the Earth". And, indeed, the case is so self-evident I feel I hardly need to argue it.'

Nods of agreement; he was preaching to the converted. Abolitionist sentiment ran high among the Cambridge undergraduates.

'I know in this house we are used to debating the fine points of law and politics. But this is not academic. The question of slavery speaks to a higher law. To keep innocent men and women in chains, to tear them from their homes and work them to death: this is a crime against God and all the laws of justice.'

On the facing bench, most of the opposition speakers listened to his oration glumly. They knew they were on to a losing cause. One leaned forward and twisted his handkerchief through his hands. One stared at the speaker with such melancholy he looked as if he might burst into tears. Only the third seemed untroubled. He lounged back nonchalantly, his mouth set in a lazy smile, as if he alone was privy to some enormous joke.

'If you have one ounce of humanity in you, I urge you to support the motion.'

Fairchild sat down to sustained applause. The president waited for the noise to die away.

'To close for the opposition, the chair calls on Mr Mungo St John.'

The man who had been lounging on the front bench rose. No one applauded, but a new force seemed to charge the room. Up in the gallery, where a few well-bred young ladies were allowed to observe proceedings as long as they stayed silent, crinolines rustled and stays creaked as they leaned forward to see better.

You could not ignore him. He was twenty, but he loomed half a head taller than any other man in the chamber. His dark hair flowed over his collar in a long, thick mane; his tanned skin shone with a lustre that no wan English sun could have produced. His suit was cut to accentuate his figure: a slim waist that rose to broad, well-muscled shoulders more like a boxer's than a Cambridge undergraduate's.

If he felt the hostility aimed at him, it did not shake the easy grin from his face. Indeed, he seemed to feed off the crowd's energy.

'You have heard a great deal this evening about the supposed evils of slavery. But has anyone here ever been to the great tobacco plantations of Virginia, or the cotton fields of the Mississippi?' His smoky yellow eyes surveyed the room. 'That is my native soil. I was born and raised in Virginia. Slavery to me is not sensational reports in the newspapers, or hell-raising sermons. I have seen the reality of it.'

He lowered his voice. 'Is the work hard? Yes. Do rich men profit from the labour of others? Again, yes. But do not be gulled by these fantasies of brutality and violence you are peddled. At Windemere – my home, on the banks of the James River – my father keeps four hundred workers, and he cares for each one. When they work well, he praises them. When they are sick, he tends them. If they die, he grieves.'

'That is because each one is worth a thousand dollars to him,' said Fairchild.

The audience laughed.

'My friend is quite right,' said Mungo. 'But think of something you own that is worth that much. A fine horse, say, or a necklace. Do you beat it and disdain it and leave it in the mud? Or do you take superlative care of it, polish it and watch out for it, because it is so valuable to you?'

He leaned on the despatch box, as comfortable as if he were leaning on the mantelpiece of his drawing room enjoying a cigar.

'I am a guest in your country. But sometimes, it takes a stranger's eye to observe what the natives do not see. Go to Manchester, or Birmingham, or any of your other great manufacturing cities. Visit the factories. You will see men and women labouring there twelve, fourteen, even eighteen hours a day, in conditions that would make my father sick to his stomach.'

'At least they are free – and paid,' said Fairchild.

'And what use is freedom, if it is only the freedom to live in a slum until you are worked to death? What use is a wage if it does not buy you enough to eat? The only thing that money buys is ease for the consciences of the mill owners. Whereas at Windemere, every one of our people enjoys three square meals a day, a roof over his head and clean clothes to wear. He never has to worry if he will eat, or who will take care of his family. I promise you, if any English loom worker or coal miner glimpsed life on the plantation, he would swap his life for that in a second.'

On the opposite bench, Fairchild had risen. 'A point of order?'

Mungo gave a languid wave to allow it.

'Even if we accept this preposterous picture of African slaves holidaying in some benevolent paradise, the gentleman is rather coy about how those persons came to his country. Will he admit that the slave trade is nothing but a trade in suffering? Or will he try to convince us that millions of Africans willingly took a pleasant cruise to America to enjoy the benefits of the climate?'

That drew a laugh. Mungo smiled broadly, enjoying the joke with everyone else.

'The slave trade has been illegal in Britain and America for over thirty years,' he said. 'Whatever our fathers and grandfathers may have done, it is finished now.'

Fairchild's face flushed. He tried to calm his emotions – gentlemanly behaviour in these debates was prized just as much as sound arguments – but he could not hold them in check.

'You know perfectly well that despite our government's strenuous efforts, traders continue to flout the law by smuggling blacks out of Africa under the very noses of the Royal Navy.'

'Then I suggest you take up your complaint with the Royal Navy.'

'I shall,' said Fairchild. 'Indeed, I may inform the house that as soon as I have completed my degree, I shall accept a commission in the Preventative Squadron of Her Majesty's Navy, intercepting slavers off the coast of Africa. I will report back from there as to the accuracy of Mr St John's picture of the *delights* of slavery.'

There were cheers and approving applause. Up on the ladies' balcony, more than one corset strained with admiration of Fairchild's manly virtue.

'If you are going to Africa, you can report back how these negroes live in their own country,' Mungo shot back. 'Hungry, filthy, ignorant – a war of all against all. And then you can go to America, and say if they are not better off there after all.'

He turned to the room. 'My virtuous opponents would have you think that slavery is a unique evil, a moral abomination unparalleled in the annals of civilisation. I urge you to see otherwise. It is merely a name for what men practise wherever they are, whether in Virginia or Guinea or Manchester. The power of the strong and wealthy over the weak and poor.'

Fairchild had started to object again. Mungo ignored him.

'That may be an awkward truth. But I say to you, I would rather live my life as a slave on a plantation like Windemere, than as a so-called free man in a Lancashire cotton mill. They are the true slaves.'

He looked around the tight-packed chamber. Only the briefest glance, yet every person in the room felt that his gaze had settled directly on them. On the ladies' balcony, the fans fluttered faster than ever.

'Perhaps what I say offends your moral sensibilities. I will not apologise for that. Instead, I beg you to look beyond your distaste and examine the proposition with clear-eyed honesty. If you sweeten your tea with sugar from the West Indies, or smoke Virginia tobacco, then you support slavery. If your father owns a mill where they spin Alabama cotton, or a bank that underwrites the voyages of Liverpool ship owners, then I say again you support slavery.'

He shrugged. 'I do not judge you. I do not lay claim to any superior moral virtue. But the one sin of which I am wholly innocent is this – I will not play the hypocrite and weep false tears for the choices I have made. If you agree with me, I urge you to oppose the motion.'

He sat down. For a moment, silence gripped the room. Then, slowly, a wave of applause began from the back and swelled until it echoed around the chamber. The undergraduates might not agree with his politics, but they could appreciate a bravura performance.

Though not all of them. As the applause rose, so too did an answering barrage of boos and catcalls. Yells of 'murderer' and 'blood on your hands' were heard.

Mungo sat back, revelling in the discord.

'Order!' shouted the president. 'The house will divide.'

The audience filed through two doors, one for 'aye' on the right, and one for 'no' on the left. The queue for the 'ayes' was noticeably longer, but a surprising number turned the other way. Mungo watched the count from his seat, the grin on his face never wavering.

The president announced the result. 'Ayes to the right, two hundred and seven. Noes to the left, one hundred and eighteen.'

Mungo nodded, accepting the result with perfect equanimity. He shook hands with his teammates, then took two glasses of wine and crossed the room to where Fairchild was talking with his friends. He pressed a drink into Fairchild's hand.

'Congratulations,' said Mungo. 'You spoke with great conviction.'

Fairchild took the glass reluctantly. By convention, the society's debates were about rhetorical skill and argument; winning or losing was less important than behaving like gentlemen afterwards. But Fairchild could not hide his disdain for Mungo.

'You take your loss in good part,' he conceded.

'That is because I did not lose,' Mungo answered, in the soft drawl of his native Virginia.

'You heard the result. I carried the motion by almost two to one. You lost.'

'Not at all,' said Mungo. 'I wagered ten guineas that I could get at least a hundred votes against the motion. Nobody else thought I would get more than fifty. And though the glory of victory is very fine, I would rather have the extra gold in my purse.'

Fairchild stared. All he could think to say was, 'I should have thought you had already made enough money out of slavery.'

'Not at all. My father has vowed that when he dies, he will free all his slaves. The will is already written. I will have to find some other way of making my fortune.' Mungo clapped Fairchild on the shoulder. 'So, you see, I will never make a penny out of that institution you revile so much. Whereas you –' he grinned – 'will depend entirely on the slave trade to make your living.'

Fairchild almost choked on his wine. 'How dare you—?'

'You are joining the Preventative Squadron, are you not? You will be paid to capture slave ships.'

'Yes.'

'And that is a very fine and noble profession,' Mungo agreed. 'But if you ever actually succeeded in exterminating the slave trade, you would be out of a job. So it is in your interest to see that slavery endures.'

Fairchild stared at him in horror. 'Arguing with you is like arguing with the Devil himself,' he complained. 'White is black, and black is white.'

'I should have thought you of all men would agree that black and white are created equal. They—'

Mungo broke off. The room was still full with undergraduates milling about, talking and drinking and carrying on the argument. But a young man was barging his way through the crowd, upsetting drinks and knocking people out of his way.

As he reached the front, Mungo recognised him. It was Sidney Manners, a stocky young man who had only got his place at Cambridge because his father owned half of Lincolnshire. With his thick neck, squat shoulders and heavy breathing, he looked like nothing more than a prize bull.

'I have been looking for you,' he said to Mungo.

'I hope it did not tax your energies. I was not hard to find.'

'You have offered the most grievous insult to my sister.'

'Insult?' Mungo smiled. 'You are misinformed. I offered her nothing but compliments.'

'You seduced her!'

Mungo made a dismissive gesture. 'Where I come from, gentlemen do not discuss such matters.'

'Then why have I heard of it from five different people?' Manners took a step closer. 'They say you had her in the organ loft of Trinity Chapel, while the choir were rehearsing.'

'That is not true. It was during Evensong.'

Manners's eyes bulged. 'You do not deny it?'

'I deny that I made her do anything against her will. Indeed, I could hardly have resisted her advances if I had tried.'

Mungo carefully put down his drink, then gave a conspiratorial wink. 'I may say, your sister is a perfectly devout young woman. Always on her knees in chapel.'

Manners's face had gone a deep shade of puce. His collar seemed to have shrunk around his neck. He struggled to breathe; his mouth flapped open, but no words emerged.

Eventually, his anger burst out the only way it could. He drew back his arm and swung a fist wildly at Mungo's jaw.

His size gave him power, but he had no training. Mungo boxed every week, taking lessons with a former champion of England who had retired to Cambridge. He dodged Manners's blow easily, grabbed his arm, then swept his feet from under him and dumped him on his backside.

Manners jerked on the ground. Mungo looked down at him and, for a second, his eyes flashed with an anger so fierce, anyone who saw it would have feared for Manners's life. In that moment, you could not doubt that Mungo was capable of anything.

Then the anger faded, as sudden as a summer squall. Mungo's smile returned. He nodded to the circle of spectators around him. They edged back, though they could not look away: captivated by the spectacle, yet frightened of Mungo's power.

'If you will excuse me, gentlemen.'

The crowded room emptied in front of him as he made his way to the door. He heard Manners staggering to his feet behind him, but he did not look back. Outside, he put on his hat and strode back towards his college. The summer night was warm, but not as warm as it would be at home in Virginia. Windemere would be turning green now, as the young tobacco plants were transplanted from their winter seedbeds out into the fields.

He had enjoyed his time in Cambridge. He had learned everything he could, made some influential friends who might serve him well later in life, and met more than a few young ladies like Clarissa Manners who were eager to share their charms with him. But he would be glad to be home.

The moon was rising behind the tower of Great St Mary's Church as he turned into Trinity Street. It was past curfew. The gates of his college would be locked, but that did not trouble him. He had an understanding with Chapman, the porter.

'St John!'

An angry voice hailed him from the end of the street. Mungo kept walking.

'St John! Stop, if you are not a coward.'

Mungo paused. Slowly, he turned back. 'No one has ever accused me of cowardice.'

Manners stood there, silhouetted against the street lamp. He was not alone. Two of his friends flanked him, sturdy young men with ham fists and broad shoulders. One of them carried a poker, and the other a wine bottle, which he gripped by the neck.

'If you were a gentleman, I would challenge you to a duel,' sneered Manners.

'If you were a gentleman, I would gladly accept. But as that is clearly not the case, I will bid you goodnight.'

Mungo tipped his hat and turned away – as if completely oblivious to the armed men behind him. Manners stared after him for a moment, stupefied by his opponent's insouciance. Then anger took over. Snarling like a dog, he charged.

Mungo heard the footsteps on the cobbles behind him. As Manners closed on him, Mungo pivoted on the balls of his feet and delivered a perfectly aimed uppercut to Manners's chin. Manners stopped dead, howling in pain. Mungo followed up with three quick jabs to the ribs that sent Manners reeling away, clutching his abdomen.

As Manners retreated, his friends moved in. They circled around Mungo, with the shambling gait of men who have been drinking. Mungo watched them carefully, calculating the effect the alcohol would have. It might make them slower – but also more unpredictable.

They waited, calling encouragement to each other. None of them wanted to suffer the same fate as Manners, but they did not want to look weak. At last the one with the poker stepped forward.

'I will give you a lesson, you American bastard!'

He swung the poker at Mungo. Mungo took the blow on his shoulder, moving away so that he barely felt it. As he did, he grabbed the poker with both hands and tugged it forward, pulling his opponent off balance. Mungo thrust the poker back so that it hit him in the stomach, then twisted it out of his hands and cracked him over the shoulders. The man stumbled back.

Now Mungo was armed, he liked his odds better. He swung around, brandishing the poker. Manners's friends edged backwards. They were not so devoted to Manners that they wanted their heads cracked for him.

'Are you afraid of this Yankee upstart?'

Manners had stood up. He snatched the bottle that his friend carried and broke it on the cobbles so that he was left with a jagged and glittering stump. He advanced again, more cautiously this time. Two encounters with Mungo had taught him that much, at least.

'I would not do that,' Mungo said.

If Manners had been sober, he might have heard the lethal warning in Mungo's voice. But he was drunk, and angry, and he had been humiliated. He jabbed the bottle at Mungo, swiping the broken glass towards his face.

Mungo avoided it easily. As Manners brought the bottle back, Mungo whipped the poker through the air and cracked it against Manners's wrist. The bone snapped; the bottle flew out of his hand and smashed against a wall.

Manners howled and dropped to his knees. His two friends took one look at Mungo, the poker raised like the sword of an avenging angel, and fled. Manners was left alone with Mungo.

Mungo could have walked away. He had done so once already that evening. But Manners had tried to kill him, however incompetently, and that had unlocked a rage he had rarely felt before. He stood over Manners like an executioner, the poker raised. Strength coursed through his arms. He was not minded to be merciful. At that moment, all that existed was his rage. He would break open Manners's head like an egg.

But as he moved to strike, a firm hand gripped the poker and stayed the blow. Mungo spun around to see Fairchild's earnest face, teeth gritted with the effort of holding back Mungo's arm.

'What are you doing?' Mungo hissed. 'Do you think you can save this loathsome rat?'

Fairchild's grip did not loosen. 'I am not saving him. I am saving *you*. From yourself.'

'I do not need saving.'

'If you kill him, you will be hanged for murder.' Fairchild prodded Manners with the toe of his shoe. 'Is he worth that?'

The two young men stared at each other, both holding the poker. Mungo knew that what Fairchild said was true, but he could not bring himself to let go. He tried to twist the weapon from Fairchild's grasp, heaving with all his might. Fairchild's fingers flexed; he was not as strong as Mungo. His grip threatened to break. But he had an iron will and would not yield.

They might have stayed locked in that position all night, but at that moment footsteps sounded on the street. A sturdy man in a long dark coat emerged from the porter's lodge and came straight towards them.

'Mr St John, sir?'

It was Chapman, the college porter. If he was surprised to see Mungo with a poker raised like a weapon, Fairchild wrestling him for it and Manners kneeling helpless at his feet, he made no comment. Chapman had known Mungo since he arrived three years ago, and nothing the undergraduate did could surprise him.

'A letter arrived for you, sir. It was marked "urgent".'

Mungo blinked. The poker dropped to the ground. Manners took advantage of his reprieve to scuttle away, whimpering and clutching his wrist. Mungo wiped his hands with his handkerchief, then adjusted his cuffs and his cravat. Only then did he take the letter. It was franked from Norfolk, Virginia, dated six weeks earlier. The address was written in a clear, large script, careful letters formed by a hand that was not used to writing.

Mungo showed no emotion as he slit it open and read the contents.

'What is it?' Fairchild asked.

Mungo ignored him. 'Have the servants pack my trunk,' he said to the porter. 'I must return to Virginia at once.'

TWO HEROES. ONE UNBREAKABLE BOND.

COURTNEY'S WAR

An epic story of courage, betrayal and undying love that takes the reader to the very heart of a world at war.

Torn apart by war, Saffron Courtney and Gerhard von Meerbach are thousands of miles apart, both struggling for their lives.

Gerhard – despite his objections to the Nazi regime – is fighting for the Fatherland, hoping to one day have the opportunity to rid Germany of Hitler and his cronies. But as his unit is thrown into the hellish attrition of the Battle of Stalingrad, he knows his chances of survival are dwindling by the day.

Meanwhile Saffron – recruited by the Special Operations Executive and sent to occupied Belgium to discover how the Nazis have infiltrated SOE's network – soon finds herself being hunted by Germany's most ruthless spymaster.

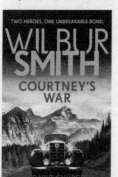

Confronted by evil beyond their worst imaginings, the lovers must each make the hardest choice of all: sacrifice themselves, or do whatever they can to survive, hoping that one day they will be reunited.

THE SAGA CONTINUES IN *LEGACY OF WAR* COMING SOON

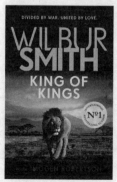